Earths Immortal Guardians

By

P.M. Humphreys

The Astrotars have been around for millions of years, unbeknown to us, helping evolve and protect the earth from the Galympites. Is now the time for them to reveal to the world their existence? Is the world ready for the truth?

1

Fear!

Fear and terror of the unknown filled my whole being. A millisecond previously I had been lying in the heather on a quiet Scottish hillside, enjoying the warm summer sun following an afternoon hike over the moorlands. An instant later, I was blind, my whole body seemingly entombed in ice as I fell into a stomach-churning abyss.

My God! What fear I was plunging through blackness; my very breath being dragged from me, my whole being aware that this was to be my end, falling to my death, alone in the bowels of the earth. I was aware that my eyes were open, and yet I could see nothing, hear nothing, feel nothing. Was I now a celestial body floating in limbo? Was this death? I closed, then opened my eyes yet again; I felt I was floating giddily in a black abyss, without sensation of weight or pain.

At this point, as with a drowning swimmer, my whole life started to dash before my eyes, but in a strange, reverse order. I remembered setting out from the local inn which had been my headquarters during my stay in the Scottish Highlands I remembered the heat and sultriness of this particular day so hot and warm was it that after having driven up the Loch Garry, Loch Loyne road for a few miles, I decided to park the car and go for a short walk off the beaten track, enjoying the Highland peace, tranquility; and beauty an idyll which was to be so fundamentally shattered a few minutes later.

I remembered noticing that here by the side of Loch Loyne the shrubbery was much sparser, and that whereas ahead of me there were hardly any trees; yet back along the road the Forestry Commission had acres of trees. Also noticeable by their absence were the wandering, black-faced sheep; and the quietness was eerie without the usual sounds of birds. My curiosity was roused why was this place so quiet and still? I had crossed over the road from the Loch and set off walking up a small trail across the grassy mountainside covered all over with assorted heather. I clambered off the small trail, which was becoming heavy going with its steepness I laid down in the springy softness of the heather. Overhead a large projection of rock shaded the sun from my head, whilst I rested and steeped myself in memories of Scottish folklore. Suddenly my eyes focused on a beautiful, nearby plant of unusual colour and shape. My curiosity aroused, I stood up to walk over to take a closer look when the earth opened up, and I experienced the fall into what seemed to be to the very middle of the earth my departure from life into my present state of limbo. What had brought me to this horrific end? Me, Glen Henderson Grant- Wallace, nationally renowned correspondent of one of Britain's largest newspapers?

Self-pity suddenly flooded my being to join my fear and terror as my strangely reversed drowning dream sequence brought me back to my origins and advancement to my national renown. I had been born on 12 September, only child of Meg and Donald Grant-Wallace, the local doctor, in a village outside Edinburgh, and had been called Glen Henderson Grant-Wallace. My childhood had been happy, and I had spent many hours listening to my grandfather relating stories and scary tales of Scottish folklore and inexplicable happenings in some of the isolated Scottish Highlands. Throughout my school life, I had worked hard and enjoyed both primary and grammar school and later university. And with my natural curiosity of life, I longed to be a journalist or even a foreign correspondent with some large newspaper, meeting people of different nationalities.

My first job was in a small newspaper office, learning the rudiments of journalism but I still dreaming of my 'big break'. My chance came through a conversation and exchange of ideas with a colleague being overheard by an editor of a large London newspaper who, apparently impressed with my ideas, offered me a job with his company. That, in turn led to my career taking my present position of roving correspondent, an international figure on a current commission to check out a sighting of the Loch Ness monster, a celebrity about to be consigned by some unknown force into eternity. My mental flashback faded, and my feelings condensed. I felt as If I were lying suspended in a large bubble. I pushed my arms up and around me, but in all directions, I felt as if I were cushioned in a large, plastic ball floating on air. A noise like a whirring sound perpetuated the blackness into my semi- conscious bewilderment, as my ears were filled with the noise of a regular beat which, had I been alive, I might have thought was my heart.

Fear started to fill my very being again. Perhaps it was my heart, but if it were my own heartbeat, then I couldn't be dead, and if I were not dead as I had imagined, then what was that whirring, whining noise that was getting nearer and louder, as if some unknown object was being propelled towards me Peering intensely into the blackness, as I began to recover partial vision, I perceived a small dot of light gradually enlarging as it approached, like the eye of some large, sinister, unseen monster.

It was as if I were trapped in a railway tunnel, frozen with fear as the fast-approaching searchlight on a locomotive engine bore down on me. I could do nothing there was no escape, no room for me to step outside the tracks and press myself against the wall of the tunnel and pray there was enough space there to provide a safety bolt hole. Run! The adrenalin was pumping wildly through my bloodstream, but to no avail. There was nowhere to run. So, this was approaching death! In a few seconds, I would be nothing but a smashed, broken, and bloody lifeless corpse. A foreboding chill seeped through what seemed to be the shell of my body, and strange emotions filled me, as I thought of so many unanswered questions. Perhaps, after all, this was just a nightmare of horrific dimensions, and I would wake up in the sun-dappled heather. Frantic alternative ideas tumbled through my mind. Perhaps this was the domain of a dinosaur from the distant past, trapped in an underworld of dark- ness into which I had somehow tumbled. Perhaps 'Nessie,' the Loch Ness Monster, had wandered upon me; perhaps that was why she was not often seen swimming in the loch by those who came to investigate. Worse, perhaps, was the feeling that I was now at the entrance of hades, and this was the life-form of one of those gargoyle-type monsters depicted in pictures from mythological stories. Logic! I tried to reason frantically as the eye of the monster grew closer and closer, larger and larger, and the roaring sound filled my ears. If I were really buried deep in the rocks of time, it should be cold and damp, and if perchance this was hades well, hell, I knew that place was supposedly hot. But I knew that my body had not experienced any sensation of heat, and the air my hammering heartbeat told me I was still breathing seemed neither fresh nor stale. As the monster eye charged nearer, I tried to wake up. 'Please, God,' I inwardly screamed, 'let me be dreaming'. But I knew that my eyes were open as I stared into the blackness. Perhaps, I thought, if I do not move, whatever approaches will pass over me; but the luminous eye grew huge, and the rumbling sound an ear-splitting roar, as this creature of darkness loomed terrifyingly nearer. That which I presumed to be an eye now seemed to be almost upon me. My heart seemed to miss a beat, and then stood, still, and I suddenly felt as if something unseen was pushing me down, lowering me yet further into the bowels of the earth, but without touching me. Now the light appeared to be above me, and all I could hear was my thumping heartbeat, which by now seemed like a drumbeat and, of course, the non-stop whirring sound. In the dimness, I could just barely discern what appeared to be a large mouth, gradually opening.

At this, I knew then, that my last moment was upon me. An unseen force appeared to be sucking me forward into this horrendous, gaping mouth. If I weren't already dead, this was surely to be my end. A different whirring noise sounded in my ears, and the dim light which had hung above me like the illuminated eye of some demonic monster disappeared from view. My mind could take in nothing further too much horror and fear had been concentrated into what appeared to be such a short time, and fear, even in the bravest person, increases a hundred-fold in the dark into which I had fallen. With this last thought, I passed into blissful unconsciousness. When I opened my eyes and looked around me, rather hazily at first, I realized immediately that I had obviously passed out in fear. I now found that I appeared to be lying flat on a clear table like construction, in the middle of a well illuminated, circular room that appeared to be painted in a silvery colour. On taking stock of my surroundings, I came to the conclusion that there were no apparent exits on view, and a large panel resembling a television screen was set in the wall ahead of me, with innumerable switches and small lights in rows beneath it. I suddenly felt as if I were not alone in the room, as if I were being watched, and I looked backwards as best as I could from my prone position, directly into the kind but impelling eyes of a strange being dressed in a long, white robe. His white hair was shoulder-length, and his complexion was fair and unlined, giving him an ageless appearance. I blinked in amazement and attempted to sit up, whereupon my unknown companion gently, but with apparent unbounded strength, placed a restraining hand on my chest and firmly held me in my horizontal position, saying in a calm voice of resonate depth, 'Earthling, do not be afraid. You are still in a bad state of shock, so do not move. Our great leader Astro has been informed that you are in our midst and wishes that first you must rest; then you are to be taken by aqua craft to his domain.'

Earthling! He had called me earthling. This, then, must be an alien being from another world, another planet. Shock, incredulity, curiosity, fear a gamut of emotions flooded my senses. And, strangely, mixed in with these was a feeling of a sense of relief. This was no alien monster of the like I had seen in the comic books and films of my early teenage years. No unearthly, green-hued being with six tentacles and one eye, breathing Sulphur and exuding menace, so beloved of the makers of science-fiction films. His whole demeanor was impassive, remote, neither threatening nor non-threatening. And he spoke English! His words to me had been spoken with authority, and although my strength had not yet returned, I was overwhelmed with curiosity, and this impelled me to ask: "Who are you, and where do you come from?" in an admittedly dazed but curious voice. The curiosity which pervades the being of all journalists had taken over, wiping out any initial feelings of fear I might have had; fear that this alien being might be a threat, not just to me but to the whole planet. The prospect of a worldwide exclusive story of a face-to-face with an interterrestrial traveller erased all feelings, other than an intense, professional interest. "I am called Botami, and I come from another galaxy many light years from here. But that is all I am at liberty to tell you," he said. "Astro, our leader, has both the right and knowledge to explain our history and the reasons for our interterrestrial existence on your planet earth. Rest now because soon I must conduct you to our aqua craft terminal, and this necessitates you regaining your strength without delay. I do not want you to be afraid, but I must lower this shield around you. Those are my orders!" As Botami pressed a button on a panel at my side, I looked up and saw a large, clear shield descending down and felt a strange but pleasant sensation I was awakened by the voice of Botami, who I recognized immediately, saying, "Earthling, your rest is now complete; drink this special juice, and then follow me." I sat up with ease and took the beautifully carved goblet being offered and drank deeply. The taste, at first, was strange but most refreshing. Finishing it I passed back the empty goblet and swung my legs from the bed-like dais on which I had been lying. Standing up beside Botami, I noticed that he was about my height; six foot in my stockinged feet, but slimmer than I in build. His eyes were of a cornflower blue colour and deep-set, appearing to hold my gaze when I looked, with a strange, hypnotic power. His nose was of a Grecian style, and I noticed that his distinctive, white hair reached down to his shoulders. His manner was impassive, neither intrusive nor condescending, neither fully informative nor open. Who was this being? If he was from another planet, what was his purpose on earth? Was he a friend or a foe, a threat or a saviour? How could an alien speak such perfect but admittedly stilted English? How long had he been on earth? How many others like him were here? How had they got me here? And what did they want of me? Obviously, I had been selected for a purpose but what was that purpose? Was I just a specimen of the human race to be experimented upon? Had others been abducted like me? Was I going to be taken to some far-off planet for some obscure reason? And why had I been selected? Suddenly, I had the overwhelming feeling that my innermost thoughts could be read by Botami without any effort. He stood waiting impassively, his hands resting calmly at his side, and I found my eyes drawn to the middle finger of his right hand, which was adorned with a strange ring, silvery in colour and inset with a large, green gem. As Botami stood silently awaiting me to gather my thoughts, I was now convinced that he was obviously well aware of all that had passed through my mind. I smiled, more with embarrassment, owing to having been caught like a curious child staring, and was quite relieved to notice that he half smiled. His smile gave me a curious sense of warmth and relief, at least this alien being shared at least one emotion with the human race: a sense of humour. But was it a vindictive, superior sense of humour, or one of a shared amusement? And what other emotions did he share with we humans? Clearly, his race was of superior intelligence to ours at least in technological terms; to have made the journey from whichever star was home to him, to be able to communicate in what must have been a foreign language to him, to have made a base here without one whisper or rumour of his presence. Botami interrupted my thoughts, as he once again read my mind. "Please follow me now," he said firmly but not unkindly. "The hour approaches for you to begin your journey to meet our leader, the great Astro." With this final remark, he held his ring close to a small, concave disk in the wall, set about shoulder level. Immediately a panel in the wall slid across silently, and I stepped out behind Botami, my guide, to face, once more, what lay ahead? I still could not believe that I was not dreaming, as so much had happened to me since I had first set out on my walk through the heather. Had I fallen into a new world? Who were my rescuer, was I their captive? All this I had yet to find out. I followed close behind Botami as we waked along a smooth-walled, tubular-like corridor, wondering as we moved forward in single file what mysteries lay ahead. As the end of the passageway loomed nearer, I realised that it was a dead end, no branches off, and I could not see any way out.

Botami stopped a couple of feet from the wall that blocked our path, and once more stretched out his right hand, adorned with the unique ring, towards a small green cut-out in the wall. Once more a silent movement sideways of this walled obstacle happened, and we were inside another circular room with a ceiling of a green opaque colouring. A strange, eerie light filled the room, and I felt a chilly creepiness steal through my bones. What a strangely coloured décor, I thought. Almost immediately I noticed a quick flash of silver and pink amongst the eerie green colouring and realised that it was a small shoal of unusual fish and that we must be at the bottom of some deep water. "Botami," I ventured to speak, quite overcome with curiosity, "Where are we? Is this circular room surrounded by very deep water?" There was a moment's silence and then my guide looked at me and said, "As to where you are, at this stage all I can tell you is that this is the aqua craft terminal, and you are quite correct on the other count. We are indeed surrounded on almost all sides by exceptionally deep water. "It will not be that long now till you meet out leader, Astro, and he will answer your questions, although I must say you earthlings are noted by us for your curiosity, even sometimes at your own cost." He smiled, and then turned from me, looking out silently once more into the unfathomable depths ahead. The conversation was ended, I thought, and I wondered what we were waiting for to happen. Following Botami's gaze, I saw something dank and large apparently approaching us at some speed through the murky green waters outside. A whale or huge shark, perhaps, I thought, as the dark shape loomed closer. And then to my amazement, I perceived at least a dozen, small dots of light radiating from the object and infiltrating the gloom. Portholes, I guessed, and immediately knew that this must be none other than the aqua craft that we were awaiting. But how, I wondered, would we be able to be admitted without the pressure of those green depths being forced inside this circular room where we stood, even if Botami were to be able to use his ring to slide open an entrance for us to pass through. As if reading my thoughts, Botami half-turned, and said, "This is the aqua craft that we have been awaiting; it will only be a short time before we are on board. "Do not worry, through extensive advancement of our marine engineering over a span of thousands of years, we have made possible feats which you earthlings would not find even remotely possible at this depth." The aqua craft slid closer, and a large, oval, rubber projection slid out from a hatch on one side of the craft like a six foot by four-foot mouth and adhered to the side of the room. Botami pressed a small switch on the wall and waited. Suddenly a red light by the side of it came on, and Botami pressed his ring onto the wall into a small, green socket. Immediately the wall in front of the projection, joining the aqua craft to the room, appeared to open, and we were about to move forward and cross into the adjoining craft without any problem. I followed Botami, who was the first through, and entered into a small chamber, watching intently once more as my alien companion pressed his ring to the wall, over the entrance way, and silently the passage disappeared from view. How amazing! I thought. A throbbing noise attracted my attention, and I turned to Botami. "Does that throbbing noise mean that the engines are in motion and that I am once more in transit into the unknown?" I asked my travelling companion. "You are indeed a questioning man, earthling, but I expect you find our ways strange," replied Botami. "You are nevertheless correct; the engines are propelling us forward now, and we have already left the boarding terminal far behind, as our speed is greater than I'm sure you would ever imagine. Now let us go and eat, and whilst we do so, you will be able to behold some of the wonders of the deep." Botami walked towards a closed door, which opened on our approach, as if by magic, and closed behind us after we passed through. Obviously controlled by computers or ray circuit being broken, I thought, and Botami turned his head and smiled, leaving me without a shadow of doubt that my alien companion had strange powers, amongst them the ability to read my thoughts.

We crossed the passageway and by way of a further set of 'magic eye' doors, similar to those that we had just encountered, passed through into a small, well-lit room. It appeared to be devoid of any furniture or decoration except for a small panel in one wall, comprised of switches, small light bulbs, and a couple of minute dials. Botami crossed the floor with a few, silent strides and commenced, touching dials and switches with obvious dexterity, which to my unmechanical but highly observant brain, seemed to be an extremely technical electronic control for something as yet unknown to me.

I watched with interest, wondering what amazing thing would now surely take place and, of course, once more I was not to be disappointed. First, the bright room that we were standing in started to visibly dim, creating a more relaxed light and atmosphere. Then almost immediately, two, small panels on the floor moved aside, and from beneath them, two, large, bubble-like objects commenced to be extruded, as if growing rapidly. As they grew, they developed into the shape of two, large armchairs with an elongated portion protruding in front. Botami pointed to these two objects and said in his deep voice, "Earthling, these chairs are called Relaxairs, and they are for our personal use. Just sit down, and you will find they are extremely comfortable. "I moved slowly towards the one provided for me, and with trepidation, in case it burst when my weight was lowered on to it, as it appeared to be only similar to a large bubble. Botami gave a small laugh, and I looked at him in some surprise, as this was the first time, he had indulged in any show of humour. "It is quite safe and strong, earthling, being a material of extreme strength and durability," he assured me, and with this remark, he walked across to his own Relaxair, as he had called it, and settled down. As he did so, I noticed a large portion of the wall in front of me start to divide, and very gradually slide aside, revealing once more the wonders of the deep to be unfolded before me. The dark green of the watery depths was penetrated by two, deep, searching lights, which seemed to bring everything to life. I felt as if I were actually in the water, as the screen was so large that nothing was lost to view. I turned to Botami and said simply, "This is unbelievable." No sooner had I spoken than a slight noise from behind made me aware that we were not alone any longer. With that, between Botami and me, stepped a beautiful woman. She was ageless and slim, with long, white, shining hair cascading down to her waist, and at the same time, framing her face with soft waves. She was clothed in a similar attire to Botami, in material of a delicate nature; long, white, and flowing to her feet, with a silver plaited throng around her waist, conveying to one's mind the sudden vision of an angel. Her eyes, like those of Botami's, were deep set and of the same cornflower blue colour, and her mouth was kind and beautifully curved, I noticed, as she half-smiled at us both. She then turned and addressed Botami and said in a voice that sounded musical to my ears, "Botami, I expect both you and our guest, the earthling, are ready for some nourishment, which is prepared for you now. Please take it, and may it give you strength." With this remark, she passed Botami a goblet filled with liquid, which appeared to be similar to that which I had previously been given, and with this we were also given two, triangular tablets. She then turned to me saying, "Earthling, welcome. I am called Eafi; please enjoy your nourishment. "This juice and tablets, which I am instructed to serve all travellers on the aqua craft, you will find represents as equal satisfaction to your needs as any of your earth meals. I hope all your wishes are fulfilled." And with a slight smile at us both, she departed from our company as quietly as she had entered, as if she were weightless and had drifted on the breeze given off by the air conditioning. So, I thought, these aliens have both male and female people like we of the planet earth, and they are not unlike us to look at, except I mused, for the quiet, compellingly peaceful attitude that appeared to exude from them. Mind you, I thought to myself, I have only as yet met two of these aliens. What was there yet in store for me perhaps hostility or were they peaceful? Botami glanced at me, and I looked straight at him and said, "I'm sorry, Botami, I keep allowing my thoughts to wander, forgetful of your strange and mystical ability to read my very mind." "Yes," said Botami, "that is true, but please don't worry; you are bound to be curious about us 'beings' from another galaxy, as you have only previously imagined that you people on earth were the only living beings in the universe. But you were wrong, were you not, earthling?" There was a short pause in the conversation, and in it I realised how true were the things that he had said. "I am sorry that so much as yet must remain a mystery to you," he said, then hesitated for just a second before continuing. "Soon you will be able to speak with our great leader, Astro, and I'm sure all will be explained." I sipped my juice and chewed the tablets. They filled my mouth and excited my taste buds with a delicious flavour that was hard to imagine came from something so small, then I continued sipping my juice and reflecting quietly on all that had transpired so far. Gradually I became aware that Botami was gazing out into the depths, and I began to stare out myself, thinking perhaps I would be able to spot some clue as to my whereabouts. By the light of the aqua craft, the mysteries of the deep were unfolding before me. Where was I? Without doubt, I was not in a loch, as we had been travelling too long, and the watery depths had already shown to my watchful eye tire obvious signs of oceanic life, but which ocean or sea was still a mystery? Perhaps if I was observant, I might solve my journey's destiny. I had always been interested in all aspects of geographic studies. My eyes had grown accustomed to the greenish colour by now, and all around me, I watched with increasing interest, as I passed through all species of marine life. With great fascination, I suddenly spied the rotting shells of two, different ships. A clipper and a whaler's frame had their timbers interlaced and covered with a thick seaweed, as if fate had decreed that they should share the same watery grave but had decided to camouflage their nakedness. Seaweed was drifting along like tentacles of an octopus, as it wrapped itself around any inanimate object that it came up against. It surprised me how vast and thick was the amount of this seaweed and wondered with fascination whether the surface was as thick and densely covered. If so, I was really certain that we must be in the vicinity of the Sargasso Sea that was situated in the mid-Atlantic. Suddenly, the fearful vision of a huge shark glided past our large screen, and it appeared to be within reach which, of course, with those teeth, was quite unnerving. Watching its sleek passage through the water and by the comparison of speed, I realised that we were travelling ourselves faster than I had imagined. We appeared to be passing through an underwater mountain range and using a route of specific navigation as we moved, first one way and then the other, passing enroute the rotting shells of many ships of varying uses and dimensions, which kept coming into view yachts, steamers, whalers, clippers, and even a large Spanish galleon, which could be recognised by its carvings and mast. I trembled as sudden realisation confirmed my previous thoughts, and I knew that this must be the large North-South underwater chain of mountains, which are to be found in the deep Sargasso Sea, characterised by its deadly calms and treacherously abundant growths of seaweed known as sargassum. This sea, in the middle of the Atlantic, I knew was feared by sailors and had, through the ages, claimed the legendary rights to be known as the Sea of Lost Ships. My thoughts were interrupted at this point by a slight rustle, which caused me to become aware once more of my silent companion, Botami, who was staring at me with a strange look in his eyes. "Earthling," he said, breaking our long silence, "you appear to have great knowledge of your world, with keen powers of observation." And with this remark, he closed his eyes and leaned back in his Relax chair. My thoughts had obviously been well-interpreted and followed, once again, by this alien with his extraordinary, mind-reading powers. We were now entering a very reefy expanse, and by watching the vegetation, rocks, and some species of marine life that I had never seen before, obviously it was because I must be passing through exceptionally deep waters, which man normally is unable to reach. Occasionally I spotted a fish I recognised from books I had read and studied over the years. And, of course, one often came face to face with sleek, silvery grey, evil-looking sharks, and the beady, peering eyes of enormous black octopus, clinging to the coral reef edges or busily entwining their long, rubbery tentacles round a newly caught prey. I had noticed that although the aqua craft was only about the size of a small submarine, nothing seemed to hinder our progress, and even the turbulence from the currents seemed negligible. How strange, I thought, perhaps they recognise that this is an alien craft and are therefore a bit wary of it. Realistically, I thought, it was probably protected by a type of forcefield of rays. I smiled, wondering if Botami was still reading my thoughts, but I resisted the temptation to steal a glance at him. Once more the female called Eafi entered carrying two goblets containing some juice for Botami and me. Without warning, before Eafi could leave or Botami could reseat himself, the aqua craft was thrown to one side violently and shuddered to a stop so abruptly that we were all three thrown to the floor.

2

Although shaken I quickly stood up and bent to help Eafi, who was very pale, to her feet. I turned to Botami and noticed him still lying in a prone position on the floor, face down. Without hesitation I rushed to his side and dropped to my knees, and with the slight knowledge of first aid I had, I started to turn him onto his side. Immediately I realised what had happened, he had fallen on the silver-coloured goblet, and not only was his temple pouring with blood, but he was in a state of unconsciousness. I felt his pulse; it seemed erratic, but I did not know whether this was normal or not. I quickly said to the alien, Eafi, "Are your pulse counts like ours? Come here quickly and help me. Botami appears to be badly hurt and unconscious." She nodded and rushed to my side, saying urgently, "Earthling, I am sorry I hesitated, but I am still shaken." She knelt at Botami's side, and at the same time, she pointed to the panel on the wall, saying to me with a note of urgency in her voice, "Quickly go over to that panel and call for immediate assistance by pressing the large, orange switch downward whilst I help Botami."

I rushed to the panel of switches, my eyes immediately focused on the re- quired switch, and I pressed it hurriedly. Within seconds, or so it seemed, the wall behind slid across, and a man entered the room, rushing across to the prone figure of Botami, who was unconscious. Before I could speak, Eafi jumped to her feet and, addressing this elderly man who has come to our assistance, said, "Xedato, when our aqua craft was abruptly halted and badly thrown about, Botami sustained head injuries in his fall and has not recovered consciousness. The earthman and I are alright, and we have done all that was possible for him." Xedato, as he was called, nodded and knelt down by Botami, quickly exerting pressure to his head and neck. He then took from the fold of his gown an object similar in shape to a small gun and pressed the trigger type-switch on, and immediately a purple-coloured spray was ejected from it over the temple of Botami, and the flow bleeding was stemmed. Xedato then proceeded to apply pressure again to Botami's head by placing his hands on either side of his head and staring into his face for some seconds. There was a slight movement, and Botami opened his eyes. During these events, I had been studying the new arrival of Xedato with interest. He was tall and slim with white, shoulder-length hair tied back. He resembled Botami, except for the hair style. Although dressed in a similar white robe, he had on certain additions. Around his neck a large, six-pointed silver star pendant was apparent, and around his waist was a green corded belt, enhanced with small, silver stars. The cuffs of the sleeves were banded at the wrist with three, red stripes, obviously denoting the rank he held. After a few seconds, Botami opened his eyes and started to sit up slowly, and Xedato turned and said, "Earthman, thank you for your help and, more importantly," he hesitated for a second, "for remaining quiet whilst I attended to Botami." He obviously noticed that I was puzzled, and so he continued to speak "It was necessary for complete silence, so I could reach through into Botami's temporary brain inactivity with an exchange of manual strength to activate the brain impulses. This, of course, is because of a complicated advancement we have made in telepathic communications eradicates the possibility of irreparable brain damage, if completed quickly enough, which, of course, this time was made possible by your swift action in calling for my attention. "I am aware that our leader Astro will explain much of our world to you, but I feel that we owed you that much of an explanation. As you will have noticed, I am known as Xedato, and I am trained in the ways of healing as used in our world, which still differ greatly from the ways of earth. I also feel at this point we should address you by your name, as you have shown compassion towards our race, although we are aliens to you, so what may we call you other than earthling or earthman?" I was pleasantly surprised with this latest development, and without further hesitation, said, "I am Glen Grant-Wallace, please call me Glen." On completion of these few words, Xedato turned to Botami and started to speak once more. "Botami, we have been lucky in meeting with this earth man called Glen. He has helped greatly in your recovery. The reason I must hasten to add for this extreme turbulence to our aqua craft is that we have come into contact unexpectedly with a new, severe forcefield set up by the Galympites, in order that they might damage our aqua craft in its passage to our headquarters. They have obviously tried to annihilate our craft and crew, but we were lucky, and our safety forcefield finder ray, which we have now installed in and around all our craft, took the impact, eliminating their forcefield, causing only slight but negligible damage to us. "Our leader, Astro, will be content to learn that a further danger area has been averted." He turned back his gaze to me, remarking, "I am sorry that all this must seem confusing to you, but I am sure that the great Astro will understand if I explain briefly our immediate problem. We are of the race called Astrotars from the planet Astrola in a far-off galaxy and have only contributed to the advancement of earth and its people. Unfortunately, we have to constantly eliminate the hazards and evils and major disasters that occur on earth owing so often to the practices and desires of the Galympites, an evil, cruel race who keep entering your planet's atmosphere in their spaceships and causing havoc in your world. Our leader, Astro, who is good and kind and wishes only for peace and understanding between people of all planets and galaxies, is constantly breaking down their network of infiltration, although it becomes increasingly difficult as the world increases in scientific knowledge and simplifies the work of the Galympites in their continual attempts to place country against country, increasing their strength at the cost of the people of earth." He paused momentarily before continuing again. "Unfortunately, every so often, they manage to enter your atmosphere without our knowledge and give earthmen and ourselves grave problems to deal with, although you still on earth think many of your disasters are of a natural determination. Now, perhaps, you will realise that we are originally from the planet Astrola, bear you on earth no harm and only desire to live in peaceful coexistence, helping the continued existence of mankind on the planet earth." All the time Xedato had been talking to me, I had been listening with amazed interest, however, at the same time, I was aware that Botami was sitting on a Relaxair with his eyes constantly focused me, obviously reading my thoughts; in case, perhaps, I was unable to grasp all this information. I smiled at Xedato and Botami and said without hesitation, "Although it is good to know that I am among people who wish earth no harm whatsoever, I still feel a strange feeling of unrest within me, as I am now aware that perhaps the destiny of the world may be in the hands of peoples from another galaxy." At this point, Xedato interrupted me. "Glen, I am sorry our conversation must end for the moment, as our troubles will not be over till, we have made sure that we do not come into contact with any further forcefields dangers, as our aqua craft is now working and travelling forward to Tri Base 1, but our safety forcefield finder ray is working under par, and all will not be satisfactory till we have been recharged and electronically examined." I knew the conversation was now ended, as Xedato smiled and hurriedly left the room. Botami, at this point, walked across to the panel on the wall and commenced pressing switches and moving dials. I walked to the window of the aqua craft wall and gazed out wondrously once more into the dark green, watery depths perpetrated by the silvery lights emitting from the sides of our craft suddenly a small, silvery fish close by, small only by comparison, which recognised as a hatchet fish found in the black depths, was grabbed in the jaws of this large, black predator, whose mouth seemed to stretch as wide as its body. I knew, without doubt from my marine study days, that this alone could only be the Black Swallower, a huge fish found in the waters of the abyss; a fish which can enlarge its mouth so much that it can swallow its prey even larger than itself. I shuddered but remembered happily that we were surrounded by our own forcefield, which safeguards us from the perils of the deep, as long as it is held firm and not permanently damaged by the alien called Galympites. The silence enveloped me, and I forgot about everything, staring out into the dark green water depths, as if hypnotised. Suddenly the silence was broken by Botami's voice. "Glen." The name, although so quietly spoken, brought me back to reality. I turned from my panoramic view and faced Botami. "I'm sorry, Botami," I said, "can I help?" Botami just smiled and walked across to me, saying, "Glen, it is only the start of your adventure. I hope that you will allow me to be your friend. You saved my life. You will not come to any harm with us Astrotars, as I'm sure you already sense. Now, come and sit down whilst I point out on our navigational screen where you are and where you are about to enter. You are about to pass into what you earth people call the 'Bermuda Triangle,' which actually is only a complex set up of forcefields to try and deter the Galympites from being able to pass into the earth's atmosphere, as this was the safest place of entry for them, before we set up these strong anti-rays. Unfortunately, at times, earthlings are caught in these rays when we are trying to eliminate the Galympites when they attempt re-entry to this atmosphere on another of their forays to cause further disasters on your planet. Innocent people of your planet become victims of these attacks, apparently to all concerned, disappearing forever off the face of the earth. "Luckily enough, we are nearly always able to save them, and they live in our underwater city of Bermartus, where we can control the time warp, they entered, being badly affected by the rays, to the extent that they would not be able to exist if returned back to their previous lives, but here they live a happy and full life." Botami paused, then added, "Let me assure you that these people are happy and well cared for, but it is so sad that these accidents actually happened and separated them from their real world, which they cannot return to, as it would kill them to pass through a reversal chamber. Far worse would have taken place, had we not deterred so many of those brutal and destructive Galympites who cause major disasters on your planet from time to time, and you earthlings always seem to think it's either natural phenomena or terrorists." He shook his head and looked so distressed. I knew, beyond anything else, that these people from Astrola were really good, and they were probably earth's only hope for survival. The actual monstrosity of the whole thing left me feeling dazed and very shaken, realising that we were all surviving through a daily battle between galactic forces for good and evil, survival or disaster, and it was actually out of our hands. Suddenly we appeared to be slowing down, and the turbulence appeared to decrease. As I looked towards the windows, I realised that the wall panels had closed and that the windows to the outside were now no longer visible. A slight feeling of panic started to well inside me and a realisation that something was about to happen. Botami walked to the far wall and started pressing switches and buttons on a large panel, which had become uncovered by the pressure of Botami's ring on the panel face. Suddenly all movement and sound stopped, and we appeared to be in a vacuum of stillness. A slight whirring noise behind me made me turn around, and I was once again amazed, as the whole side of the wall slid back, and I was facing several people, obviously Astrotars, standing in a group, all dressed in long, white robes, all with the same blonde long hair and cornflower blue eyes. Two appeared to have the six-sided silver cord, similar to that which the man called Xedato had worn on the aqua craft, with the same green cords around their waist, decorated with tiny, silver stars. These two also had the cults of their sleeves banded with three, red stripes, obviously denoting a rank held of some esteem. Others in the gathering were dressed like Botami and Eafi, except for the tall man that appeared to stand out from the others, although dressed in the same white robes. Around his neck was a large, gold, six-pointed star, set with a large, green stone in the middle of a triangle and hanging on a gold chain. The waist of this man was girded with a wide, golden sash, set with some strange letters made out of beautiful, green stones. He stepped forward, and with a kind of smile on a face of ageless wisdom, he directed his gaze at me with an intensity that looked into my mind but filled me with warmth, not fear. In his resonate voice, for the first time, said, "Welcome, earthman Glen Grant-Wallace. You are the first outsider who we have been able to communicate with, and to feel that you can help in our struggle to save your planet. I am Astro, father leader of my people the Astrotars, from far off Astrola, which has long ago burnt out and become a black hole in the universe. We were fortunate enough to have warning, some of us managed to make the journey safely to your planet many, many years ago, hundreds, in fact. We were appointed back in the eons of time by the Power Lords of the Galaxy Adrominicus to be the guardians of earth, and before our planet imploded, we had already visited earth when your earth people were only just in the beginnings of civilisation. 'We helped them, and they thought we were gods. As your planet evolved, we spent less time here, and only when our planet was about to destruct did, leave it and journey to your planet, hoping that we could live in harmony with you, sharing your planet, but not actually letting you know that we were here. "I am sorry that you have been abducted from your part of the world, but the time has come to make contact with the people of your planet, and it had to originally be done through someone like yourself, who is able to communicate intelligently with others through your writing. It is imperative to make the people of earth aware of why disasters are happening with such frequency on this planet and why there is so much disruption in all parts of this world." Astro half-turned, and with a semi-smile, gestured for me to follow him. We passed along a beautiful corridor that shimmered with light reflecting from the walls, although there were no signs anywhere of lights, and yet I had noticed that it slightly darkened behind as we passed along the passageways. This I had observed by looking back over my shoulder and found it very mysterious and rather eerie, adding to my feelings of excitement. Astro and the two men dressed like Xedato, which I had described, walked by his side, and I hear them referred to by Astro as Erup and Neek, suddenly stopped at what appeared to be a blank wall ahead; fitted, I noticed, with a strange, triangular shape. Astro touched the panel with his ring, and an opening appeared for us to walk through. We then entered a room resembling a huge garden. Happy and contented groups of people of different colourings stood or sat around talking, dressed in lovely, blue robes. Immediately I knew that these were the earth people victims of the Bermuda Triangle rays, saved by the Astrotars. Astro raised his hand, the talking all around the rooms ceased, and he smiled benevolently and started to speak in a friendly but deeply resonate voice. "Glen, an earthman like yourself is only a visitor for a short time. He is to be our ambassador to the outside world, to explain why this planet earth is suffering the huge increase in world disasters." Astro, this man who obviously everyone admired, but who had complete control, turned his head to me briefly and half-smiled, then continued, "My friends, Glen has only just arrived, but will be leaving us again shortly. I know there is so much you would like to ask him. Of course, tell him, but he will only be here a short time, so make him welcome, but when he has to go, you must have patience." The people around listened, smiling and nodding to this remark. Astro touched my shoulder, saying, "Join your people, but it will be for a short time, and then I shall send for you, as I have much to speak about." The next minute he was gone, and I was alone with all these different people, different nationalities, trapped in an alien world. Everyone turned to face me, and a split second of total silence fell. A fear ran through me. What would be their reaction to me? They knew I could return to the outside world. A tall, blond man of about forty spoke first, "Glen, welcome, I am John. You have no need to fear us; we are lucky to be alive. I have been here for many earth years. We each have had an escape from death, only to be saved by the Astrotars, who tell us they can in time build a time reversal machine, which could transport each and every one of us back through what we know as the Bermuda Triangle, or time field rays or be trapped here for as long as we live. We have everything we could ever want, everything we could ever wish for; except, of course, freedom. But freedom from here is death, as our bodies are life supported by the Astrotars. They are a good people, and we hope you can help them. We knew they have been trying to get the right person for a long time." My eyes became drawn to a dark-eyed, dark-haired girl about thirty. She moved forward with purpose and held my gaze. A smile started to flicker around her mouth, and I felt almost hypnotised. I felt as if I was drowning in her eyes, when suddenly, the spell was broken and John's voice said, "I see you've met Leanne? Take care, Glen, you are only here a short time; don't fall too heavy." And a hearty laugh rang out. A new voice, new person spoke behind me. 'Welcome, Glen, I'm Gerry. I'd like to introduce you around. We would all like to meet you, as this is an unexpected pleasure to meet a person who can return.' People gathered around. There was Sandy, Jean, Arty, Chesco, Martin, Vechenzo, Angie, Lizzie, Billy, Mark, and so the names went on. My brain felt battered as everyone was speaking and telling me tales of planes being pulled from the skies, fishing boats, and yachts being drawn under. One minute they were enroute, the next minute passing through lights and flashes of colour, a crushing feeling of wind, and then blackness, finally finding them- selves here with the Astrotars. Kindness and survival and all the necessities but not freedom, that had gone, stories abounded, stories of friendship, lost loves and families, fears. I looked around, and there was the dark-haired girl again, sitting with an elderly couple who looked not unlike her, a family look. LeAnne, that was her name. I walked across and said, "Leanne, wasn't it?" She smiled. "Yes, that's me. Sorry I was so forward, but I felt drawn." I was pleased beyond measure. I could not believe these strange feelings and sat down beside her. "This is my mother and father, Marge and Cliff Duckett," Leanne said, introducing the elderly couple to me. I was overwhelmed with a feeling of completeness, everything seemed unreal. I tried to pull back I could see that there were many people still trying to talk to me, but I would not move. I smiled at people and temporarily excused myself. I was talking to Leanne as if there were no tomorrows, and we knew that time was running out. I felt as if I had always known her. I could not take my eyes off her, or her from me. I placed my hand over hers, and her fingers curled round mine in acceptance. She smiled at her parents and then back to me. "Come," she said, "I must show you around before we are parted, but you will return. I know it." Holding hands, we started walking. Everyone had gone back to whatever they were doing or disappeared to other parts from sight. As we came to a wall across our path, Leanne pressed her hand to a groove in it, and I noticed a small ring on her finger, which touched a small stone in the groove, and immediately the wall opened, and we entered a passageway. I looked around. The opening had gone again as if by magic. Leanne was beautiful. She was smaller than me about five feet, nine inches, and slim and mysterious. I was hypnotised and, keeping hold of her hand, followed without question. Suddenly she stopped beside a small waterfront. "Drink," she said simply and proceeded to fill small glasses by the side of it. It tasted so refreshing, and I felt a warm glow filling my whole being and a feeling of total relaxation. Taking my hand again, she led me to an entrance of a room I had previously not noticed, and as we entered it, a profusion of beautiful perfumes surrounded me, and

I felt lightheaded. All around were beautiful flowers and small birds singing; a mini-paradise, I felt. There were Relaxair sofas all around set in small arches, and she said with a voice of husky mystery, "Glen, let's sit and talk" I must be dreaming. Here I was in a strange, idyllic piece of paradise, far below the waters of the world, with a beautiful, mysterious woman who had only eyes for me, and I knew that at first sight I loved her. I was almost too scared to close my eyes in case it all disappeared. "Oh, Leanne," I said, "how lovely you are. Am I dreaming?" To which her reply came, "No, but if only it could last forever. Our time together is limited this time, but I know, Glen, you will return." Suddenly she was in my arms, and I was kissing her with a passion I did not know possible, caressing her brow and whispering words of adoration; hearts beating in unison, everything around stopped, and we were as one. Slowly, I came to my senses, and Leanne was beside me, looking at me with an intensity I returned. But it was so hopeless. What was our future?

      She straightened her clothes and I mine, and she smoothed her hair with her hands, then we just sat with my arms around her for some time, close and warm in our unity of love. Shyly, Leanne took my hand and, standing up, she said simply, "Glen, we have been allowed a while together. I have asked Astro for this favour, and when they are ready for you, I will be informed. Come with me now. I want to take you somewhere special." I stood up and followed, as if in a dream. How wonderful and mysterious she was. We walked through this beautiful hall of flowers of all colours, small waterfalls, and singing birds in paradise. Tremors kept running through my body, my whole being was filled with love and desire for this dark-haired nymph who had stolen my heart. Suddenly I realised we had entered a corridor with dome-shaped indentations of about six feet high and three feet wide. After passing, Leanne stopped and loosened her hand from mine. I looked surprised, but she just smiled, and with her other hand, placed it on a silver inset plate. Slowly the wall moved sideways, and together we stepped into her private apartment. It was obvious straight away a piece of coral reef was inset with an image of her parents. Everything was soft and feminine, and a large, oval-shaped Relaxair type bed was to the side of the room, covered with a beautiful, green cover of the softest looking down. She pressed a tiny button in the wall, and the room became bathed in a sultry light, and soft, dreamlike music surrounded us. Leanne gently reached up to me and brushed a soft caressing kiss on my lips, causing my heart to miss a beat.

"Darling," she whispered, "our time is limited. Please love me." She slipped from the blue robe that had cloaked her figure in mystery, and before my eyes stood a goddess of beauty untold. My body became tortured with love for her, and I slipped from my worldly apparel and folded into her arms onto a cloud of love. Our bodies moved as one, our lips sealed in passion¡ my hands, her hands caressing, searching, the world became on fire, love fusing our souls together in an explosion of passion, then a sensation of floating held in an embrace that both hearts could not bear to part from. Slowly our eyes opened, and both could see as we gazed into each other's hearts that no one else would ever matter. "I love you, darling," I whispered. "I love you forever, Glen," she said simply. "How long I've waited for you." And with the passion fulfilled and the dream-like music, we drifted away on a cloud. "Glen, we must rejoin the others, but before we go back, how do you feel? Is it like something you have never experienced before? Because it is for me, and I shall love you forever." I gazed at her and said simply, "Leanne, you are my destiny. Whatever is ahead, I shall return. I feel that I have loved you through time. Come through time to meet you, and I shall return through time to be with you. One day we shall be together again. Please wait for me." And with this I tenderly pulled her to me, kissing her eyes, her nose, and then held her to my heart. Our lips sealed in a kiss of foreverness. Then gently we parted as Leanne said, "It is time. We must return." We slowly retraced our steps, and as the door in the wall opened and we stepped through, all eyes turned to us and all knew a bond had been forged forever. I noticed that Erup and Keek and two other Astrotar men, who I later found out were called Sehtor and Ennovy, were giving out refreshments and talking to some groups of people who were all in quite earnest conversation, and I realised that there were strong bonds and friendships between the earthlings and the Astrotars and a harmony of life through trust.

A shudder went through the room and vibrations started, lights flashing, and people moving quickly to different places. The outside view of sea life suddenly disappeared behind a shield, which slid across, and everywhere seemed to be heavy with a sense of purpose, or at least deliberation. "What is happening?" I asked Erup. "Serious underwater vibrations from another of the Galympites earthquakes," replied the Astrotar without hesitation and then looked wary as if he shouldn't have spoken. I looked with obvious curiosity and fear. "What do you mean? Who are the Galympites?" I asked. "I am sorry," said Erup. "I have said too much. I forgot you were not one of us; you must wait for our great leader, Astro, to explain. I hope he will forgive me. My surprise turned to concern. What was going on? I was a reporter, correspondent, with a natural curiosity and I had to know. Tremors continued, and panels started moving in the walls, creating fortification, I presumed. I felt uneasy. I looked around to see small openings had slid back in the inner walls, and everyone was starting to move through. Leanne, who had excused herself from my side a few minutes earlier, was back and taking my hand said. "Glen, we are all to go into the inner chambers to ensure our safety." We followed the others; the passageway was long. Small, button-type lights flickered along it. The walls were smooth, and although they looked like wood, they were cold like marble, but there was warm air around us. Suddenly we were in a large, spacious hall-like room. The ceiling was divided into sections and huge panels of little lights glistened and sparkled above our heads. Small tables and Relaxair chairs were all around, and there appeared to be about a hundred earthlings dressed in blue robes and about half as many Astrotars, both male and female with blond hair, blue eyes¡ white robed people from another world, and yet protective of us from whatever was threatening. Leanne was scared, I knew that. We were already close in our feelings, and I could feel her tension. I, too, was scarred, but why? Then a dull explosion in the distance and the lights started going out, flickering and dying, and all around a feeling of panic gripped the air. Seconds passed, then they started flickering back on again. Through all the panic came a voice, a voice of authority, but kind. "This is Astro. Stay calm, my people. Astrotar and earthling, fear not; we have had worse moments. We have an extremely safe inner sanctuary, built with an attack from the Galympites in mind, but calmness must remain.

"If we ever panic, we will forget things, and then problems will occur. Trust in goodness and unity, and we will prevail. Allow chaos to enter our lives and the Galympites will win and civilisation of earth will end." The lights were now fully on, and he continued, "You must have patience. It is imperative that no time is wasted. We have a new friend amongst us, Glen, who must return to his work, so that the cause that we are fighting for can become the cause of all the people of the world. "Only Glen can write our message to the people of the world and make them believe. They would destroy us if we tried, as 'suspect' aliens, and we all know a setback to us is a victory to the Galympites, but Glen will come back to us, I'm sure, and next time he will have more time to relax and get to know you all." The Great Astro looked at Leanne and Glen and then said, "Glen now has added reasons for return because when he goes, he will take only ambition to succeed in his human frame, but his heart will stay here." The people around listened, smiling and nodding to this remark. Then Astro said, "My people, relax again, danger is over. The Galympites have been dispersed by the outer Astrotars, and the triangle forcefield had been increased. Unfortunately, this could bring more people from earth into a danger zone of the so-called Bermuda Triangle which is, of course, of our making for the safety and survival of our created world below the sea, but we have no choice. We are the guardians of earth, and we must preserve life here at all costs." Astro then looked at me with a deep look that I felt penetrated my very soul, locking my eyes into an almost hypnotic state, and I knew that whatever it cost, I must do whatever I could to help. Then he spoke again, "You must take your leave of Glen now, as he must come with me, for I have much to discuss with him before he leaves us to act as an ambassador, I know that I have chosen wisely and that he will one day return." I was holding Leanne's hand, and I felt her hand tighten in mine, but I knew as I turned to look at her that our special love that had been ours for only moments in time was to be subjected now to a heartbreak separation, and nothing could change that from happening. "Goodbye, Glen," whispered Leanne, tears glistening on her cheeks. My heartbeat like thunder, but with heart and soul on fire, I bent and kissed her tenderly, whispering, "I'll love you always; please wait." I smoothed her tears off her cheeks and looked again at Astro. He was smiling, but a depth I could not understand was on his face, and he said, "Glen, please follow me." The people around listened, smiling and nodding to this remark. I called a goodbye to them all, glanced at Leanne with heartbreak in my eyes, let her hand go, and followed Astro as he had indicated, towards the side of the room, leaving the Astrotars behind. Once again Astro, by using his ring, took me through an apparent wall by touching some hidden ray or mechanism with his ring and causing the wall to move, leaving a doorway to pass through. For a moment, my sense of humour bubbled up, and I thought 'No draughts in this place.' Astro turned his head and smiled, and I knew he had read my thoughts. The room we entered was very relaxing, with a warm glow to the air and a form of subdued lighting that appeared to come from nowhere in particular. Around me I sensed I could hear the calming sound of water gently lapping on a beach. Two, long Relaxair chairs were placed side by side, with the most marvellous oceanic view set in front of us, through what appeared to be a huge porthole some twelve feet long by about six feet high. Astro beckoned me to sit down, and I relaxed back into a long-type Relaxair, whilst he settled into the other. Immediately from behind us, startling me slightly, as I had not heard the approach, came another girl just like Eafi. She passed us both silver goblets. Astro acknowledged her with a smile, and said, "Thank you, Rinka, we were ready for some refreshment." She smiled and glided out. They were so beautiful, these female Astrotars, I thought, and then flushed knowing my thoughts had probably been read.

Astro sipped his drink and closed his eyes for a moment, so I did likewise, relaxing and enjoying the drink I could not identify, but found delectable in flavours, being more refreshing and nourishing than anything I had ever previously tasted. Suddenly my wandering thoughts were interrupted by Astro. "Glen," he said, looking at me with a very serious look, "I have yet some more to say to you before you leave us." "I am aware that your feelings, although new, are deep for the earth woman Leanne. My heart is sad for you, though, as she never can re-enter the world as you know it. There are many things you do not know about us as yet, and one is 'that as you see' is not always as it would be seen outside of our complex. We have saved all these people from earth that you have met but, unfortunately, they have had severe damages done to their human body which, although now appears alright, would not withstand outside the complex for any time. Only time will bring you back to her, and you will always see what you want in a woman, in Leanne." How did he know? "I know also that you are aware that we have a complex ray system set up here, at this part of your planet, to destroy the Galympites, as this was the easiest place of entry before it, for them to wield destruction, and we have two other bases in deserted parts of the world. But, unfortunately, the people of your planet are increasing the difficulties for us, to keep out and destroy these evil beings. The pollution caused by earthlings is causing havoc with the atmospheric layers of your planet, amongst other things. When these layers, which are protective to your planet, are affected, they cause breaks in the layers, leaving 'holes,' which have already been noticed by knowledgeable people on earth who realise that the sun's radiation is no longer being sufficiently screened. But they do not realise that this also allows easier access to your planet for these cruel perpetrators of earth. This is making it more and more impossible for us to protect earth and to stop the Galympites from causing these horrific disasters worldwide. Think about it, Glen, lately there has been so much trouble everywhere: fighting, earthquakes, volcanic eruptions, floods, and airplane and train disasters of a magnitude not experienced before. "People on this planet are starting to wonder why things are getting worse and are frightened what will be next. Glen, you must tell them, warn them. We will help earth but for how long can we manage to hold out. We are few in comparison to them. If the earthlings do not help to look after their planet themselves..." Astro paused, and overwhelmed, I held out my hand to him and said, "I am deeply grateful to have met you and to have learned of your galactic protection for us for so long." Astro leaned across from where he sat and grasped my hand. I felt a surge of strength flow through my body from this great man and an intense feeling of a bond being formed between us. Astro started to speak again and looked straight into my eyes. "My friend, you do realise that people on this planet will be hard to convince? You may be laughed at, or it be even suggested that you are mental, or at the least, highly imaginative, but if you persist, perhaps, together we may stop the Galympites from succeeding. "I cannot impress on you enough that they are a destructive and evil race of beings from the far-off Galactic planet of Doomstare, many light years from earth and led by Golupus Diavelo, who is evil beyond imagination, but will be destroyed one day, if only we can all work together, and with combined strength destroy him.

The earth people are many in number, and basically an intelligent and good people. If all nations continue to talk and befriend each other, they will gain strength, and we can work together to save this wonderfully beautiful planet earth." Astro stood up, a touching my shoulder, said, "Now rest, my friend, and thank you for listening. I will send Botami to you presently. He thinks very highly of you, as do others who have met you." In what appeared to be the conclusion of his conversation with me, and in saying this, he smiled, inclined his head in a gesture of farewell, and walked away from me to the side of the room, touching the wall and leaving through the exit which had appeared. I was alone with my thoughts, on his words. I was suddenly made aware of a presence, and was quite astonished to find Botami, my aqua craft companion, standing beside me. I had not heard him enter the room and obviously showed some surprise." I think you were miles away in your thoughts," explained Botami gently, "but I'm sorry I startled you. Glen, would you follow me, please? I am to take you back to the aqua craft station, as we are about to depart from this underworld complex. Please follow me." We walked towards the opposite wall that I had appeared to pass through, and no opening even showed afterwards. In the wall there was an unusual stone carving of three arrows pointing downwards and three crossing upwards, centrally placing an indentation where a beautiful, green stone was seen Botami touched the stone and the wall slid back, and I couldn't believe it. I was back in the landing craft area where I had first arrived by aqua craft. So much had happened. I had met so many people, I had learnt so much, things that I found so hard to take in, and yet knew that so much depended on me, who was so unimportant in worldly matters, had been selected. Oh, I must not let them down. And then the thoughts of Leanne came flooding through my mind and a feeling of hopelessness and loss filled my very being. A slight noise came and by my side stood Botami and Leanne. I gasped. Botami quietly spoke, "Glen, the Great Astro said you were to have a few minutes to say goodbye, but then we must leave." There was a small anti-room off the hallway, and we walked in there together, gazing into each other's eyes. I knew I must succeed; I must return. No woman had ever meant so much, and with that single thought, she melted into my arms and embraced. Our lips locked in a desperate goodbye; how long off would the next time be? "Glen," a voice called, "it is time!" Botami came into sight. "We cannot wait longer because of tidal circumstances, diverse currents, and anti-rays, which must be avoided. The aqua craft is ready." There it was the hatch was open. I turned, and as if by magic, Leanne had disappeared. "Where is she?" I asked Botami, to which he simply said, "Waiting for your return." I entered through the doorway after Botami into the craft and flew that in that second it was closed behind me.

3

What lay ahead now that I had left Bermartus, the secret underwater world? A slight feeling of turbulence and whirling noise and I knew that there was no turning back I was in this with the Astrotars, and I must try and convince the world through the tabloids the true but dangerous facts. I was brought back from the depth of my thoughts by Botami's voice. "Glen, you can do it. I feel sure. You have believed and trusted us, so I'm sure you'll find a way." Once more I knew my thoughts were just as a conversation, no secrets. Botami laughed. "Quite right, my earthling friend; no secrets. We know you now have a warmth in your heart for the dark-haired earthling they call Leanne. Do not worry. I will not interfere with your deep thoughts. Relax and gaze once more on the wonders of the deep." He pressed the panel in the wall, and once again, the huge wall panel slid across, leaving a vast screen into the waters. For a second, a nervous shudder went through me as a huge shark's face with colossal teeth leered in at us, seconds and it was gone. We must be travelling fast, I thought as I sank into a Relaxair, leaning back. I closed my eyes for a second as Botami left me with my thoughts. A faint a touch on my shoulder, I jumped my eyes opening in surprise to see Eafi my female travelling companion from before, was standing beside me. "Glen, I am to call you that," she said, "We have problems." The side panel had reclosed, and I noticed that the lights were much dimmer in the room. She continued, "Botami is busy with the others, trying to strengthen the shield around the aqua craft, as we appear to have entered an area which must have been set with de- charger detector rays by the Galympites. This means unless we can act fast, they will discharge our forcefield around the aqua craft and destroy us." Eafi was trembling, and I took her hand gently. "I'm sure," I said, "that the Astrotars will think of something." "I wish you believed that" she answered, and I knew that my fear was being intercepted. The aqua craft lights flickered and almost went out then. Suddenly we seemed to swell from side to side, as if being shaken. I stood up and held Eafi close. Then we seemed to stop. The lights went out, and the whirling noise decreased, then stopped. I was scared. Suddenly the whirling started, and we seemed to leap forward. The lights came on again, and Eafi broke the silence. "They have been beaten again; we are safe." At this moment, Botami and two other Astrotars came into the room. "Well," said Botami, "That was a bad moment, but we still have many powers that work that the Galympites have not been able to decrease. We are travelling through an area now that we have a secret channel through, so we will bring you some refreshments, and you can rest. I'm sure that your head must be reeling with all that has transpired." A drink and some of their tablet refreshments were brought, and I partook of them. Then, relaxing back, I slowly felt myself slipping into sleep. How long had I rested? I thought as I opened my eyes on hearing Botami speak. "Glen, I'm sorry, but I must ask you to come with me now to the Zoom-ray departure bay. We have reached our destination already." As we reached the side of the room, he touched a button I had not noticed. It looked like a green, triangular-shaped gem set in a rock-type carving of arrows. I had seen this before so often in their complexes but never thought about it. So, the aqua craft had docked, and we were still safe. We passed through a dome-shaped room. Suddenly a very important, unanswered, unasked question stopped me in my tracks. "Botami," I said quietly, "I have just realised no one, not even the Great Astro, has told me what the Galympites look like and where they are. I feel I am so unarmed against questions that I will be forced to reply to when I tell my story."

Botami, who had been just a step-in front of me, turned to me and said, "Dear friend, we have not been as remiss as you think We are hoping that the Galympites will be destroyed before long, but should these battles, these destructive forces continue, you will be helped by us when you least imagine. The Galympites cannot breathe the air of earth, so they cannot just mix freely or intermingle with your people, but they have forces for evil beyond imagination. Their appearance to your kind would be fearful. They have the upright stance of man but the appearance of a horned goat. They breathe not air but a Sulphur like substance, which they would have to transport with them to survive your atmosphere, outside of their earth entry vehicles or spaceships as you call them, as on their far-off planet of Doomstare, where all of us would find it impossible to survive" My mind raced. Was this the origin of the devil: evil and Sulphur smelling, goat like in appearance? It all fit, but who had actually seen one, or had they infiltrated already into our life through black magic? "What is their leader's name?" I enquired, and the answer came back, "Golupus Diavelo." Diavelo was Spanish for devil. The puzzle was starting to fit together, but what a puzzle. How could the world be saved? Why did the Astrotars think I was any use? "Stop." A rather commanding side of Botami's voice interrupted my thoughts. "The Great Astro, our leader, has exceptional faith in you. You are a world travelled correspondent. You have been at many world disasters reporting and relating and have been monitored at the Base 2, which you have not visited as yet, but more is known about you than you can imagine. Be brave, forthright, and compelling, and the world will one day believe, but Glen, when you return to your world, you will not be alone; you will have our constant support. You are to be the Great Astro's ambassador. Wear the mantle proudly." Botami stopped and looked at me with kindness and depth, then quietly said, "Glen, it is time for you to depart "A large, tube shaped bed was in the middle of the room, and Botami advanced to it, lifting the lid and thus causing the tube to be divided into two halves. Botami turned and faced me and said in his kind voice, "Don't be afraid, Glen, but our great leader Astro thinks it would be safer to send you back by Zoom-ray. It is a form of atom transportation whilst in a dormant state. You will awaken on your arrival at your destination, perfectly aware of all that has happened whilst you've been with us. Please, could you climb into the bed of the Zoom-ray?" I nodded but felt a cold sweat breaking out all over me. Botami looked into my eyes and said calmly, "Don't be scared, Glen, you will be home faster this way." He stretched out his hands to grasp mine, and I felt the feeling of strength and reassurance that I had experienced with their great leader Astro, and as this feeling surged through me, my fear left me knowing that these people were good and would not hurt me.

I lay down, and Botami fixed the controls on the side of the Zoom-ray shield that were just at the side of me. Finally, he took from his finger a second ring, one he did not wear when I had seen him previously saying, "Our great leader Astro trusts you, Glen and has asked me to give you this ring as a token of our love for your planet earth and our friendship for you. One day this ring will enable you to return to us and perhaps stay longer among us, learning our ways. But take care, my friend, and do not lose it ever or let it out of your possession. I shall think of you often, but I know that we shall meet again soon." Botami touched my forehead, and with the other hand started to lower the small, dome-type lid over where I lay. I felt my eyes growing heavy and vaguely saw Botami's hand leave my forehead as the lid closed.

I heard in the distance a faint whirring sound, and I felt myself moving through space as it were, just a feeling around me of speed, then a floating sensation and intense cold, then wetness. I was unable to see anything as either it was pitch black or I could not open my eyes. I moved my hand, everything was black, cold, and wet. Where was I? Then my eyes started to focus on the darkness, and shapes started to form.

I was on a hillside, damp heather around. It was dark, nighttime. Oh, so that was it, I thought. I had fallen asleep on the hillside in the sun and slept till night, and it had rained. Oh, what dreams I had dreamt. I remembered them clearly, and I started to get up onto my feet, glad I was not stiff, and then everything stopped for a second as I realised I was wearing a small, triangular, green stoned ring. The unashamed tears ran down my face, I felt bereft she existed, the one love of my life, but out of reach. I had to see her again. I knew that I would pledge my life to that end. My Leanne, and with that my life took on a dedication I had never previously known. I started walking. It was quite dark, and as I stumbled over rocks in the dusk, trying to find the outline of the pathway, I was drawn to look up at the stars. A full moon glided out from behind the clouds, and I felt that perhaps there were stars for good and maybe the moon for bad. With my head full of thoughts, I came upon the path that led to my car. Still there I breathed relief and was amazed to find my key in the lock of the door. Jumping in I took off down the track, back to the main road and civilization. I looked at the clock in the car it was 21:37 But, of course, it was late September. No wonder it was already dark. I knew that I was passing along Loch Garry's perimeter and would soon be out on the main A82. My mind kept wandering. I must concentrate. I thought, how many miles had I driven? Another signpost in the headlights said six miles to Fort William. It was 22:15 on the clock. I would stop there. Time for a quick drink before bed. At last, the hotel sign showed I had arrived: The Wayfarers Rest. I remembered I had stayed here once before; clean, hospitable, small, family hotel, run by, what were their names? Oh, yes, Pat and Jack Buchan. I jumped out of the car, grabbed my suitcase, locked the car door, and moved swiftly to the entrance. Thank God, it was still open. As I walked into the light, music, and chatter of the bar, I was met by Pat, who said, "Hi, can I help you?" "I've stayed here before. My name is Glen Grant-Wallace," I replied. "Any room tonight?" "Aye," she replied, "follow me." We climbed a steepish staircase and stopped at a door numbered 7. "Make yourself comfy, and then why not come down for a wee dram before bed?" I nodded, threw the case and briefcase into the room, closed the door, and nipped quickly down to the bar. There was still an assortment of people around the bar, although by this time, it was nearing closing time. I asked for use of a phone, as I needed to contact my editor. It must have been how long? I suddenly thought. How long, indeed? I dialled the number in London. "Hello, editorial" it was answered quite sharply. "Glen here, Is that you, Sam?" "Yes," said the editor. Then sharply he said, "Glen where the hell have you been? No calls...in fact, total silence. What's the deal? we thought you'd fallen off the planet." "Well," said Glen slowly, "I did, and you'll never believe what happened, what I have learnt, who I've met, where I've been...What a story I've got for you..." Then I paused and added, "...and the rest of the world." There was silence for a few seconds, then Sam said, "Alright, Glen, it had better be good." "Well," I said, "I was at Loch Loyne for a bit of relaxation after doing the follow up on the Loch Ness Monster for Colonel Easterbank, when I fell down this crevice in the rocks and thought I was dead, but thank God, I was caught safely and transported by the Astrotars to their underground Loch base."

"Stop," Sam's voice commanded. "Have you been drinking, Glen?" "No," I said adamantly. "Whether you like it or not, I can prove it. I'll be travelling back tomorrow, and it is imperative that we treat this whole matter with urgency." "Yes," said Sam in what sounded like exasperation and simmering temper. "I'll see you tomorrow, Glen."

The phone went dead. Oh, Leanne, I thought, how can I make them believe me? My eyes caught sight of the ring, that special ring, a green triangular stone, which I wore on my hand a present from Astro. What was the benefit of this to me? Was it a keepsake, or was it a key to the puzzle that had yet to be uncovered? I went through to the bar and ordered a double whisky. By now the main door was locked and a stay behind was in process. The landlord Jack called me over to join two, elderly locals and himself, they were busy recounting tales of long ago. After a while, one of the elderly men, who had introduced himself as Angus, asked me in a lovely, soothing lilt about what I did for a living, to which I replied, "Reporter, correspondent; I'm Glen Grant-Wallace. I originate from Scotland, although I am based now in London." "Do you travel a lot?" asked the old man. "Yes," I replied, "to places no one else has been to." "What do you mean?" asked Angus. "Well, I'll tell you an amazingly strange but true story you may mud it difficult to believe. But please, please hear me out, that's if..." I asked, "there's sufficient time." "Well, wait a minute" said Jack, "I'll get us all some more drams, and get Pat and we'll all listen to your tale. It's a good way to wind up an evening with a good story." "Well," said Jack, the landlord, "we're ready. What's this amazing tale?" So, I started to recount my tale. At first, they were listening, but only half-heartedly, but they became absorbed, in parts my voice broke as I spoke of Leanne and her forced exile and our separation, and they became more and more amazed as I went on. Sheer disbelief turned into sheer incredibility, and then as I finished and showed them my ring, which I kept on my finger, old Angus leaned across and stared at it. "I've seen something like that before "he said. "I'm sure it was in some museum." "Can I see it here, laddie?" asked the other old man call Dodd. I went to take it off my finger, but it seemed stuck fast. "Can't get it off," I said, and twisted it around. Immediately the lights flashed and faded, flickered, and came back, and in my mind's eye, I could see Botami standing there, gazing at me, and telling me never to lose it. We all looked at each other, bonded by the story; they believed me. If I could do it once, I could do it again. The silence was broken by Dodd. "Well, lad, that was some tale, and I don't know why, but I believe you. But then I think you have an honest face. I wish you luck, and I wish the human race luck." "Aye," said the others "We better hope the world believes Glen, or there won't be one anymore." "How are you going to work the oracle, lad?" said old Angus. "I suppose you're going to splash it all over the television and the newspaper. Mind you," he added, "no one believes them these days." "Well, you believed me," I said, turning to the group sitting round the dying embers of the fire. "And as far as I'm concerned, that's a damn good start" I yawned. "Oh, God, I'm tired. I'll have to excuse myself and go to bed. I've a long journey tomorrow to see a most disbelieving editor at the end. "Not forgetting a period of days when I was missing without any communication, but rest assured, when I come back up to Scotland, I'll stay and let you know how I'm getting on. Watch the newspapers and the T.V for any hint of the story and watch for those so-called natural disasters, disasters without explanation increasing steadily. You will know, like myself, that it's all a power struggle, good against evil, Astrotar against Galympite, survival or destruction of the whole human race" "Well, Glen, lad," said old Dodd, "it would be more than marvellous to us Scots if it was a Scot that saved the world." And with a nod and a smile of acknowledgement, I climbed the stairs to my room. Tomorrow was another day. Although it was September, it was cold and overcast, with a hovering London mist, which, in the past would have been fog not I thought like the highlands where the mists I had just left at six o'clock this morning, were refreshing and inspiring, and quite mysterious at times, but back to work. Here I was now outside the huge old building which towered up in front of me. An area known in the past for its many newspapers, editorials, magazines, but not as many now as used to be the famous Fleet Street, news centre of London, capital of England but most now had moved or transferred to Wapping East London in the late 80's. Deep in thought, and sadness for having left the beautiful Leanne, so warm and loving, and to have fallen so much in love, and not knowing when I would see her again. Perhaps I might never see her again, or for us to be together and yet perhaps if I achieved success with my mission, who knows what could happen. I pushed open the old door, which must have been there for at least a century, and entered the building, which I had entered so many times before but this time it was different, so much rested on my shoulders and ability to overcome disbelief from others. I started climbing the stairs, the boards were well worn, and I thought how the walls could do with painting or perhaps a good clean. As I climbed the stairs to the third floor, I was wondering what my editor boss's reaction to my amazing story would be, and how would I convince him to believe me. As I reached the third-floor landing, the door to the office was pushed open hurriedly and a young reporter burst out, quickly turning back as he saw me, and shouted to the general office to anyone listening. "It's Glen, he's back from Scotland, I wonder what news he's managed to get". I entered and nodded to the few around that looked up from their desks and computers. Only a few of us remained here at the Fleet Street office with Sam the editor most had either left or transferred to the Wapping office, with the changes in the late 80's and 90's. The world was certainly changing fast. I made straight for the editor's door, knocked and waited. A bellowed "ENTER" was the answer, in his usual bad tempered and bossy way and continued with the following words. "So, what mythical concoction am I about to hear". The look I got told me the whole picture. He was sprawled in a big leather chair, his shirt open at the neck, his tie undone, his sleeves rolled up, the appearance scruffy and to complete the look was a narcissistic grimace on his face which did nothing for his looks with his puffy red cheeks and his big reddish nose.

In between words he was puffing a big cigar, totally illegal these days, but he did not care. The air in the room was thick with the smell and quite Smokey. "Right talk, Glen" he snarled "I'm all ears". I, with great difficulty, suppressed an inward laugh, imagining this supercilious fat, bullying individual with 'ears' all over his head, but quickly suppressed my thoughts and said "Sir, I am going to relate the whole story that's if you do not interrupt", the editor coughed and said "Ok Glen, get a move on, I've got work to do, and really do not have time to listen to your ramblings". "Believe Me" I said and continued "by the end you will realise it is a fantastic piece of unbelievable news for not only you, but for the whole world, but if you do not want to listen", as he had already started to interrupt, I continued. "I am sure other editors would be delighted to be the first to know how and why I am so desperate to make the world aware of that which I have learned". Begrudgingly Sam Juste, who was only 'just' in name, not in nature said "Well continue for god's sake I can spare a few minutes" to which I reported that it would take more than that. I was sure that he would want to hear it all. As I began to tell the tale of how it had begun on the Glen Loyne hillside, the fall, the monster, the journey through the Atlantic Ocean about four kilometres down, stating things that were impossible for me to know otherwise. The journey through the Sargasso Sea in the very depths in an aqua craft. All about the Astrotars and the Galympites. The Good and Evil struggles, the rescued people from the depths of the Bermuda Triangle area, of course leaving out personal details of my lost love Leanne. The necessity to plug the holes in the atmosphere to stop the Galympites gathering strength and destroying the earth as we know it. I finished by telling him about my return to Glen Loyne hillside by the Zoom-ray reversal chamber which acted as a transformer of matter and how I woke up and was amazed by how it was all true and I needed to find a way to tell the story. He looked puzzled, but still not convinced and asked what proof I had. I showed him my hand and said that he would see a triangular green stoned ring to which he replied, "Bloody hell, Glen anyone can buy a ring" I looked at him and said, "If I twist it something will happen" and I started to twist the ring on my finger, as Botami had told me to do and he promised that although I must never take it off but by twisting it, something dramatic would happen. I gently twisted the ring, and the lights went out and a quiet commanding voice broke the silence with "Believe Glen it is all true". It was spoke in a strange accent and with that the lights came back on again. I looked at Sam, my unbelieving editor, who no longer had that sarcastic disbelieving look on his face, but a rather shocked white, wide eyed look, saying "Oh my god, Glen, which way forward" and "My heart missed a beat". Now it was going to be a major planning operation, and I knew that I had achieved the first step. I was being offered the way forward. Sam's final words to me as I was leaving the office were words, I shall not forget. "This is so very important Glen" he said with a very serious face, "Let's keep this to ourselves for the moment we must not open a can of worms. How we publicise this is extremely important, so that it helps the planet, not destroying it. So, whatever happens I will help you, but please keep me informed, but the story stays with us". I commented at this stage that I was probably going to have to travel away, as I had certain aspects to check which had been told to me, and I had also been informed that certain people would be contacting me when I was with the Astrotars, as they have another two bases but where? That is one of the things we need to know, and I need to find them with help from certain people. As I reached the office door, I turned to Sam and said, "I may need to take a few weeks off call it holidays, but it will be work". As I left and the door closed behind, I heard Sam reply "Glen, take whatever you need, please, be careful and let me know at all times how you get on". I was grateful for the turnaround in Sam's attitude, and felt grateful of his offer of help and belief. I felt happier now, than I had when I arrived and ran down the stairs and out of the main door into Fleet Street. I had business to see to, prearranged by Sam for four o'clock, and it was with some dissatisfied politicians who had asked for a meeting at their gentleman's club. These politicians wished us to write an article about their views on certain matters. I would have to be careful as certain topics would have to be looked into, and I would have to pass it over to Sam as I was going to be too busy. The gentleman's club was not far from the office. I arrived a little late but explained that I had been away in Scotland. The men were pompous, and all knowing or thought they were. I listened to their arguments, making notes and wondering why I was listening to such self-important rubbish and worse write an article on it, why? Who but them wanted to read it? I said that I had enough notes, and I would see what I could do. They asked me to stay and have a drink, but I explained that I did not have time, thanked them, shook hands and left, it was five thirty and I decided that if I nipped into the big library nearby, I could do some research on U.F.O.'s and such like, remembering what I had been told about them entering into our atmosphere. Some of the notes I read on the microfiche about sightings were extremely interesting but the majority of them appeared to have been made up. I thought that as it was now approaching seven o'clock, I had better get home, as I had still had not been there since returning from Scotland. I was full of promise and excitement and as I crossed the road I suddenly remembered a little library near the train station, I went to the door and realised that I only had fifteen minutes 'till closing time so I went inside and asked if they had any literature on sightings or strange happenings in the world or any strange places, to which the librarian took me down a narrow aisle and lifted down a book of ordinary size saying, "You will have to be quick, I'm afraid, we are due to close shortly". I sat down and started thumbing through the pages, amazed to see so many names of places in the world where strange, unexplained things had happened. I was interrupted by a loud bell and a man's voice on the tannoy "The library is now closing, please return your books and exit the building", I was sorry that I had not come here sooner so I asked the librarian if I could borrow the book, she made me leave a deposit and asked how long I wanted it for, I said "About three weeks". She charged my credit card and told me to have a good evening. I was made up I would have a good study of the book when I got home. As I got outside, I realised it had started to rain, so I rushed to the place where I had left my car, reserved for journalists in Fleet Street. As I got outside I realised it was still raining, so I went and dived into my parked car and made for my flat. Whatever lay ahead filled me with excitement and journalistic curiosity, obviously I knew there would be danger, who would I meet? Someone was going to contact me, but who? After parking and locking my car and extricating my luggage, I found that by the time I reached the door I was drenched to my skin and cold. Now at last I was home, I put my key into the stiff lock of the door and went inside the cozy warmth enveloped me, I was so glad I had left my heating on a timer before I went away. First things first, I thought feeling secure and out of the weather, so what was I standing there for move I thought. I took off my wet shoes, soaking coat and hat, and hung them around the radiator in the hallway. I went into the lounge, switched on the lights and pulled the curtains closed by this time I was famished, opening the freezer, I took out some bacon and put it into the microwave to defrost and then got some bread ready by the toaster. Nothing better I thought as my bacon started fizzling under the grill, popping a couple of eggs into a frying pan, I said, "Glen you are multi-tasking, now for the toast" and "Nearly forgot the coffee, the most important part". I got my tray ready and plated up the bacon, eggs and toast, grabbed my mug of coffee and headed to the lounge to settle down and enjoy my meal. Half an hour later I was sitting on the sofa with my notes from the meeting, my borrowed library book about 'strange events & places' and other junk I thought might come in handy. I idly turned on the television with the remote, what for? Habit, I guess. I wanted to read, so I just had the volume on low, in case, I thought, anything interesting catches my attention. After some time of looking and reading the book and learning of amazing facts and anomalies from around the world, some of the information I had gleaned, I had already known a little about, but I was now intrigued to find out more. I read of the fires in Sicily, the marble caves in Chile, the great blue hole off the coast of Belize and lots more. Suddenly and for no apparent reason, my attention was immediately drawn to a group of individuals on the television screen, men of different ages appearing to be discussing something, I quickly turned up the volume and started to listen with intrigue. They were discussing the News, the latest world disasters and wondering why so much was happening, so often these days. I became much more interested in the programme and listened intently. My eyes were suddenly drawn to one of the men in particular, a man who used his hand to express his words it was then that I saw it on his finger, he had a ring which was an identical copy of mine, a triangular green stoned gold ring. Where had he got it from and who gave it to him? My mind started playing tricks on me was I going mad? The men talked and talked, I was spellbound with him, listening for all my worth, my eyes glued to the ring and wondering. I had to know who he was and how I could contact him I know I thought I'll ring up the news desk. I looked up the telephone number, and seconds later I was answered by a female voice asking if she could help me. I told her that I was watching the debate on world disasters and wondered if she knew who had arranged it. She thought for a minute, and then looked at a script in front of her, "Hello" she said, "Are you still there, sorry for keeping you waiting, it was someone called Arthos Grant". I then asked her if she knew whether it was the man with the blond hair, wearing a blue shirt and black suit, because he seemed to be in control of the conversation, and I added that I thought that he might be a long-lost cousin of mine that I had lost touch with, due to all of my travelling as a reporter and correspondent, and that I was quite desperate to make contact. I then asked if she could possibly catch him before he left the studios, as I knew it was an actual programme live not recorded. Maybe, I went on, could you give him my telephone number and ask him to call me my name is Glen Grant-Wallace, and my telephone number is she stopped me and said, "I have it recorded on the phone". She finished the conversation by telling me that she would do her best to pass on the message and said goodbye and that was that! Would he call? Maybe it was just coincidence, but it seemed surprising the ring was so special and identical to mine. Twenty minutes passed, it seemed longer, and then the shrill ringing of the phone bursting into life, I grabbed it and answered it. A deep resonate voice spoke "Hello Glen, I am Arthos, I thought that with a little help I could make contact with you we both own a very special item, which is our link, and which helped to make the contact. We must meet tomorrow." I agreed and asked where would be best. We decided the ten a.m. would be fine, and that we would meet at the steps that go to 10 Downing Street, a definite landmark. Remarking as our conversation was finishing "Oh Arthos I shall be wearing my leather jacket, black trousers and a cap" the answer was simply "Fine Glen, I will see you at ten", and the call that would change my life forever more, was ended with a click of the phone. I felt a weird feeling as if I knew him, but that was not possible. Right, I thought, perhaps it was time to go to bed, as I suddenly realised how tired and exhausted, I really was. It was after midnight and I had been us from around four in the morning, travelled from Scotland, spoken to Sam, interview, library visits and then this magical connection. Dreams of a peculiar nature disturbed my sleep of Botami and the Great Astro and Leanne, my love then visions of those Galympites, all mixed together and then with a start I was awake. It only my alarm clock, nothing sinister. I showered and shaved, and then to keep things right I called my boss Sam, to say I might not be in as I was meeting a new contact evolved from a surprising source, and that I would speak to him later. This done I decided to have a couple of cups of coffee and some toast to set myself up for this meeting.

Would I have difficulty recognising him I thought, as I reached the steps at the entrance to Downing Street, so many people were toing and froing and perhaps I might miss him. A tap on my shoulder, and we were face to face as I turned. I reached out to shake his hand and we both looked at the pair of rings and smiled, contact had been made. We needed to talk, and an agreement was reached to find somewhere to have a coffee and have a leisurely and private talk. I could feel trembling in my stomach was it fear or excitement, the future hour or so would decide. We walked across the busy street, dodging traffic, and getting several hoots from irritable motorists. Turning a corner, we walked down a side street to a small cafe I had previously used ages before but found it had changed. We asked if we could get some coffee or would that not be possible. He nodded and disappeared. A few minutes later he re-appeared with two coffees and biscuits and brought them over to us, in a quiet corner we had found. Mind you because it was bad weather and only mid-morning the place was empty. I paid the man and asked him if he was the owner "Yes" he replied "Owner and loner today, glad to see someone else I will be in the back, please give me a shout if anyone else comes in or you need anything. I am doing my bookkeeping whilst I get the chance". We smiled and thanked him. It suited us fine, and we settled down to talk. Arthos started by explaining that the force of Astrola would always help us in our future forays around the world. I interrupted him briefly, asking him what exactly he meant by 'around the world'. He smiled and began to explain to me, that alone, I would have difficulty, and that we would be meeting up with some other people who were in it with us. I was mystified, Arthos", I said, "I am confused, what are you telling me?". Arthos sighed, took a deep breath and then continued with a tale of unbelievable things.

4

Firstly, he told me that he had been studying all types of disasters in the world for many years and reporting facts he found out to his friends and colleges, the Astrotars. He paused "Now" he took another deep breath "there will be things you don't understand, but you must trust me, things I will confide as our friendship grows, but we are not alone, but will be helped by thought transference, my Astrotar contact, through my ring is the Astrotar Yatoo, and someone else you will know called Botami who will always be your contact". I looked puzzled I knew I did, I even felt my face frown, and asked him how he knew all this. "It will gradually unfold Glen, and you will learn all".

He had a map and put it on the table. It was a world map, with crosses and arrows on it. I looked and studied it intensely and wondered what it all meant? As I looked up, I noticed he was smiling and said "Glen your curiosity is good these crosses are marking the journeys we will be undertaking. On route we will be meeting others that will be as us, sorting out and reporting if we can see the evil forces that are destroying the planet earth. We must organise our route and we will be starting off by journeying to Sicily, we must be prepared to travel light, washing or buying things as we move on, when we need them. So, remember, Only necessities. Tonight, I have things to do and arrange, but at nine o'clock tomorrow morning I will call at your flat, is that all right?" I was surprised and said, "I will give you my address", "That's a good idea" said Arthos, I'm not that psychic!" It was great we were so at ease in in each other's company, like old friends, peculiar as that was, as we had only just met. We shook hands and left the cafe, shouting a goodnight to the landlord. I was making for the underground, and he was going in the other direction, where too, I had no idea as he had not said.

Although it was only mid-afternoon, I had decided to go straight home, as it was raining once again and I still had those notes to sort out for those politicians and then fax it to Sam. Plus, and it was a big plus, I had to let Sam know that the following day I was off on my travels with my new contact, to where in Sicily I had no idea?

The underground was crowded as usual everyone needing to push their way forward to the front, everyone in a hurry, running down flights of stairs onto crowded platforms. Everyone determined to get on the trains when the doors opened, people exiting with difficulty as others pushed in. We were packed like sardines. Next thing we were at the station at which I needed to change. Then rushing up the escalator and onto another underground train connection. Great, nearly home! At last weary and wet, although it was late afternoon, I rushed down the street and with a sigh put my key into the door lock. Home again I wearily threw my wet things over the radiator, went into the kitchen and grabbed a TV dinner of roast beef and popped it into the microwave and bingo five minutes later, complete with a mug of coffee, I sat down to enjoy my dinner and started weighing up all that we had talked about, and what lay ahead!

So, I thought, Sicily according to Arthos was to be our first destination. I wondered why? And then suddenly started to worry about how much this was going to cost. I wasn't flat broke, but travelling from place to place, trains, cars, planes, hotels that was going to stretch my savings account. Suddenly the phone rang, and as I lifted the handset to answer I was immediately met by Arthos's voice "Glen, stop worrying the cash side of this endeavour, has already been sorted." I couldn't believe my ears, amazed as I said to him "Arthos, how did you know my thoughts?" to which his immediate answer was that there was more to him than I could possibly know at this stage, but to accept his sincere friendship with trust, and that all would be well, his word and solemn promise upon it. What felt like a minute of silence ensued until his deep voice said, "Goodnight Glen, see you in the morning," and he was gone leaving behind dead air.

The next morning, I awoke, it was only just after six, but I was awake, so I got up and showered and shaved as usual. I was amazed that I did not feel tired as I had been working late into the night finishing up my editorials and then faxing them off to Sam to print. After this I had become engrossed in my borrowed book, which was all about strange facts, and after I had packed my backpack with the things I would need, indeed very sparse amount, plus my camera, passport and my credit cards just in case I needed them. So of course, it had been after midnight when I eventually dropped off in bed. I checked that my lights would go on and off at regular intervals, put my heating on very low, washed up and tidied the lounge then with some toast and coffee sat down and telephoned my boss. The phone rang and he answered "Sam Juste, Editorials." I told him who was calling and that I was just about to leave with my new contact but would try to keep in touch as much as was possible and that any information that I gathered would be for use by him and no one else. He pleasantly thanked me, and I wondered if he was ill taking no chances I immediately excused myself as my doorbell was ringing. I certainly did not want a long and involved conversation and did not want to let him in on what I had learned already. The door rang again, and I hurriedly opened the door, and yes here before me was my new friend Arthos. I brought him in saying "So you found me alright"? And an unusual answer followed "Yes Glen it has taken a long time to find the right person for these missions, you were suggested long before you visited Scotland. That visit was preordained by me and the other Astrotars. I have known of your skills in journalism for a good long time and coupled with your ability to get people interested in your stories. We physiologically persuaded you to go for a walk on the Glen Groyne hillside. Botami said you were a good man and an excellent team member for our expedition. Everyone you met liked and respected you and were sorry to part company with you." I sat down in a state of confusion "Arthos" I said, "I am no longer me?" I wasn't sure if this was a statement or a question. "Of course, you are" explained Arthos "But without intervention, you would not have visited the Astrotars." I quickly said, "Have you been there?". Arthos looked long into my eyes holding my gaze steady, then said firmly but quietly "One day I will tell you all that I know, but for now let what I have spoken of be enough, I can trust you and you should feel easy in trusting me. Arthos sat down on the chair next to me and said "we were going today but, but our plans have altered slightly, I have to send some very important messages to Bermartus the city under the ocean but enjoy the extra time that you have read your new book and find out all that you can about Sicily, I must go home now to arrange flights to Sicily, organise our schedule and cashflow, there's nothing for you to worry about. I see that you are already prepared so today you can relax. I am glad to see you have a backpack, as we cannot take a suitcase, please don't forget your passport." Arthos got out the map from the day before which was marked with crosses and pointed out a small town by the name of Canneto di Caronia which was situated beside the Tyrrhenian Sea, he advised that this would be our first destination. This interested me greatly as I spoke a little Italian and felt perhaps this would be of help. Arthos looked at me and commented on the fact that it was indeed good that I could speak some Italian and that it might well come in useful. I frowned and felt bewildered, confused by how he knew what I had been thinking, to which he said gently "Glen, I have the ability to know what you are thinking, it is my gift in this life, and one day it might also come in handy if you should find yourself in trouble." "Thank you Arthos for your kindness" I said. I made some coffee for us both, and we continued talking at length about each of the crosses highlighted on the map these were places that I had never visited during any of my travels, but I was enthralled as the conversation conjured up all sorts of things in my mind. First was the Cave of Crystals in Naica, secondly Hang Son Doong, which is a mountain cave in Vietnam with a subterranean river and the caves in Chile with amazing blue and grey chambers, submerged to some extent and formed over 6000 years. After this he went into a story about the Great Blue Hole off the coast of Belize, where he had been with some colleagues and needed to go back at some time. He finished by saying "I could speak so much more on this subject, but everything will unfold for you as we travel and we will even travel to the Nazea lines in Chihuahua, Mexico. There are so many things to see in this wonderful planet Earth". I was spellbound as Arthos was so knowledgeable and his storytelling was simply mesmerising. The hours had flown by and I had made us both some sandwiches and coffee for lunch awhile Arthos continued to tell me of his travels. I was elated and filled with excitement, but still I felt scared, as we were bound to come across dangers, visas, passport control, people with evil intent and nerve cracking adventures. Arthos smiled and commented that I had got it in one but added that I would meet some very wonderful and important people, some that would be known from the news and others of which you will never have heard of. He finished by saying "Actions speak louder than words". Arthos arose from the chair and told me that he must leave in order to get everything organised, and that he would meet me tomorrow at Heathrow Airport, and that I must remember to come complete with 'Passport' and 'Backpack', and that our meeting would be at Departures coffee lounge. "I will ring you later on today with the time to meet but I am off now, and I will look forward, till tomorrow when we start our mission". As Arthos left I waved and thought tomorrow was another day. There I was dosing on the sofa, dreaming of a mix of things, travelling, airports, things I had read about, then returning my mind to my time spent with the Astrotars pondering on the connections between the recent pass, Arthos and then the future. My dreaming thoughts were sharply interrupted by the ringing of my phone. I lifted the receiver and was immediately greeted by Arthos, the deep even tone easily recognisable, apologising for the lateness of the call. I glanced at the clock surprised that it was already 23:30 "Yes" came his voice "It is late isn't it?" "No matter" I replied, "I have been dosing the night away". Arthos continued in a decisive manner "Please Glen be at Heathrow Airport tomorrow at 10:00 as we have to book into the Alitalia desk two hours before our flight which is at 12:35 to Rome and then we go on to Palomino in Sicily. The rest of the details I will let you know when we meet. Goodbye Glen" and he was gone!

    I rushed around the flat grabbing the last few things that I had not as yet put in my backpack which lay ready behind the front door, checking as I did that, I had already packed my passport, camera, driving license, credit cards and sunglasses; my check list was now complete along with all my usual journalistic things except for a notebook and pen which I suddenly remembered to pack. Sleep came quickly, but so did the ringing of the alarm clock, which I had set for 6:30am. I hated to rush with last minute things! A quick shower and shave the to my usual list of necessary 'does', alarm set in case of intruders, switches off, fridge door and freezer closed properly, water turned off in case of leaks and lastly, I made sure my heating was set on the lowest setting. Now I knew I had enough time for a cup of coffee while I rang my boss Sam. I told him that I was just about to for the airport to catch a flight to Rome and then on to Sicily with my contact, and I advised him that was all the information I could share with him at the moment as I was running out of time. He started to speak but I cut him short "Got to rush Sam, bye for now!" With that I donned my jacket, put on my cap and hefted my backpack and swung it on my back opened the front door, making sure I had my keys to hand closed it and I was off! I made for the underground, hopped on two buses and finally concluded the last 10 minutes of my journey in a taxi. As I walked into departures in Heathrow, there was Arthos already, my travelling companion! I knew that somehow, he had become the sort of friend that lasts, someone that I had always known and yet it was such a short time. Arthos had the tickets already, plus the boarding passes, so with only hand luggage we went straight through security to the Departure lounge. Only 90mins remained before our flight was due to leave. There was time for a sandwich, drink and perhaps a paper for later. It was nice to relax after all my rushing about. Our flight was called, so we proceeded to gate 12 where the boarding for the flight to Rome had been announced. A helpful team of air hostesses met us and welcomed us on board as we took our seats which were located near the front of the airplane. A pleasant flight ensued, with not too much turbulence, our needs attended too by a staff member with a beautiful smile, coffee for Arthos and a whisky for me only one though! because I did not want to fall asleep, my journalistic nose was always twitching, listening to people around me. I read some of the paper I had bought earlier and enjoyed the lunch that was served. Squealing noise, a couple of bumps, and we had landed at Rome airport. It was noisy and crowded with security police very obviously placed around there were queues and more queues, people of many various nationalities shouting voices nearby alerted my attention to a group of men involved in a heated argument the row was escalating by the minute and very vocal. Without warning several police surrounded them and separated them from the queue and escorted them to a side room. I wondered what was so bad that they had felt the need to cause trouble for themselves, but Arthos turned to me and said to me to forget it, as it was not our problem. I guess once a journalist always a journalist, but I had noticed one of the policemen fingering his gun and it could easily have turned nasty. It is always good to watch what goes on around you! Arthos looked at me and smiled, obviously he knew what I was thinking.

  Through passport control, and off to the next stage of our journey the flight (though much shorter) to Sicily. Arthos went and asked about the time of our flight, and I looked for the new security control point which we needed to pass through, all the while I was watching the different groups of people passing by. One group that particularly caught my eye looked to be important people, dark suits, dark sunglasses, very Italian looking, and seemed to be surrounding one individual, I wondered who he was? Maybe a politician or a Sicilian God father who knew? Before my interest was fully engaged Arthos was back with our boarding passes in hand, and he hurriedly led the way always in a rush. He turned and smiled saying "Glen we still have much yet to do today!" We passed through security and were awaiting our gate information being displayed and at last we were boarding a plane for the second leg of our journey, having only just caught this connection by the skin of our teeth. Palermo here we come! We arrived at Sicily airport, a few bumps and that dreadful thrust back on stopping, and next we were being ushered through the gates to Security. Once again, we saw armed Sicilian police ready for any unusual occurrence. Quite a relief to be through without there being any trouble. Before we knew it, we were out of the terminal and looking for the car hire cabin situated outside, or so we were told! But we eventually found them by the arrival's entrance. We chose a Hertz desk, as they offered us a good deal, two drivers, insurance and a good weekly rental. We were told where the nearest petrol station was to Palermo Airport and it was an Esso garage and to reach it, we were to leave the motorway at the Villanueva di Cinisi, so it meant we had to drive past the airport, turn left to Cinisi and the garage would be further up on the left-hand side. We got there, filled up, paid and then returned back to the motorway, getting off again at the airport exit and heading the seventy odd miles to the place Arthos had told me about Canneto di Caronia, which would take us about one and a half hours to get to. Arthos said that he would be driving as I did not know the road and he had been there before. The road dipped and as we wound our way along the coast, and it was another surprise to me as I did not know that Arthos had been here before, he had never mentioned the place in any of our talks. All this I was only thinking, not saying aloud but Arthos remarked reading my mind again "And there is a lot more you will learn about me as we move forward together." the miles went on and on, and as dusk was turning more into night, it was not so easy to see any of the passing scenery; just vague shapes becoming cleared as we got closer to our destination. I was wondering where we would stay, but I am sure there will be a hotel or a bed and breakfast place, I thought to myself. Arthos interrupted my thoughts and told me we were going to meet an old friend of his called Pietro, and that he would sort out our accommodation for our time here. That was reassuring as I did not fancy sleeping in the car, which I had done many times in my younger reporting days. I am ashamed to say I must have dosed off as suddenly Arthos said "Glen we are here". He had stopped the car and was already getting out, waving to the man coming towards us. "Here is Pietro" he said, "Let me introduce you". We shook hands, exchanging names and smiles. Then Arthos said to Pietro "My friend, where can we stay for about a week?" We were answered with a shout "Glen, Arthos, follow me" a short walk and a welcoming chat, we came upon a small inlet harbour. Pietro pointed to a two-berth cabin cruiser saying, "So this, you two is your home for the time you are here, it is well stocked and ready for you both as promised".

I smiled as everything was organised and I had not had the slightest idea about any of it. I turned to Arthos and said, "You are most organised and wonderful at planning". They were talking to the side of me, as I lifted the back packs out of the car, saying to them "I shall just get these aboard if that is ok?" and this was agreed. Arthos turned to me after a few minutes and said "Pietro is going to show me some photographs, would you like to have a shower or perhaps a rest? Just help yourself to something to eat, or have a beer if you fancy it? It's been a long time since I saw Pietro." I understood their need for some privacy and it had been a very long day, indeed I was ready to settle down. I boarded the boat and made my way down to the lower deck. There was a table, 2 chairs, microwave, fridge and even a filter coffee machine. Two doors located off to the right were closed, so I opened the one nearest me, it contained a ready-made up bunk bed. Great I thought and then crossed over to the other door, the same identical layout greeted me in this room as well. I made a sandwich ham and cheese but in the Italian style, some pickle accompanied by a yoghurt and a nice cold beer, Great! My little repast looked most enjoyable. The gentle rocking of the boat felt very comforting and made me feel very cosy, ready for a nap even. I decided after I had eaten and drank my beer to settle in for the night; and not knowing the drill for boating life, I climbed onto my bunkbed, closing my door behind me. Wearing only my t-shirt and boxers in case I had to get up. That was that! Darkness crept over me as I sank into a deep sleep.

  I do not know what woke me up. I called for Arthos, but there was no reply. I climbed out of my bunk, but the place was in total darkness. I looked around for Arthos, but he was nowhere to be found. I opened the door to the stairs, and it was still completely dark. Wherever were the harbour lights? Suddenly I realised we were moving fast. How could we I thought? The engine is not on. Nobody is aboard! I wondered if it could be a figment of my imagination, but by the light of the moon my eyes quickly adjusted, there was nobody here with me and the engine was stone cold definitely not switched on, I was shocked! It was as if some unknown force was driving us through the water. I began to feel terrified, I was no sailor; how could I get this boat to stop? Why was the boat no longer in the harbour with the anchor weighed? Where was Arthos and Pietro? A thousand thoughts and different questions transcended through my brain, my panic was escalating, and I needed to find a way to calm myself. I was not even in sight of land! I rushed down to the cabin, threw on my trousers, jumper and shoes no time for sock. Rushing back to the wheelhouse I tried to start the engine, hoping that I could turn the boat around. Oh, by the Great Architect in the Sky, where was I? "Help me someone" I shouted out. I looked at the dials and was frozen with fear then I suddenly remembered my ring "Twist it"

I thought and then a quiet voice seemed to whisper, "Keep calm Glen, fear is not good, you must prevail, dispatch the flares, you will find them if you look carefully." I found a cupboard in the wheelhouse, which contained flares. I grabbed them rushed onto the deck. I sent two into the air, and then another two. What was that smell? Was it the flares or was it something else entirely? It was a Sulphur scent and Oh, the fear made me tremble. Was I in the hands of the Galympites? Would help come in time? The boat appeared to be slowing down, rocking from side to side as if it would capsize. What should I do? Perhaps if I tried again to turn on the engine and turn the wheel gently, then I could compensate for the rocking. This was all guesswork as I was not even remotely navigationally skilled. I started to try and turn the boat, praying with my whole being that this tin can would not capsize! I felt the boat turn slowly, or was it my imagination? I couldn't even remember which sea I was in. I felt stupid, so unwise, but nothing ventured meant nothing gained. Suddenly I heard a hooting noise and started trembling, if it was a big boat, I'd had it! I had no control there it went again, so I ran back on deck and let off another flare I immediately heard three sharp hoots, thank goodness someone had seen the flare. I waited and prayed for help, out of the mist a larger cabin cruiser, it was Arthos, Pietro and some of Pietro's friends. They pulled up alongside and Pietro and Arthos jumped aboard "Glen are you alright?" they said in unison. "Now I am" I replied "What happened? How did I get out into the sea, the boat was moving so fast that the rocking motion woke me up, and I didn't know what to do, eventually a voice seemed to tell me to use the flares, and I thank God that it worked! Was that you Arthos?" Before he could answer I saw Pietro's hand, and yes, my friends were both wearing identical green rings. "I think there is something I need to know. Now, can you and Arthos please explain it all to me?" To which Pietro answered immediately with a kind smile "Glen, when we get back to the village, we will tell you everything. It is time we fought as a team." I went ad sat down in the lower deck and left the two of them to start the engine, turning us around and heading back towards Cannito di Caronia, whilst I enjoyed a cup of coffee. There was more to this place, I thought shivering there were still unexplained happenings occurring, still forces of evil at play as well.

At last, we were back in the inlet of the harbour and there we found that the anchor which had moored the boat in its lodgings, was no longer there! This amazed Pietro and he said he would secure us with a double anchor next time and if necessary, block our boat in the inlet. He laughed and said, "You two must be making our enemies nervous for that to have happened and now we are stronger as we are three, they had better beware!" It was two o'clock in the morning and we were all hungry, it seemed an age since we had eaten, Pietro said, "Give me half an hour and then come over to my house and I will have something ready for you to eat," He hesitated and looked across at me "Glen we will tell you our stories?"

They entered Pietro's house. What a fabulous smell greeted them. It was bacon cooked in maple syrup, scrambled eggs, mushrooms, Italian tomatoes, loads of warm crunchy bread, lovely salty butter and a large pot of steaming hot freshly ground coffee. "Fantastic" we seemed to echo in unison "It smells great and we are starving." "Well, there is plenty for all of us" said Pietro "Come and sit down, don't let it get cold." Once everything was eaten, and the dishes cleared away, apart from the coffee, Pietro said "Right Glen are you ready for a long story from Arthos and I?" Arthos immediately followed with "Yes Glen, and when we have finishing telling you our history, you will become part of this forever, this is a lifetime experience of trust and friendship, there will be many of these friends that you meet along the way, all a part of our story, gradually you will become totally absorbed in what we are trying to accomplish. You will come to see how important you are to the grand scheme of things, our cause will hopefully become your cause! In turn it will become a world cause and you will help us to save the Planet."

Arthos leaned back into his chair, started to speak "Long ago when your planet was young, many of the Astrotars visited earth, and helped the people to advance their civilisations. They thought, they were being visited by Gods, because we arrived in spaceships and we looked human in form. We wore long robes and walked as humans did and thus, we were able to communicate with them and in time teach them. We taught them how to read the stars and gradually move forward advancing their cultures. They thought our spaceships came directly from their Gods. The people of Astrola were given the task of becoming the Guardians of the planet Earth, this task was given to them by the Power Lords of Adrominicus and they visited the earth many times to assist and advise. As the people became more advanced the Astrola inhabitants visited less and less, and so earth progressed ever onwards, sometimes to its detriment but mostly in a wise fashion. We developed bases that we used when we visited earth.

Then we received warning of the imminent implosion of our home planet Astrola and as many as of our people as possible managed to make the journey to Earth, escaping before Astrola became a black hole in the Galaxy.

Luckily, we still had bases set up on Earth and were able to move into them, as we had maintained them. They were named Tri Base 1, 2, & 3, Glen you have already been to Tri Base 1. "Now Glen I will continue to explain us! Astro chose me to join your people and co-exist, not making waves, just waiting for someone I could team up with difficult to imagine I know! I have looked, listened, watched and waited in the hopes that The Great Astro would point me in the direction of the person destined to help me. He did that's you Glen! It's a lot to take in but now I must rest and so I hand you over to Pietro".

Pietro looked straight into my eyes. He had the same blue eyes as Arthos his hair was tied back securely in a bun, but his hair was brilliant white, and I realised that Arthos had the same-coloured hair but much shorter, now I was studying the two of them I could clearly see that Arthos's glasses hid similar piercing blue eyes, as his glasses had slipped down his nose while resting. "Well," said Pietro "So you now know that we are both Astrotars! I have read your thoughts, which like Arthos, I am able to do, and I know you are aware that we can do this. Please, I beg of you don't let this ever annoy you as it may prove very useful to you in the days to come. I came here when there were fires erupting all over the town, but nobody knew why they were happening. The Great

Astro, in his infinite wisdom, suspected that the evil Galympites were behind these awful fires, and sent me to investigate. I settled in the area and mixed with the local inhabitants always watching and listening to try to solve the mystery. Astro always feared that the evil ones were trying to gain a foothold town across earth to sow the seeds of dissension and ultimately create widespread havoc. I was actively working against the Galympites which of course was very dangerous, I would go out throughout the night, watching through my telescope, and after observing for many hours and travelling around the coast I was able to convey to one of our aqua crafts in the ocean where I thought some of the Galympites might have been situated, and the Astrotars who were situated at a hidden location were able to destroy several of their small spaceships as they took off out at sea. That was reported to the authorities as bright flashes out at sea. As the fires had already died out people had started to move back to the area, and I was gradually absorbed into the community, and considered a retired eccentric. The Sicilian powers and their Government never could find out the cause of those fires and decided to put it down to strange happenings. My job is like a security blanket, if they ever return, I will be watching ready to report on any strange occurrences". "I met up with Arthos some years ago when he was told to make contact with me, and he has since visited me several times, whilst we awaited Our Great Leader Astro finding the right person to aid us, I was so overjoyed to hear that you had been found. Our team is gathering strength all around the world, and 'Yes' we 'WILL' succeed!" He lent back in his chair, and then said "Glen I miss your friends in Bermartus in the wonderful ocean Tri-base 1. A city of happiness and wonder an accomplishment that has saved the many lives of the people trapped in the Bermuda Triangle. I believe you met Erup and Neek whom I used to work with, but Glen there are still so many for you to meet on your travels, we are all stationed at different locations trying to destroy the Galympites and not get caught." I looked at them and marvelled at how they were so involved as a people trying to save the planet earth. What a hard job lay ahead!

While I was listening, I was trying to consider how I would personally bring all this to the world. Ideas kept formulating in my brain but for now we had to face whatever lay ahead, and deep down I wondered if I would ever return to the Tri-base where I had met my love Leanne. By now it was morning, and we had talked the night away, sadly out of time and due to return to the boat, so Pietro said, "I'll give you a quick run back in the car in case the boat has gone." he ended this with a quick laugh. We thanked Pietro as he dropped us back at the boat, which to our relief was still where we had moored it. Aboard for only a few minutes, was long enough for us both to say we would see each other later, within minutes I was gone away to the land of nod!

The next few days we either spent together, or went for walks, mixing with the local people, Arthos was always asking questions; I noticed his ability with languages was fantastic. We even went for a run in the car, the three of us to the base or rather as near as we could get to Mount Etna. I was a little apprehensive in case it suddenly erupted, but luckily, we had a great day out shopping stopping at a small hotel for a bite to eat. I tried to pay, but as usual was told by Arthos to sit down I was their guest. I said that I was part of the team and they laughed saying "yes, but you are the newest." After about four days, Arthos and I decided to borrow Pietro's boat the one we were currently residing in with Pietro's permission of course! Pietro was going to Palermo on some business and had no issue with us borrowing the boat. Athos was an accomplished sailor and Pietro lent him a map and some instructions on rocky places once he knew where we were thinking about sailing out to a little uninhabited island called Le Guglie. It was situated past two islands that were inhabited but we could easily pass between. It would take us about four hours to get there, so to turn back quickly before the night comes in. We looked at the time and it was around 09:30 as we set off on that pleasant October day.

  We reached the island of The Guglie after around 4 ½ hours of steady sailing, we had lessened our speed as we passed through the straits nipping in-between the two larger inhabited islands, while being ever so careful of any hidden dangers. Arthos's expert sailing saw us safely there and I lent a hand as was needed and eventually we sailed into a little harbour and moored the boat. The island was indeed desolate but intriguing with a large protrusion of rock towering above us, forming a cliff face on one side, I tried to calculate the dimensions and said to Arthos "I will climb up this shaley side and have a look around." Arthos said grimly "Look Glen, be careful, go forward slowly, and be prepared to rush back to the boat quickly at the first sign of trouble, I dare not leave the boat unattended as we do not want to be marooned on this island." I moved slowly one step at a time, and this slow steady pace created an eerie feeling in the air, as I neared the protection of a dark rock, I noticed it was concealing a large cave entrance, which had been unseen from the angle where the boat was moored. I stopped and peered into the darkness, and there it was a putrid Sulphur type of smell similar to rotten eggs. Oh, bloody hell I thought immediately, and tried to dash back to Arthos, shouting "I think I have found an exit for the Galympites", without warning I slipped falling heavily to the ground with a thud. The next thing I knew, Arthos was trying to help me down to the boat. "Glen are you all right?" he asked anxiously as I was now sporting a rather large bump on my forehead which was grazed and oozing blood sluggishly. "I think you knocked yourself out for a minute Glen" said Arthos. I felt dazed but tried hurriedly to get into the boat. We were both understandably nervous as Arthos started the engine ready to set sail out of the little harbour and out onto the Tyrrhenian Sea. A sudden rumbling sounded, and I could see that Arthos had become extremely nervous, he then said, "Quickly Glen get under that big tarpaulin and lie down, I will keep the engine running but try to keep us under cover whilst I make for land." We started forward, Arthos was steering the boat while crouching down and was covered over with another tarpaulin. I only saw this because I was peering out from underneath my makeshift hide away. Suddenly we could hear a terrifying roar and I could just make out a large silver coloured object, shaped like a cigar shooting up out of the water. "Keep hidden" hissed Arthos while the silver object came ever closer and resembled a ball of light above us in the sky. I knew I needed to pray to the Great Architect in the Sky who protects all races, creeds and galactic strangers from harm. Aloud I said, "Oh Heavenly Father Protect Us," I was terrified while I prayed silently that they had not seen or heard us! My heart was in my mouth, my body paralysed while the object hung directly above us for what seemed like an age, without warning it shot off at great speed upwards and was quickly lost from sight. I panted heavily while the boat continued to move and tried to find the strength to crawl out of my hiding place. I stumbled across the deck towards Arthos, where I was horrified to find him gasping for breath "What's wrong Arthos?" His breathing became more regulated within a short time and he then replied "Please Glen, help me to sit down, we need to keep the boat moving forward, whilst you were under the tarpaulin an unknown force in the form of a bolt threw me to the ground, luckily it was glancing blow as they aimed badly and hit the steel top of the wheelhouse and fortunately, we Astrotars are stronger than average. We are obviously onto them and must let the Great Astro know what has occurred here. The Astrotars from Tri-Base 2 and 3 may be ordered to break into action. Let us get home as quickly as we are able." "How are you feeling now" I asked him, and he replied, "Glen I have felt better, but I will live, although it's not thanks to those evil monsters who are hiding in this area waiting to cause harm." He was quiet for a moment, having taken over the controls for the boat keen to return home as quickly as possible in case of the Galympites return.

5

As dusk was falling, we passed peacefully trough the inhabited islands of Santa Mauina Salina and Lipaurie paying close attention to the straits which were around three quarters of a mile wide, we kept moving forward thinking on what had occurred previously at Le Guglie, we kept our eyes peeled for anyone fishing along the banks, in the hopes that we could chat with them and learn about the area. We continued on ploughing through the Tyrrhenian Sea which seemed to be endless. Eventually through the far-reaching darkness, we spotted pin pricks of light appearing from the harbour at Porto di Santo Stefano di Camostra, which fortunately was our intended destination to berth the cabin cruiser. Finally, we arrived, safe and if not completely in one piece relativity unharmed, after spending the last four and half hours keeping a close watch all around us for the 'evil ones' return. What a long day it had been! As if by magic, Pietro appeared at the quayside and I could not help but notice that Pietro had been twisting his green stoned ring, I noticed this only because I was so nervous that my eyes kept darting about watching every little movement. It was clear to me that these rings held powerful magic, both men smiled at me and these smiles reached the depths of their kind eyes and I knew without a doubt they would do their best to keep me from harm.

"Arthos, Glen thank Goodness you are both safe, I saw some strange sights in the sky, a ball of light coming from your direction is everything well?" We looked at each other and then proceeded to tell him about our adventures that day. Pietro was amazed by our ordeal and upon completion of our tale, told us about a time when he had been out fishing, and had stopped in a little harbour for a short while before continuing on to Lipouis. There he moored his vessel and spoke to the locals, who mentioned that they had seen bright lights in the sky it was hoped that it was not related to the episodes of 2004. Pietro went on to explain how he noticed it was quite desolate, and with his binoculars had looked upon the cliff like peninsula but could not see the hidden cave entrance, it looked solid. He had stayed only a few minutes before journeying on as the weather had deteriorated rapidly. Both Arthos and Pietro said that the days happenings had to be reported immediately and that it would take them around half an hour to do this, Arthos asked me if I felt well enough to prepare a small meal for the three of us after the knock to my head. Pietro laughingly said, "He would bring an extra chair back with him." They both left quickly heading to Pietro's house to report to Astro. I wondered how they would communicate with Astro, but they left me in the dark and I did not bother to ask for an explanation. While Pietro and Arthos were away I gathered all of the ingredients to make three large omelettes, mushrooms, juicy tomatoes, crumbly mature cheese, mixed herbs, fresh Sicilian ham accompanied by several beaten eggs, two table spoons of water, salt, pepper and combined everything in a large mixing bowl.
I found the largest frying pan, added oil and heated it gently before adding all the ingredients and letting it cook gently on the heat. When the omelette was nearly ready, I removed it from the heat to rest, whilst I made a beautiful salad drizzled with olive oil and sliced some fresh crusty bread to accompany the omelettes. Dinner was ready but there was no sign of Arthos, or Pietro and I began to feel anxious the events of the days catching up with me, my hand found its way to my ring absently twisting it while thinking about the dinner spoiling due to no one appearing to enjoy the meal. Presently they both appeared and jumped upon the deck of the boat, Arthos was the first to speak "Please Glen, only use the ring for emergencies, it is not a mobile phone it is a guardian against distress" Arthos spoke firmly but not unkindly and I immediately apologised for my

mistake feeling embarrassed by the whole affair. I soon relaxed as they had brought some lovely wine back with them which complemented the meal perfectly, after eating and drinking our talk turned to the episode on the water and I was informed that it was being looked into the hopes that this small Galympite base could be destroyed. We talked long into the evening until Pietro said "I'm afraid I must go home, I am far too old to be sleeping on the floor and much prefer the comfort of my own bed, I will see you both tomorrow ready to face the next challenge that is thrown our way. Remember brothers. Our greatest Strength is our Togetherness." We bade each other goodnight, and each make our way to bed, ready to sink into oblivion.

The sun was shining as we went up on deck, we had risen later than usual it being passed nine o' clock before we ventured forth and although it was still relatively early in the day and October it was already hot and sultry with the sun promising to be unseasonably warm. Pietro had just arrived bearing warm fresh rolls "I'll go and make us some coffee" I said and disappeared below deck. Once the coffee and the rolls were distributed between us the conversation turned to our departure which I felt sure was in the next few days but not as imminently as that very day. Arthos told me that it was today we would leave, which I found very surprising, but I still had no idea on where we would be travelling too. Arthos glanced across at me "Well Glen I hope you are ready; we are going to be having our first public meeting with some very important men, they have agreed to listen to us, but we must be very careful in what we say and not give away all of our secrets. If we can get these gentlemen to believe in our cause it will be extremely beneficial as they have connections all over the world. The meeting is to be held at noon tomorrow in a secret location near to Palmerno airport and Pietro will join us about 11am so that we can fully answer their questions and concerns.

That night, having enjoyed a leisurely drive through the countryside we stopped for the night at a little inn located just off the beaten track but quite close to Palmerno. We were greeted by a cheerful Sicilian woman who welcomed us into her house with a warm-hearted smile, her name was Rosanna, and I was amazed to see Arthos chatting away to her in Sicilian, again I thought what an amazing man! I nodded and smiled along with the conversation as my language skills were not up to much and there wasn't any way I could converse fluently in Sicilian. Rosanna showed us to our rooms, and according to Arthos she also invited us down to join her for dinner. A very enjoyable spaghetti topped with an Italian meat sauce, dressed side salad, crusty cobs and of course a 'home-made red wine'. The food was good, but I found the wine rather strong and slightly bitter. During the meal talk turned to what we were doing here were we on holiday? Our hostess told us that she used to live in Canneto di Carona but that fires of 2004 had driven her out of her home, forcing her to relocate here. Arthos continued to chat with our hostess in Sicilian and I excused myself from the table as I wanted to retire for the evening. The wine had made me sleepy and listening to the soothing Sicilian murmurs of my companions had sufficiently relaxed me that I was in danger of falling asleep.

Next morning after breakfast Arthos settled our bill and we made our farewells with much thanks given to our hostess. Arthos told me that our hostess had spoken freely about the events of 2004 describing how things would burst into flames, even if the electricity had been disconnected. She spoke of how the electric companies, government officials and even the army came to investigate the fires but, in the end, they were all stumped and could not find the cause of them. There were many suggested explanations including aliens this of course nearly made me choke, as we were nearly sure that it was the work of the Galympites in their bid to take over the area for themselves. When the Astrotars had become involved, the attacks had ceased, and it was thought that the Galympites had ceased their warfare and fled in their remaining spaceships. The talk returned to the topic at hand and I asked Arthos "Who are these people we are meeting tomorrow?" to which he replied, "I do not really know them, I was contacted by a friend prior to our leaving London and he advised me that it would be very useful to our cause to meet with them and get them 'on board' as the saying goes. I was given a telephone number and advised to contact them at my earliest convenience and thus we shall meet them tomorrow at twelve noon. And so, the following day we had arrived at our meeting place in good time, followed perhaps ten minutes later by Pietro who parked his car behind ours and jumped out of his car and climbed into ours to greet us. Twelve o'clock arrived, and with it the arrival of a large black Cadillac, out of which jumped a couple of men. They were dressed in dark suits and brought with them an air of menace! We also climbed from our car in readiness for their arrival and they greeted us in broken English "We sorry you must come; we mean no trouble, but you must come in car with us, we blindfold you as our friend's location must remain an unknown to you." "OK" we answered looking at each other nervously. My heart was beating madly it was like a scene from the Godfather, but thankfully there had been no signs of guns so far, and that was definitely a blessing. Once our eyes were sufficiently covered and we were safely ensconced in the car, the engine started, and we were underway each hoping that the journey wouldn't take long. We were packed together in the back seat like sardines in a can but thankfully about ten minutes into our uncomfortable journey we were told to remove our blindfolds. The car pulled up outside a beautiful mansion, set back amongst tree lined gardens an idealistic setting. A large man, black hair liberally sprinkled with grey and dark piercing eyes was dressed immaculately and stood serenely on the veranda with a well-defined air of distinction about him. His face broke into a welcoming smile upon our arrival and he greeted us with a hearty handshake saying "Welcome my friends" he seemed to bestow an extra smile upon Arthos, and I wondered why as the man continued "We would all like to hear what you have to say, and so I welcome you to my home. Please come in and be welcome we should not waste any time." Again, he nodded and smiled at Arthos, I thought this particularly strange as I had studied the man's hands while he had been conversing and I couldn't see any sign of a triangular green stoned ring, so what was the connection between these two? "I hope we shall all find this meeting both enjoyable and enlightening" said the man who had also told us to call him Francesco. We followed him into a large octagonal shaped room, which had a large beautifully polished mahogany table located in the centre and spaced evenly around it were six smartly dressed men of various ages. Francesco addressed the room at large "These three gentlemen will, shortly become well known to us and perhaps even become good friends, we have important matters to discuss so please treat them with courtesy and make them feel welcome in my home. We in the craft are honour bound to carry out only good deeds in this world, and I believe that which these gentlemen reveal will help to set us on a new path." He turned to us and said, "I am sorry you were brought here in such a disagreeable manner, but I wish for my home to remain out of the public eye, thus allowing me some semblance of a normal existence when I am not travelling on business. Therefore, bringing you here without letting you know your exact location will allow me to get to know you and to make sure our paths lie in the same direction." Once again, he nodded towards Arthos saying to the company "This gentleman Arthos is known throughout the world to be a man of honour, one of our own has vouched for him." This intrigued me but then so much about Arthos did, he had many layers waiting to be unwrapped. I listened to the words of our host, whom everyone seemed to hold in the highest regard and hoped that when we imparted our story, he would believe our words. Whilst wine was handed out to everyone in the room I glanced at both Pietro and Arthos who appeared completely at ease in the strange company, whilst I felt apprehensive about the whole affair. Once everyone was refreshed and seated comfortably, Arthos looked around the assembled company and started to talk first filling in a bit of background about the Astrotars and he continued on in this vein "I have been selected by the Astrotar leader The Great Astro who has several bases hidden across the world in the most magnificent places several of which I have visited to help in this fight. Some history for you fine gentlemen first. The Astrotars visited the planet when civilisation was young and helped the citizens to advance and move forward, teaching them new skills such as the written word and this is where written language evolved. As advancements occurred, these early Astrotars were worshipped as Gods for descending from the skies, and so as man grew and evolved the Astrotars visited less and less, knowing that they had secured bases throughout the world if the need came for them to return. Some time passed until they were given warning that their home planet Astrola was about to implode, as many Astrotars as possible left their home to travel and settle here aiding the planet and people wherever possible. In life there is always order and disorder, good and evil. The Astrotars are good but the evil forces are the Galympites who want nothing more than to destroy the human race! They are led by Galumpus Diavelo the evilest of evils, his people have the stance of a man but the head of a goat. Their breathing is sulphuric and so they must wear specialist breathing equipment as they would die if they breathed in the air in this atmosphere. They have established their bases in sulphur type conditions but as we uncover them, we will destroy them! He gazed into the eyes of everyone present and asked earnestly "Have you not noticed the increase of explosions, volcanic eruptions and floods?" a few coughs and some uneasy shuffling could be heard throughout the room but this was totally ignored by Arthos "Gentlemen please" he begged "Do not let yourselves be bored and please do not let yourselves believe that this is a fabrication, 'believe me' we have so much proof and I am sure that the more we converse the more your 'minds' are going to understand. Now, I am going to introduce you to my colleague Glen, who will tell you his story. To start with, he is a reporter and correspondent with a large

British Newspaper, and he is not afraid to impart the truth to you fine gentlemen." "Glen" I coughed to clear my voice and said "Gentlemen, firstly let me say that I am sorry I cannot speak to you in Sicilian but hope that you will understand my English". I delved straight into the story from start to finish, telling them the highlights of my interactions with the Astrotars, and when I eventually finished there was silence. Francesco who seemed very much in charge said "This seems very reasonable, but I must ask you where is the proof? This is very hard to take in on blind faith of which I am sure you can understand my position." He looked at us in turn his gaze resting on both Arthos and Pietro the longest, as they both stood up straight, raised their arms in the air and spoke "Astro! Great Father, Leader. Turn off the lights!" In that moment everything went dark and a loud resonate voice emerged "Believe them, they are my voice we wish only to save this planet. Help us please believe!" There was silence as light returned once more to the room. No one moved as they had realised that this was not a trick. Pietro spoke "I am also here to impart my story to you fine gentlemen and so I shall begin I came here when all of the fires were spontaneously erupting in Canneto di Caronia and no one ever found a reason behind these strange occurrences. I am sure that you can remember the events of 2004, but I am here to tell you that although nothing was ever proved, the Galympites were the evil force behind these tragedies and these events were only concluded with the intervention of the Astrotars. The Astrotars managed to attack one of the Galympites bases bringing a close to the fires, unfortunately some of our forces were injured in the fighting but we were able to save them with our advances in medical technologies. Lately, it has come to our attention that the Galympites may be lingering on in this area, there are definite signs of them in the Tyrrhenian sea, more specifically, an uninhibited island known as Le Guglie. This has come to light thanks to Arthos and Glen who recently made the trip between Santa Marina Salina and Lipari. They had the most terrifying experience" At this point Arthos interrupted "It is important that intelligent people must believe that we speak the truth before it is too late. It is our intention to set up small groups of people around the world and then call a meeting that everyone would attend and eventually bring this to the attention of the Governments around the world. Until that time, it is essential that our actions be carried out in secrecy, it is necessary that we have the backing of almost 100% of the worlds powers before we gather the governments together. My question to you now is this? Are you prepared to be my

Sicilian contacts? I have trusted you all without even knowing the address at which we are currently residing, it is a lot to take on faith from both sides but please 'Believe Me' this is important!"

The "Boss man" stood up and said "I am amazed, and although it may seem strange, I do believe you! You are the return of the three wise men, may everyone follow your star. You know my name and number, please keep in touch and let me know if you would like to meet again. We will keep watch over this area and inform you of any strange occurrences."

He clapped his hands, and a tray of drinks was brought in by a middle-aged lady, she was very smart in appearance, her grey hair tied back sedately in a bun at her neck and her purple dress made of a silky material, I presumed this was his wife. On the tray were numerous cut glass goblets, each full of wine they were given to everyone who was present once distributed he stood up tall and straight and said "Salute" the equivalent to cheers, tow which everyone present replied the same. Once the meeting was over, hands were shaken, and we were once again blindfolded for our own safety we were told and driven back to our cars. Once deposited safely I muttered "Oh my god" as it was dusk already and we had been at the meeting for over five hours, that meant it was time to say goodbye to Pietro as we would go our separate ways. Pietro shook our hands and hugged us both, saying "Please come back soon, it has been great to be amongst friends again." We returned the sentiment before Pietro climbed into his car and headed back to Canneto di Caronia. Now it was our turn to set off back towards the airport. Once there we returned the hire car and Arthos settled the bill from the weeks hire. On route to the airport terminal, I asked Arthos "Are we off back to London now? Or somewhere else?" to which he replied, "Why Glen? Have you had enough already?" "No, not at all Arthos I'm just very curious about our destination." Arthos gazed at me "Patience Glen, we still have much work to do, all will become clear in time, I have some information that I need to check at enquiries." Arthos went to the desk and returned a few minutes later saying, "Ah well, that's a pity, there's no flight available till tomorrow at 12:30, we will need to be back here about an hour before the flight leaves, will you excuse me for just a minute, while I make a call Glen?" While Arthos made his five minute phone call I idled away the time by gazing around the small airport with its basic but sufficient amenities. Once finished he returned to my side saying that "A friend of his who worked in the airport would be with them shortly and he had agreed to help them out with accommodation for the night". Arthos then informed me that he still had to finalise the tickets for tomorrow's flights, and suggested I get a coffee whilst I waited. Before heading to the enquiries desk, he said "See Glen your patience has been rewarded, we will be flying to Tunisia or more precisely into Tunis Airport." I went and got a coffee from the self-service kiosk remembering to say "gratzie" to the lady behind the counter. I sat in the waiting area letting my mind drift, just watching people and listening to the way the spoke, they all appeared happy and contented. My trance like state was broken by Arthos reappearing and saying, "Glen this is Antonio, a long-time friend of mine" and I knew before he could say any more that that he would be wearing a green stoned ring upon his finger. Antonio had greyish white hair, blue eyes and looked very smart in his uniform he was not however, particularly Sicilian in looks and knew he must be another Astrotar. Arthos smiled at me saying "Glen your exactly right, and we are going to stay over at Antonio's flat. He lives very close to the airport and so we will be able to spend an enjoyable evening with an old friend while we compare notes and get each other up to speed. You will continue to meet many new people while we are on our travels, so do not be surprised by all the new friends you will make while we try to do our best for the good of the Earth." Antonio led the way out of the airport and the corner to a small path that led the way to Antonio's home. His home was not huge, but it was nicely furnished and provided adequate space for us all. We settled in quickly while Antonio busied himself organising us a meal, he took from the fridge a selection of cold meats, a home-made Italian sauce, pasta, fresh salad and of course some wine. He said, "I hope you do not mind but it will be duvets and sofas for you both but don't worry the sofas are very comfortable, I promise you." The food was soon finished, and the storytelling began, we talked long into the evening and it was 'wee hours' as they say in Scotland before we found our beds. I was asleep as soon as my head hit the pillow, falling into a deep and blissful sleep that ended only because the smell of coffee and fresh rolls filled the apartment. Once we had breakfasted and helped to tidy up, we collected our things, thanking Antonio for his hospitality. Arthos wanted to converse with Antonio, so I headed outside to give them some privacy. After ten minutes Arthos appeared "Sorry to keep you waiting Glen, we have been friends along time and even served together on Tri-Base 1, I honestly do not know when we will see each other again." I replied saying "That no explanations were needed." Our journey continued as we headed back to the airport, heading swiftly through security and straight on our flight to Tunisia, which would hopefully land at Tunis airport around an hour after take-off.

The plane journey passed swiftly and in no time at all we landed and had to make our way through customs again, how hot it felt with the sun streaming through the windows making me feel clammy and the air stifling. As we walked through the building, I noted that this airport was far larger than Palermo with V.I.P. lounges, bar, restaurants, ATM machines, disabled facilitates, snack bars, cafes and duty free available to the many people who must pass through the airport's doors. Outside of the airport I could see palm trees waving gently in the slight breeze. Once through customs, Arthos excused himself and disappeared. I walked over to a small cafe and ordered coffee and a piece of cake, which I ate while watching all of the travellers milling around some rushing to their destinations. After about half an hour Arthos appeared apologising for leaving me for so long but that he had been checking our options for our ongoing travel as we were off to Casablanca that very evening. "Glen I am waiting for some friends that you can meet." This circle is dramatically increasing in size I thought to myself as I heard Arthos laughing to himself "Oh Glen you are so funny with your thoughts I am sorry for laughing but I told you we are many!" There were two men heading towards us both dressed in Arab type clothes and I looked at each of them closely, they introduced themselves to me as Marien and Ahmed, embracing Arthos like a brother. I was studying them looking for any tell-tale clues, they both wore head attire, and both wore glasses. Ahmed bent across to me and whispered, "Yes we have blue eyes" I felt my face flush as I had been caught staring and while he was talking, I caught a flash of a ring on his finger and yes it was a green stone set in a triangular gold band, so we were all "Brothers together bound by our green rings, own beliefs and own minds", I was so proud to be included. My immediate thoughts were interrupted by Arthos "Come on let's go into the restaurant and find a quiet corner so that we can all four eat and chat". Arthos turned to his two friends and said, "What do you suggest we order, or shall we leave it to you, surprise us." They studied the menu and gave the order in a strange tongue obviously Tunisian I thought. We were all seated at a lovely quiet corner out of earshot of others and so many had left obviously catching their planes. The meal that was served was delicious, lamb appeared to be the main dish, but there were so many extras added to it plus a beautiful salad; and of course, wine. I was getting used to my glasses of wine rather enjoyable. We were eating and talking, and the meal was finished, but we talked on and on. I realised that they had all known each other for a long time even Antonio and Pietro were mentioned. We started to tell them all about the happening we had experienced in our week with Pietro in Canneto di Caronia, and they were extremely interested saying that Tunis airport is only straight across the watery straits that join both the Tyrrherian sea and the Mediterranean Sea, with that in mind they would concentrate on that area, letting others know. We told them all about our meeting with the group of businessmen of some importance; with the main contact being a man called Franchesco. They had all listened to our stories and wished to be kept informed giving us a name and telephone number of our contacts. Franchesco also promised to help if any of us ever needed it, and with that we gave the information to Ahmed and Marien should they need it.

Time passed so quickly, and it was soon time to pay and say goodbye and consider our flight to Casablanca. Mohammed Airport my god I thought where to next they all looked at me and burst out laughing "Oh! Glen" said Marien the taller of the two "By the time you act as our ambassador you will feel you are one of us, what a shame you are not grey or white haired yet, and those green eyes, well don't worry we still accept you as one of us. One day you might even be given the gift of mind reading" we all laughed and shook hands. Arthos and I moved across the airport to check-in and security. We entered the departure lounge and worked out that we still had about half an hour before take-off. There were many people sitting and standing around the large room with a couple of desks at the doorways leading onto the tarmac. Arthos left me sitting down and said he was going to walk around and check on a few things. I started looking at newspaper which I had just bought, occasionally looking to see where Arthos was, in case he disappeared. I noticed that he sat down near a group of four men with olive complexions and beards who appeared to be studying something in their hands. Then he got up and started walking round again, as I watched him, he neared the desk where a couple of officials were standing. Suddenly he dropped to the floor by them, they rushed to help him and of course I dashed across the lounge to see what was wrong. They were helping him to a seat by the desk, he appeared to be in deep conversation with them, showing them something. As I approached him, he said to them "This is my colleague we'll stay here if it's alright?" They nodded and one had left the departure lounge.

Many people had started queues as the gate number was showing. Then an official came into the lounge and said over the tannoy "I'm sorry there will be a short delay, we have found a fault with the plane and will be using the next one that arrives. In the meantime, would people with young children and the elderly please come and sit at this end of the lounge so that we can make sure you embark first" Many people streamed across the lounge and took seats leaving not so many people on the other side. The main door was thrown open and a bunch of armed police entered hurriedly and went straight to the four men, arresting three of them, but the fourth man made straight for one of the air hostesses but before he could reach her Arthos pointed something at him that looked like a pen, the man dropped to the floor. The police handcuffed him as he was coming around, he had only been stunned, it was obviously a type of taser. There was great excitement in the room, and everyone was told "Sorry about the disruption but those men were going to cause trouble and we have had them removed. When the luggage had been sorted and the men's removed, we will be flying as agreed, but you will all be pleased to know there is nothing wrong with the plane we were just buying time". The two officials turned to Arthos and said we were so lucky that you overheard those men and in your capacity of F.B.I. to advise us. Great act you pulled off, everyone thought you had fainted, will you please come with us the police would appreciate you making a statement, but we will not blow your cover, seeing you told us you are on a special investigation in Casablanca. In my mind I looked at Glen and said my mind. "Are you really in the F.B.I?" Arthos smiled and looked at me and said, "The world is full of surprises Glen". It was all over, and we walked across the tarmac an hour later than expected, but thankfully owing to Arthos's ability to read people's minds the hijack plot had been foiled, but we would not arrive in Casablanca now till about 22:00hrs, so once inside the plane and seated in business class seats as a thank you for Arthos's speedy intervention in a near crisis, I knew we had at least two and half hour's flight. I allowed the chair to recline into a semi bed, the wine had obviously taken affect, told Arthos I was going to have a dose, but with eyes closed I found sleep took over. A screeching noise, a couple of bumps and we were down, I could not believe I had slept the whole journey. I apologised to Arthos who just smiled saying that I should not worry because he had also slept. I realised we had landed and were slowly taxied to a stop at the terminal. The doors opened after the steps had been put in place and gathering our bags from the overhead locker, we commenced our exit. The pilot and stewardesses made a big fuss over Arthos thanking him repeatedly and asking him if everything had been ok on board. He answered with a smile saying, "Thank you we slept well". The warmth outside hit us, October evening yet it was lovely. Looking upwards I could see how large the airport was with continuous windows covering the whole of the airport building and a huge sign 'CASABLANCA MOHAMMED V AIRPORT'. Although I had travelled worldwide this was one airport I had never been through or visited, so I intended to take in as much as possible. It was very spacious and clean with all the amenities you could possibly need, from ATM's currency exchanges, telephones, pharmacy and various food outlets, even a prayer room and a smoking area. There was also a VIP lounge under the name of 'CONVIVES OLE MARQUE' I then realised Arthos was making for the lounge area having completed our security checks at customs. "Where are we going", I asked "To meet some very special people, friends of mine from long ago" answered Arthos. We walked across the clean mosaic floor towards the lounge, out of the hustle and bustle of many people, the chatter and noise of the flow of multi-nationalities and into the peaceful beautifully decorated lounge with an array of foods and drinks. Once we had entered those swing doors Arthos was addressed by an official on the other side in uniform and asking for identification. A minute later after being accepted we walked across this rather luxurious lounge scattered about with various types of armchairs and couches. Arthos waved an acknowledgement to a far corner where three gentlemen in Moroccan dress had arranged themselves around a table in the corner. They stood up as we approached Arthos warmly greeted them and immediately introduced me to them "This my friends is Glen, who I have told you about, he is not by birth right one of us but by his sincere and loyal friendship, he was chosen by the Great Astro and has proved his worth".

They all smiled in acknowledgement. First there was Mohammed then Khalid and lastly Youssef. All with strong handshakes and smiles but when they looked into my eyes there was a strange depth, as if searching my very soul. I did not even look at their hands I knew without looking they would all be owners of the triangular green stoned rings. These wonderful Astrotars where scattered all around our planet helping to save it. I suddenly realised that all four men were looking at me, so I broke the silence "And so you all know what I was thinking, but I am getting used to it" I said. They all laughed. After sitting down, we all ordered some coffee and cakes plus a few morsels to snack on whilst we talked as there was much to discuss. Arthos started telling them about meeting up first with Antonio at Palermo where he works, then into Tunis and our enjoyable time with Ahmed and Marien, and of course about Pietro who was our marvellous contact at Canneto di Caronia. So much conversation ensued as they knew all these people and had not seen them for a while. The next topic of course was our meeting with the man called Franchesco, not one of them, but an important businessman and his colleagues who all said they would support the cause, and to keep them informed. We only got his telephone number Arthos told them from a contact of Pietro's from Catanio called Yatop who as, yet I had not met. Arthos said to them he had met Yatop in London and that was why he had found out through Pietro where I was, as I would most likely be the most able to make contact. They asked him why, and of course I said we are both members of a London type of club who can recognise others by certain signs. The conversations went on thick and fast, sometimes I became a little lost with all the strange names, but they tried to keep me informed. Arthos noticed the time, it was 23:00hrs. I wondered where we would be staying, "No problem" replied Arthos to my unspoken question "At the airport hotel we are already booked in, I did it earlier", and then to the others he said, "Shall we say midday to meet as we have much to discuss?" With much handshaking and 'goodnights' we parted. Arthos and I went out of the airport doorway. Outside. there were seats and palm trees and a lovely welcoming exterior to the airport, with the hotel situated nearby. There were still many people milling around or just using the seats in the warm night air waiting perhaps for a late night or early morning flight, but all around I felt an intoxicating atmosphere of mystery and excitement, what would happen next? It was nonstop like something I had never experienced, although I had travelled widely with world correspondence and reporting a multitude of things. This was different and I admit I had never felt such warmth and friendship and a feeling of belonging. I followed Arthos as we entered the hotel, passing the doorman attired in a smart uniform and went through the foyer to reception. Arthos had booked two adjoining single rooms and the cards were given to us by a pretty petite dark-complexioned girl, with stunning big brown eyes dressed in a very attractive uniform. She had welcomed us to the hotel saying, "Your rooms are on the second floor, please use these lifts and follow the arrows upstairs" and smiled. She was lovely but she was not my Leanne. I felt bad as Arthos paid for everything saying, "It's all for a good cause, I have been well paid." We reached

the rooms, they were lovely, smallish but adequate, the bathroom had all necessary items of soap, shampoo etc. Then I realised I had a small balcony when I opened the French windows. I went out on the balcony and found Arthos already standing on his balcony. Voices below could be heard, and the air was still warm. I decided to take a quick shower, I knocked on Arthos's door and asked him what time I should meet him in the morning, to which he said, "Please yourself I will be down about ten as I have some calls to make, but we are not meeting the others till midday". I said goodnight, going into the bathroom I took my shower and enjoyed the fancy gels and shampoo that were there for me to use. Luxury after so much travel. After the shower, I found a small fridge in my room with some beer in it on the house! If not, I'll pay for it tomorrow. I opened the balcony doors put out a chair, opened a bottle of beer and was enjoying the atmosphere when I suddenly remembered my editor Sam. Bloody hell I cursed! No peace I will have to give him a quick call just to whet his appetite and let him know I'm still alive, or he may stop my salary. The number rang it was late here, nearly one in the morning. 'Ring, ring, ring' "Hello, who's that?" angrily he answered. "It is Glen" I replied, "I have not forgotten you. Unbelievable the things I have been involved in, and when I get back, I will tell you amazing things, I have lots of ideas for the paper, but as yet say nothing." He started to ask questions and I interrupted with a lie "Sorry Sam, got to go, my plane is leaving." I just imagined him roaring in temper because I had not phoned before, and he did not have my private mobile number, so he could not ring back and ask questions. I finished my two beers, closed the balcony doors, closed the blinds and snuggled down, and ….
Next thing I was awakened by what by what sounded like horns, but it was just traffic outside I had left a window open. Just as well I thought as it was already 09:30. Dressing quickly into things that I thought could really do with an iron, I made my way down to breakfast. Lovely strong coffee, warm rolls, cold meat and cheeses, more than enough. I had bought a paper that I found in English and was having a quick glance through it when I saw Arthos rushing out of the main door, and I hoped he had not forgotten I was with him.

I sat on drinking coffee and another one, glancing at the clock in case they wanted me to move. When in rushed Arthos it was 10:30, he came over to the table and apologised for being late, I told him it was fine. He then proceeded to tell me he had been making our future 'ongoing' plans. I said to him "Another destination?" "No" he said not planes, something else and that was that, as he quickly grabbed some coffee.

We wandered around the airport for a short time looking at all the weird and wonderful things for sale and enjoyed studying all the different people, as they rushed about as if there was no tomorrow. They actually reminded me of ants the way they rushed backwards and forwards. We decided to go and collect our things from our rooms as it was after 11:30, and back packs on we went down to the desk, I told the girl at the desk I owed for two beers, she just said "Compliments of the house". Arthos paid and we handed back our key cards. Exiting the hotel, it was just twelve noon and there was Youssef on the dot. His car was a black Volkswagen, we climbed in, it was comfortable, and we were off. Youssef explained "Casablanca is one of the largest artificial ports in the world. The primary naval base for the Royal Moroccan Navy is situated there. It is also one of the largest and most important financial centres on the continent". He continued "We are now on our way to the centre of Megarama, where there is a shopping and entertainment complex in the Morocco mall. Then you will see there is a complete renovation of the coastal walkway". We spent about an hour touring around which I found most interesting. "Khalid and Mohammed will be meeting with us shortly in a nice quiet place we know where we can talk, eat, drink and plan. It is a very pleasant place as you will find out". We drove off the main beat and down some side streets eventually pulling up at an off-street parking place. We drove in and parked, as Youssef pointed out ahead to a darkly lit building, rather somber looking, no windows appeared on the side we were at, just a door. He locked up the car and we followed him, he knocked, and we were ushered in, down some stairs and through some beaded curtains into a beautifully furnished room with secluded lighting. Your feet sank into the carpet which was red and gold. All around the room were semi-circular recesses complete with table and fitted seating around half of it, armchairs in the front, each recess giving a private area for a group of people. In one such corner recess were Khalid and Mohammed, who jumped up to welcome us with great enthusiasm. We all sat down and Arthos and I exclaimed how amazing the place was, from the outside no one who did not know, would ever guess the beautiful quiet luxurious layout within the walls. A waiter came and orders were given. I sank back in the comfort of the chair, oh! This place was something else I thought. In what appeared to be seconds, we were served with lovely cool flavoured drinks; I sipped away with pleasure as I had been hot and thirsty, the others were busy talking and although

I was listening, I found much difficulty in understanding their so-called plans. Something about a boat, tides and when it would be safest. "What time had the messenger said" commented Youssef. I was bewildered and thought this was obviously is another plan. Arthos turned to me "Glen forgive us for talking so fast we are making plans and speed is of the essence, but do not worry you are in them, but too difficult to explain for the moment". "Oh, I will trust you" I replied and smiled. The waiter returned for us to choose from a menu. We passed it around. I said, "You choose I like most things because I spent years travelling". They all laughed, I thought what nice men they all were, Arthos turned to me and said, "And so are you Glen" and I realised that once again my thoughts had been read. The meal was served and more cool drinks, it was all delicious, loads of different dishes and we helped ourselves, so many new tastes, but so good. At last, we had finished, and the dishes were collected, and coffee was bought to the table. Youssef said "Glen you and Arthos are coming back to my house for a while. When we get there, we will explain everything to you". Then he turned to Khalid and Mohammed saying, "See you tonight, we will meet you where and when we said". With that Arthos, Youssef and myself said goodbye and left. We were shown out of a side door and back into the car. I looked again at the door and thought no way would you ever imagine the place inside. How lucky I thought I am... I sat back in the car and wondered where Youssef lived, but it did not take more than twenty minutes to arrive. Arriving at the house Youssef showed us in and pointed out to a small bedroom saying "Glen, please do not be offended, but I thought you might like to use the bathroom, and perhaps short nap. Tonight, we are all going out and before I should like to have a chat with Arthos as we did not get a chance to meet very often and it's ages since I last saw him". I smiled and answered, "Good idea, sounds like another adventure, I better have a nap". I went into the room and wondered what lay ahead, realising I was quite tired. I took a quick shower and lay down and that was that!

"Glen quickly get dressed", I awoke with a start, it was Youssef in an extremely agitated state, "We have got to leave quickly because we might not be back tonight", I rushed around and made it in minutes, wondering what the problem was and seeing Arthos already waiting in the car, I jumped in myself. We were off immediately I noticed we were making for the direction of the port. Moving along the coastal road towards a little inlet I had been shown when touring in the car. We stopped alongside what appeared to be a large boat house, parking behind it, we got out of the car and I turned to find what was the problem, whatever was wrong. At that moment another car arrived and out of it rushed Mohammed who said with great agitation "Has Khalid answered yet", "No" said Youssef frantically "The last time he spoke to me he was checking the engine and compass, and said they were playing up and then he noticed a bright shape up in the sky, further out in the ocean. He said he was just getting ready for us making sure we could go without any hitches". Youssef and Arthos were dragging out a large motorboat with a big engine and in a very dark green colour I was closing and locking the doors of the shed and checking the cars were all locked. "Whatever is wrong" I asked, "Where is Khalid" I asked, "That Glen is what is wrong, the boat which is a small cabin cruiser is missing, and so is he; so, we are all going to look for him, are you coming, are you game?" said Arthos "of course" I replied "thanks" they said, and we pushed off and all jumped in and set off. They tried contacting Khalid, but his phone was not answering. The Mohammed said we are trying to set our navigational unit onto him using a signal we have set up before between the two boats, but so far, no luck. May the great architect of the heavens look down on us, and keep all of us safe, especially Khalid. It was dark, only the stars brightened the sky, we kept watch for anything evil we might spot. The water was dark and obviously very deep, after all this was the Atlantic and this was only a large motorboat. Suddenly Arthos said "stop the engine, tune in all of you think of Khalid I'm sure I got something very faint". Then Mohammed said, "Khalid is hurt, he's whispering, keep going straight ahead".

6

My fear was stupid the others were coping so I must we had been travelling for about an hour and then suddenly we saw it. The boat was on one side and Khalid was hanging on to it. We reached him and as we did Arthos grabbed the side of the boat, and Youssef jumped into the water and assisted Mohammed to drag Khalid into the motorboat. He was very white and his head very bloody, with a deep cut on the top of the head. I helped Youssef back into the boat also soaked to the skin; then Arthos attempted to tie an object to one side and then moving around the other boat Mohammed tied somewhere to the other side, then like magic the boat turned the right way up and as it had now been fastened to the back of the motorboat, we were all in. The five of us started back to land. They had opened a back shelf in the boat and taken out two blankets which Khalid and Youssef were wrapped in. Arthos had put a temporary dressing on Khalid's head, but he looked so ill.

No one was speaking, everyone was trying to do their best watching for any problems. It was a slow journey and we wondered if we would make it without running out of gas, but when I asked, they said we have a special compartment in this boat, we'll easily make land, don't worry it's only the sky you have to watch. Just once we thought we saw something behind the clouds, a bright light then nothing. Perhaps we were mistaken but we knew we were vulnerable. Eventually we made it back to the little harbour, Arthos jumped out and held onto the anchor rope whilst everyone got out, then I helped him and Mohammed pull it up, unlock the boat house and lock it inside. Then Youssef said, "I will take Khalid to your house Mohammed and make him some hot tea and have a hot shower" All follow me once you have berthed the cabin cruiser, we will sort that out tomorrow. We double anchored it as a safeguard, and covered part of it with tarpaulin out of the car boot. We then got into Mohammed's car and set off for his house, where we were all meeting up. Twenty minutes later we arrived, locked the car and went inside. It was a smallish house with about three bedrooms, a large lounge and kitchen and a couple of bathrooms, and he showed us a slightly extra staircase behind some curtains which led into two attic bedrooms. "OK" said Mohammed as Khalid had started getting back some colour "I am so glad that you are safe, now Khalid, you and Youssef go and raid my wardrobe and get yourself showers to warm up. It maybe four in the morning, but we must know what happened". "All I know is we were all going out to check on some weird sightings that had been noticed in the sky out over the sea. We were going to try and work out where they were coming from, which exact direction if possible".

Having spoken at great length Mohammed went into the kitchen and made a large pot of coffee, bringing out also a selection of cheese, ham and biscuits for us to eat. We all gathered around in the lounge, which he had put the heating on as I guess we were all suffering from the coldness of the sea trip. We were all waiting for Khalid to tell his story. He began "I was in the cabin cruiser, and I thought I would go for a short ten-minute trip and check that everything was fine for all of us to go out at night, when suddenly the boat appeared to jolt and then started moving much faster without my help. I turned off the engine, but it would not stop, I tried to turn it back to land but it appeared to be stuck in the forward position. I tried to phone or make radio contact, but nothing would work. Everything seemed jammed and I was going further and further out. I kept telling myself not to panic, but it was very hard. I was just about to send up a flare when suddenly something like a beam of light or a ray hit the boat with a huge jolt, I fell to the ground as I tried to stand up the boat started rocking furiously with a terrible force and I was tipped out into the ocean, grabbing the anchor rope as the boat turned onto its side. I thought it would sink and I would be lost, but the new things I had fitted recently in case of problems, stopped it from sinking. Thank God we perfected them, or I would surely have been lost. As I was hanging onto the anchor rope, I managed to try and keep at the part that I could hook myself under so I became less visible, I also realised I had cut my head open and all I could do was send whispering messages and hope that you would receive them, as we are so in tune".

"As I was hanging on to the anchor rope and trying to keep hidden, I saw a bright torpedo shape shoot across the sky back towards Casablanca and then veer off southwards. We must report it, but I am so tired I must go and lay down if nobody minds? But the Galympites are still definitely around in this area. Mohammed have you got room for us all?". Mohammed answered "Yes, enough room for the five of us, but you Khalid use the downstairs one, Youssef and I will use the other two, and maybe Glen and Arthos will use the two new attic bedrooms?". Everyone agreed and we all said goodnight, Mohammed said "Sleep till noon and then we will meet up in the lounge for coffee and rolls, for tonight blazes, to the Galympite, now I will show you the way". Arthos and I took the two rooms upstairs, and before I knew it, I was asleep.

The smell of freshly brewed coffee and fresh warm rolls woke me up. It was noon and we had all slept well. Khalid still looked a little pale, but his head appeared to have healed, almost no sign of it. I could not believe it, I tried not to stare at his head, thinking to myself that they were something else these 'super-beings'. Mohammed must have tuned into me and said, "Thankyou Glen that was a lovely compliment, I hope we are worth it". I had been caught out with my thought again being read. I felt myself redden with embarrassment, but really, I should be used to it by now. They were all talking about something that had happened at about seven this morning. Khalid was saying that he made a quick call when we got in from our night experience and had been contacted just a short while ago with some news. I finished cleaning away the dishes and cups feeling that I must do something to help in some way, when Arthos said "Glen, come in and join us, you need to know what is happening, you need to know what the latest news is". Before we went to sleep Youssef and Mohammed were in contact with some friends quite a lot further down the coast southwards, at a place called Agadir. With some new equipment that we have that has just been perfected made contact with that torpedo shaped object, like that which nearly destroyed Khalid, may be even the same one. Our friends said when the ray hit the spaceship, bang, and it was a ball of fire, it was history one less Galympite craft to worry about. I asked are these people also from Astrola that destroyed another earth enemy. Arthos replied "Yes one day you will meet them, they have lived amongst your people for many, many years, they are called Ochnat and Tamit, if it is a case of your meeting with them don't know where, don't know when but with our travels, you certainly will. "Right" said Khalid "I believe that because we have worked out all that is necessary in this area, tonight only three of our group are going to sea. Youssef, Arthos and you Glen". "I thought I was to go" said Khalid, "No" said Youssef "You are staying with Mohammed as our land contacts, especially after what happened last night". "Now this afternoon we dry out the cabin cruiser and check it is not damaged. It will not take us long if we all work away at it. Then we will get out the large motorboat and check it is all ready for tonight's ocean foray, always keeping in contact with land". We started working on the cabin cruiser which against all the odds was not damaged, it had only the glass in the wheelhouse that was cracked, but Khalid said he would soon fix that, and had measured it up already. We took out several of the things in the cabin to put in the boot of the car to take back to the house as they needed drying out. Khalid said he would see to that tomorrow, when he fixed the glass, he would bring everything back and store them away. Several of the things in the cabin had been broken but easily replaced I was told, but it was such a pity because the cabin cruiser was really smart, and Khalid obviously loved it. Whilst we were working on the boat Mohammed said, "Look Glen there is a pod of dolphins just within watching distance", leaping out of the water and one huge one leapt clean into the air it was amazing. Khalid said "Sometimes the older ones leap up at the side of the boat and show you a young one they bring up with them. Sometimes", he continued "They follow your boat for a good while diving and cavorting around, as if showing off. It is amazing to watch, and they appear to be smiling at you when they leap up and look at you". He then said, "Do you know what Glen, they are such curious mammals but not dangerous, there is absolutely nothing menacing about them, and there are many stories how they have saved shipwrecked sailors or people who have fallen overboard." Arthos then said "But Glen not in the Bermuda triangle, that's where the Astrotars help instead, remember you have met many of them Oh! Glen are you blushing?" they obviously all knew about Leanne and started laughing. After we finished cleaning and checking up on Khalid's cabin cruiser, we opened the big shed's door to get in and check the motorboat over. `Youssef checked the engine, compass type dials and the amount of gas that was left, saying "I'll fill the reserve container later, before we leave, let's get the dry blankets out of the shed cupboard and fill the boat cupboard with them, you never know when you may need them. I must dry the other ones we took back to Mohammed's house last night, or rather this morning", we remembered it well. After we had finished cleaning up the boats, we covered Khalid's cruiser with a heavy tarpaulin and made sure everything was very strongly tied down and double anchored. We then locked up the big shed climbed into the cars and made back to Mohammed's house. On a quick chat all around, we decided to order chicken curry and rice from the local takeaway, to save mess and work. We all relaxed at Mohammed's until the food arrived and Arthos and I made ourselves useful making coffee, getting plates and cups for the coffee to which Mohammed said, "would you two like part-time jobs?." We all laughed it was a great feeling of companionship between us all, I no longer felt an outsider. 20:00hrs it was dark as we all five arrived in two cars at the large boat house. Parking up the cars Arthos said to me "Do not forget to bring our bags Glen we may not be coming back here tonight" I asked "Why, where are we staying?" "That is the million-dollar question" Arthos replied. We could only see each other by moonlight as this inlet was not lit. We had torches which we only used sparingly. We pulled the motorboat out of the shed, and Khalid and Mohammed were busy looking everything over. As we were about to climb into the boat Mohammed said, "Stop, Arthos, Glen, in case you reach where you need to go, and do not come back for quite a while, I want to say, how much I have enjoyed your friendship". He embraced both of us and shook our hands, and as Khalid did the same, I noticed both of them were quite tearful. I thanked them and said, "Thank you, all of you I have never in my life known such friendship, and I will count the time till I see you all again". With that believe it or not, I was almost in tears myself as I said later to Arthos. Youssef said, "As I am coming with you for so much of the journey, I will wait to say goodbye, but my friendship and love goes deep for you both". With this we three, Arthos, Youssef and myself, were pushed off by the other two and that was us in the dark motoring through the water, hardly believing that this was the Atlantic Ocean, and we were off to I did not know where, dressed in two pairs of slacks, shirt, jumper and of cause my life jacket. We had put so much on to save carrying it, and as Youssef said that it is very cold on the ocean at night. I wished I could read minds then I would know where we were going. Arthos looked at me and smiled. We were going further and further, the water was so deep, I knew about depths I had been a good while ago with the aqua craft when I first became involved with the Astrotars, but this time I was on top of the ocean not beneath it. I was glad it was not stormy, but it was so cold, I was glad I had so many clothes on at least this kept me warmer. I watched Khalid studying the compass and some other dials, he seemed to be speaking but he could not be doing so, because Arthos was sitting by me, so I thought it was a bit strange. Suddenly the boat appeared to be slowing down, and we almost stopped. I said, "Oh my God Arthos what is wrong we have been travelling for about two hours, has the engine seized?", "No" said Arthos. Then suddenly I saw at the side of the boat a large black sort of round shaped object appears out of the water. I thought it was a whale, Youssef said "Well Glen, Arthos safe journey, see you again soon, take care as you enter" the huge opening appeared and Arthos said "Jump in Glen, I am behind you with our bags, bye Khalid take care, keep in touch. Safe journey". The opening closed over us my heart was thumping, as we slid down a chute into a passageway, I could not believe it I was in the aqua craft and there was Botami. He embraced Arthos and then myself and said "Follow me quick we have to dive right down before our signals are recognised and we need to build up our strong force field for safety. I thought I was dreaming. How could I be in the aqua craft? Had I drowned? But it was Botami so I must be awake. We followed Botami, the wall slid open and once again I was in that opaque room with the little shimmering lights and the wall with all the switches. I remembered it so well. Next thing Botami pressed some switches and once again panels in the floor moved over and there they were, three relaxing chairs for us.

Botami said "Take care we are starting to dive steeply, and I do not want any accidents should we fall" and nodded to me Botami laughed and said "Arthos look at Glen he is in another world, metaphorically speaking or is it a dream like trance". The Aqua craft although diving must have done it in some magical way, because it appeared quite a smooth transition as we moved down to the depths. I still could not believe what had happened I thought we had been going out, checking whereabouts of Galympites, forgetting that we had been able to have another one of their crafts destroyed after we had saved Khalid from his awful escape the night before. I looked at Arthos and Botami and said "Arthos, when was all this decided? I had no idea". Botami answered the question "Glen, the Great Astro was so pleased with you both, and your companions, with all that you have related back to him, and all that you have accomplished on your travels, not to mention the adventures you have come through and survived the experiences, that he risked much to bring you both for a short stay in our underworld city of Bermartus, on Tri Basel and then return you both back to the city of London. You will both have to collect all your information together and remember all the people you have met. Your ambassadorship is a heavy mantle to carry, but you are doing well and all that have met you hope that one day others will be like you and live-in harmony".

    Suddenly I was aware that the lovely Eafi was with us, quietly returning to the room looking just like an angel with long white robes tied with a simple sash and her silvery blonde hair down to the waist. She was carrying a tray holding three goblets of refreshments for weary travellers. I thought immediately of something else, "Arthos have you heard if Youssef returned safely?", to which Arthos said "How thoughtful you are Glen, yes he has just arrived back to join the others. He was exhausted as it started getting a little stormy, but thankfully he is safe. We will meet up with them again before too long, they are quite willing to travel to meet up with us when we next take off on our travels, but let's enjoy now, it will be only short but wonderful it is so long since I visited Bermartus", "And it's great to see you" said Botami "And Glen" he added. Eafi, who had been talking to Botami turned to Arthos and said "Oh, it is really wonderful to see you again Arthos, we all do miss you and worry about you as we do for the others. Perhaps when you have a few minutes you will catch up with me and tell me about so many of the others. We are all scattered these days, but if it saves the planet it is worthwhile". She smiled excused herself and like magic disappeared through a panel, by use of the green stoned ring once again. Suddenly I noticed Botami had slipped back to the panels on the side, and we were looking once more into the depths of the Atlantic. A huge shark peered at us through the glass or whatever it was made of, obviously something stronger than we used on Earth yet, because no one could come down to these depths.

 I asked Botami "What is depth of the ocean where we are now", he replied casually about three kilometres, I could hardly believe the miracle of it. I was once again amazed at the different types of fish that you only see in literary books, or only seen washed up on a beach dead. Some of them no one could expect to see, as they couldn't go this deep, so they were probably unknown. I noticed some squids that were luminous at the back, then I noticed a fish that was quite large, brownish in colour with an illuminous part at the back, I asked why they thought they were illuminous at the back, Arthos said he thought it was so that others would think the head end was safe and be gobbled up so continuing with deep ocean fish have to grab what they can, when it is available whatever the size, he stopped for a minute, then pointed to something else "Look Glen quickly, see over there, it's a Fangtouth it is orange in colour it has a huge mouth and swallow something almost as big as itself, as its mouth stretches to match the prey, I was fascinated. Then, suddenly Botami started pressing switches and panels on the wall were closing so quickly, as the Aqua craft started shaking as if in a grip of a monster. Arthos jumped up and asked Botami if he could help, but Botami told us to try and keep sitting less we fall. "What is wrong? I asked fearfully", Botami said "Fear not Glen, we are cutting through a section of vast currents as we pass in the craft through an opening in the Atlantic Ridge Mountains, and there are many force fields in place protecting our underworld and also the earth, we are at a part of the Bermuda triangle". As you have seen before there are many ships lying at the bottom of the ocean covered mostly with seaweed, or half sunk into the ocean bed sand, I was thankful it was not the Galympites this time, I

87

had certainly had enough of them for the moment. Then I realised the craft appeared to be slowing down and I wondered what could happen. Botami said "Well Arthos, Glen are you ready?", we touched the wall, it opened, and we were here in Bermantus and there were lots of people waiting for us. Dressed in their white robes were the Astrotars with their different ranks obvious by their cuffs, and groups of other people in blue robes who were the people saved by the Astrotars. In the middle of all these people was the figure of the Great Astro, clad in a flowing white robe embellished with a wide gold belt studded with green gemstones, around his neck was gold pendant with a large green stone in the middle. Around his wrists he wore cuffs with bands on them. His flowing hair and deep blue eyes completed the picture. My eyes filled with tears, it was so wonderful to be back, as Astro moved forward shaking first my hand, then Arthos was greeted in the same manner. Speaking to Arthos he said, "Welcome home, you are always sadly missed, we shall enjoy every moment of your short stay, and to you Glen, I welcome you as one of us, as you have proved my faith in you, enjoy your time again with us". As I looked around Arthos was being greeted by the Astrotars obviously he was very popular with everyone, then my heart missed a beat, she had come from behind the crowd, and it was my beloved Leanne. I ran to her and embraced her saying "I told you I would come back, but I certainly did not think it would be this quick or happen in this manner". A commanding voice called my name, I turned around and found it was Astro who said "Glen, enjoy sometime together, then I need a meeting with both Arthos and you, enjoy what time you have, but always remember time is of the essence for all of us, as we cannot let the evil ones have time to rebuild. I will call you when I need you", with that I watched as he walked up to a panel, touched it, it opened and shut, and he was gone.

"Come Glen" said Leanne "Let us not waste time, we are only spared a short period before you leave, and we have to relish it". Holding her hand, we walked down a lovely corridor and as she touched what appeared to be a dead end, with her small ring, it opened, and we were once again in a beautiful garden, glorious perfumes and small birds appearing in the bushes. I was once again mesmerised wondering how this could all be possible. We sat for a while in a beautiful bower and talked, then she said shyly "Please let us go to my private quarters", a short walk later a panel touched, and we were again in a room of shimmering light, her own personal space. A lovely oval shaped bed was covered with a light gossamer spread in a pale blue; I took her in my arms, my beautiful Leanne and covered her face with kisses, and as love took over, we were wrapped in each other's arms in an embrace that was for eternal love, our hearts beating in unison we whispered our love for each other, and with such emotion tears were on our cheeks as we knew our love was only for minutes in time. She was one of the people saved by the Astrotars that had been caught in the protective rays of the Bermuda Triangle. The rays were also trying to stop the Galympites from arriving in the Earth's atmosphere. Unfortunately, those saved although it did not show, had been damaged irreparably and could not return through the reversal chamber, but were only kept alive by the experts of the Astrotars in Bermantus, so I thought Glen here is the love of my life, and I can only be with her when I am here. Perhaps wishfully I thought one day they might let me stay, I don't know how long we lay together, close as bodies permit. I told her that we can only meet when the Great Astro allows, as I have to help the Astrotars to save the Earth and the human race from the evil Galympites. I told her "I will never love another; your heart is mine and mine is yours". We must have drifted to sleep when a knock woke me up "Quick Glen and Leanne, you must come now to the great gathering hall, the Great Astro wants to talk to everyone". We dressed quickly and holding hands we moved forward as Leanne opened the sliding panel with her ring, and we rushed to the gathering hall.

Everyone was there, lots of blue robed figures which I knew denoted those that had been saved by the Astrotars, although still thought dead and lost by the outside world. No one knew about Bermantus. People I had previously met waved to me but were good enough not to break the spell between the two of us, almost a futile hope we had of a lifetime together. It was wonderful to see how happy everyone seemed to be. Astrotars all in their white robes and their ageless complexions, long silvery blond hair and their deep blue eyes, mixing in friendship with all the other people. It just showed how people should get on with different races and nationalities, when everything worked here even from different galaxies. This is how life should be. Then I saw Arthos, he was with a bunch of Astrotars talking deeply with them and dressed in similar robes with cuffs and embellishments. He waved and I felt the pride of our friendship almost overwhelm me. My thoughts were suddenly interrupted as the Great Astro appeared and everyone gathered around to listen to him. "My friends", he started his strong resonate voice loud enough for all to hear. "We are continuing our fight against the Galympites, but we are as yet far from winning, but we have marvellous people on the outside relating the whereabouts of Galympites, when spotted in the skies and if any place they come from on this planet. Sometimes through speed of action, crafts have been obliterated by some of our people on the ground. We have now perfected a special ray that if we can get it locked onto them in time, that is their demise, and one less for us to worry about. Nothing of course can stop till they are all eradicated completely. Now I am about to call Glen and Arthos to my side for them to keep me up to date with their worldly adventures. When I have learnt all, I will endeavour to let you all know anything of interest to you". Then he beckoned both Arthos and myself to follow him to his inner chamber, letting everyone know with a parting shot, "You will be pleased both of these two people will be with you for a couple of days and then you must say goodbye again". We followed him immediately as he pressed the panel with his ring, and we all passed through, and as soon as we through it closed. It still amazed me the powers of the green stoned rings.

Arthos and I followed Astro along a passageway clothed in a shimmering light giving an impression of silvery marble all around us. Then he stopped and pressing a small dent with an arrow marking with his ring. It opened and we entered a lovely room. Once the panel closed Astro indicated to the three relaxing chairs which had emerged from the floor spaces, as usual bubble like in appearance but so strong and comfortable. "As you both know I am kept informed of your progress by you Arthos and your other companions along the way, but I would just like to hear some of your stories and for you to tell me exactly how my Astrotar friends are keeping. I miss them all" We started to relate our journeys and happenings and as names were mentioned he smiled and nodded; he knew them all. We must have been talking for a few hours when he got to the Aqua craft part and he said "So Glen, did you think it was a monster from the deep, I warned them all to keep it as a surprise for you", he laughed a deep resonate laugh and we joined him, because it was so true, then he said "Actually Glen, that was a very dangerous operation, because if the Galympites had known about it, they could have blown the Aqua-craft and all of you out of the ocean, as the powerful force field had to be turned off whilst you came aboard". After a silence of around three minutes, he suddenly said "I was relieved to hear Khalid made it safely back to harbour that night after Youssef's experience the night before. I must say you all did so well to save him, I am proud of you all". At this point Rinka glided in through an opening behind us carrying a tray of goblets containing their special refreshing drink, we were grateful after talking for so long. The conversations resumed for a short time at which Astro said "You are both welcome to stay for a while longer, but unfortunately Glen I will be sending you home first as our Zoom-Ray transporter over such a long journey, must have space between transportations. Arthos will stay a little longer, maybe a day or so but will contact you as soon as he arrives home". Arthos turned to me saying "You first in case anything goes wrong", and then added "Glen I am Joking!" Astro smiled he obviously enjoyed a bit of humour.

Astro stood up and shook hands with both of us and we were dismissed with "I will see you again before long". Arthos led the way as we left the room, it was just a short walk before we re-entered the Great Hall, where there were still many people. Here Arthos said "Glen I am going to join my friends, I would take you with me, but I see that the Earthling Leanne is awaiting you". I thanked him and looked across the room, he was right she was sitting down patiently waiting for my return. She ran to me when I beckoned her, how heavenly we could spend time together again, I said "Leanne let's make the most of it, because who knows how long it will be till the next time, I may have a day or it may be less, before I have to leave". We spent hours talking, sitting again in the beautiful garden. It was then we went to her private room, where she had goblets of refreshing liquid and some of those tablets, that are each a meal, and we partook of them. We had talked about our lives to each other and felt we had always known each other. Leanne said "Come on Glen, I love you come and curl up with me, so that we can be as one. When you are gone from me, I will imagine you are here". It was two hearts beating as one I wanted to stay forever with her in my arms, but that was impossible. I felt a tear trickle down my cheek, then I remembered the course was important, I must think of my duty and be proud I had been chosen, so I relaxed once more taking her into my arms and whispering how much I loved her.

Suddenly Leanne said "Glen someone is knocking" she went to the door panel and opened it. It was Erup one of Astro's top men who said simply "I am sorry to awake you and Glen, but the Great Astro in the company of Arthos and Botami await you. Please collect your things together, I will come back in a short time for you, but we can't keep them waiting there is some reason". I held Leanne close to me and whispered to her through our mingling tears "I will come back somehow to you, but in my thoughts, you will always be with me and I with you". I embraced her again and with a quick goodbye, I left following Erup who was hurrying ahead to where they were waiting for us. Astro was the first to speak "You are now as one of us, you are indeed a true ambassador because I now have worked out how you will tell everyone about us, and the fight between good and evil", I said "How do you know? I hardly know myself." Astro put his hand on my shoulder and stared into my eyes "You will write books for all the world to read and advertise them in the papers, give interviews maybe they will even want to make films, but always be careful not to give too much away. You know many secrets and many people so when you write make sure the names are changed, so that our people can continue to live and exist in their new communities letting us know anything they hear that we need to know about the Galympites and stop their evil practices." I realised that was the method that I had being thinking about but was going to ask the permission of Astro on whether I would be able to do this, of course guarding top secrets and people, but there it was, handed to me one hundred percent permission. Botami said "Great Astro may I explain what is about to happen?", "Yes tell Glen what the next move is going to be". "Well," said Botami "We have made ready the Zoom-Ray transformer but as we have to send you all the way to your home in London, we can only do this with a few hours between, as it must be fully charged, so my dear Glen you are leaving shortly", with this Arthos piped up "Glen I will be following a day later and will contact you as soon as I am home. Don't get in touch with your editor straight away, enjoy a day or two of peace, and as soon as I am home, I will come round to your house and we will plan the way forward, we are brothers now, but you still can't read my mind". They all laughed including me. "So, Glen" said Botami "Someone behind you has just been bought here and wants to say goodbye", "So while I let Arthos, leave I will prime the Zoom-Ray".

I turned and there she was "Leanne I love you" I said and held her close, our lips met in a goodbye kiss, and that was that as Botami entered the room and said "Erup please take Leanne back, I have to seal the area far for a short time with us alone.", Botami opened the panel with his ring and there it was, the large Zoom-Ray machine, Botami lifted the top and I climbed in as I did Botami shook my hand and said "Dear friend it won't be long till we meet again, your journey will be safe.

7

Now you understand why I wanted your absolute correct address, or I might have made the address and exact place of your landing in the house of someone else". I felt nervous it was only my second time and maybe it might go wrong I thought, to which Botami reading my mind said, "No Glen it is very well tested by many Astrotars". He bent over me and touched my forehead as he closed the top of the machine, I could hear a faint noise then nothing.

    I opened my eyes I was lying on the carpet in my lounge, with my bag beside me. So, I am home and in one piece, it was certainly better than wet heather which it was the first time. Well, I will wait till I hear from Arthos I thought as I got undressed and climbed into bed, Sam my editor can wait till I see Arthos, I need a long sleep and I closed my eyes. 'DONG' that was the church clock striking 13:00hrs, definitely time I put the coffee machine on. I had decided to recap all that had happened recently and make more notes, wondering at the same time whether Arthos was home yet from Bermartus. So much had happened to us, perhaps he would not come back for some time. Then an awful thought, perhaps the Zoom-Ray transporter had gone wrong. I started to get worried, so much depended on our future as a team, and in all my life this was the best friend I had ever had. I knew the Astrotars were relying on me. The great Astro and all his people were trying to help earth survive, and I needed to write my books letting the world's people know all that I knew, in the hope we could make them believe. I wondered if Arthos would phone me when he arrived home? I went to check the coffee and the quietness was broken by with the shrill ring of my doorbell, making me jump. I hesitated in answering, as I was certainly not expecting anyone, and hoped it wasn't my editor Sam. After a few seconds of hesitation, I thought better of it, and as I opened the door a voice said, "So you were going to leave me outside, some friend!". It was Arthos reading my mind yet again, we both laughed, and he came indoors saying "Got the coffee on? I can smell it; we have a lot to talk about so let's get to the coffee then we can chat". "By the way have you managed to keep your boss at bay?".
I replied "Yes, I haven't phoned him, and he probably doesn't know I'm back yet, so Arthos the answers are no to the boss and yes to the coffee". It was good the humour we had between us. We

poured the coffee and started to talk, we mused about our adventures and how we narrowly missed disaster a few times, the great people we had shared our time with at different places and of course the unexpected end to our journey. Arthos laughed and said, "Oh! Glen your face was an absolute picture, when suddenly our boat was met by a strange projection in the middle of the ocean" "Don't be mean", I said "You knew what it was, I thought it was a monster". We laughed helplessly together. Then Arthos said "Before I left Bermartus The Great Astro decided that as you have now become almost one of us, it is time we told you our stories so that the world can hear them from you." "He also said that he meant it that you writing books would be an excellent way forward, because interviews and questions would follow. He thought that when you told him you were already writing notes, he expected that you probably were using each set of adventures would make a book. Is that right?". I agreed with him but told him I wasn't prepared to let my boss know the stories yet but would tell him that all would be revealed as soon as I could, and his paper would be 'Number One!'. Arthos then said, "Well Glen, we will shortly be off again in just a couple of days, are you ready for it?". "Of course," I said. Arthos continued "We are off to another part of the world and need to investigate further the trouble spots where the evil ones the 'Galympites' are making their bases and report it, so that they can be destroyed before they can cause more trouble". "Anyway, my dear friend I have so much to tell you. Do you remember The Great Astro telling you that we Astrotars have been visiting your planet since the dawn of civilization? The power lords of the galaxy made Astrola the guardians of planet earth, and to assist in the evolvement of civilization". Arthos stopped for a moment whilst he drank his coffee and I said, "Go on Arthos I want to hear everything so that I understand so much more about my planet". Arthos smiled saying, "I hope I will not bore you? I have so much to tell you before we leave, so that you will understand more about our journey". He stopped for a minute then began again. "People today say how could the people of those days build like they did. How did they move great boulders and stones like they did? How did they build the Pyramids, build colossal structures by stones being placed in certain ways? Other people these days come up with all sort of answers, some sound feasible, but I tell you Glen, the people thought we were Gods that took human form and came down to earth in heavenly chariots. Of course, these were our galactic crafts capable of light year speeds, and when we told them certain things, they were amazed. Our 'Magic' tools were lasers and tools that you could not even know about today". "Although the earth had existed for millions of years, having many 'Ice ages' which formed the different rock formations and mountain ranges. We only started our visits from about 10,000 BC. Intermittent at first and then more regularly, we even prepared and built our bases in different parts of the world. You have visited Tri-Base 1 and the city of Bermantus, but we have others as you will eventually come to know".

"Amongst our first flights were the Azores where they built structures to live in, which are still standing today over 5000 odd years later. There are more examples of this in other parts of the world. One nearer to you than you realise, on islands off Scotland. Your history books refer to this as 'Stone Age Man'.

They were primitive and difficult to teach and understand, as their language was very primitive and more like noises and signals." "Around 2000 BC we were visiting different tribes of people, the biggest groups were the Maya civilisation which were a Mesoamerican civilisation developed by the Maya people, to start they were growing crops of maize and beans, but we found them easy to teach, so with help they developed a writing system which was extremely articulate. They learnt about the stars, the equinox's more for their ceremonies which unfortunately involved human sacrifice. Their mathematical achievements were excellent, they even developed the 365 days of the year, and a type of calendar. No matter how hard we tried though, even they thought of us as gods. They would say in their language which was well developed that they had to appease their rain god, or they would starve. They spread over vast areas of Mexico from the Yucatan Peninsula, Guatemala. El Salvador and Belize to the Mexican state of Chiapas, just to name some parts. Unfortunately, although they were clever and industrious, they were warlike and power minded, so constant battles raged, and we moved to other parts". "In Peru there were also great and intelligent people called the Aztecs who worked with gold and silver and built great monuments and buildings, but cruelty and human sacrifice along with famine depleted their numbers. We did help them with their evolvement of learning, but like the Mayans, the Aztecs were eventually killed and scattered till their numbers were few, by the Spanish Conquests in 1500 – 1600 AD approximately." "Please realise Glen I am only giving you brief details and dates, or we would be here forever, though at a later date I will give you more for your books, so that you have all the correct dates." "Then of course going back to centuries BC we were around during the Egyptian period. They lasted for quite a few centuries and the Astrotars played a part in teaching them many things. Building the great pyramids were done using many slaves, but we taught them the technique, and it was our teachings that aligned the pyramids with the stars. The hieroglyphics on the tombs and pyramids show their god like creatures, also human type gods which they thought we were. I know now when people say they must have had help from other planets and archaeologists try to disprove it, but I can assure you we were there." "They were cruel and immoral people and extremely warlike and with their constant leadership and royalty intrigues, feuds and jealousies they destroyed themselves from within." "The next long period of time from before the second century BC and onwards were the 'Romans', who came into power after the Egyptians. Once again, we tried and, in many ways, succeeded in helping the evolvement and ideas of those prepared to learn. Unfortunately, once again jealousy, feuds and battles and even madness, over the centuries they went from greatness and we hoped they would continue, but gradually they also were suppressed.

The great Astro kept trying to help the people of your planet become less hostile and use their learnings for a greater civilization. The power of greed and hostility are such destructive forces, this is when we decided that we Astrotars would help when and if it was thought it would be to the advancement of mankind all around the world, with quite long intervals between visits". "It was around this period that we found in time that our own planet of Astrola was about to implode, and escape was necessary, with having many galactic spacecrafts we were able to make the journeys to the earth crammed full of people. Most Astrotars were already used to visiting the bases at different times around the globe, that is why we not only wanted to the save the planet for your people, but for the Astrotars as well. Unfortunately, during the exodus from Astrola, many of our own spacecrafts were attacked by hostile aliens, we think it was the Galympites, some still managed to make it even though the spacecrafts had been damaged. You met one of the survivors Youssef when we at Casablanca".

"It would be wonderful if all the people of this planet could live in harmony as we did on Astrola. If they could realise what a wonderful place it is, and how the past wars and vast amount of suffering and deaths should be the past. Why cannot different races and religions with different opinions and customs live in harmony. We must strive to get rid of evil influences, and most certainly destroy the Galympites as those evil ones have caused so much devastation over the years". Arthos had stopped talking and then said rather hoarsely, "Glen I hope you are not bored, I am actually skipping over so much but trying to put you in the picture of how we Astrotars fit in, before we once again set off on our travels. By Jupiter Glen I'm so thirsty". He leaned over and poured himself another coffee. Earlier I had made a tray of ham sandwiches, cheese and pickle with crackers, and covered it all with cling film. Thank goodness I had otherwise it would have spoilt, as I had just noticed it was now late evening and we had been talking since early afternoon. Mind you we had managed to go through several pots of coffee. We tucked into the food with relish as by now we were both hungry. By the time we had finished it was nearly ten o clock and Arthos said "Thanks Glen that was great, I'll give you a ring tomorrow sometime and we can make plans". I asked him if I could call him a taxi, but he said not to bother as he would catch one down the road at the taxi rank. I told him it was no trouble, but he insisted, so with his coat on my special friend was gone. I cleared up the lounge, washed up the dishes and within thirty minutes was in bed. What a lot of history I thought, I knew about some of it, but it was amazing to think how much the Astrotars had been involved. Then a strange thought went through my mind, what was their family life? There was no mention of parents, how did they have young, did they live forever?

      Or what had I missed! Ah! Well, Arthos always told me everything, obviously my questions would be answered soon, and that was when sleep enfolded me.

The shrill ringing of the phone bought me abruptly from dreamland into reality. What time was it? The bedside clock said eight o' clock. I reached for the offending item, but before I could speak an abrupt voice shouted down the phone "Glen, I've been trying to get you, I'm waiting for blasted answers, where is my news and my world shattering stories?". It was my editorial boss Sam. I answered as loudly and gruffly as I could "Sam when we are ready, we will tell you all, but it would spoil everything for part of the story to come out too early, before disasters have been averted and evil beings destroyed. All these extra calamities have got to be stopped". I hesitated for a minute and then continued, "You will be the one to publish our stories, when we are ready". He laughed and said in a loud voice, "Look Glen I have been hanging on for weeks and weeks, whilst you are travelling all over and I wonder what will happen if you get hurt, captured or killed,

I won't get a story". "You will" I said "But thanks for your concern. Sam I will leave all my notes and photographs to you and you'll have to do it yourself. It will be in my safe, which of course you will have to open, but not whilst I'm alive. I guess that will make you more bad tempered and stroppy?". I laughed and before he could come back with more I said, "We've got a lot to plan and long distances to travel so wish me luck, bye"; I put the phone down fast. I imagined his ugly red scowly face, with his purple nose as he stomped around the office. Sam hated not being in charge, god help my colleagues in the office I thought. As I got out of bed the phone rang again, knowing Sam's mood I guessed he was ringing back for another go at me. I answered it and without waiting I said sharply and loudly "So what do you want now? Thought of something else?", to which I was shocked to hear Arthos say, "Glen what's biting you?". I apologised profusely, explaining about Sam on the phone previously. Arthos laughed and said, "So Glen, you are not always mild mannered, there is a hidden fire lurking below the surface", which made us both laugh. "Glen" said Arthos, "Can you be ready to leave tomorrow morning for Chile. We need basic clothes, shorts, couple of tee shirts, one shirt, one decent pair of light trousers, warm jacket, swimming trunks, wet suit if you have one, don't worry if you haven't. A towel, shaving kit, passport, driving license, small camera, notebook and pen, oh! And your phone. I'll get the visas and tickets; you need very little money. I've been provided with it all, so our cash flow is organised." "Maybe in case you suffer from travel sickness at all, bring some Dramamine tablets, we can't afford to be ill. Most important I must contact some friends of long ago, who will help us from Balmaceda airport." "It's a long journey that we are about to undertake with some difficulties, we might incur on route, or might not. So, my old friends could be very necessary to us, and I know you will like them." Arthos stopped talking and I said "Arthos I'm sure I'll like them; all your friends have been so good to me." "I'll ring you back later with the details of meeting time at Heathrow International Airport. It's just as well I took down your passport details, as I need them for the visas that we need. So" Arthos stopped for a minute then continued, "Are you looking forward to us venturing once more into the almost unknown? Mind you I'm glad we trust each other so much." There was another short pause, so I interrupted with, "I do really value your friendship and that of your many friends and I know we'll cope come what may." Arthos immediately spoke, "Glen, it is really good that we have formed a true friendship, I was once told many, many years ago that a true friend is a precious jewel in the path of life, and I thought that was so true." I had listened to all he said, and I thought this is what real friendship is all about, complete trust. Arthos then said, "Ok Glen, may think of something else and if so, will call you, otherwise I'll just ring you with our meeting time, bye for now." Then the line went dead. I made some coffee and scrambled eggs and sat down at a small table by the sofa, with a large atlas open in front of me. Having first of course devoured my eggs and coffee, excitement seemed to make me hungry, because it certainly went down fast. After getting myself a second coffee, I turned to the atlas looking up the page for South America and finding Chile, Patagonia. I had a large reader's digest atlas book which was fantastic for its detail and interesting facts. I found what I needed on page 192 and thought as I looked at it, somewhere else I've never been to in all my previous journey with the job. "Hell" I muttered as I realised how far we had to travel, "That's some journey," I exclaimed loudly. Starting at Heathrow I knew but where to next, so I started working out or rather wondering which routes our journey would take. I stretched back on the sofa and started thinking about the dangerous things that I had heard about in my days as a roving correspondent. I'd heard of many happenings in South America, but of course I knew that good and bad things happen all over the world, no exceptions. My thoughts were overtaken by an over imaginative crisis, with strange happenings, and myself involved, with the typical zeal of an overzealous correspondent and my very special friend who could read my mind. Probably in the end if we were in trouble, he would save me with abilities from danger, I hope! Suddenly I was snapped back to alertness and I think this was caused by the church clock, situated opposite my flat, booming two strokes. I was amazed I had been asleep again, mind you once we start tomorrow on our journeys, sleep may be intermittent, so I was making the most of it now. I decided to get my things together so as not to have a big rush tomorrow. I would need to nip out for a few things, but I had plenty of time, but I knew how easy it is for the hours to pass when doing odd jobs.

    Having popped out and bought what I needed, I tidied my flat, done my washing and sorted out my books, papers and notebooks, not forgetting some wonderful photographs. I just put my story notebook in the safe, I didn't want them to go astray or fall into the hands of Sam, in case his curiosity and bad temper got the better of him, and he broke into my flat. He was certainly ruthless enough with all this in mind I wrote him a note addressing the envelope to him and putting it on the hall stand. Next came a meal which I pulled out of the freezer. Roast beef, potatoes, vegetables, Yorkshire pudding and gravy, an easy option from the supermarket, ten minutes for the meal in the microwave and my dinner was done. I had finished the meal when the phone rang, and as I answered a voice said, "So you have finished your meal", it was Arthos, so I replied saying, "So you can even concentrate and read my mind from a distance? Maybe very useful if I am ever in danger." Arthos started to talk, and I said, "Hang on a minute I'll get a pad and write down the instructions", to which he replied, "No need, we meet at Heathrow main entrance at 22:00hrs and we are booking in to fly first to Madrid and then onto Santiago, South America. Have you got a large duffle bag to pack your things in, making sure your weight does not exceed 23kgs, and for safety put a label on it with your name, mobile number and destination Santiago? Then we can always check on its whereabouts. Ok I'll be off still sorting out things, see you at ten tomorrow" and he was gone. I know I was busy all evening, but when I thought about it, I could hardly see what I'd done or achieved. By the time I had gone to bed and got up again in the morning, I had managed about nine hours sleep, but thought to myself that all would be well by the time I had a shower, shave and some coffee and toast. I was on my way to Heathrow Airport before I felt as if I wide awake. I had left my flat early and headed for the underground, which I could get to from the top of my road, down some steps onto a train, then after a few stops, off that one onto another platform, onto another train for several stops. The station I needed arrived at last, I got off the train, up an escalator and out onto the pavement. There was the usual taxi rank with several taxis jostling for business. A man jumped out of the first one and said to me, "Ok, Guv? Where to?", I replied smiling at his local introduction, a typical London expression not 'Sir' but 'Guv'. "I need Heathrow main entrance." "Ok Guv jump in" and off we went, darting in and out of traffic as only a London Cab driver can. We arrived, I paid him and thanked him then walked through the main Heathrow entrance wondering what was before me and tingling with excitement of the unknown future.

 Ten years I had been a correspondent travelling and reporting on disasters and world affairs, but now it was different, people from a different planet, a super friend who was actually an alien and chasing around the world checking the whereabouts of an evil alien race.

 As I entered the airport, I immediately spotted Arthos and gave him a wave. After greeting each other we decided to go and have a coffee. We made for a nearby café sitting in a corner where we could chat in peace. Whilst having our coffee I became aware that some men who had come in after us and sat down quite close to us, although there was plenty of free tables were talking but seemingly trying to hear our conversation and eyeing my duffle bag. They appeared rather shady characters and their apparent interest in us was quite baffling. I said this to Arthos, who said, "Ok I'll tune into them" and then quickly and quietly said, "Glen put a couple more labels on your bag, have you got any more?", "No" I replied but of course from his pocket Arthos took two bright orange labels saying, "Put your name in capital letters on it, and the hotel name where we are going to stay, it's Hotel Heaven Dela Patagonia and pin them to your bag, for some unknown reason as yet I think their interest in your bag is definitely not healthy." I fitted the labels on the bag, one you could see, and one you couldn't, and we waited. Nothing happened so we both thought maybe we had been hasty in our ideas and suspicions, but as Arthos said, "Better safe than sorry." When the Iberian Airways desk opened and it was time to check in, we made our own way to the queue which was already starting to form.

Then amazingly enough we found the four men right behind us, which we thought peculiar. One minute they were nowhere near, but one I hadn't seen was behind us keeping a place for the other three. I whispered to Arthos, "What's going on?", to which he put his finger to his lips and just whispered, "Shush", I noticed one of the men was concentrating on our bags, or rather our duffle bag. I was watching Arthos, he had a glazed look on his face obviously finding out what they were thinking about, it was obvious to me that he was like myself suspicious of their behaviour, but I couldn't work out why. The check-in lady behind the Iberian desk was very smart in her uniform and not to mention her attractiveness as well as her slightly foreign accent asking us the usual questions as we stood before her, "May I have passport Sir?", and then, "Did you pack the bag yourself?", then, "Have you any of these things in your bag?", pointing to a notice; to which I answered, "Yes to your first question, and no to your other questions." She smiled at my answers, I noticed that when she smiled, she was even more attractive. I lifted my duffle bag onto the weighing scales, and saw it register nineteen kilos, that's good I was under the allowed weight. She touched a button and it moved backwards and was gone. Then Arthos went through the same procedure. I noticed his duffle bag was very similar to mine, except his zipped across at the top with a lock on it, where mine gathered at the top and I tied it in a strange knot and put a small lock on it. Mind you I noticed that mine was not actually sealed at the top, but no-one would possibly get into it, unless they cut the ties, so it was perfectly safe like Arthos's bag. Mind you I hoped it didn't go missing as it had my little camera in it that didn't look much but had been very expensive. Also, I suddenly realised I had left my credit cards at the bottom of it. What an idiot I was, but I guess they would all be ok. I had some money in my backpack along with my phone as well. Arthos smiled at me and said, "Oh! Glen what a worrier you are I've got more than enough for both of us in my backpack. Relax and enjoy life for the moment." We already had our boarding passes so were without luggage, except for our backpacks, it was good knowing the luggage would not reappear till Santiago. No pickup at Madrid, I still wondered about the four men and what prompted their apparent interest in us. Arthos said breaking into my thoughts, "Glen you must be very quick when we get off the plane at Santiago and retrieve your duffle bag from the departures carousel, as from what I understand they, those four men I mean, seem to want to make an exchange with your bag, but for what reason I'm still clueless, unless they are being watched and they have slipped something into your bag without us even noticing and then hoping to retrieve it later." Arthos continued, "I have no idea what it is yet, but maybe we will find out more on the journey? I shall keep my eyes and ears very alert." As we got to security and passing through with shoes, belts, watches and jackets all off we were in turn indicated to pass through the shield one at a time. I overheard an elderly gentleman in the next lane say in a rather loud voice, "Before long they'll have us running across the tarmac naked!", which caused a general laughter, though the remark was treated with scorn from the official in uniform who said, "Surely you'd sooner be safe than dead?", which of course these days was a valid remark. We passed through but of course it had to be me, to trigger off the alarm, I had forgotten the ring I had on which I always wore and normally remembered to place it in my phone case till after security. The ring had been my grandfathers and I always thought that whilst I wore it, I would have a guardian angel looking out for me, as I was close to my grandfather. Now through we gathered up our things, put on our shoes, belts, jackets and watches not forgetting our backpacks. "Funny" I remarked to Arthos, "The four admirers of ours are noticeable by their absence", "Was that sarcasm?" Arthos said and laughed. Suddenly over the tannoy an announcement was made that the Madrid-Santiago connecting flights IB3173 Iberian had been re-scheduled from 12:30 midday till 19:20 hours to Madrid and we would be advised at what time our Santiago flight would be but that having already handed in our luggage it would be on the new scheduled flight and passed through Santiago. We heard this and knew we now had ages, but the best thing was to make straight for the American Express Club International lounge, show our boarding passes and enter into and enjoy extremely comfortable surroundings in a peaceful atmosphere with choices of food and drink, whatever you wanted inclusive.

This was indeed marvellous no tiredness a very pleasant and convivial atmosphere. Newspapers available to help yourself to on a stand, and attendants always ready to avail you of their services if you needed help. Normally when I had travelled with my job it was economy, not luxury like here. We settled down in a nice corner of the huge lounge, partitions were all around which made it a bit more private, but still open plan. The chairs we chose were comfortable with a table in front of us. Arthos said, "I'll contact my friends in Balmaceda and let them know about the re-scheduling of our flights and as we don't know the time of the Santiago one yet. They will find it out before we arrive tomorrow because we then must get an internal flight to Balmaceda which is 870 miles south of Santiago. That is where we shall be met by two people, he knew very well but hadn't seen for years. Arthos smiled "Now Glen", he said, "Stop wondering whether they are blonde haired and blue eyed, try and judge for yourself", and he really started laughing, "Anyway" he continued, "They will have a car and we are all booked into a hotel on route for a couple of days before we eventually make our way to the famous marble caves." He went quiet for a minute and then said, "When you were filling in the labels on your duffle bag, I told you the name of the hotel, we will be staying at, do you remember?". Of course, I didn't and said, "No sorry Arthos, I was too busy writing and keeping an eye on my bag", "Well" said Arthos, "It is called Hotel Heaven de la Patagonia, and I'm told it is perfect for travellers wanting beautiful scenery, good food and luxurious amenities. Not forgetting perhaps having a bit of an outdoor adventure, perhaps whether we want to or not." "Apparently by car it takes a couple of hours to reach the hotel, so I guess you'll nod off. I'm sure you will like my friends, their names are, Ricardo and Paulo, quite normal names for my friends, but then perhaps they are normal?" He smiled; what a tease he was! I am led to believe the marble caves at Puerto Tranquillo Patagonia are unbelievable, so whatever else we will have to take a trip and visit them. When we are met, we have a long journey to Puerto Tranquillo, it takes at least four hours, but we are staying only one to two hours from Balmaceola at the hotel and sticking around for a couple of days. "Many years ago, I visited this area and found Chilean Patagonia so interesting and beautiful and the people I found very friendly, of course there is a dangerous element I was warned about bandits or something, but I was lucky and only met warm friendly people. The Chilean food I found scrumptious. My attention was brought to this area by the eruptive nature of so many volcanoes, and even earthquakes which of course I hope don't happen whilst we are there, but they have become more frequent in the last century. As you know from what I have told you, it is usually a place we like to scrutinize for sightings of the Galympites, where are they hiding? Where are their secret bases? They must be found and destroyed.

There will always be disasters and volcanoes but that is caused by the movement of the earths crusts and molten core, but these extra ones are caused by the evil Galympites and they do need eradicating." Having spoken for so long he suddenly stopped and said, "Glen are you still awake", "Of course", I said "I always find you so interesting and knowledgeable." I stood up and said, "I'm going to the gents and then I'm going to get some food and a drink, how about you? "Good idea" replied Arthos, "But I'll wait till you get back and mind our bags, and at the same time make a phone call". I went off to do what I'd said. I was soon picking from the varied food and treating myself to a glass of cider. I could have whatever I fancied hot or cold but decided on fish and chips with a side salad. Straight back to the table and Arthos was off to get his food. When he came back, I saw he had chosen a very full ham and cheese salad with a baked potato and a pint of fresh orange. We both enjoyed our meals only speaking occasionally. The food was excellent and the armchairs comfortable. I could easily get used to this I thought. Arthos smiled and commented "Make the most of it, I'm sure we won't always have it easy on this trip", If only we had known how true this was, but we didn't! The time passed quickly, we always managed to find so much to talk about. Arthos was so interesting telling me about the long past years of the Astrotars visiting our planet and the advancement of the human race one minute, and then sinking back again into the dark ages then progressing again. Unfortunately, with the huge steps in the twentieth century from nineteen hundred onwards and into the twenty first century much advancement was owing to their being wars which bring out a natural development of brainpower, machine wise and medically. Arthos continued "We did assist although it was to bring peace from behind the scenes. We could no longer allow the cruelty that was happening to continue." And he drank after talking for so long. Arthos sank back in his chair and then said, "Glen, you really should stop me once I start, I just can't stop wanting to let you know as much as I can. Actually, there are still things that I'm not permitted to talk about yet" I assured him that the stories and information he spoke about were always of interest. When I came back from getting another drink for us both, I noticed that the two of the men from the café had come into the lounge and were not far from us, but only two. I wondered when the other two would appear, perhaps I had an overactive imagination about them, but as I was thinking this in came the other two and joined the others. I alerted Arthos who was apparently dozing, and he grinned and said, "No chance Glen, I am focusing on them and guessed that they are about to come and speak to us". I picked up their whispers, they know we are going to Santiago and are going to ask if they can show us around. Say nothing when they send over their spokesman, leave it to me." We sat back in the chairs and waited.

After about five minutes a tall lanky man with a beard and moustache walked over to our table and said, "Excuse me gentlemen, but I overheard you are going to Santiago. We are from there and would love to show you around", to which Arthos replied, "How kind, may we let you know after we arrive, as we have business appointments?" The man smiled and said, "Fine we'll talk again" and went back to his friends. Arthos looked at me with a knowing glance, "I told you that they were up to no good" said Arthos continuing, "I'm sure they are trying to involve us in something, could be drugs, whispers are easy for me, I've been listening into their conversations, but although mind reading is more difficult, I'll concentrate. I've had an idea; I have a friend in the Santiago police, and I'm going to contact him and let him know because they are definitely up to no good. This way we will be met, and our problems should be over." Next thing Arthos returned and said, "OK, Glen all organised. I was told they will try and check on them, but they could be using different names, but I was told drugs are high on the suspect list."

As we settled back in our chairs watching their body language which gives so much away, and pretending to do the crossword puzzle, it was obvious that we were being talked about. Suddenly two security officials came into the lounge and started walking about, speaking to different groups. Then they stopped in front of the four men, and we heard them say, "We have been advised by the American Express desk that it has come to their attention that two lots of two persons have slipped in here without the correct club facilities authority, please show you boarding passes." We heard one official say, "Will you four please come with us?" They all got up and sheepishly followed the officials out of the lounge trying to look as if there was some mistake, but we knew better. A couple of hours passed without incident and we both wondered whether they would get fined, anyway we could relax now.

Eventually the time had come for us to check the indicator board and saw that the Madrid flight was due out at 19:20hrs, so we got prepared for the gate to show and gathered our things together, exiting and starting to walk along the area where the shops were, many shops, cafes and bars, were all full of many different nationalities. "Look" said Arthos, "It's gate 12", so we made straight for the area of gate 12, which entailed a hike and a half to get there. It was IB3173 our first part of the trip to Madrid. Into the priority queue across the tarmac and up to the steps, welcomed on board and into the first part of the plane, separated by a curtain from the rest of the plane. I was woken up by an air steward asking if I would like a drink, and at the same time apologising for having disturbed me, although half asleep I said, "Oh! Yes please, may I have a glass of wine?", "Would you prefer sir, a small bottle of Champagne?", "Why not" I said, "Thankyou". I looked at Arthos who only wanted a glass of fresh orange and said, "Don't worry I'm only having one drink I promise, I won't get drunk." He laughed at me and said, "Glen enjoy the trip" I sipped the Champagne and felt this was just like the start to a wonderful holiday, when I now look back on that relaxing trip, I realise how very wrong I really was.

Here we were at Madrid it seemed so quick and yet it was late as we disembarked from the plane into pouring rain and darkness and had to run across the tarmac, guided by men and women in yellow jackets, to make for cover in the Madrid Airport building. Along a passageway to passport control and quite quickly through as we had been amongst the first off, the plane. Now make for security priority again and unbelievably I set the alarm off again. I had put on my ring again, but of course we had very little time between landing and getting ready for security again. Once more I had to be frisked down, was accepted as ok, then on with our shoes, belts, jackets etc.

Pick up our back packs, we knew our new flight was IB6833 and as we made our way to gate 21. I noticed all the bars, cafes, shops, book shops, cut price alcohol, toilets, disability areas and so on. A humming multitude of people all seemingly in a rush, assorted nationalities with a general air of needing to speak louder than the next. An obvious sight was many Spanish Police or security around, all with guns in their belts, ready for anything I thought. We went via the priority queue out of gate 21, across the tarmac to our plane, we were now with Latin Airways for an hour-long flight to Santiago, expected to arrive local time 07:20, a flight of over twelve hours. Thank god Arthos had told me we were in business class with the luxury of chair beds and covers, and many other amenities that would surely make the flight another good experience.

The night was a mixture of coffee, food and watching the flights progress on a small television in the front of my seat. Also, I must admit to just one more glass of Champagne, then oblivion a few hours' sleep. I apologised to Arthos for my sleeping, but as he said he was rested as well. I just couldn't believe it we were almost there, and the air hostess was suggesting we got ready for landing in about ten minutes, as we were due to land at 07:20. A few bumps and a roar of engines and we were down to a different world almost. So far from home and I wondered what to expect, it was then Arthos reminded me, we still had a little local flight to take to Balmaceda flight LA7083, which was only an hour and half flight in total. We made our way to collections to get our bags, not rushing like we meant to, in order to get there before the four men. I rushed up to find that they were holding my duffle bag and starting to walk away. I said, "Excuse me that is my bag", "I think not" said the man holding it by the top strap. As I was arguing Arthos had bought a security policeman over to us. The man still insisted that the bag was his. He had pulled off my label on the top, unknown to him though I had hidden in the flap out of sight, and I pointed it out to the security policeman who asked me to show him my identification which I did. He looked at it, then the label and then said to the man, "Senor you are mistaken this bag belongs to this man, that must be yours going around on the carousel." The man grimaced and let go saying quietly, "Take your bag, idiot." "Why speak like that?" I said, "You just made a mistake." "Did I", said the man, "You'll be sorry, just wait." The security man was talking to Arthos whilst another couple of security came over to the men, which I noticed now where only two. Then the man with Arthos came over to me saying, "Bring your bags and follow me", and he took us into a small room nearby, closing the door. Opening the top of my bag he said, "Here you are, they stuffed this in your bag at Heathrow, because they obviously knew we are watching them." He had pulled out an envelope A3 size, "Ok, I'll keep this and let Arthos know what happens". "Those types have their luggage well and truly checked, so they look for some way to get things through security. The envelope obviously has drugs in it, but I don't want to handle it", he said pulling off his gloves, "Could be fingerprints on it", Arthos said, "By the way Glen this is Anton we go back a long way, thanks again Anton. I'll contact you when we arrive at Balmaceda". We all shook hands, and we went over to the desk to book in for our flight, to find Anton right behind us, "Arthos", he said, "I'll have to explain to them you've missed your booked flight, I'll get you on the next flight". We went to the Latam Airways desk, and as we did Arthos' friend Anton was already talking to the airway's lady at the desk, and as we approached said, "These are the two people that need you to change the Santiago-Balmaceda tickets", "Alright Senor, no trouble", in a cheerful voice, "You have done well gentlemen, although I don't think the two other men will think so". I interrupted and said, "But there were four", "Wait a minute" she said and called security, "Please send Anton 195 security to the Latam desk". Immediately Arthos's friend appeared again from the security office and she told him that the two that had been taken into custody, were two of four, and two were therefore still free". The security man Anton turned to Arthos and I and said, "Be careful these damn people get dangerous when their plans are thwarted, so watch out. Mind you knowing you, Arthos of old, there is no need to issue warnings". We laughed then he continued, "But let me know if you need help". Arthos and I went through their security and into the departure lounge. Our flight LA1B7084 and now re-scheduled to 14:50 just twenty minutes, but it was already 14:00, so we quickly bought some coffee and sandwiches and sat down and waited for our gate to show on the information board. There it was gate 13, I shivered, oh! My God I thought hope it is lucky 13. The gates opened we were off across the tarmac and onto the plane. It was a smaller plane for domestic short flights, this was an hour and half according to the information given and approximately 870 miles south.

Arthos said to me, "Glen I have in touch with my friends at Balmaceda, who are meeting us there. They have a car and will be driving us to the hotel, which takes about two hours. It'll be great seeing them, and I'm sure you will like them. They are going to stay with us for a while, so you'll hear loads of stories. I bet you Glen, will sleep for a week when we get to the hotel", said Arthos. I smiled but couldn't resist saying to him, "When I was a roving correspondent over the years, getting stories, reporting disasters making our papers well off, and a name for myself, I was never treated to business class or good hotels with Sam, my mean employer, it was economy and cheap places to stay. No luxury flights unless I paid myself", I took a deep breath, "Honestly Arthos, meeting you and being with you on our journeys, has been a wonderful experience." I continued, "I suppose I was luckier than most, as my parents were quite well off and they left me enough money to buy a flat and have enough over to always have enough when emergencies happen, so I am not completely dependent on Sam, thank goodness". "Mind you", I added, "I'm still embarrassed that you pay for everything", "Don't worry", said Arthos, "I have substantial means and I will explain all one day, but just let me tell you so much at a time and gradually all will be revealed. I know you have many questions you wish to ask me, but please give me time, your queries about the Astrotars are many and varied, I have picked up upon them and I promise you, you will be told everything in time. You are a special friend and one day I will surprise you". By this time, we had been sitting in the two back seats for about an hour, and although there wasn't anybody directly in front of us as he said quietly, "You really don't know who's listening". About thirty minutes before we were due at Balmaceda we were offered drinks, we both had fresh orange juice and ice, we were thirsty and very tired. A thought suddenly penetrated my sleepy brain and I said, "I wonder if we will ever see those two men again, who didn't get caught at the airport?", "I hope not" said Arthos, "I really believe they are big trouble, but I don't think they saw where we went from collecting our bags and going to Anton's office, then round to the Latam airways desk. I hope not because I think that the one with the beard was the leader, but he disappeared and left the others to take the rap. That is why, if his minions grabbed the bag, no fingerprints. "Do you think he was a drug chief?" I asked, "Who knows" answered Arthos. "Anyway, don't worry we have left them behind and will be landing soon, about five minutes". He was right it was the same time announced by the air hostess. Engines roaring, I thought how I hated the decent when they put the engines in reverse to slow down. Then with a bump and a bounce we landed, the roar of the engines slowed down to a stop then peace. It was the pilots' chance to thank us for flying with Latam airways. They only opened the front door, so we were last off, though this time it was not a rush across the tarmac.

Through passport control and an array of security we reached the carousel for our two bags and it was then that I noticed again the difference. Arthos had a different top with a zip and lock, so I guessed why they had chosen my bag, "Yes" said Arthos reading my mind yet again. Arthos was looking so happy as he was greeted by his two friends, they hugged like true friends who had not seen each other for a long time. Arthos turned to me, "Sorry Glen, this is Ricardo and Paulo", he turned to them and said, "This is Glen, he is not an Astrotar, but he is to me we are very special friends". What praise I thought, as in an instance both men hugged me saying, "Welcome to our world and hearts, if you ever need help, we are there for you". They then told me they had lived in South America for a long time and travelled around so everyone here excepts us, but let's face it they don't really know us, like you do". They then said, "Come let's get to the car, we can talk as much as we like there with nobody listening", we went outside it was hot, though not really it was my tiredness kicking in, I was so tired. We were packed into the car and sped along to our destination, their voices were getting further away, when I awoke the car had stopped and we were at hotel 'Heaven de la Patagonia'. We went into the hotel which was beautiful as described in our literature. A meal was suggested but we decided to go to our rooms first and clean up. We had been travelling for so long I had stubble beginning to look like a beard. Arthos wasn't, though this didn't surprise me. We signed in at reception, I was impressed with the luxurious surroundings, we were given our key cards, going up the stairs I said to Arthos, "Would you be offended if after I wash and change that I come down and just have a drink and a sandwich and leave you three to talk? I feel overwhelmed with tiredness, but do not want to appear rude", Arthos said, "Look if you are fit, come down for an hour, then disappear for the night, we really do understand". Arthos then said, "After all Glen you are only human", we both laughed and made our way to our rooms. I kept my promise, had a quick shower, shave and changed and went down for a pint and a sandwich beautifully decorated with a salad, I made my way back to my room, locked the door, threw off my clothes and fell into an extremely large and comfortable bed, and fell straight to sleep.

I wondered what the knocking was, why don't they ring my bell? I sat up and then realised

I wasn't at home, but in a hotel in Chile, Patagonia. I jumped out of bed and rushed to the door, I opened it and Arthos said, "Ok, Glen? We began to think you had either left or died, thank goodness you were only being human! see you downstairs, we are about to have breakfast, I assume you are ready to eat?". I hurriedly agreed washed, dressed and rushed down to join the others in the breakfast room. As I sat down, I noticed two men sitting at the far side of the room, not knowing why, I thought one of them looked familiar but of course knew that was impossible, they reckon everyone has a double after all. I ordered my breakfast, when it arrived, I relished it eating hungrily and sipping my hot fresh coffee, I had some more toast, then that was me full. Arthos and his two friends had already finished when I arrived so were talking. I caught Arthos's eye and said in a whisper, "Who are those two men just going out of the breakfast room, I know I'm being highly imaginative, but thought I had seen the tall man before". Arthos watched them depart and said, "I think some people came last night, quite late but I didn't really see them arrive, to be honest I was so pleased to see and be with my friends that I didn't take much notice of them. We are going out for a short trip in the car today and taking it easy. I want to check maps and find out where all the volcanoes are situated and if any sightings of the Galympites, such as sightings of spaceships by the locals, that is if we can find some locals. Then we will look at making a boat trip to the marble caves and playing at being tourists. We all got ready to go out in the car having first put any valuables into our room safes. As I started to empty my duffle bag, putting all the clothes out of it on a big chair and checking that my money and credit cards were deposited safely. My attention was suddenly bought to an object that had slipped to the bottom of the bag. It was a strange object about nine inches long, by about an inch wide in a plastic/metal covering, with some type of lock on it. Obviously not mine it must have been another thing put in my bag by those men at the airport, but had not come to anyone's attention, would they follow me to retrieve it? Anyway, how would they know where we were staying or where we went to in Santiago, or was I just letting my imagination get carried away? A knock at the door, I froze, then Arthos's voice said, "Are you ok, Glen? Or have you gone back to bed?" I opened the door and told him what I had found, "Ok", he said, "As long as you have hidden it, we'll keep our eyes and ears open and if necessary, I will contact Anton at Santiago airport to alert the authorities, come on Glen let's go but make sure the key of the safe is hidden". As we started towards the car, I with my natural curiosity asked Arthos, "Where are we going?", "Exploring" he replied laughing. Into the car and off down the road from the hotel we were in very mountainous territory, with scattered vegetation all about with boulders and rocks of various sizes, a few bushes and immense amounts of bracken around on one side of the road. On the other side of the road, it was sheer rocks, part of the Andes mountain range. And as far as we could see it was a typical Andes landscape.

Eventually Ricardo pulled into the grassy side of the road and parked up. It was then I saw this small lake nestling in the not so far rocky enclaves, around which were scattered large and small boulders and rocks, obviously been scattered during volcanic eruptions or great ice age movements of rocks. After a brief chat we decided to walk around it, making sure that the car was locked, as we heard that sometimes there were bandits in the hills. I asked what had determined this sudden step and was told by Paulo that Arthos thought we were being followed, but as the road was twisty, we were going to make them show themselves. There were some huge boulders which we got behind. They were right on the lake side but out of view from the road on the way we had come. We chattered, waited and watched for around twenty minutes. Perhaps Arthos was wrong I thought, but Arthos immediately tuned into me saying, "Ok Glen in about five minutes a car will appear, maybe pass by when it sees the car and park around the next twist and then they will sneak back". They smiled at Arthos's words and Ricardo said, "Look, quiet here comes Arthos's words", and a car came slowly into sight, slowed up and almost stopped by our car, then continued slowly round the next bend of the road. We waited; next thing two men appeared around the bend of the road slowly trying to blend in with the surroundings trying to look as if they were examining rocks etc., but at the same time looking around seeing nothing they continued getting nearer. It was the two from the hotel, so we waited and as they came up to our huge boulder, we stepped out in front of them, all four of us and Arthos spoke to two very surprised men saying, "Can we help you gentlemen? I guess you are looking for someone, would it be us?" The two men were noticeably shocked firstly by our sudden appearance, and secondly by the directness of the question that they were looking for us, but quickly gathered their composure saying, "Oh! Oh! Err, we saw the car and thought someone might be in trouble" That is where Ricardo said, "No we are not in any trouble, just enjoying the rocky, bracken covered hillside, and walking around this small lake enjoying the scenery. We were wondering if there have been any volcanic deposits left from bygone ages. I am a geologist and my colleagues, and I are studying rock formations then moving onto volcanic areas, where we can trace the origins of them, and or the reasons for their eruptions" He stopped talking and the tall man of the two said, "That is very interesting by the way my name is Nicholas, and I come from Santiago, my friends call me Nick, and this is my cousin Juan. We are originally from Sicily, but we live in South America now. May I ask your names and where you are from?" said the newly bolden Nicholas. "Different places", replied Arthos, "But for now my friend and I are temporarily living in London", pointing at me. Then pointing to Ricardo and Paulo and said, "Our two friends are from around Santiago area at the moment". Arthos still hadn't given any names or residences. In fact, it was quite funny, but so well done, "Anyway", said Arthos, "We will bid you goodbye, as we want to talk and stretch our legs", he offered his hand to shake and we did likewise. The niceties over, we smiled and the four of us continued our walk around the lake. They were left standing as we glanced back, we noticed they were talking and the one called Juan appeared to be talking on a phone. Ah! Well, I thought whatever is going to happen next, because I really felt that this was far from over. We were continuing walking and talking and every so often as we knew they would be watching, examining rocks and pretending to look at a little notebook, as if we were making references, then walking on again. We had reached the corner of the lake when we would have to go right along the far side, so we stopped to decide. Whilst doing so I stopped and felt the water, it was icy cold. Anyway, this was very south and almost glacial in parts, so it was bound to be cold. Arthos suddenly said in a commanding voice, "All stand still for a minute, now I want Juan and Ricardo to concentrate with me on those two men, to find out what is going on and then we will let Glen know what's transpiring". The four of us appeared to be studying a large boulder on the far side of the lake, that must have been about ten feet high, but it was just to throw them off guard. Who would ever guess mind reading capabilities of my three friends, yes, you've guessed the three were all Astrotars although I guess they had coloured their hair, as it was silvery blonde, but of course they had to fit in with people around Santiago? Suddenly, Arthos said, "Am I right they are getting someone to join them?" Ricardo joined in with, "That's what I understood, how about you Paulo?" "Actually" said Paulo, "I think they are out of their depth. I'm sure they are dealing with forces other than human; if so, we could be in trouble. Let's get back to the car as soon as possible, but don't look as if we are in a hurry". Arthos made a pointed effort of rolling up his sleeve and looking at his watch, and with that we started walking back the way we had come, as it was nearer than going right around the lake. We were soon passing the huge boulder we had previously been standing behind, walking a steady pace towards the car, and appearing to have humorous chats, giving them a wave as we passed the two men sitting by the roadside. The other side of the road had become steep and craggy, sloping upwards to the mountains the Andes. I remember hearing Andes pipe music and never forgetting the magic sounds, so eerie and mysterious, and now I was actually here. "Glen" Arthos said, "Come on, stop being miles away we've got to hurry, turn the car around here and back track to the hotel as we don't know what's ahead". Ricardo started the engine, and it was so quick the turn around and we were on our way. He drove like a racing driver, Arthos was beside him, Paulo and I were in the back. We waved to the two men as we passed them and were given a grimacing nod.

    Arthos spoke first, "Wait my friends, get ready for trouble I sense we are about to find life not so easy. Paulo has already advised a nearby Astrotar base, and help is on its way". A thought suddenly came into my head, a picture in fact, a face, I realised who the tall man was, he was the leader at the airport who had disappeared and was now without a beard and moustache. Arthos said interrupting my thoughts, "Glen I had only just realised the same thing, this has become more troubling than drugs, I don't know how but I think the Galympites are involved, but how?", "I also think so" said Ricardo, "I'll repeat my message to the nearest base of the Astrotars and they will send out a decoy with a destruct rocket on it. Those evil forces will not be expecting that". A loud noise overhead and we looked up a torpedo shaped object shot across the sky. Fear is a horrible feeling but I'm sure we were all feeling wary. The road was twisty, but Ricardo made the car move at what seemed to be an unbelievable speed. Then again, the blasted thing went over us again, at an extreme height, but still we saw it in the clear sky. Again, the peaceful sky was pierced by this object passing overhead at great speed but lower. Arthos said, "It's definitely Galympite" then said, "Ricardo, slow down and let the car get nearer if by any chance they are in cahoots with each other the Galympites will not want to hit them, and we can use them as a shield, anyway we are getting near the hotel". From the mountainous side of the road, the side we were travelling suddenly something shot southwards high in the sky, and the shape disappeared. "Astrotars to the rescue" said Juan, "I hope all will be well", "Unfortunately" said Ricardo, "No success is written in stone."

8

We slowed down to about forty miles per hour, the other car was not behind us but not far away. When high in the sky there was an explosion like a clap of thunder, and we froze. Don't let it be the Astrotars, let them have won, our thoughts were all the same. Suddenly Ricardo said, "Don't worry, I've just received a message, one less Galympite spacecraft and its contents", we all cheered then Arthos spoke, "Just keep going, five minutes and we are back to the hotel. It will be interesting to see what the idiots have to say if they try to speak to us when they see us", "Certainly not what we expected today" said Juan. Arthos turned in his seat and said to me, "Glen are you ok? I told you life as an Astrotar has its problems, now you are getting the taste of the bad bits", with that Ricardo laughed and said, "Oh! It's good to laugh again". "Another five minutes", said Arthos, "And Glen will be getting a stiff whisky", they laughed again, "No comment", I said.

As we went into the hotel the other car came around the corner and drew into the car park. Ricardo couldn't resist saying, "Come on my friends give the men a wave that will unnerve them".

I mentioned to Arthos before we left for the day about the object, I had hidden in my room in the safe which I had shown him before we left. Arthos said, "Right we are all going to Glen's room to examine this object found in his bag, and we must determine how we can benefit from it". We went into the bedroom and locked the door, opened the safe and started to study the object. Arthos spoke first, "I don't yet how those two men were contacted, but I think somehow that this object is a translator, to aid them in communication. Somehow, I think this could turn out to be very important. Mind you I think it will also cause a great deal of trouble, I'm sure we are up to it. Ok Glen lock it away and hide the key under that wardrobe as far as possible, in case your room has visitors". Let's go down and have some sandwiches and salad with plenty of coffee. It's mid-afternoon and a while to dinner. We ordered and sat down at a corner table. The lounge bar was very luxurious with red and gold upholstered chairs, lovely carpets and attractive lights, as well as being spacious, allowing private conversation if spoken quietly. The two men came into the lounge, "Leave this to me" said Arthos to us. A waitress came over to the table and placed our orders which looked very appetising, nicely decorated assorted sandwiches with salad garnishing, plus a large bowl of potato crisps and a large thermos flask of coffee, with milk and sugar. The waitress said, "Let me know gentlemen if you need anything else", we thanked her, then she departed. The two men who had entered the lounge bar showed extreme brass neck, by walking over to our table, and interrupting our conversation with, "Oh we meet again, shall we join you?", Arthos replied "Why?", "Oh" said the tall man, "I thought we could have a good chat", Arthos replied, "No, now go away and leave us in peace". The men glared at Arthos and continued, "Have you got a problem? Or even more, an attitude problem?", "Yes, my problem is you, you may have shaved off your beard and moustache, trying to change your appearance, but I don't take kindly to being followed, as you may have noticed? I didn't try and become friendly when we met by the lake. Do you know why? I know what your game is and will soon find out how dangerous it is. Now go away and leave us in peace and remember my words, you are involved in more than you can handle, your life is no longer your own". The look of mixed hatred and fear on the man's face was there for all of us to see, as he walked across the room, and sat almost out of sight. Arthos looked at us and said, "Was that ok? How did I do?", we all agreed he was excellent then Arthos said, "Wait for it though, he will be back". We drank more coffee and talked quietly and waited. Arthos was seldom wrong, Ricardo said, "Glen, you might wonder why we listen so much to Arthos, but he has always been an excellent leader", "Thank you" said Arthos, "I only hope I can live up to the praise." Paulo said, "Arthos are we going to travel down to the large lake tomorrow and meet up with our friend we've contacted for a motor-boat to visit the blue marble caves, or should we just do the tourist thing and book on one of those trips?" Arthos thought for a moment and said, "It's a long drive down to Puesto Tranquilo, it's a four hour drive down the Carretera Austral Road, so I guess we need an early start. How about breakfast at six in the morning, ok Glen?". We laughed Arthos said, "Give you a knock at five, and we'll go for breakfast then pack up. I'll sort out the bill and we can leave. Maybe before our followers are awake?" We decided to go outside and have a short walk around the hotel. It was very classy and lived up to its name 'Hotel Heaven de la Patagonia', hopefully I thought it won't turn out to be 'nightmares'. It was early evening but as it was summer being early January the sky was still lovely to look up at. Saturn was visible all night I was told by Paulo, then Ricardo said, "Look Glen, Venus is visible at the setting and rising of the sun", as he pointed out to me the moon which no longer a full moon, but it was so interesting as they pointed out different stars, suddenly they spotted Jupiter and pointed it out, I was told watch out when the sun sets, you'll be able to see Mars. We were so engrossed we didn't see the two men come outside. They stood smoking a short distance from us, obviously trying to hear our conversation, but we were only discussing the stars. The smaller man must have been selected for the mission, he came over to us and said, "Excuse me, please don't get angry with me for interrupting you, but we really want to apologise for any inconvenience we have caused you, I think you may have judged us wrongly. Only time will tell, but please don't think we want to annoy you, we are just taking a long-earned break from Santiago. Arthos turned to the man saying, "No trouble, enjoy your break we certainly mean you no harm. We are also having a break to study some rocks as geologists". The man smiled and went back to his companion obviously to report. At this point we started down the road for about half a mile talking about the two men and agreeing that we didn't trust them at all. Having decided that maybe it was time to go and get a shower and shave before we met up for dinner, as we didn't want to eat too late with an early start.

We meandered up the road wondering what tomorrow would hold, then Arthos said, "Glen, you are at it again, don't worry if it's going to happen it will, so enjoy tonight and let tomorrow take care of itself", "Well said" chorused Ricardo and Paulo together, and it bought back a touch of humour to the situation. We went back to the hotel and to our rooms, agreeing to meet up around eight. I went into my room and locked my door. Some of my clothes were on the floor, I wondered if anyone had been in when we were out, but I thought that was just a silly idea. I had a quick shower and shave and changed into my lightweight smart trousers, which I thought were more appropriate for dinner than shorts. I still had time before going down for dinner, so I decided to fold some of my clothes and open my duffle bag and fill it with my folded clothes. I had plenty of room to pack the remainder in the morning, not forgetting the mysterious object locked away in the safe, which I decided to leave until just before we were due to leave. As I exited my room to go down for dinner, I checked and double checked my room door was locked, didn't want any undesirables in there. I made my way down to the lounge bar where we had agreed to meet. As usual I was the last one, even though I thought I might have been the first. We went and chose some seats and made ourselves comfortable. Immediately a well-dressed man in a black suit, with crisp white shirt, black waist coat and with very highly polished shoes to complete the look. He appeared to be the manager, or head waiter, he spoke, "Good evening gentlemen" he said, "May I presume you wish to dine with us this evening?", "Yes we certainly would" replied Ricardo, speaking for us all. "May we have a look at the menu whilst we wait?", "Well sir, if you are ready, I will take you through to the dining room where you can decide from the menus and you won't need to be moved again" the waiter replied. Arthos said "Thank you, you lead the way, and we will follow", the manager gave a slight smile. We stood up and followed him out of the lounge, across the hallway into a very salubrious room. The décor was of a bygone age with red and gold armchair seats around the tables, which were covered in starched white table clothes. We were led to a table situated next to a bay window which gave the impression of a framed picture with dusk setting over a mountain view. The garden of the hotel was well illuminated, which made the setting fantastic. I was hypnotised by the view as I sat close to the window. The other three said, "Oh! Glen, it's good you are enjoying things, and may it continue", I don't know if they chorused it or just interrupted each other. We were all in a happy mood. The waitress came over to take our order, Arthos was the spokesperson, "We have decided not to have starters, but we are looking forward to the main meals. Can I order two wild boar with fresh pineapple served with dauphin potatoes and mixed side salad, and two meals of roast lamb served in a special Patagonian sauce with a mixed salad and sautéed potatoes. Can both meals be served with salad dressing and onion rings please?". The waitress replied, "Yes sir" and then asked, "And would you like wine?", "Of course, maybe a bottle of Uco Malbec and a bottle of Calsernet Sauvignon, have you got these very good reds?", "I will check sir" said the waitress, and she went off with the order. She was pretty with lovely black hair, dark brown eyes and high cheek bones, slim and petite in statue and I imagined she was of south American ancestry. "Well done Glen" said Paulo, "I think that's the waitress's family history". With my thoughts laid bare we all laughed, "It's not fair, your minds are secrets from me" I said. It wasn't long before our food was served, which was excellent. "They must have a very good chef", remarked Arthos between mouthfuls. The food was that good that we ate and drank with hardly a word uttered between us all. We decided on a cheese board and coffee for dessert for the four us. It was a lovely evening telling stories and feeling as though I had always known my companions, but as I thought back all the Astrotars I had ever met were friendly. I started thinking of Pietro, Ahmed, Youssef, Mohammed and Antonio and the times we had together. Suddenly a voice bought me back, it was Arthos, "Glen, we also like those people but you are with us for tonight". I apologised saying, "I was only thinking what a wonderful race of people you really are".

    We finished the wine, coffee and cheese board and noticed it was getting late, so we said our goodnights noticing our not so friendly friends were nowhere to be seen. "Must be planning tomorrow", Ricardo joked, "Hope not, I don't like their playmates" said Paulo. We parted company, Arthos reminding me he would knock me up at five in the morning, I grimaced and laughed when they all called me sleepyhead. I opened my bedroom door and was met by a very disturbed mess. Someone had been searching my room, my duffle bag was emptied out and drawers were left half open. I checked the wardrobe it hadn't been moved. I checked the key was still there where I had left it. Now I must concentrate I closed my eyes and concentrated on my friends, "ARTHOS, RICARDO, PAULO" I said over and over, "PLEASE HEAR ME IT'S GLEN I NEED YOU". Five minutes passed I began to think it hadn't worked, when a knock at the door and the three came in, "What's wrong?" they asked, I explained, and they saw the mess. "Did you lock your door?" they asked, I explained how I tried it several times to make sure, "Right", said Arthos, "I'm going for management, don't touch anything", I said to Ricardo and Paulo, "It must have been whilst we were eating, well I'm glad I wasn't in bed when they got in". The three of us stood and waited the other two said, "Don't worry Glen, we'll sort this out, and you will be fine tonight, we'll make sure of that, we Astrotars always stick together", then added, "Even for adopted ones", "Thanks", I said. Another knock on the door and in came Arthos, with a rather stout gentleman, with a grey beard and moustache and elegantly dressed. He started off by saying, "My heartfelt apologies, who could get in? Was your window open or door unlocked?", to which I replied, "No" to both questions, then the man said, "Have they stolen anything", "No", I replied but obviously they have acquired a key card from someone, I will change your room", "Never mind that", said Arthos, "I want to know who it was because how did they get supplied? If it wasn't staff, I have a strange feeling we may know which of your guests it could be". The man looked perplexed but said, "Don't worry gentlemen this will be sorted", and he left. We locked the door, got the key from under the wardrobe and opened the safe. "Yes" said Ricardo looking into it, "It's still here, I think I'll put in my safe, as it will be a very sorry person who breaks into my room. I have an object like your police have Glen, you call it a Taser, but what I have is stronger, so let him or her try. Also, I am physically extremely strong", to which Paulo and Arthos agreed. They are super friends I thought. Then our investigating gentlemen, who was actually the manager and was horrified that anything like this could happen said, "My son was on reception last night and only left reception for about ten minutes to go to the bathroom. When he came back, he noticed two men going up the stairs and presumed that they were going to get changed to have a meal, all the other guests were still in the dining room when you left after your meal, you were the first ones to go to bed". With that Arthos said, "May I speak to your son? I wonder if he could describe those two men, because I have a feeling, I know who they are", "Of course", said the man who had told us his name was Pedro Lopez and he was the holiday replacement manager, but his duty covered many hotels since his semi-retirement and was very upset", Arthos said "Ok, I'll come with you if I may?". They left the room and whilst Ricardo and Paulo were talking, I quickly repacked my bag, leaving my shorts out as I could wear them if it was hot the next day, and save my good trousers for the evenings. Then I said, "Ricardo, do you really want to take the object to your safe, when I leave my room?", "Yes" Ricardo replied, "I don't think he'll have a key to any other rooms, but it's his problem if he does try". We waited around ten minutes when suddenly there was a loud knock at the door. It was Senor Lopez and Arthos. Arthos spoke first, "The description fits those two idiots, but without proof, we'll wait. I've advised them that we are leaving tomorrow, but we will return in a few days. I hope you don't mind senor Lopez but our whereabouts at the moment we would prefer to keep to ourselves, but we will return to stay with you again in a few days", "Ok, thank you gentlemen", replied senor Lopez then gave me another key, "This key is to next door to this man", he pointed to Arthos, I thanked him and said, "I'll hand both keys into reception in the morning", with that senor Lopez left. I got the key from under the wardrobe opened the safe and gave Ricardo the object, then locked the safe. I then put my shaving kit into my duffle bag, checked I had everything so not to leave anything behind and said, "Ok, Arthos lead the way, we had better see Ricardo to his room first", to which they just laughed at me and Paulo said, "Don't worry I'm next door to him and will look after him". We opened the door and I said, "Goodnight my very special friends, thanks for being there for me, and thank you for hearing me though I was far away", the door closed, and I noticed it was nearly midnight, I went straight to bed as I only had five hours before I was to be up again.

    Lying in bed, just about awake I wondered who was delivering a parcel, as a knocking on the door persisted, I wasn't even expecting a delivery. The knocking got even louder, then it dawned on me it was Arthos, I was in Chile not London. I jumped out of bed and opened the door. Arthos was laughing, "See you downstairs sleepyhead, you don't even know where you are, that is so funny", I replied, "Sorry, I will join you as quick as I can." Never has anyone showered, shaved and dressed as fast as did, I would tidy up after breakfast. Locking the door, I rushed down to the breakfast room. The other three were finished but still drinking coffee, I quickly helped myself to some cold meat, cheese, butter and a couple of warm rolls. Arthos excused himself and went to reception sorting out the bill and advising the hotel as to when we would return in a few days. We arranged to meet outside in the carpark in fifteen minutes, just enough time for me to go to my room, put everything in my bag, and checking the room to ensure nothing had been forgotten. I handed in my two keys at reception and made to depart to the carpark. As I did a young man behind the desk came over and said, "Senor, I am senor Lopez's son, I wish to apologise to you for any trouble I unwittingly caused you last night", I smiled and replied, "Don't worry it all ended ok luckily".

We were chatting away in the car as we drove down the long Carretera Austel Road, we had at least a four-hour journey ahead of us, and fortunately we hadn't seen the two idiots at breakfast. Our early start must have fooled them, more importantly we had hoped it had completely fooled their evil alien colleagues. We certainly didn't want to play hit and miss again as we drove to Puerto Tranquillo. Suddenly I had a thought, "Oh! My god, we have forgotten the object, I gave it to you Ricardo, didn't I? And I forgot to remind you about it before we left". Ricardo slowed the car down saying, "We will have to go back for it, that will spoil our advance start to the day". I was upset and said, "It's my fault I should have kept it. The object was really my responsibility". They all then started laughing and said, "Glen, don't worry, we have hidden it where no one will expect, or looks. The car has many hiding places invisible unless you know where to look", "You bunch of torments", I replied, "I was so upset I thought I had spoiled the day". We talked at length about the problems of yesterday's outing, and wondered if the two men who had been following us had found out where we were going. The weather was fine, a warm spring day, which pleased me, as I wasn't too keen on the cold. The landscape was an extremely mountainous area, which lends a certain magic and mystery as a backdrop to travelling. National Parks were advertised in several areas like Perez Razoles and others situated on small islands on the west seacoast of Chile, Patagonia. Small villages were scattered around from Balmaceda to Puerto Tranquillo nestling in the areas, carved out between the craggy rocks and mountains, tall grasses and bushes gave some of the land a Savanah type appearance, but the boulders and huge rocks even on the not particularly mountain side gave the impression of past volcanic debris and ice age deposits. As we were driving southwards, we were aware that there was a heavy mist coming off the mountains, giving an eerie feeling, not unlike the Scottish Highlands I knew so well. We chattered about so much, their stories were innumerable and so interesting. Some I felt had been passed through the generations as they couldn't be that old, or could they?

How Ricardo escaped from a site of the Galympites, when he found one of their smaller sites and crept inside. Unfortunately, some came back, he was hiding in a crevasse high up, so no one saw him, but as the last one left, they sealed up the entrance. He thought he was done for, they must have suspected something he thought, and called for help, worried that the Galympites would come back too quick. Luckily two of his colleagues intercepted his call for help and came and released him. He added they had great difficulty but thankfully succeeded. This might happen to anyone, so if it does find a nook out of sight and stay quiet and hidden, sending brain messages to your colleagues. I'm sure they were going to keep me prisoner was his final part of his story, we had all been so absorbed in. We hadn't noticed that a grey torpedo shaped object was hovering about five hundred feet above us. "Not them again", said Arthos, "Get out of the car and do as I say". Ricardo, Paulo and I got out but Arthos stayed in the car, using his phone I noticed. He said, "Now look up and start waving, it will confuse them, I'll get assistance if they stay around, it will make them think we are more in numbers". It appeared to move away and then come back over us. As we waved again, they appeared to go up a bit higher. Suddenly a bat shaped craft came from nowhere and made towards the torpedo shape by the mountains. No impact was made but something was directed at the torpedo shape, as it streaked away followed by the bat shape. In the distance we heard a noise that sounded like a strong clap of thunder, then immediately a very bright light, we all stood there and about fifteen minutes passed and Arthos said, "I think but as yet I'm not completely sure that the Astrotars are safe, I'm waiting for news".

    We got back into the car and started back on our journey. None of us were speaking, all worried about the Astrotar combater and craft. "Do you know who it was in the Astrotar craft?", I asked, "I know who it could be", answered Paulo, "And I hope that he is ok". He turned to Arthos and said, "I think you know Oracet don't you?", "Yes", replied Arthos quietly. We motored on when suddenly Ricardo said, "Oracet is ok, but the spacecraft needs a slight repair, but that is another Galympite spacecraft obliterated, gone for good". We all cheered; our spirits being revived. Travelling on for a few miles and all feeling much better, we rounded a corner of the twisty road known as Route 7 or Cavietera Austrail Road and came in sight of a lovely hotel called, 'Hotel Loberias del Sur', we continued on as we only at this time wanted a coffee and some cake. It was shortly after this we came upon a little café just off the roadside, with chairs and two tables outside. As the car stopped an elderly lady came out, she had long grey hair tied back her face had dark brown eyes and a Latin colouring, which made her ageless.

She was wearing a colourful dress and welcomed us with a beautiful smile that was very hospitable. She asked if she could help us. Ricardo answered her in Spanish, ordering some coffee and cakes for four. Within minutes a pretty colourful tablecloth was spread on our table, then plates and napkins, followed by the milk and sugar and a large jug of coffee and homemade cakes. "Please help yourselves", she said in broken English. Ricardo spoke to her in Spanish, and she spoke to us in broken English, "I happy lady to see you gentlemen, how you be happy and eat your cake and coffee". When we decided to leave, we paid for our cakes and coffee and Paulo gave her a tip, and was embarrassed when she said, "Gratzie Signor" and gave him a big hug and kiss. Once we were in the car the teasing started, we asked Paulo what special charms he had that we didn't as we didn't get a kiss, he just laughed and said, "What's your earthly expression Glen? If you've got it, flaunt it", we all laughed. The peace was disturbed again, another oval shaped object swooped over us, too close for comfort, we all knew then, we had a hard job ahead. Once again Arthos called for backup but insisted, "Take care these idiots mean business", Arthos then spoke to us saying, "Don't worry, I'm formulating a plan". As he spoke, he was looking at an area on the map, "Keep going", he said, "Shortly you will see a small lake on the left-hand side, stop and watch what I intend to do". At the same time, he was sending some strange instructions down the phone and Ricardo commented, "Good idea, if they are listening to our conversation on the phone, they won't understand Astrolish". Ricardo turned to me and said, "Glen, one day we'll teach you Astrolish how about that?". I smiled and replied, "I had trouble with Italian and German at school and can only just get by in French. When I did my correspondent travel, I was always grateful that most people spoke English, as it is recognised as a world language, I guess also when it comes to languages the British tend to be lazy, not all of course, but I am one of the lazy ones". Arthos then said, "Ok, all concentrate I've just found a screwdriver in the glove compartment, I need something heavy, and it's black. Now we are just coming to the small lake, I want you all to watch outside the car, whilst I get ready to throw the screwdriver. No in fact Ricardo you can throw it harder and further than me, so you can do it when I give you the signal". We spotted the lake and pulled up off the road, onto the grass verge. It was quite hilly around us and craggy on the other side of the road. The lake was quite near us, so we approached it a little then waited. Almost on cue the hovering monstrosity about five hundred above us, we all waved and then Ricardo with all his might, swung round in a circle and threw the improvised screwdriver black object into the middle of the lake, looking up he shouted, "If you want your object so badly, it's in the middle of the lake, so get it." The alien craft hovered even lower then shot off southwards. By this time Arthos had advised the Astrotar base and wanted to see if the alien craft would return. Half an hour passed and just as we were about to get in the car, Arthos said, "Don't get in just yet, let's stay at least ten metres from it, we can hide ourselves by this big rock. I've noticed there's a deep crevice in it and the top is protruding over it, all get inside and let's see what happens, we have plenty of time, and I just received a warning from Oracet, so let's see what happens. It's not worth taking chances it's certain that base has received some intercepted transmission and passed it on". I asked Arthos, "What do you think will happen?", the answer came from Ricardo addressing Arthos, "You have been advised that they may laser the car, do you think they will expect to kill us, then move on?". We all ducked out of sight and waited.

Arthos said, "Look, I was right it's back, but it's in for a surprise" a bright ray shot from the hovering craft and the car lit up for a minute and smoke hung around it, which as Arthos whispered hid the fact that we were not in the car. Suddenly an Astrotar craft came from the mountain side and although the Galympite craft was taken by surprise started off, but it was too slow, there was an almighty crash like a double thunderclap, then even though we were hidden we experienced seeing a strong brilliant white light as the alien craft imploded and dropped into the lake. The Astrotar craft came down very low as we emerged from our hiding place, flashed a light at us, dipped on way then the other way, then turned and zoomed off the way it had come. "Well,", said Arthos, "They certainly don't like us and definitely this time they meant business, but thank the masters of the universe for looking after us", Ricardo turned to Paulo and said, "You are very quiet, are you ok? You are so depressed", he replied, "Yes, I was remembering how fatal those rays can be from the distant past when I was in a similar position and only by throwing myself out at speed into a roadside ditch I was saved, but my companion was not so fast and was lost as he tried to throw himself out, he caught his foot in something which slowed him down. I have always felt guilty that I survived, and he didn't". Ricardo gave Paulo a hug and said, "We have it written in the stars that we have an obligation to try and stay alive and help the earth people and our people". Arthos spoke to us all saying, "We must wait for about another ten minutes and make sure the rays have dispersed". After a time, Arthos took something from his pocket and flashed it at the car, it showed a green light and he said, "Ok, it's safe to enter now". Arthos turned to Paulo and gave him a hug, "Sorry I was so involved with the situation I had temporarily forgotten that incident. You are right that indeed was a long time ago, but I like you will never forget Pollich, he was always brave and a great companion with which to travel.

We climbed into the car, it had a peculiar smell like bad eggs or some chemical I couldn't remember, "Sulphur" said Ricardo reading my thoughts, "It's their smelly trademark", "Thanks", I replied. Ricardo started the car, I was relieved when it started, apparently it wasn't damaged, "No" said Paulo, "It was only us they wanted to damage". "Perhaps we can make it to Puerto Tranquillo now without further interruptions", exclaimed Arthos, Ricardo added, 'Oh, Glen that was a practice, the real stuff hasn't started yet", they all laughed. It was a good feeling to look forward to a few days of relaxation, though nothing in life ever goes to plan as we would all find out. An old car came around the corner from where we were parked, just inside the village near the lake. We watched the car and immediately realised that it was Arthos's friend Ottol. He waved out of the window and honked the horn a couple of times as a welcome, laughing, he jumped out of the car and embraced Arthos who had rushed to meet him saying, "Ottol dear friend so long since we met but you don't forget me, that's so good these are my friends, Glen, Paulo and", he interrupted, "I know Ricardo, we meet again, it must be at least five years ago?", "Yes", replied Ricardo, "We meet again, I didn't know you were down here in Puerto Tranquillo. You were living in Casablanca when we met up, and later I heard you had moved. It was Botami told me when I visited Barmartus for my relive programme". I picked up my ears wondering what this relive programme was and looking at Arthos for answers was just met with a smile, no explanation. "Ok, Ottol this is Paulo who works with Ricardo in Santiago and this is Glen", pointing at me, "He is half Astrotar by adoption, we'll explain later", the others all smiled. "First question" said Ottol, "Have you had any further trouble from the nasty ones? I heard from the base that they have been busy, and I might add successful, but warned it could happen again. My instructions are to tell you to garage the car for the time being, so that they would be confused as to where it had gone", Arthos replied, "Where shall we put the car?", "Follow me, I've got a large garage nearby, we'll put both cars inside then get you sleeping quarters organised". We got back in the car, following Ottol down the road for a couple of minutes and then we were there. He had stopped at a large shed, which when he opened the doors, we realised was his garage. It was certainly large enough for the two cars. We piled out of the car whilst Ricardo put it in the garage. "We'll come back later for our stuff", said Arthos. "Let's go find accommodation and eat", Ottol put the second car inside the garage and locked the doors. We all walked down the street, all five of us, I was happy whatever happens I thought, I've never before in my life known how great it is to be part of a group of dear friends, a band of brothers I thought. It was a wonderful experience, no matter what happens, but it has some frightening moments and some curious ones also. Relive programme I mused but didn't dare ask I knew they would tell me one day, but I didn't catch their eyes in case I got them reading my thoughts. We stopped at a small hotel which looked inviting with a pleasant aroma drifting from the kitchen. I excused myself and went to the toilets. As I came out, I gave them all the thumbs up. The others had acquired a table for five and ordered a menu. Arthos was checking for rooms. They had four rooms left, so he booked them for two nights initially, but maybe more if needed, he would let them know shortly. The menu was quite simple, so it wasn't hard to choose what we fancied. We all chose the homemade ham and vegetable soup with warm rolls, followed by roast beef salad and potatoes. I didn't think it would be appreciated to ask where the Yorkshire pudding was, with that thought in my mind, I caught Arthos's eye twinkling with amusement, so I put my finger to lips and to tell him "Shush". It was all very enjoyable with a large carafe of red wine to make it even better. I noticed Ottol not having any wine, only a bottle of water, I asked him if he drank, "No Glen, I might be called out with the boat tonight if there are any problems, they will call me out. I'm a lifeboat helper, you never know the moment when a call comes". "I'm going to lend you all my motorboat tomorrow, especially as I know Ricardo is a good sailor and you'll be safe, hopefully", he added. We finished our meal with coffee and decided to all walk round to the garage and get our bags and have a reasonably early night. We arrived at the garage chatting as we walked. Ottol opened the garage, and we collected our bags, waiting whilst he locked up again. We thanked Ottol and arranged to meet him in the morning, when we said goodbye, as he lived near the garage. We headed off to the hotel, decorated in a lovely bright colour where we met the lady who was obviously the owner. She was smartly and colourfully dressed, with an attractive face and a pleasant manner, with long black hair wound around her head in an unusual way, I also noticed how dark brown her eyes were. It was Arthos speaking to her in Spanish that gave me time to take this all in. With that Arthos said, "Would you all like a night cap before bed?". We all agreed it was a brilliant idea, so we followed her into the lounge with a tiny bar built into the corner. Suddenly I whispered to Ricardo, "What about the object?", to which he answered, "Safer where it is, so are we in case it has a tracking device on it", "I never thought of that" said Arthos, "Well done Ricardo", we all ordered a glass of wine and chatted for about half an hour. As we went up the stairs, we agreed to meet for breakfast at 08:00hrs. I then was on the receiving end of their parting shots, "We'll give you a knock around thirty minutes before Glen, is that ok?", "Torments" I replied smiling. I wondered if I was tired as I entered my room, locking it and deciding to have a shower and shave. After that and getting clothes ready for the morning, I climbed into a lovely crispy white bed, I snuggled down, and sleep enveloped me.

Morning arrived with a knock on my door, and bought me back to reality, what would today bring? I shouted "Ok, thank you, will be with you soon". I hurriedly dressed and washed then locked my room when I left and followed the delicious smells of breakfast. A dark-haired woman with very dark smiling eyes, a bright dress and a starched white apron welcomed me with a very cheerful voice, "Good morning sir, my name is Rosella, I think you be sir with the three gentlemen waiting on you?". Her English was fairly good but not her natural tongue. I followed her to the table and joined my friends, "Are you ready for eating gentlemen?", she said in her cheerful accent, we all agreed what to have, and she departed. I immediately told the others that I don't know why, but I had a peculiar feeling of apprehension, if something bad was going to happen. Instead of their usual banter of laughing at my strange ideas there was general agreement that each one has similar feelings. "Well,", said Arthos, "Lets enjoy our meals and just be prepared for any eventuality". A few coffees later we were ready to make tracks. As we walked up the road to meet Ottol, from whom we were borrowing a motorboat, I noticed that like myself, each one was carrying a small backpack, except Ricardo who had a much larger one over his shoulder. I looked at him to ask why the big bag, but before I could speak Ricardo laughed looking at me saying, "Glen, you are so curious let's just say it's our insurance for today", I replied, "And I didn't even have to speak!". This caused them all to laugh, I just smiled.

Ottol came out of his house as we approached and said, "Come, I've got something to show you". He opened the garage door and there were scorch marks on the roof of each car and the garage roof. "How on earth did those evil beings know your car was in here?", he asked. Quick as a flash, Arthos replied, "Now we know the object that we have hidden in the car is a tracking device, and if it's all right with you Ottol we will leave it hidden. There's always a chance they will think we are all dead". When Ottol was told all about it he was shocked and thankful we had left it in the car and now said, "Arthos now I know why you told me don't move the cars last night, was that just in case of what might happen?", "Yes" replied Arthos. Ottol said, "Let's not waste any more time I will take you to the boat house". On arrival he took out a large red and white motorboat with plenty of room for the four of us. Ottol knew Arthos of old and said, "Well I certainly don't need to show you how to work the controls, or do I?", "No", replied Arthos, "Many years of experience I confess to as you well remember and some very tricky situations." Ottol's final words rang in my ears, "Don't forget any of you, if you need help at all, think hard all of you, say my name over and over and I will bring help." We all thanked him, but it made me think obviously our apprehension needed to be heeded. We headed off waving Ottol goodbye. The water was so blue and clear, about which I commented, Paulo answered me saying, "Glen, the water of the lake in this part is the Chilean Patagonian side and the other side comes under the Argentina name, but of course it's only one lake." "The marble caves plus the large rock formation in the middle is called the 'Chapel' and we will see the marble rock formation near the far side called the 'Cathedral'. Where we are staying is called Rio Ibanez Puerto Tranquillo, that is your geography lesson", we laughed at him, then he said, "By the way have you noticed how turquoise blue it is in some places and bluer in others? It's exactly like that in the marble caves, and it's different blue colours are caused by the excessive amounts of rock flour in the water", I was leaning over the side peering into the clear water, I could make out all sorts of different rock formations deep down, obviously lots of underwater caves, anything could hide down there I thought. A tap on my shoulder and I nearly fell overboard, it was Ricardo and Paulo, "Are you planning a swim Glen?", they asked in chorus, jokingly, "No thank you" I replied feeling the icy cold water, "But I bet there are some wonderful caves down there, but I don't fancy finding out", Ricardo's deep laugh rang out.

We had travelled in the boat for some time, I noticed that although quite far from land we were following the contours of our side of the lake, moving round a bend in the land, so that our actual part disappeared. At this point we were passing a large rocky edifice with many cave entrances visible, though still quite a distance from us. This I was told was called the chapel, mind you I noticed an almost impossible thing, there seemed to be a small tree growing out of the top of the rock near the top, rather amazing I thought there's no soil, Paulo said, "Glen may I tell you something? That tree has taken root from a seed a bird has passed perched on the rock and the droppings have allowed a root", "Isn't nature magic?", I replied. We talked about going and have a look at the chapel later if the weather held. About this time, I noticed we were getting close to a section of the marble caves, that appeared on the left-hand side of the way we were passing, which I was told was called the cathedral, a huge grey colossal marble unique structure, that certainly must be something that had taken centuries, to become so large. There were many apparent entrances which we could see, but I certainly didn't fancy entering them. These structures were carved out I was told by the endless battering of the waves, and the times when water levels had risen dramatically. As we entered the marble caves only reached by boat, we were mesmerised by the beauty all around, the different hues of blue and turquoise and even grey glistened from every angle. Although the water was turbulent on the lake, inside the caves the water was clear and totally tranquil and peaceful, like I had never experienced before. Ricardo said, "Isn't it just worth coming to see?", to which I agreed with a nod. All the time we were motoring through the different caves, I noticed Paulo noting which way we turned as Arthos steered the boat. When I asked him about it, he said, "Well Glen, we never know the moment we might need to make a hasty retreat". I couldn't imagine why; it was so peaceful.

My dreaming was shattered by a tall, large black shape about ten-foot-long and about five feet high approaching from around the curve of the marble cave wall and making straight for us. As it moved nearer Ricardo and Paulo sprang into action, grabbing large oxygen cylinders out of a concealed cupboard at the back of the boat, and at the same time Arthos jumped up as they threw him something that looked like a larger version of his laser stun gun, shouting, "Glen, take the wheel and steer". Everything happened so fast, but I managed to quickly take over and hope I could manage. The weird craft by now was no more than six foot from us, as the roof slid back and

I saw three Galympites standing there, and all around was the pungent smell of Sulphur. Ricardo and Paulo were too fast for the evil ones and delivered oxygen at high pressure at them. At the same time Arthos shot them with the laser stun gun rays. Obviously, they were caught unprepared as they didn't realise how prepared the three Astrotars were and so quick. They were all three Galympite caught off balance and fell into the water and with that Arthos threw something into their craft and it burst into flames. Arthos shouted, "Glen, move forward fast, press the fast forward switch because any minute their craft will explode. I steered the boat as best as I could towards the nearest exit, with Paulo shouting, "Turn left Glen". Just as we turned the corner, an almighty crack echoed within the caves followed by a couple of explosions, we all knew that the boat had sunk in pieces. I felt a temporary feeling of relief, "Thank goodness we were prepared", said Ricardo. "How did you know?", I asked, "Well everyone including you, had bad vibes today" and then Arthos piped up with, "Glen you are definitely becoming one of us, but no more talking there could still be more danger as yet. Let's get away as fast as we can, keep directing the way forward Paulo and I'll take over Glen, you have done well", "Oh! It's ok", said Paulo, "I have the directions written on my arm" with that we ploughed ahead as fast as we could with Paulo calling the directions. Then the exit came into view and we were back on the lake. Although we had intended to see a lot more, we decided without hesitation, enough was enough and we headed to make homeward tracks.

Arthos contacted Ottol saying let Base 2 know, we've experienced a Galympite attack and temporally won, but we might need cover if possible. Luckily enough we were prepared for any eventuality or hostility and it worked, but we were worried about the large stretch of open water, where they could send more evil ones to blast us with their scorch rays, like they had done with the cars. We were turning into the vast lake which although we were motoring quickly the distance seemed endless, and the water was quite turbulent. Overhead there appeared to be heavy clouds with just small patches of blue peeping out. We were commenting on the fact that we hoped the clouds did not herald heavy rain, at least they weren't black and stormy.

Our comments were interrupted by a noise overhead which made us all look upwards, Paulo broke the silence with, "Don't worry yet because I think it's one of ours anyway, let's hope so". No sooner were the words out of his mouth, then we saw the flash of a black shape not that far above us, it was certainly not an Astrotar craft.

We felt the boat behaving erratically and realised that Arthos was steering it in a strange manner. First fast, then slow to the left then to the right. I wondered what was happening and was told by Ricardo, "Glen, Arthos is making it too difficult for them to pinpoint us with their scorch beam ray, and to stop us being targeted from the air" Then the clouds started to clear, a quick flash of another space craft with marking we recognised was seen then gone. Even the black one seemed to have disappeared, but we knew that the Astrotar who was piloting the craft could not relax, as the Galympites could attack when least expected. Suddenly out of the dispersing clouds came a black Galympite craft at tremendous speed, leaving a white streak across the blue sky that was now showing. The Astrotar craft just managed to manoeuvre out of the way shooting upwards at high speed, then twisting and plunging down at the same time changing direction. Absolutely amazing skills, we were all mesmerised even though we were still moving forward we never stopped praying in our own ways for the Astrotar safety. All seemed to go quick, and we just kept moving and watching. In the distance we saw a large blue and white motorboat racing towards us. It was Ottol in a rescue boat having received our signal, he and his colleagues had come to help us.

Ottol had told his friends a slightly different version of our problems, so as not to say too much. He told them that our boat had been cutting out and we thought we were going to be stranded. At the same we had noticed some weird activity in the sky, some strange flying objects which we wondered if they were causing our engines to stop, then burst into life after. Which of course was only a figment of the truth but enough. One of Ottol's colleagues said to us when they reached our boat, "It's really strange that which happened to you, because a week ago two of us were out on the lake fishing and we thought we saw some strange things in the sky, and our boat behaved erratically, we even began to think it might be aliens", to which we all laughed. How near the truth was that, and the man didn't know how funny it sounded to us?

As we climbed out of the boat and tied it up, we noticed Ottol was saying goodbye to his colleagues, so we all shouted, "Goodbye and thanks". Ottol jumped onto the bank as they motored off, he said, "Arthos, I need to make you all aware of something", we gathered around him and he started to talk, "Listen", he said, "There are two men asking around in the village for you four, I wondered if it could be those two men who have been following you since Santiago and before". "Who else?", said Ricardo, "They need sorting out once and for all, and find out how they have become so involved with the Galympites. We need to plan our strategy carefully, come on Arthos you are usually the one with the good ideas, you have so much experience, what do you suggest?", "I'm working on it at the minute", he replied, "I certainly have a couple of good ideas, but I will have to be careful. Come on Ottol we are taking you back to the hotel, we will all eat there and do a bit of collective Astrotar ideas, well the planning anyway". As we entered the hotel door the lady who waited on us at breakfast called Rosella welcomed us in asking if we wanted to eat, I asked the others if we could do without the wash and change to which Arthos said, "Rosella would you mind if we stayed as we are to eat as we have had a very difficult day and we are all starving? Also, he added there are five of us to eat do you mind?". She answered, "No sir, you are all fine, I will get a menu for you to look at. We have a corner table that sits five people, please follow me". She was always so pleasant and obliging. It was great to get myself into the corner as the others arranged themselves around the table. We were given two menus, which had a decent sized selection to choose from. We all chose cream of asparagus soup, followed by sirloin steak, potatoes and salad. All the steaks were requested medium rare and as the waitress went to leave, Arthos said, "Please may we have a bottle of your red South American special wine", she nodded and smiled and left us to talk. We all wondered when we were talking, where the two other weirdos were staying. They obviously hadn't given up yet, but what was driving them to be so persistent. Arthos said, "When I'm on my own tonight I will give those two from Santiago some serious thought and see what I can dream up. If anyone else has any bright ideas let me know".

At this moment conversation was cut short as Rosella arrived at the table with a tray of soups and a plate holding some warm rolls. We were soon finished when Rosella arrived back at the table with a large bottle of red South American wine, a very popular Malbec and we all agreed with Arthos as he took over the pouring, that we may well manage a second bottle. As soon as Rosella left after serving the wine, she was back with the steaks, then the salad and potatoes. We were all hungry and tucked in, the food was delicious, there was very little talking, just five very satisfied customers. We all raised our glasses to success as Arthos received a message from Base 2 that the Astrotar pilot that afternoon was safe, and although the Galympite craft had not been destroyed, it had been damaged and disappeared, hopefully we all hoped it might have exploded out of sight. We sat and talked for a while after the meal and then Ottol said that he really must be going, in case during the night he might be called for an emergency on the lake, not that it happened often at night, but you could never be sure. Mind you he added, that after all the red wine and good food, he might just not wake up easily. We all laughed at him; he was so funny. We decided we would all have a general scout about in the morning after breakfast, and then maybe after saying goodbye to Ottol we would move on. According to Arthos we still had a fair amount of investigating to do. We said our goodnights and went to our rooms. I locked my door and opened the window a little fixing it on the safety catch. Mind you I thought I've had to come upstairs to my bedroom, so should be safe as not on the ground floor. I decided to have a shower and shave as I felt it had been a long day, and put things out ready for the morning. Then just in my underwear I slipped beneath my lovely thick duvet which was comfortable, and I was soon asleep.

I was having a weird dream and feeling I was fighting, but I couldn't move I couldn't see my dream, it was like one of those situations where you can't move. I tried to wake from the nightmare, but I felt I was being held down, and I couldn't breathe properly. I felt there was something over my mouth and head, then I realised it wasn't a nightmare. It was happening, I tried to struggle to free my hands to kick out, I couldn't my body felt as if it was tightly wrapped in something and I couldn't even shout. I seemed to have tape over my mouth, I was terrified, this was real. Then I remembered what Arthos had told me repeatedly, that thoughts transferred could save you. I started saying "Arthos, Ricardo, Paulo help me, it's Glen I'm in trouble, Quick help me, help me". I felt myself being pulled from the bed and being forced out of an open window, like a package. I had thought I was on the first floor, but there must be high ground outside, my side of the hotel. My mind was screaming, "Help, please hear me someone, wake up, Glen needs you. I'm outside now I think, HELP ME, HELP ME", my mind cried as my body hit the ground, and I was being dragged. Then I heard an engine running and I thought, no one can hear me, I'm lost, I cried out in my mind again, "HELP ME ARTHOS HELP ME", then a terrible bang on my head then blackness.

9

I came to the sounds of shouting and wondered what was happening. Fear is a terrible feeling, especially when you are helpless and unable to do anything. Suddenly a voice I knew it was Ricardo "Glen where are you? Give me a signal", "I'm here I shouted", in my mind as no voice came out. Then a familiar voice, it was Arthos, "Look Ricardo, I think, in fact I'm sure that Glen is that bundle in the back of the car". The door was opened, and the tape gradually eased off my mouth and eyes. They pulled of the tapes that were wrapped around the sheets that had bound me so tightly, I tried to help but found I was too weak, maybe I had been drugged, "Yes", said Ricardo, "I'm sure you have been infected with something, we'll soon sort that out with an antidote". "Thank you for hearing my silent pleas I thought, I was a gonna" I said using a London slang word. "Where is Paulo?" I asked, "Guarding the two evil servants of the Galympites. You realise they were going to use you for bait to trap us".

Amazingly we have found out something when Ricardo punched one of them, his faced cracked they are not what they seem, they are robots, not of this world made by the Galympites to be able to penetrate the human race. Now that we know we will perfect a way to catch them. We will get Base 2 to recover them, when I dismantled their works then we will be totally free of them. It is now our job to destroy them, as they are not real people just an excellent replica of a human in looks and speech, but digitally controlled. Whilst we were talking Ricardo and Paulo using some object pointed at them, caused a most peculiar happening, weird clicks started resonating from their two bodies, and strange whirring noises from them, then from their mouths came strange words getting slower, then after about five minutes absolutely nothing. "They are done, scrapped", said Ricardo, "But I think we will have to get rid of them quickly". Ricardo then turned to me and said, "Glen you are freezing, you are actually shaking, climb back through your window and lock it, we will be with you shortly". I was still in shock and with their help I climbed back into my bedroom and closed and locked it. I watched Ricardo, Paulo and Arthos bundle the two bodies of the two robots into the boot of their car, into which I had nearly been taken off to some unknown place. It was terrifying to think what could have happened. Then they moved the car just out sight around the bend of the road, I watched for them coming back. Shortly I saw them coming back on foot, and they knew they would be with me soon, and I waited for my rescuers. A knock at the door, I called out, "Who is it?", "It's us" came Arthos's voice, "Let us in", as they all came into my room. I was overwhelmed with the friendship we had and how by a miracle even though they were asleep, they received my desperate screams from my brain. Ricardo spoke first, "Glen, we meant what we said we are all tuned into you and will always help you. You will never be alone. Unfortunately, as we were all in bed, we had to throw on some clothes, I guess we nearly fell over each other, running down the stairs having all received your thought transference of desperate pleas. We are all tied up together in Astrotar friendship, which you have truly earned". To this Arthos and Paulo said, "We agree", then Arthos took control and said, "With a bit of luck we can all go back to bed, it's 02:30 and breakfast is six hours from now. Will you be ok Glen? No more nightmares. Lock your door and windows and we will see you at breakfast". He turned to the others saying, "Ok, come on we need a quick word, goodnight Glen" they then all left leaving me to re-lock my bedroom door and climbed into bed. I still felt shivery so I left my jumper on and hoped as I snuggled down that I would sleep, but sheer exhaustion took over and that was all I remembered.

    The sun coming through my window woke me up and I realised that last night after the terrible happening I had been so intent in locking the windows I hadn't pulled one of the curtains across. I looked at the clock, it was 07:45, so I thought I'd get up shower and shave, change the clothes I slept in, and shock the others turning up early for breakfast. I then folded my different clothes and put them all in my bag folded, as I had to take care of them, as I had not a lot with me, and we might be moving on today, according to Arthos. As I entered the breakfast room, I was met by Rosella, who asked me if I was ready to eat. I replied, "Rosella, if you could bring me some coffee, I'll wait for the other three, but it's the first time I've been up before them", "Oh no sir", she replied, "they all went out very early this morning and are not back yet". This worried me as they hadn't said anything to me last night, so I tried our thought transference under my breath or in a quiet whisper, so no one could hear me. "Arthos, are you, all right? Ricardo, Paulo are you ok? I'm worried about you, I'm in the breakfast room, can you let me know somehow? I wish I could read your thoughts". I drank two cups of coffee and wrote a few notes on a pad that I used to take down facts for my books. Still nothing, it was just gone 09:00 when Paulo came in and immediately said, "Sorry Glen, we didn't want to wake you after last night, the other two will be here shortly" He then said to Rosella, "We are so sorry we are late, but we had some very important business to see to, and it took longer than we thought. Is it still ok for us to order some breakfast for the four of us? When we have finished, we will sort out our bill, unfortunately although we love this hotel, we have to move on". She listened to all Paulo said and replied, "That is all right sir, take time no problem. I serve food when other two arrive, and more coffee", "Thank you Rosella" said Paulo with a smile and her face lit up. I thought what a pity I had no local money, as the English currency I had was of no use. I was rewarded by Paulo saying, "Don't worry Glen, we intend to give her a lovely surprise, she is far from rich, but so charming and pleasant I don't think the person who owns the hotel pays very much, but relies on her to run it, when she nips off". Next minute the door opened and in came Arthos with Ricardo who said, "Glen, you really surprised us being down so early after last night, we thought you would sleep late" Arthos then said, "Did you think we had been abducted?" I laughed at him saying, "I don't think anybody is brave enough to tackle you three, that's why they took me" This made everyone chuckle, "It isn't funny", I said smiling, "As an afterthought it means I'm nearly one of you" Ricardo said, "Look Glen we've got lots to tell you, but let's eat first, and when packed and settled up, handed back our keys, and left the premises, we will tell you every last thing, is that ok with you?" I replied, "Fine". Our breakfasts were served, we all tucked in, as usual it was perfection, not exactly a full Scottish breakfast, but gammon, scrambled eggs, tomatoes, mushrooms and a meaty rissole. After plenty of coffee and warm rolls we were ready to face another day, hopefully a little less terrifying.

    Arthos went to settle the hotel bill, which as always worried me, as I had always been used to paying my way, not taking things for granted, but Ricardo interrupted my thoughts, "Don't worry Glen, the Great Astro has made all this possible as we are on official business, and in appreciation of our work". He smiled and added, "So relax whilst we can". Arthos approached us, "Ok, can we all go and pack our bags and meet outside in about fifteen minutes?", to which we all agreed and went our different ways to our rooms, I reflected on last night when we parted all that had happened and hoped it would not be a case of 'de ja vu'. Fifteen minutes later as I handed back my key, I was pleased to see I was the second ready, which was an improvement. As we went out of the front door, Rosella was there to wave us off and gave us all a hug, which was very unexpected, as we had only been there such a short time. Then I heard her say to Arthos, "Oh, sir thank you, thank you, that is so much, I cannot believe, I very happy you come so happy". I looked at Arthos and he said, "She is a good woman and is paid very little by the woman who runs the place, but is left in charge to do everything, and let's face it Rosella is an absolutely lovely lady. So now she has had a reward, she doesn't have to hand over". I guessed he had given her a very generous tip. Outside Ottol was waiting and I just couldn't wait any longer to know lots of things saying, "Arthos where is the other car? What is the story you said you would tell me?" "Wait Glen" said Arthos, "We will all go to Ottol's house where we won't be disturbed whilst we will tell all, then we are off again on our travels". My curiosity was intense, and they all kept looking at me, obviously getting all my thoughts transferred to them. Ottol opened his door and we all walked in. It was only a small house, but very neat and tidy, with enough chairs for all. Ottol then gave us all a glass of his home-made wine. Arthos then started, "Right Glen, when we had made sure you were safe, we first got in touch with Ottol then we got in touch with Base 2 and had a word with Alima who is in charge there. We wanted his advice on which way forward was the best, having told him all the details that we had already found out about the car and the robots. He told us to take their car about a mile out of the village where we would find a secluded clearing between trees and large rocks, wait there at the entrance to it. So, the three of drove in the robot's car, which was strange to drive to the spot we had been told about. We alerted Ottol to follow us there with our car and met us there. Less than thirty minutes later we were amazed when one of our small crafts appeared to drop out of the sky, right down into the clearing, the craft opened a door and out came Oracet, the Astrotar pilot we knew, we all gave him a hug as we hadn't seen him for ages and he said", "We must be quick, put the smaller robot in the driving seat of their car, now put 'the object' that has caused you to be followed into his hands pointing forward.

Now in the front panel of the car insert this metal eight-sided disc and as you turn it the car turns into a boat". Alima remembered seeing one used by the Galympites many years ago. We did this and as it slid into the water, we noticed that Oracet had retrieved the second robot from the boot.

Arthos had been told he said to place two small explosive devices on to 'the object', and one large one on the robot. Oracet then told us the boat will go directly to the Galympite base, they will let it in recognising, it but when they grab the object it will explode, he then said, "Now quickly help me put this other body in the space craft and let me get off the ground or they will no doubt attack me. I will let you know how we get on when we experiment on the robot." He shut the door and next minute he zoomed upwards and was gone, safely I sincerely hoped. Arthos continued the story, "We waited and watched as the boat car got smaller than it seemed to move towards the far landline and disappear behind large rocks. Five minutes, ten minutes, still nothing. We thought that all our efforts had been in vain, no boat car, no explosion, then there it was a large explosion. It was like a volcanic eruption. On the distant far side of the lake just visible there seemed to be a large fire, so we left". Then he added, "Mission complete here, so Glen I'm sorry you weren't there, but I think you have certainly been involved enough. It was because of you we were able to get the two robots. By the way everyone I received a call from Alima himself, he congratulated us all and said Oracet was disappointed he couldn't stay longer, but he is safe, and the robot is being interrogated, sorry I mean dissected is more to the point. Alima also said to thank Ottol you are still doing a great service and said one day he hopes to meet you Glen. So that's all briefly, unfortunately we must be off. I'm sorry to say goodbye Ottol. I hope it won't be over twenty years next time". They gave each other a hug and I noticed Ottol had tears in his eyes, how strange I'd never seen the Astrotars show a lot of emotion. Ricardo immediately said, "You are wrong Glen, we are all heart but keep our feelings under wraps". Paulo said, "Arthos, are we going back to Balmaceda? If so, I need to ask you something", of course said Arthos, "We are going back that way so ask away", "Well" said Paulo, "There are some quite strange things around this area, and not only that I know someone who has recently come to that area that would be overjoyed to meet you again", "Who?" asked Arthos, "Is it someone I know?". Paulo smiled and said, "Oh! I really think so", "Ok" said Arthos, "I'm trying to read your mind and you are blanking me", to which Paulo roared laughing. Immediately Arthos broke through the mind barrier and said, "So it's Laximo? How wonderful, I'd love to see him, what's he doing in Balmaceda?", "Investigating" said Paulo, "There's been some peculiar sightings, so he's here from Mexico, but I got involved with all our problems that I almost forgot that I had told him we were meeting up for a trip, and I'd try and arrange a meeting before you went away again" I turned to Arthos laughing, "Is this another friend I'm going to have?" Arthos replied, "Glen, Laximo and I haven't met up for years, but we were nearly killed about fifteen years ago, when there was a terrible volcanic eruption at a time we were in Peru, and helped lots of people to escape, but we managed to escape publicity by blending into the people. Now Glen, that was terrifying and after walking miles through lovely hillside, we contacted base and were picked up by one of our space crafts and taken to Base 2, even that was extremely risky". "Arthos" I said, "My goodness what a hectic life you've had?" Arthos replied, "Glen, that's the tip of the iceberg, I have lived longer than you think, and had more escapes than I can barely remember, but I always remember my fellow Astrotars". I wondered what he meant by lived longer, he was only about my age. Arthos smiled saying, "Glen I keep telling you more and more, and one day you'll be able to join it all up". I smiled that was the end of the conversation. Ottol had been enjoying the conversation and said, "Arthos remember me to Laximo, I've met him, but I think it was in Bermantus when I was there for my relive programme". "Ok" I said, "I can't stand it any longer, what is a relive programme? It keeps being mentioned as you meet up with new people, but I always think I shouldn't know, why?" Arthos laughed, "Oh! Glen you are so curious, but I do understand" he then added, "Maybe you are too young to know?" To which they all started laughing. I felt hurt and turned away, "Glen" Arthos said, "I'm sorry but when I explain you will understand, anyway come on Ottol, put on the coffee we need to sit down, we really can't leave yet, I guess I now need to explain to Glen another part of the Astrotar history". Ottol asked us all in and we went and sat down as Arthos started his tale. "Glen", Arthos said, "Our story is long, as it has covered thousands of years. It was from when the people of Astrola were made guardians of the earth by the great power lords of the galaxy. We used to visit often helping the native people to form languages, first by pictures and symbols, showing and teaching them to move forward in evolution development. They thought our space crafts were fiery chariots of the gods and we had been sent by them. Some Astrotars became involved with natives remaining on earth with them, and in some cases mating with them, giving up their rights to return to Astrola. Their offspring's being part Astrola had abilities to read minds and transfer thoughts, also psychic capabilities which have been passed down through the ages to certain people, even to this day. Guess it missed you Glen!" he said laughing. He continued,

"Anyway on our planet relationships were not quite the same as earths, but occasionally young arrived, and they were instilled with knowledge and grew into Astrotar men and woman, but we all lived out a different cycle of life in Astrola, longer than you do here on earth, and not family based. We Astrotars all feel we are one family; we truly love each other in deep friendship, that is why we embrace each other as we never know how long it will be till, we meet again"

"When we were warned that it was probable that our planet was about to implode, as many of us that could leave, left. Some refused not believing it would happen, but three quarters of the Astrotars left as we had many space crafts. Unfortunately, they were attacked by cosmic storms and litter, not to mention the Galympites. Because of all this they had to travel at unbelievable speeds even for us, which affected everyone causing irreparable damage to our reproduction organs making us sterile. The Great Astro, knowing that this would obviously curtail our length of time on earth, as we would become old and die. We appealed to the great power lords of the galaxy who originally instructed us with the task of guardians of earth. When the Great Astro made them aware of this, they put him, and him alone in charge of the relive programme at Bermantus, which would enable each of us to live as long as we needed". "The relive programme is a very secret procedure where we are put in a coma type state and somehow unknown to us our bodies are renewed to serve earth once again. I think if I remember correctly it's about two months, we stay at Bermantus" "Now Glen, do you want to know more? Or can we move on and maybe add to your education on route. Mind you it's not that we want to leave you Ottol, but I guess it won't be that long before circumstances make us meet up again, dear friend. It seems a very long time since that terrible journey to earth, so I guess I'm older than I look Glen, mind you after all that has happened lately, I feel a bit frayed around the edges, I think that's an earth expression, but describes me well". At this remark we all laughed at him. At times Arthos was quite drool, but also could be serious and commanding. At this point I said, "Arthos when I write my books this is something too private to include, it will have to be skipped over, and all names will have to be changed to keep all my dear friends safe", "Wise thoughts Glen", said Ricardo, "We don't want to be dissected like the robots", which made us all smile. Arthos started speaking again, "Glen now you know why we are always so glad to see each other, as there is perhaps less than four hundred of us left scattered around the world. Some are at the different bases or at

Bermantus and we all know that if we were to be killed, that is the end. Obviously the relive programme only works whilst we are alive, so if we are starting to feel unwell, we get in touch with the Great Astro, and he sends for us. Oh! Glen, what a pity you are not an Astrotar, we all think so much of you". Without hesitation and to my surprise gave me a big hug with tears in his eyes, he turned away to compose himself. It made me feel extremely emotional to find such friends. Ottol had made coffee and some lovely warm rolls with local ham and cheese and pickle saying, "If you eat now, it will save you stopping, and I'll enjoy your company a little longer. We talked and ate and laughed, although everyone appeared cheerful, there was an underlaying sadness at having to say goodbye.

    Suddenly, obviously making a final decision, Arthos stood up and said, "I'm sorry Ottol, this is really goodbye for the time being, but I know we'll meet again soon, remember I am exceptionally psychic" he mustered a weak smile. We all said our goodbyes to Ottol, this time we jumped into the car, I commented to Paulo sitting next to me as to what was all the stuff on the roof to which he said, "Glen, Ottol had fixed a roof sack on it, then put a lot of empty boxes on top of it, so from the air it disguises the car so the Galympites might not recognise it, as it doesn't look the same as it did", "Brilliant", I said, "How clever" The car had moved off as we all shouted goodbye and settled down for a long drive. Ricardo took the first turn of driving, then Arthos was going to take over. I started enjoying the scenery, the mountains were very black and quite bleak with patches of vegetation. I wondered where all the volcanoes were, and if we were safe. Arthos had told me that in Chile alone there were over 6000 volcanoes, mostly still active some more than others. Even a very large one called the Llama volcano, one of the biggest and most active in Chile, and is situated in Conguillio national park, last having erupted in 1994. I sincerely hoped we were nowhere near it. "Well done" said Arthos having obviously tuned into my thoughts. "You certainly listened to us when we were telling you all the geographical information. You are quite right the Llama volcano isn't in our path, but near enough to be wary of it. Glen there has been earthquakes and eruptions here in Chile before and since 1994, even as near to now as 2014 with a magnitude 8.2 earthquake, but weird as it might sound, I must admit I really like it here. You have the feeling that nature is all powerful and stronger and more lasting than man, and you have to be brave and strong to exist, and hope that the Galympites don't make things on the planet worse". I decided to close my eyes and rest for a few minutes, I guess as usual I nodded, off as next thing I knew we had stopped at a small café and were able to visit the bathroom, order some coffee for Paulo and I, and fruit juice for Ricardo and Arthos, as well a plate of cakes. We were only there for half an hour and the man who served us spoke very little English but was very pleasant and everything was clean. Arthos paid him and thanked him in Spanish, we then bundled back into the car, we wanted to make Balmaceda at a sensible time and it was already past three thirty.

Arthos took over the driving from Ricardo, Paulo and I stayed in the back. We hadn't travelled very far when we heard Ricardo say, "Keep down in the back" and he pulled down the sun visor in the front. We asked what was wrong to which he replied, "I might be wrong, but I'm sure I saw something flash across the sky, a peculiar shape. It could be the evil ones, or it could just be my imagination, but they will be watching for us that's if any survived in that base of theirs, or it could be from another. I shouldn't imagine we are number one in the popularity stakes especially using their own car and robot to destroy them. Of course, the base we destroyed will not be their only base around here, as I've told you there has been lots of weird sightings around Balmaceda. I bet half the volcanoes and earthquakes are their fault", "Yes you are right", said Arthos, 'Quick, Ricardo keep watching, I think I saw something". Arthos kept driving and in the back, I wondered why we had to duck down on the seat. Paulo answered my thoughts, "Glen it's because they expect four of us, and if they only spot two they might not know it's us and leave us alone. The roof rack may also help to fool them with all the boxes on it" We continued for several miles and suddenly just as we began to think our fears were unfounded, a shape flew very low over the car, then zoomed back upwards. It was definitely not one of the Astrotar crafts it was the Galympites. Ricardo was speaking low and I realised he was on a type of phone and speaking in a strange tongue, obviously Astrolish, "Yes" said Paulo, "Shush". We kept going, zoom we saw it flash across the sky still too close for comfort, then shoot upwards again. All this time we kept low in our seats Arthos said, I'm worried, as I just can't work out their strategy. Do they know it's us or is it just a coincidence?" We kept crushed up and Ricardo kept the sun visor down. Then he saw the flash again, this time it was even lower as if they were trying to make out who we were. Suddenly, Arthos turned the radio full blast and opened the windows and said, "keep down, but start shouting this will annoy them and they will think it is impossible to be us and it will distract their thoughts and concentration. The noise was awful and as they passed over us again, Arthos started sounding the car horn in time with the music, it was a hellish noise but almost funny. They passed over us again then appeared to zoom up to a higher level. Suddenly an Astrotar craft came from over the mountains and chased after the other craft. They both disappeared from sight, Arthos said, "The Galympites were not expecting that, I'm pleased to say I think we disorientated them"

Arthos had now turned off the radio as he slowed down the car, there was a tremendous bang that echoed to the west of us. We all froze in fear hoping with all our hearts that the Astrotar craft that had come to our aid was safe. Although we had slowed down, we kept going fearful and wondering. We came to a cut off from the road where there were some huge boulders and parked up behind them and waited. Maybe ten minutes passed then we heard a clicking noise and Ricardo put his phone to his ear and started talking, then laughed and said, "Quick, all of you out of the car and look up its Orecet", the Astrotar craft came down low flashed his lights and zoomed up and away, "Well everybody that's another Galympite pilot and craft obliterated" "Ok" said Arthos, "back in the car the sooner we drop this at the airport the better, and Ricardo tell us what Orecet said please". "He told me that he chased the Galympite craft with the special rocket blaster they have perfected, he destroyed the back of the craft where the engine must have been, it then dropped like a stone and blew up as it hit the sea".

Then he said, "Did you hear it? It was an important craft I think, but it's gone, gone" This made us laugh. Orecet was alive and safe, and we were happy. Around twenty minutes later, more clicking, Ricardo said, "Thank you Orecet, for everything hope to see you soon, bye", He turned to us all and said, "Orecet is safely back at base, and Alimo has told him to have a short break and rest as he has been active too much lately and can't afford to get too tired". We drove back onto the road and continued to Balmaceda, "Ah well" said Arthos, "Only about another half an hour and we will be at the airport" I closed my eyes and thought a quick snooze wouldn't hurt. I always found sleep so easy to come, perhaps too easy. Next thing I heard Paulo saying, "Ok Glen, wakey, wakey, we are at the airport, to hand back the car, then pick up Ricardo's Volkswagen Beetle if it hasn't been stolen. It will be funny explaining the scorch marks, the roof rack and pile of empty boxes, but watch it's amazing if anyone can do it, it will be Arthos, maybe a little bribe! But he'll do it". Sure, enough he did I said to him, "Arthos how did you manage that explanation?" He just smiled and said, "I've got to keep some secrets!" We all walked over to where Ricardo had left his car, it was still in the same place and intact. We all climbed in and were off, to where I still didn't know and what surprises would lay ahead. "Stop thinking the worst", said Arthos, "Enough is surely enough". Ricardo was steadily driving eastwards, and we were all chatting about the events of the day. After about ten minutes we passed through a small village and Ricardo stopped outside a small, detached cottage in the middle of a large area ground. Around it were a few shrubs and huge boulders and almost hidden at the back was a two-berth caravan, with a great view of the Andes mountains as a backdrop, not volcanoes I hoped. Ricardo told us to follow him he opened the caravan. It was lovely inside and spacious with two bedrooms one at each end. The bathroom and kitchen were situated in the middle both off the dining room just big enough for a table and four chairs. Absolutely ideal said Arthos, "Is it alright if we stay about three days before we move on?", "Great" said Ricardo, and Paulo chipped in with, "It will be strange to see you go again, we seem to have all been together for longer than we actually have, but let's enjoy every minute that we shall all be together." We all agreed with this, with Ricardo saying, "Well my friends we can either raid the freezer, or contact Laximo and all meet up at the local hotel to eat", "Best idea yet" replied Arthos. "We'll all meet up again in an hour, shall we walk there Ricardo?", "No, it's only down the road but it saves our feet, I'm feeling lazy and hungry, how about you all?" replied Ricardo. It was agreed one hour and to use the car, whilst Ricardo promised to contact Laximo, who would be thrilled to see us all he told us.

We went into the caravan, I made two cups of coffee using some long-life milk I found in the fridge. Arthos washed first, then I used the bathroom, we both changed and went and sat in the dining area. It was a lovely view of the mountains at the back, I was thrilled to think these were the famous Andes, which I had only heard about. I know I had travelled far, but it was Australia, America and Europe even to china once, but never South America. Arthos interrupted my thoughts saying, "Sorry to interfere in your thoughts but I want to give you a little more information. Did you know Glen, that the Andes in geographical terms are one of the youngest mountain ranges on earth, and they include over 6000 volcanoes which I know I've already told you about? Throughout Chile there are deep valleys and high plateaus in front of these mountains, which run right down the east side of Chile with Argentina on the other side of them. There is an area called the Pampas that runs all the way on the west side to the Pacific Ocean, and as you found out as you go down towards the Southern tip of Chile, you come across the blue lakes and caves of blue and turquoise marble. I suppose seeing, it is a thin long country of about four thousand miles, it certainly contains plenty to learn about. It's not just a bleak landscape it's a land of mystery and uncertainty with lovely people who although they don't seem to have a lot, are happy and hospitable. Sorry Glen, I'm sorry I can't stop sometimes, I just get carried away. I guess my brain is full of unnecessary information gathered over the years". "No" I said, "I could listen to you as long as you talk, you are so interesting and have taught me so much about, my own planet, as I hope I will be able to tell others when I write my stories. Paulo opened the caravan door and said, "Will you please stop talking and come and get in the car we are waiting for you". We rushed out locking the caravan and scrambling into his car. A short journey of maybe five minutes and the hotel came in sight. It was very picturesque, with a small fountain and big flower tubs set around the outside. Then I realised that they were more like cactuses in the pots, but I thought they were quite unusual. We went inside and we were immediately met by a waiter, immaculately dressed, with white shirt, black bow tie and long black apron. His first words to us were, "You four gentlemen have a friend, he sits over there to meet you". His English was very good but quite quaint, he led us to a table at the far end of the room. Immediately a man came forward to meet us and gave Arthos a hug, shaking his hand and saying, "Oh! Wonderful to see you, Oh! Arthos I am so happy". He then said, "Are you Glen?" I replied, "Yes and I'm sure you are Laximo", "It's lovely to meet you Glen" he then shook my hand and said, "I believe you are now half Astrotar, so I will love you like the others", they all laughed at him. As they sat down, he said, "What's wrong with you two, no hugs you know how emotional I am". Arthos said, "Oh! Laximo, you never change, but don't because you are so genuine, and I know you still suffer because of that accident when you lost your two friends. Well, you've got us now, so come on, no tears only laughs". "Laximo" said Ricardo, "We've got lots to tell you and by the way Ottol and Oracet said to say hello to you and say to tell you if they are around here, they will come and see you", Laximo seemed to cheer up and said to me, "Excuse me Glen, but I'm not as strong as the others, I've had too many upsets but I'm a loyal friend". I smiled at him and said, "I'm thrilled to meet you Laximo the others love you so much". "Anyway" said Arthos, "Can we have a menu please? We need to choose our meals" the waiter brought us three menus then said, "Do you want wine please", Arthos smiled and said, "Yes Medoc please large bottle, if you haven't got that a good Chilean wine", "Thank you sir and he disappeared. We talked about what we should have and decided to all have steaks, as they looked good on a nearby table. The waiter came back, and the order was simple, Ricardo ordered, "Five large steaks, your best, and medium rare, potatoes sautéed, mixed salad and rolls", "Shall I pour your wine sir", he said to Arthos. Arthos replied, "No thank you I can do that you just see to the steaks", he smiled at us but Arthos meant it, he poured the wine and we chattered away.

We didn't have to wait too long, and our steak meals were served, Arthos asked for another bottle of wine, the same as before. We hadn't realised just how hungry we were, and with little conversation we devoured the excellent meals. After we had finished the meals and wine, Arthos ordered a pot of coffee, where we arranged a bit of sightseeing away from the mountain around Pampas. Laximo was upset that he could not make the trip said, "Can I meet you all tomorrow night? I work at the local coffee house, just lunches and afternoon teas but the owners are retired and the person that used to work there left suddenly, they don't know why and are desperate for help, so I offered, and they gave me the position, so I've got a little job whilst I check out the area for the Great Astro, I don't suppose I'll be very long what do you think Paulo?". "Maybe yes, maybe no, you never know when we get the calling but the answer to your other question is of course, We'll all meet up tomorrow evening" said Paulo. Arthos asked for the bill and we all got up to go and Laximo whispered something to Arthos, he smiled at him and said, "Certainly not Laximo, you know I'm in charge", we all agreed with that statement. Paulo asked what time he should come up in the morning, Arthos replied, "9am, I think is soon enough we all need a good rest". Paulo then said, "I'll walk down the road with Laximo he's living near me in a small flat, so will be company for each other", we knew he was worried about Laximo and obviously realised he needed to be able to talk to someone, it was good that they lived that close to one another.

We all said goodnight to them and the three of us got into Ricardo's car for the three-minute journey back to his house. Ricardo looked at Arthos with a worried look and said, "Arthos I'm really about Laximo", he paused and then continued, "Would I be wrong in suggesting you let the Great Astro know this situation, he's very troubled and that is why Paulo walked him home, to check he is ok, and actually Paulo has two bedrooms he just might keep Laximo with him for the night", "Do you think so?", said Arthos, "I'm going to get word through to Bermantus in that case, I do feel you are right, but I was unsure whether I was just getting too protective", "Well I think that's right" said Ricardo, "We don't want to take a chance".

Arthos and I went into the caravan and I said, "I'm going to have a word with my editor Sam, it's been a while since I spoke to him, and I believe it's daytime in London". Arthos replied, "Ok, I've got several calls to make and messages to get through to Bermantus. If I don't see you again tonight, I'll see you in the morning". I rang the number of my editor, which was answered by a female voice, I said, "Hello can I speak to Sam Juste? It's Glen Grant Wallace the reporter", to which she replied, "Who did you say?", annoyed I replied, "Who's that I'm talking to anyway?". "It's Nancy James, his secretary, I realise who you are now, but it's ages since I've seen you. Sam was always saying when is Glen coming back, I can't wait to hear his story. He certainly won't hear it any longer", "Why I replied?", "Well", she said, "Sadly you are too late, he was killed nearly two weeks ago, he's been buried now. A large conglomerate has bought over the newspaper and what with Sam's Will, life is strange as he left all his money between you and I, he said in the will he had no family and we were the only two he trusted, not only that Glen, we are all being handed a large redundancy pay from this office, so go and check your bank I was amazed, I never knew he had so much money. You and I, nobody else knows how much, they just know we were beneficiaries. We got £250,000 each and then you'll get your redundancy money, based on how many years you have been here. I have been here as a secretary for ten years and got, £40,000 but I'm sure salary was more, how long have you been here?", "twenty-seven years, it will be enough for me to publish my books", "What about?", she said, "Well Nancy, it will make the world sit up, you'll have to buy my books". I went quiet for a while and said, "Must go Nancy, this is long distance, I'm in South America", she gasped, "Oh! My god, I thought you were back in London", I replied, "Ok, maybe see you when I get back, goodbye". I couldn't believe it £250,000 plus redundancy plus what I had left from my parents which I had been careful in not spending unwisely. Wow, I thought, I never saw that coming and went into the dining area in shock, and thought I need a coffee. As I entered the dining area quietly, Arthos emerged from his room,

"Well, Glen you didn't expect that, I wasn't thought reading, you were just talking loudly, and I was busy sorting out plans for Laximo. This is what I've decided with agreement from the Great Astro who contacted me personally on the emergency frequency we have set up, to make plans shortly for the three of us to go back to London. Then for me to continue to Inverness and plan for Laximo to be taken back to Bermantus. For the moment I'll tell Laximo to start packing and for him to be ready to be moved away for a while. He can store some of his stuff in Ricardo's loft because Paulo only has a flat and Laximo doesn't know it yet, but he will be away for a while, probably coming back eventually. Ricardo, I know is here for a good while yet and we could well be coming back before too long. As for Paulo, I think he also is here for a while but doesn't have that much room in his flat. Let's go to our beds, have you got your coffee", "Yes" I said, "Did you want some?", "No thanks, I have a juice", replied Arthos. I said goodnight and went to my bed, what a lot to take in, I thought wondering where I fitted into the travel programme. It was still a bit of a puzzle but anyway I thought I would soon know, so I curled up in bed, hardly able to believe how rich I had become. However, had Sam liked me enough to leave me so much? Maybe he was trying to help the Astrotars by making me independent, with these thoughts I drifted off to sleep.

The next morning when we were going over to Ricardo's house from the caravan. We noticed the heavy mists coming down from the mountains, somewhat reminiscent of the Scottish Highlands. Where the mist hung round the tops of the mountains, it looked as if it were smoke from an active volcano. "Glen stop that", said Arthos, "We've got enough to worry about without active volcanoes" and smiled. At that moment Ricardo's front door opened and he said, "Right come in, I've made coffee and organised some breakfast. Paulo will be here in a few minutes". As he finished speaking, Paulo walked in through the back door saying, "What's that lovely smell. I thought we were going to get something when we were out?" Ricardo has worked for us instead", said Arthos, "And it will give us a chance to make some plans" Breakfast was served, and it was lovely, a type of cheese, tomato and ham omelet with plenty of warm rolls, with a big pot of coffee. Once we had finished eating and without thinking I said, "Ricardo you are a very good cook, who taught you? Where you interested when you were young?" Ricardo smiled and replied, "Life and being hungry taught me to cook, our food was different on Astrola. I can't remember what I liked when I was young because I've been made younger quite a few times although I have a good memory, I only retain the important things which help me to survive", "Sorry", I said, "I always forget about the relive programme and I spoke without thinking". "No harm done, now let's get down to around table conference and make our own plans", said Arthos. He poured himself another cup of coffee then continued, "Well my friends, I've been told to take Laximo up to Scotland and get him picked up from a loch up there, he will be taken to Bermantus. Several things have occurred recently. Glen's company has been taken over, and his boss has been killed, so he must sort out certain things in London. When I've sorted out Laximo's travel arrangements I will return to London and check my flat is still in one piece. I will then immediately contact Glen and we'll work out our new forward plan. Whilst I'm away in case I'm not straight back, start collecting all your notes and papers together, and make sure you will be ready to move away for a couple of months. In case you are puzzled I can't say anything more until I've completely formulated a plan which is for your benefit and for the story of the Astrotars. We will part temporarily at Heathrow, whilst I catch a connecting flight to Inverness, where I can hire a car to complete the journey". He looked at Paulo and said, "Could you help Laximo to store his extra things in boxes and we'll put them in Ricardo's loft, if that's ok with you Ricardo and Paulo? I sound as if I'm being unusually bossy, but I've got to organise tickets, currency and a few other things. I guess if today is Tuesday it will be less than a week before we leave Balmaceda? I'm afraid both Ricardo and Paulo will be staying here, maybe you Paulo could help out the old couple who have the teashop where Laximo has been working, till he gets back?", "Maybe", said Paulo, "It's not really my scene but I do need to do something". "Well don't look at me", said Ricardo, "I grow all my own vegetables and fruit, keep hens and amaze people with my good crops, which are so good, I also help out at the local garage, remember Arthos I was always a mechanical genius?", "Now", I said, "Arthos what can I do? I'm adopted now so must pull my weight. I may not be able to thought read but I'm beginning to find I register things far quicker", "Well done" they all said, I felt happy and proud. "Well,", said Arthos, "Let's nip up to the airport Ricardo and check availability of flight for perhaps in four or five days' time. We can see what's available and how good the connections are, you never know but when we come back, maybe just maybe Paulo and Glen will have washed up everything, and coffee will be ready on the stove". We all laughed but agreed it all made sense. "We will make the definite plans for today when we come back", said

Arthos, "Never mind", said Paulo, "It will give us something to do whilst you two are driving around enjoying yourselves", he said.

When they left, I said to Paulo, "You know it's so funny at first I was always aware of us all wearing the same green stoned triangular gold rings but now I'm hardly aware of it. I'm sure that it is the thing that not only keeps us strong, but binds us together, that truly is how I feel". "Amazing", said Paulo, "I've just thought of something, Laximo used to be so strong and independent, mind you he was always emotional, but he showed me his ring and when he had that accident a small chip broke off his ring.
I wonder if that could have any bearing on his depression and fear. I will have to mention it to Arthos, he always seems to know best. He is so learned and clever and his friendship is the greatest thing you could ever have". To which I heartily agreed. We had set up to wash our fatigues, as it was only ten thirty it had been a good time for them to go to the airport, I didn't think they would be that long, as I didn't expect it would be that busy. Paulo answered my thoughts, "Don't be so sure Glen, it may only be a small airport but it services all around here, it's a quick way of getting to Santiago and there are quite a few flights every day". I turned to Paulo and said, "Don't say anything to Arthos but I will miss him when he goes to Scotland, and of course he says he's coming back to London but if circumstances change, and I get too lonely, and I can't concentrate on my writing. I will send word to Arthos and travel back to Balmaceda isn't it funny I keep mixing up the name of this airport with the Astrotar undersea world of Bermantus", "Gosh", said Paulo, "I never thought of it before, but you are right". We were quiet for a while then Paulo said, "Glen don't worry you will be welcome, and you could always rent Laximo's flat, anyway, we will give you a number so that you can always make contact in case anything changes with Arthos's plans. As far as I can understand Arthos is going to get Laximo picked up, taken to Base 1, then onto Bermartus, we'll soon know he'll tell us more later. None of us will ever desert you Glen, you are one of us now". I was overcome, I gave him a hug and wiped away a few tears. How I had changed, I had never been demonstrative or tearful, but now I felt so different I was so content and happy with my life. Everything was done and Paulo said, "Come and sit down and tell me about your life and you're growing up years, there is so much we don't know about you, but of course I'm sure the Great Astro will know all". I started to tell Paulo how I had been an only child

and had been lucky in having a wonderful childhood. "My father had been a doctor and my mother a nurse. When they met, they had fallen in love and married within six months. My father doted on my mother and they both were overindulgent with me. Although I don't suppose I really appreciated them, but I loved them dearly. They took me on great holidays, and I was given lovely presents and all my friends were always made welcome to stay, as we had a big, detached house in Edinburgh. I was always proud to be Scottish, but as I finished at Edinburgh University I decided to go down to London and get a job in journalism. Deep down my father wanted me to be a doctor like him, and my grandfather before him. Family tradition but it wasn't for me, I wanted to travel and write, so like good parents they helped me to realise my ambitions as pay was very little when I was a junior reporter. My father used to pop down to London and slip money into my pocket, perhaps even a hundred pounds, as London has always been expensive, and my mother would either come down to see me or put something into my bank in case I didn't have enough to eat properly, they were so kind. I think they would have liked more children, but it never happened. I eventually became a senior journalist, then a world correspondent, travelling all over America and Europe, even to Australia and China, but never South America. My world was shattered when I was thirty years old when my parents were killed in a car accident. For a while my world was destroyed but I had to pick myself up and make them proud of me. So, I threw myself into my career and became well known. At this end I am so thrilled that the Great Astro thought well enough of me to bring me into the world of the Astrotars". "Oh! Honestly Glen" said Paulo, "A happy family on earth sounds wonderful, but I know that isn't always the case because I've read about terrible things that happen on earth". "Now all I want is to write my books and in doing so I will learn even more about you all and your life on Astrola", I replied. Ricardo was sounding the car horn, I said to Paulo, "It's the dynamic duo back!", we opened the door laughing. They came in saying in unison, "So where's the coffee?", "Sorry, we have been talking" I replied. Paulo rushed into the kitchen and put the kettle on, whilst Ricardo bought some cake in from the car, "Munch time" he said. Arthos then joined in saying, "Then it's time to talk". We all gathered round the table and Arthos started, "It's Tuesday today the tickets for the three of us are Saturday leaving Balmaceda I'll check the time later when I've sorted out Laximo I can go back to Inverness and I can call you Glen. I'll also ring you both here and let you know how things have gone. So, is everyone happy about everything?". "No" said Ricardo, "We are going to miss you both, is there no way you can come back? Glen could write here just as well as London and it's more eyes to watch for Galympites". Arthos looked round the table and said, "Friends, I will wait for my orders, if I get a choice I will come back, but you all know we all go where we are sent and needed, but I will miss you, I am close to all my Astrotar friends, but always closer to some more than others. My last tearful parting was from Pedro at Sicily and Mohammed, Khalid and Youssef at Casablanca, we had some frightening times, didn't we Glen?". "Yes, but I have found everyone kind and I have never known such wonderful friendships, but I shall exceptionally miss these two, I owe my life to them" I replied. "Anyway" Arthos changed the conversation, "That's number one thing organised, now Paulo could you help Laximo to pack up his things that he wants to store, and fill his large travelling duffel bag, that we all have similar ones with his necessities. Then we'll all come and get his boxed things and store them in Ricardo's loft. Then perhaps Friday night he could stay with you Paulo?". "That's fine with me", said Paulo. "This afternoon we'll call into the tea rooms and tell Laximo he's going travelling with Arthos for a short time and dropping off Glen in London. He's going for a holiday to Bermantus to get well and strong again without earthly worries. Just think Paulo that would give you the chance to meet the old couple and tell them you'll help them out from time to time till Laximo comes back. We will pay the landlord three months' rent and then he's got it to come back to". Paulo said quick as a flash, "Arthos have you seen the mists on the mountains?" to which he said, "You are like two naughty boys, I'll find out I always do" Ricardo said, "Shall I make the coffee, have you two forgotten what you were doing? The cakes will be stale by the time we eat them". We all talked about the arrangements then decided we would go for a run in the car and have a look at the Pampas area and see if we could spot any troublesome evil ones. Hopefully not. We drove for about thirty minutes, it seemed endless. After so long we came to an inlet of water, we stopped to see whether it widened out into a lake or stayed like a deep stream. I wondered how far off the Pacific Ocean was from here, and was told without me speaking, still an awfully long way. Anyway, we turned around as it was starting to rain. Arthos who was now driving said, "I'm glad we are in Ricardo's car because I'm sure I saw something that wasn't a plane, it was the wrong shape, but it was very high in the sky and they don't know it's us. I'll certainly feel safer back at the house as we really aren't prepared today". We stopped at the tea rooms where Laximo worked and Ricardo said, "We'll stop and have a coffee it will make Laximo proud to tell the old couple we are all his friends. It's necessary for us to tell him we are all eating at my house tonight, and do you need to go home Paulo or are you staying as you are?". "As I am if that's alright with all of you?" Arthos said, "When Laximo comes over to our table leave it all to me", Laximo had finished with another customer and came across to us. Before he could speak Arthos said, "Lots to tell you Laximo, first we need a coffee, secondly, I'm paying, thirdly the five of us are eating at Ricardo's tonight, and fourthly Paulo and I will collect you at your house at 18:00hrs. Just come as you are no special changes. None of us are changing is that ok with you?". "Marvellous!" he said and went for the coffee. The coffee and biscuits were soon consumed, Arthos went over to the cash desk and said, "Laximo, no messing, how much?", "Alright" replied Laximo, "But I do want to treat you", "Another time, we are off now. See you tonight", replied Arthos. Laximo smiled and waved as we left. He looked so lonely, loneliness is a horrible feeling, because I've been there, I know it. "Haven't we all?" said Paulo, "At some time we all have upsets" we were all quiet till we got to Ricardo's "Well,", said Ricardo, "You Glen and Arthos can go and read, or phone or sleep, but Paulo is going to help me and we will prepare the evening meal, so off you go it's already nearly four in the afternoon, and we are eating at 18:00, I've got to make the sauce and stuff", so we said "Bye" and went. Arthos was smiling and said, "I find it so funny", but I didn't laugh. "Paulo didn't know he was helping, Ricardo is nearly as good at organising as me!", we both laughed. I went into my bedroom and stretched out, it was comfy, and the air just had a knocking out effect on me. The first thing I knew was Arthos saying, "If you want to freshen up Glen, we'll be leaving in a few minutes. I've got to let the others know, poor Ottol has had his house scorched, thank god he wasn't in it but out on a mission, anyway, let's get over there as soon as you are ready, and we can tell the others the whole story". As we entered the house Paulo said, "What's wrong it's only 17:15?", "Well I thought I'd tell you both before we go for Laximo, Ottol our friend in Puerto Tranquillo has had his house scorched, luckily, he was out, but the garage where our car was stored next door, to his house was also burnt, they must have thought we were there, or that he was our friend. Someone has rented him a little house a bit further away and helped move his things that haven't been ruined. He was in a terrible state talking to me, his voice was shaking, locals are all saying it's those aliens again, everyone has seen strange things lately. Perhaps it's going to be like the things that happened in that Sicily town? Oracet has also said to me in a private message that they will take vengeance on them for hunting down Ottol, and there are three spacecrafts working in unison now. He said a friend has offered to paint Ottol's car for him in different colours so that the aliens won't recognise it, so there is mayhem down there, I'll ring Ottol and see how he is, and you can all have a quick word with him". "Gosh!", I said, "He must have been terrified", "Yes" replied Paulo, "Because he's down there on his own". Paulo stood up quickly and said, "Come on Arthos, Laximo will think we've forgotten him". The car roared off, less than ten minutes later they were back, he had started walking and jumped in the car.

We all sat round the table; Ricardo had managed to have five chairs. I think one was from the bedroom. The smells from the kitchen were mouth-watering, Italian food always gets the juices running. Ricardo bought some bottles out and told Paulo to get some glasses and start pouring, but not to forget him, that made us laugh. I noticed Arthos was sitting by Laximo and talking quietly to him, Paulo had also noticed and said, "Hey Glen, come and help me get the rolls and salad and help Ricardo", "Yes, good idea", I replied. We started to the kitchen letting Ricardo slow down a bit. After ten minutes we knew Arthos was ready when he shouted, "Are you lot preparing the meal, or eating it? We are starving", "We're coming", shouted Ricardo, "In case you didn't notice, we were being discreet", "That's unusual!", said Arthos laughing. "Ok, I've told Laximo he's having a short holiday at Bermantus and that the Great Astro says it's his turn. He's going to travel with Glen and I, we will leave on Saturday. Also, I told him we are all here to help him, and that we start tomorrow, so we'll come over to his flat in the morning and if he shows us what he wants us to pack up we'll do it for him, whilst he lets the old couple know he's got to go away for a while, but that his friend will help them occasionally to give them a break and that he will be back in a couple of months and will help them again. Is that ok Laximo?", "Oh! Yes", he said, "You are all so kind to me. Are you sure you don't mind storing my things Ricardo?". "Of course, not you're my friend", Laximo looked so pleased when Ricardo said that to him. Ricardo was serving out pasta with a beautiful meat source, real Italian style. Hot rolls with garlic butter and parmesan cheese, a good red wine, it was perfect. We were talking, drinking eating and occasionally dripping food down our fronts, real Italian style! It was superb. Ricardo asked if we would like some cheese and biscuits to finish, but we were all too full, overflowing was the comment from Paulo. We all agreed coffee would be nice to finish, so out came the coffee. We talked and talked, they were asking me about my life and about Scotland. Then Paulo even said, "Well Glen, as you are the baby here, we will gradually educate you, as we've all been through the relive programme, not that we know much about it, I can't always remember how old I am, so I just pretend I'm young!". The others laughed at Paulo and Arthos said, "Well I'm going to stay as young as Glen wants to be our friend", Ricardo joined in with, "Glen do you really feel comfortable with us, and love us like brothers?", To which I replied, "Love and trust you all even more than that". Perhaps it was the wine, but they assured me it wasn't, but Ricardo said, "Well come on you two" to Laximo and Paulo, "I'm taking you home we are coming to your flat in the morning Laximo about 10:00hrs. Before we arrive let the old couple know you've got to go away on urgent business so you won't be able to work, but you'll do tomorrow afternoon, and tell them your friend will call in next week and have a chat with them", "Thanks", said Paulo. Arthos and I gave them a hug and went to the caravan, the other two gave Ricardo a hand to wash up before they left. "I feel bad not helping them" I said to Arthos, "Oh! Don't worry they will be impressing Laximo about how lucky he is, obviously a favourite of the Great Astro" Arthos replied, I smiled and felt better. I said to Arthos, "Well I'm now going to make a call to London, I want to check on this redundancy payment, I find it hard to digest. The money from the will is unbelievable but this as well". My first call was to the bank, I explained it was a long-distance call from South America, and I needed immediate attention. For once they were quick, I explained who I was then had to answer several security and data protection questions. Eventually they were satisfied I was who I said I was. I told the bank person that I believed I had not only received a large sum of money from a will, but also was in receipt of a large redundancy payment from the newspaper, as I had worked there for over twenty-seven years. "Please hold the line a minute Mr. Grant-Wallace, do you know how much the amount is?" I replied, "I have a good idea as I have been advised." The woman replied, "The first figure was £250,000", "Yes", I said, "I know". She then said, "The second figure was £180,000, plus what you already had, which makes your bank account at just under half a million pounds".

10

I replied to her, "Very good, it's about what I expected, thank you for your trouble, goodnight", she answered, "Oh! It's daytime here", "Oh! Yes, sorry, bye", I replied. I came off the phone, I was absolutely in a dream, I couldn't believe it. I was sure I would wake up. My god I thought, money in the bank, lots to write about, wonderful friends, oh! Please don't let it be a dream. A knock at my bedroom door it was Arthos, "Ok, Glen?" I looked at him and said, "Was I shouting?", "No", he said, "But I felt your emotions through the caravan. You have always tried to help people, now it's your turn to enjoy your life, maybe sometimes have more excitement than you want. But don't worry we all look after you and make sure that life continues to be good. Now my dear friend as your much older friend, get to bed and have a rest because tomorrow and the next few days are going to be busy", "Thanks", I said, "Goodnight and I can never thank my triangular green ring enough it has changed my life". With that Arthos left the room and went to bed. I know it was bad, but I didn't even get a wash, I first jumped into bed and went fast asleep.

Next morning, I awoke early and when I went to the bathroom to get a shower, Arthos was already having a coffee and said, "Sorry did I wake you? I was making a few calls", "No", I said, "I think I'm improving at waking up", he smiled, and I went to get a shower and shave. As soon as I finished and was dressed, I made myself a coffee, and noticed it was only early, pretty good without an alarm clock. A knock at the caravan door, and a voice shouted, "Anyone at home? Come and get some breakfast, Paulo is on his way up to join us". It was Ricardo as usual organising us I thought if only I could do something for them. I felt it was always me that was receiving not giving, I so wanted to show how much I appreciated everything. "Oh! Ricardo", Arthos said, "Before you go, I have heard from Bermantus, Limrod and Flipsi who tend to often work together, are being sent to Puerto Tranquillo, where they are going to buy a house, large enough for Ottol to move in, and have his own quarters. Limrod is a carpenter and will make a separate entrance for Ottol. He will be safer with company, it seems to be very dangerous down there, especially, it will be good if they buy the house, it can be always passed on if they move, to other Astrotars. They will be given the money by The Great Astro as he worries when he hears that someone like Ottol is being threatened". I said, "Arthos where have these two Astrotars come from, I haven't heard you mention them before", Arthos replied, "Glen, there are lots of us scattered around the planet and every so often they get moved. My duty was charged when the Great Astro chose you to become our ambassador. I was worried at first as I didn't know how it would work, but I think it was great for both of us, I have thanked the Great Astro for choosing me to be your guide, partner and friend, for good or in trouble". "Will you two come and eat and stop talking?", "Sorry", we shouted and joined Paulo and Ricardo.

That was the last quiet time, because as soon as we finished eating and cleaned away, we all went down to Laximo's to start packing up his thinks. The hours passed, we all worked hard only stopping for a coffee shortly after midday. Laximo had gone to work and to explain he was leaving that night. Early afternoon we stopped for another coffee. Paulo had told Laximo that we had nearly finished for the day, and to meet up at the hotel tonight around seven thirty. Paulo also told Laximo to ensure he packed his duffel bag with anything extra we may have forgotten. It needed to be a small bag with no sharp edges as it will go in the hold. Laximo thanked him and agreed to meet up at the hotel. Having accomplished a great deal, Ricardo opened his boot and we filled it with boxes, filling the back seats too. We locked Laximo's flat, and Paulo said, "I'm going back to my place now, I'll see you both at the hotel tonight at seven thirty, bye", he started jogging up the road as it was only a couple of minutes away. As the car turned when we left, we could see him entering a building. Ricardo and Arthos were in the front seats, whilst I was surrounded with boxes in the back seat. Arthos laughed, "Are you comfortable Glen? Perhaps you ought not answer that!" We went into the caravan and Ricardo, went to his house. We had only been in there for about half an hour when there was an explosion. We rushed out to see what it was. Outside was Ricardo and further down the road we could see other people. "What was that?", we asked almost simultaneously. Ricardo said, "A volcano blowing it's top, but thankfully not to near, but look over there". We could see in the other direction he pointed to plumes of smoke reaching into the air, I think the lava was on the other side away from sight. I hoped everyone was safe in that direction. Another huge explosion, even nearer and Ricardo said, "I'm not very happy it seems to be getting closer, like a chain reaction", "Are we safe or in danger?", I asked. "I think we are ok, we'll see what happens" said Ricardo, as we were talking an old police car came up to us and stopped saying, "It's the valley about twenty kilometres from here, and the far side is getting it, I even think it may be nearer the Argentina side of the Andes", he then added, "Not our time tonight", and moved off. Ricardo turned to Arthos and I and said, "I bet it's those damn Galympites, I've never known volcanoes this close before, I think it's still safe though a little unnerving. Right, I'll go and get my shower now, glad I wasn't in it when the explosion happened, I might have lost my reputation, caught running out of the house with no clothes on!". We all laughed at that. It was nearly the time we arranged to meet, Ricardo, Arthos and I got into the car ready to leave and have our evening meal. The hotel service and meal were excellent, the wine hit the right spot too. We all had the steaks again, and by nine thirty we all had finished and settled the bill. Paulo and Laximo left us, as we drove home. "Meet at Laximo's at 10:00 in the morning" we said as we drove off. When we got to Ricardo's I was glad there had not been any further explosions, Arthos said, "I contacted Base 2, they said it was far enough away that it wouldn't cause us any problems, but there was one a lot nearer that was showing slight signs of life, and Base 2 will advise if it becomes dangerous". On that note we said our goodnights and went to the caravan. I made a coffee, Arthos had a juice, I said, "Maybe I'm getting old, but I'm shattered tonight", "Don't worry", said Arthos, "After all those boxes, I'm not far behind you, just a couple of phone calls, then I'm going to bed", I smiled had a quick wash and went into my room I knew that contact with my bed was dreamland, and I was gone. Thursday followed the same pattern as Wednesday with breakfast at Ricardo's filling boxes at Laximo's, cleaning and polishing Laximo's flat and arranging with the landlord to pay for three months' rent, and that the flat maybe used during this period, but Laximo should be back before too long. Then we had a meal at the hotel, Laximo stayed with Paulo and we went home exhausted.

Friday dawned; we had agreed we would take it easy today. I wanted to take some photographs and have a walk around the area, taking in the Andes mystery in case I never came back. Ricardo and Arthos went to the airport to collect the tickets and boarding passes and said they would bring back something good for dinner. As for Paulo and Laximo they were going to lock Laximo's flat and put his travelling things, duffel bag and backpack at Paulo's then walk up to Ricardo's after Laximo had said a temporary farewell to the old couple and told them he would be back. Ricardo as usual had excelled himself and made a wonderful smelling curry, which I was assured was not hot, but a medium chicken one with cream and stewed apples in it. He had bought some long French rolls and made a lovely garlic butter, spread it on the rolls and put into the oven to crisp. They had also bought wine. We all felt a little sad as we didn't know when we would be together again, but I said, "Let's make the most of our time together as fate has bought us together and why shouldn't it again? I for one will keep in touch so please give me your phone numbers so I can contact you, and I'll give you my number. Your friendships mean more to me than anything else in the world and I relish the times we've had together". I didn't mean to upset them, but we were all a little tearful. So, I added, "And I still can't 'thought read', so you can say Glen is a soft idiot or maybe drunk, but I'm not". With this they started to smile and talk again. At about

22:00hrs, we decided it was late enough as Arthos and I still had a little packing to do, we thought we might be even later going to bed, especially as we hadn't cleaned up yet. We all helped to tidy and soon everything was cleared, washed up and put away. Ricardo got the other two into the car and said, "I know it will be crammed but we are all coming to the airport even if we have to sit on each other's knees. This raised a laugh he said, "Tie up the duffel bags well, as I am going to put them on the roof rack, otherwise it will be a physical impossibility to all fit in. We all said "Goodnight" and Arthos and I went into the caravan, whilst the others left for Paulo's flat. We were all feeling a bit emotional.

Morning dawned, Arthos and I took turns with the bathroom, I had hardly slept. I was so sad at leaving but Ricardo had said as we parted on Friday night, "I'll collect these two at seven thirty as I want to have breakfast ready by eight. Can you two Glen, Arthos come over at eight and we'll put the bags on the roof rack, then eat?". Breakfast was a quiet affair, but we all managed something, not a lot, though plenty of coffee. We locked the caravan and the house, squeezed into the car, having first counted three very large duffel bags and three back packs. Arthos said, "Has everyone got everything? Glen, Laximo, have you got your passports?", "Yes" we replied. Then Ricardo trying to sound cheerful said, "Now no hysterical laughter", which was about the last thing we were about to do, and we were off. Balmaceda here we come! We parked up the car, collected our bags and all went inside. We followed Arthos who took us up to the desk, handed in tickets, and got our boarding passes. It was an internal flight, so we only had about an hour to wait, once we had said goodbye had a few hugs, dried a few tears and passed through security. We waved goodbye; I felt a great loss as we went into the departure lounge. LA1B7083 was our flight number, and it was due to depart at 13:40, it was now 12:55, less than an hour I thought. Arthos was talking to Laximo who appeared extremely stressed. I kept looking at the different people imagining where they were going, and what their stories would be. When you do that time passes quickly, next minute our gate was showing. I was glad when I went through security that I hadn't put my grandfather's ring on, I had enough trouble coming. Next minute we were going across the tarmac into the plane. It was not a large plane but after all it was only an hour's flight to Santiago airport. We collected our duffel bags to hand in, answered some questions, then that was the last we would see of the bags till Heathrow London. Next was security, I noticed Arthos was leading us into the priority line, when we suddenly spotted Anton his friend the security guard Astrotar, who had helped us when we were arriving. Anton rushed over to give Arthos a hug, and shake my hand he then said, "Oh! Laximo, I haven't seen you for about fifteen years, how are you?" Arthos interrupted, "He's fine just a little emotional leaving his friends", "That's fine as long as you are all well", "Myself likewise", he uttered. He then said, "Thanks for letting me know Arthos about those two individuals that disappeared, but I can assure you the other two were from London and had been paid a lot of money to work for them", he took a breath and said, "But after treatment they got for being with undesirables they slunk back to London. They really didn't know the other two, and I didn't let anyone else know the full story." We had to say our goodbyes and went to security, but he took us over to the priority line and told them, "These are my special friends". It was then the usual paraphernalia, shoes off, belts off, watches off, jumpers off, stand here, look this way; now collect your things, get dressed, make sure you have everything, and let's go and find somewhere for a coffee and something to eat. We made straight for the priority lounge for business class, as we showed our boarding pass we entered, into a different world of peace, the staff determined to assist you. Food was there to help yourself too along with an array of liquid refreshments. I had a glass of wine, and a cold meat salad with a couple of rolls. Laximo and Arthos chose salads and buns with fruit juices I said, "Sorry about the wine, but I'm not really a fruit juice lover, give me wine or coffee, they both laughed at me. Although we were there for nearly an hour and half, we checked the board to see what time our flight to Madrid was. IB6943 at 19:00, so we decided to have another drink, this time I really did have coffee as I didn't want to get sleepy till on the plane. Although we were business class, I thought I would try and stay awake and enjoy the trip. Mind you it was twelve hours from Santiago to Madrid, then security and a plane from Madrid to Heathrow flying Iberian airways about three hours. I reckoned it would be Sunday by the time we got to Heathrow. I thought I'm so glad I'm with Arthos, I'll leave it to him, Arthos said, "Glen take note, you never know when you have to do this alone, to meet me or one of the others", I grimaced at him and he grinned at me. Ah! There's gate twenty-one, we made our way to the priority queue which was only short, and we were quickly waved through and onto the plane. We were shown into the business class front part of the plane, divided off from the rest of the passengers. A real touch of luxury and I must admit I loved it. Mind you, I hoped I would manage to stay awake for at least part of the journey this time. Finally, everyone was on board the plane, then the usual lifesaving procedures were demonstrated, then the engines roared, and we were hurtling down the runaway, and up in the sky on our way. Warm flannels were given to each of us to wipe our hands and faces, then we were given a choice of drink, I looked at Arthos and said, "Well I'm not turning champagne down, one won't harm me then I can sleep", Laximo and Arthos both had a glass of it as well, it made me feel a little less of an alcoholic. This thought made Arthos and Laximo laugh, I pulled a face at them. I know I finished it but before much else happened I had got myself comfortable and of course the rest goes without saying, I fell asleep! A few hours later I was awakened by an air steward asking me if I would like something to eat, I thanked him and said, "Yes please, and a coffee or I'll be asleep again". He thought that was funny and went away laughing, but I meant it. Arthos and Laximo were very involved talking and I knew Arthos was trying to talk Laximo's problems through and help him. Suddenly the plane started moving erratically with terrible turbulence, everyone was told to make sure they fastened their seat belts and put their seat into the upright position. Then an announcement we are sorry for the extreme turbulence, but we have hit a bad storm, we are trying to rise above it. The plane was rocking and pitching as if in the hands of a great monster. The lights had been dimmed and the air hostesses and steward were trying to calm down passengers in the economy end. There was an airhostess speaking over the tannoy, "Please remain calm the pilot is trying to ride out the storm". It was a very frightening experience, and I was secretly praying for a calming miracle. Then the plane appeared to make a type of spluttering noise, I thought, I hoped the engines were still ok. This went on the dropping sensation then as if we were moving up again, then rolling from side to side. I have travelled in planes many times all over the world with my job as a reporter, but never experienced this before. The steward came to us and said, "Are you all right?" I answered, "Well I guess we are all nervous wrecks, but the pilot must feel worse". Like a well-trained steward he said, "Oh! We have an excellent pilot, please don't worry", but he was white as a ghost, that did little to calm us. To make matters worse the lights flickered and went out for seconds, then came back on. It had been nearly thirty minutes, storm or no storm I was getting worried. I wondered if we were going to make it or was this the end of my good luck. Another announcement came over the tannoy, "We are now going to try and change flight levels to a high altitude. Anyone feeling faint use the oxygen masks above your heads. I checked on its whereabouts and looked at Arthos and Laximo. Arthos was talking quietly to Laximo who was visibly shaking, so I said, "Don't worry Laximo we'll soon be ok" I kept thinking positive, Arthos looked at me and said, "Well done, Glen". It was a miracle, we suddenly started flying as if nothing had happened, smooth and normal. It was my miracle my prayers had been answered. I looked at Arthos again, who said, "The power lords of the galaxy are on our side I feel". Just then the steward came around to us saying, "Would you all like a drink?" I answered without hesitation "A whisky please". Glen and Laximo took some champagne but I was thankful of the large whisky the steward gave me. Then he said, "When everything is calmed down with the other passengers, we will bring you some food, but I'm sure you understand us helping some very frightened other people", "Yes certainly", Arthos and I said together. Laximo was just sitting looking white and dazed, I said to the steward, "Our compliments to the pilot and navigator, they were marvellous to ride out that storm and keep us safe", "Here, here", came the voices of the other business class section. Our food was duly bought, I noticed that not only myself, but Arthos and Laximo along with many others were having extra drinks. It had been a terrible experience, but hopefully I will never experience that again. The pilot bought the plane down safely at Madrid where daylight had broken. We thanked the crew as we disembarked the plane and walked across the tarmac. I noticed that it was very cold this morning or perhaps I was exceptionally tired as I hadn't slept the nearly whole journey like I did the time I was flying to Santiago. Through customs and security and we needed to find out the gate we needed for Madrid to Heathrow. It was only about an hour to wait, and we would be flying out at eight this morning, arriving at Heathrow three hours later, but with the time difference it would be about ten o' clock, if I had worked it out correctly. Our flight was IB3271, I was a little nervous of yet another flight, but I had survived lots of things and the next flight was going to be fine. Think positive and things go well. The plane was waiting, once again we were in the priority queue, before we knew it we were climbing the steps and being shown to our seats. I sat by the window and Laximo and Arthos took the middle two seats. I was happy because they might not notice if I fell asleep, it made the trip quicker. After all were aboard and the formalities were finished, an attractive air hostess offered us a choice of drink. We all chose coffee, she bought some warm rolls, butter and cheese, ham and cake. More than enough. My stomach still hadn't settled after the last flight and after a couple of coffees I was starting to feel more my old self. Everything finished I settled back, putting my feet up and you know I fell asleep! I must have been in a deep sleep but as we neared our destination, Arthos gave me a little push saying, "Wakey, wakey Glen, we are nearly at Heathrow. You have been asleep for nearly two hours". I apologised but as Arthos said, "Don't worry I think we all had a doze after the flight we had". We landed safely and we were on a way across the tarmac. We were through security without any problems, as we were let off first and we went to where the bags and cases were coming around the carousel. Good three bags all together that was another miracle, nothing lost! It was time to say goodbye. I gave Arthos and Laximo hugs not caring what anyone else thought. This was London where you shook hands and remained cold and impersonal, but these were my special friends, and I didn't know how long it would be till I saw them again. I held back the tears, but Laximo couldn't. I said, "Ok Arthos ring me when you know what is happening, and please don't forget I'll be waiting for the phone call with eagerness. Laximo take care and enjoy your break, Bermantus, is heaven on earth". I looked at them with a smile turned and walked quickly away.

To hell I thought today I'm not getting the underground, buses etc., I'm going to treat myself and spend some of my money on a bit of luxury. I walked over to the taxi rank, opened the door gave my address asked him if he knew it. He laughed and said, "Look Guv I've been driving taxis for twenty years in London, course I know it". He started off then said, "Been away on holiday Guv?" To which I replied, "No, business and I'm absolutely bushed", "Ok Guv" he said, "I'll wake you when we get there". I thought no chance, I'm staying awake I might end up dumped in the wrong place". I was wrong, he was far quicker than I imagined, and I was home. I paid him and gave him a decent tip, because he could have easily taken me for a longer ride. He waved goodbye, I opened the door to my flat, I was home, but I wished I was still with my friends. I realised that all my life although I had many acquaintances, I had always been lonely, searching for something I never had, now I knew what it was 'real friends'. I turned on the heating, opened the curtains fully as I had left them half closed, turned off my security lights that turned on and off at various times, and went and put the kettle on. That's it I thought a coffee, take something out the freezer for dinner, have a couple of shortbreads, then have an hour on the sofa and relax.

I woke up to the phone ringing, how could anyone know I was in? I answered, "Hello Glen speaking", I was amazed to hear Arthos's voice, "Glen, it's me Arthos, I've just rung to let you know I've hired the car from Inverness, but I've just stopped for something to eat, because I'm not being met at my destination till later tonight. Just thought I'd let you know what's happening", "Thank you", I said, "It doesn't matter how late it is when you are on your way back to the airport or at a hotel, give me another ring and I'll know how things have gone", "Ok", said Arthos, "I'll be in touch later" and he was gone. I looked at the clock I couldn't believe it, how time flies. It must have been my body getting over the shock of the flight, plus the time differential's. So, I thought where's the destination? I thought it was to be Loch Loyne, but it's obviously changed. I was still lazy after all the travelling; I don't know I thought how Arthos does it. He's always ready awake and on the go, Amazing man! I had my meal and coffee and sprawled back out on the sofa with a book and the telephone within reach. I put on the television quietly for background company and settled down to wait for Arthos's call. It was only early evening and I started watching a programme on the television about ancient aliens, how they were starting to believe that aliens had been to our planet thousands of years ago, and there were different types from different planets. Some of the information was true but some I'm sure Arthos would say it was rubbish. I waited for Arthos watching television, but no phone came, I couldn't understand it. I felt something was wrong, but I knew he would call eventually. Time passed I looked at the clock, it was already past midnight, I dimmed the light making sure the phone was near at hand on the coffee table with my other bits and pieces, pulled the big rug off the back of the sofa and closed my eyes. I thought a short nap would make time pass quicker, and I would be able to answer the phone fast as it was just by myside, so even if I fell into a deep sleep, I would hear it. The phone started ringing, I grabbed it, it was Arthos, "Thought I might not be able to wake you up", "No Arthos, I was dozing waiting to hear", "Well operation Laximo is complete, but it had problems, all sorted now, I'm going to the Travelodge and book in for a few hours. My plane is at 18:00, so I will be at London about 19:40, so much I want to tell you, but won't tonight I'll give you a ring tomorrow, Tuesday. Glen I'm so sorry to call you at this time. You will probably sleep till afternoon", he laughed. I said, "Bye" as the phone went down, and went straight to my bed, leaving the curtains closed and putt off the lights. Good I thought, I'll get up when I wake up, and no alarm clocks. The next thing I knew I looked at the clock and it was already afternoon. Mind you as I stretched, I felt so rested.

I'll get up in ten minutes I thought and have a shower, then some coffee, but there is no rush. Work was no longer a pressure it was hard to believe. Oh, the hell with it I thought the shower can wait, first things first. I spent a leisurely afternoon and evening gathering my books and notes from the safe, adding all my new notes to them. I remembered Arthos said to get everything together, we can then make quick arrangements if we want, and I can take all stuff with me. I found a briefcase and fitted it with all my paperwork. Once that was done, I spent an hour opening all the mail that had come whilst I was away. It was mostly rubbish, but a couple of bills. Most of accounts were on direct debits so being away was not a hardship. Then of course there were letters of my redundancy and letters from the solicitor in connection to Sam Juste's will. I thought perhaps they had changed their mind, but no everything was status quo, as they say. I tidied the mess throwing all the rubbish away and started thinking about supper, I wasn't that hungry I thought I'll eat then have an early night. A frozen lasagna did the trick with a piece of defrosted chocolate gateau to follow. Thank goodness my freezer was never allowed to be empty. In no time at all I was finished. I had done all my jobs and as I looked around it was tidy, so if Arthos came instead of ringing the place was respectable. Ok I said to myself bedtime calls, early night and I'll get up early, well maybe!

    I woke up and looked at the clock, it was just light enough to make out with the curtains closed and the light off, eight o clock. Well, I'd make a coffee and have a piece of toast. I would have had cereal but had forgotten to take the milk out of the freezer. I took it out whilst I thought of it, then I needn't go out today. I could hear the rain on the kitchen window, but the heating was on and it was quite cozy. My flat was only bedroom, lounge, kitchen and bathroom, but it was adequate for me. Many years ago, I had been seeing a girl for over five years, both of us were very career minded. At last, I got around in my mind to the proposal bit, but she said she was accepting a journalistic career in America, and she realised she didn't want to tie herself down. I was hurt but thought that maybe we would sort things out because I had genuinely thought we were in love. Then the bombshell she said, "Glen" and it was over the phone from America, "I did meet someone through my work job in London and didn't like to tell you, and we are getting married next month". I put down the phone now I had been made to realise why she had left for the last month, been busy, not available, unable to meet me for dinner, or very unresponsive to any love I tried to show her. That's it I thought I'm never getting involved again. Friends great but no involvements. The phone rang, as I answered it, Arthos said, "Gosh Glen, you are deep in your past today, aren't you? I'm coming over to your flat at about two o' clock this afternoon", I replied, "Oh! It's really good to hear you. I look forward to this afternoon, bye", and he was gone. One minute you have loads of time, next you are dashing around like a lunatic, but what for? I suppose I was getting out some things so that I could make food for us, if he wanted to stay for dinner. Knocking on the door bought to a standstill, hoping it was Arthos, not wanting to be bothered by any other visitors. I opened the door and Arthos said, "Hi! Glen, how many people are you expecting?", "None" I said, "Except you of course, but you never know do you?", "Yes I do" replied Arthos, and we both laughed. We sat down, I had a tray ready with a thermos jug of coffee and milk, and a nice cake I had also defrosted with the milk. "Alright, I want to hear all the news", I said. Arthos sat back in the chair having drunk his first cup of coffee and started, "When I left you at Heathrow, we did security, no problems, and caught the plane to Inverness. We picked our bags up after the flight, and I hired a black car, just a 1.8cc Peugeot which was enough for us. At Heathrow we had bought two black jumpers, black trousers as they don't show up at night. I had my instructions as you know, but couldn't go where we used to go, there has been changes so had to drive down to Loch Ness to a certain place, out of view of everyone. I had received my destination on a type of text map, so it was quite difficult to find the spot, on the map but before we left, we sensibly went and had a quick meal, and bought some juices for the car. We didn't start down the long Loch Ness road till after 20:30. I found our meeting place in more than enough time. Botami was bringing the aqua craft to the place out of sight, below water and would come into the bank where it was deep. I had an attachment to Laximo in case he fainted, or did something silly like falling in. I was given my signal, clicks remember them. We were unnoticeable on the bank, trees behind us, the car concealed behind bushes when suddenly the black object you will remember in Sicily came above the water and opened. I helped Laximo into the craft. It then closed and disappeared beneath the loch. They were gone, I got click, click and silence, they were on their way. They made their way through secret loch tunnels which join up he lochs, then they make their way out into the North Atlantic and home to Bermantus at tremendous speeds to keep from trouble. When you think about it, how many of the times that Botami has been collecting Astrotars from the Highlands of Scotland and using parts of Loch Ness and other lochs to pick them up, in the aqua craft which is green on top, with the part that come out of the water and opens up to let you get in, looks like a huge head, and people think they are seeing the loch ness monster, as it quickly disappears again beneath the water, it certainly has helped keep the story alive! Anyway the climax of my story, they are safe had quite a lot of turbulence going through the area in the depths of the mid Atlantic under the ocean mountain range, which I'm sure you remember well", "I most certainly will never forget my voyages in the aqua craft", I said, "Botami is so kind and when I first met him and of course I was scared, he was so reasoning", "Yes" said Arthos, "He is a wonderful man and greatly loved by everyone, and although he doesn't look it, is much older than any of us". He reached over and poured us both more coffee, "Well", he said, "There is more they eventually reached Bermantus I believe about 06:00, but I had already booked into the Thistle Hotel in Inverness, had a few hours' sleep, paid and left around 11:00. I took the car back to the airport, got back my deposit and went and had breakfast in the restaurant at the airport. That's when I heard they were safe, it was then I found out that my flight to Heathrow was at 15:00, and so I went through security and rested in the American Express lounge, I had a few hours to kill, so in your words I had a quick snooze, but asked the security men on the door to make sure I didn't miss my flight. A small tip helped the problem. I didn't actually receive the message that they were safe till late, I thought you might be sleeping. Next, I have some rather sad news for you, and I am scared to tell you". "I'm not needed anymore?" I said, "Oh! Glen don't be stupid, you are part Astrotar now of course you are always wanted, no that's not it I'm afraid sadly, Leanne has been very ill due to her human body only being temporarily repaired, as she was so damaged, and unfortunately, she died. Her last words to the Great Astro were thank you for allowing me to love Glen, tell him I'll love him till the end of time. The great Astro stroked her head, and she closed her eyes, with a smile passed into the great beyond". He was silent the tears were running down my face and I said, "I feel I let her down because I was with her so little", "No, you gave her something she met a wonderful man even though she actually would never have done so had the Astrotars not made her able to live with a make belief body, she was given extra time to meet you, and it's better to have loved and lost then never to have loved at all. I have never had that experience", said Arthos, "but then I'm an

Astrotar". I tried to pull myself together and said, "Do you mind if I go and make some coffee and compose myself?" All the time I was speaking I was sobbing and Arthos put a brotherly arm around me and said, "I'll watch television for a few minutes, and I'll ring the boys in Chile and let them know Laximo is safe in Bermantus". Ten minutes later I came back to Arthos and said, "Sorry about that, I secretly knew it was a hopeless love, but you always think a miracle could happen. It did really I met her and now she has gone, I will devote my life to be a trainee Astrotar", and with that we both smiled. "Finally," said Arthos, "We have a short time to make up our minds the Great Astro wants me to go to Bermantus for my relive programme a little earlier than usual so that we can go Galympite destroying in the summer, he also wonders whether you would like to come there with me, you will be given a study to do your writing, and a computer to type out your stories. They want to check how well you are, maybe they can find a way to put you through the Relive Programme one day, who knows. Would you like that? Or would you sooner go to Chile and use Laximo's flat?" I couldn't believe the things he was saying I was in no doubt what I would choose, but I tried to blank my mind against Arthos and said, "What do you think I should choose?" He laughed at me and said, "In two weeks' time we are off to Bermantus is that right?". I said, "Yes, Oh! Yes", then I said, "But how will we get there?", "That will be figured out, don't worry and we will be informed. So, I was right? I already thought this would happen, when I told you to start getting your things altogether, ready for the trip". Arthos stopped for a minute then said, "One brief case of papers and notes, one duffel bag of essentials clothes etc.", "That is all we each can take. We both need black jumpers, black trousers and black ski hoods for pickup. Make sure you leave your flat all sorted, put with drawing pins, something like a black bin bag so that when the mail is through the letter box it's hidden in the bag, pull your curtains across, make sure your security lights are all working, and you leave no trash to go bad in your flat. I'm going to bring an Astrotar friend round for you to meet and he will keep an eye on both our flats. His name is Yatop, he lives near me in London. He is an accountant and obviously goes under a different name in business. I know I'll give him a quick ring and see if he can pop round this evening around 18:00, for half an hour.

  He has a car and maybe he'll have to help us in our travel arrangements, is that all right with you Glen?", "Absolutely fine", I said, "I remember you saying you had a friend in London when we were visiting Franchesco in Sicily", "That's right, you certainly have a good memory", said Arthos. Arthos made the arrangements with Yatop and before we realised it was 18:00, and a knock on the door heralded Yatop. Arthos opened the door and gave Yatop a hug saying, "Now you'll meet Glen that I've told you all about". Yatop came straight to me and shook my hand saying, "Before you ask, I'm an Astrotar and I have a ring like you". We had to laugh it was so unexpected and highly amusing he said to us, "You will have to excuse me, I am going to the theatre tonight there is a play on, which I'm told is marvellous but honestly I have forgotten the name, isn't that terrible? I can only stay a few minutes but of course I will help checking on your flats whilst you are away. Don't forget to leave me a key for both flats. Anyway, that's enough I'm sure you have much to organise. I'll see you both as soon as you need to leave the day after tomorrow, Arthos at 06:30 and you Glen at 07:00, I'm off now" He gave us both a hug and he was gone. Arthos said, "Night Glen, I've got lots to organise so will be going shortly", "Should I make us something to eat ", I said, "No thanks, I'll only start talking, again and we both have so much to get ready. You need your duffel bag with some clothes etc., and your briefcase with your notes. I'll get the dark clothes we need for when we get to the loch. Yatop is taking us all the way in the car, so will be able to have long chats then, that is if you stay awake" replied Arthos. This made me laugh. "We've got to get everything thing ready for a couple of months stay at Bermantus as we venture forth to the bottom of the Atlantic Ocean. The people of Bermantus will make you very welcome and you will get so much time to do your writing and acquire lots of knowledge. The next time we meet we will be on our way" Arthos said, as he gave me a hug opened the door and was gone. Ah! Well, I thought I must get all my papers together, my things I wish to take, make sure I don't have any food in the kitchen, check my lighting switches are all working giving the impression I am at home. When all is done, I will have a good rest as there is much travelling ahead. With excitement mounting for what lay ahead I started my preparations. Arthos had told me we had about a month.

    Eventually the time came, our plans were put into action. It was dark and cold as we stood hidden behind a huge bush trying to blend with the scenery. Yatop had stayed with us to see us safely collected by Botami. The moon light played eerie images on the loch in front of us, I could feel that shivery feeling. Arthos had looked at me and told me not to worry, but the minutes ticked by and seemed longer than they were. Yatop had parked the car quite a bit further down the windy road to avoid detection. Then from nowhere it happened.

11

Click, click, click, click, it was Botami's signal then from the depths, the loch's surface broke and what appeared to be the head of a huge monster appeared in front of us where we were standing near the edge of a deep part of the loch. Immediately the top of the head flapped back, "Quick",

Arthos said, "You in first Glen, then me and Yatop will throw in the duffel bags and your briefcase". We all did exactly as we were told, the top closed and the monster, and the aqua craft sank below the surface. We slid down the passageway and without warning the door in front of us opened, we passed into the aqua craft's large opaque coloured room, where we were greeted by Botami. He had not immediately spoken as he was busy pressing switches on the wall, then turning round to us he said, "Sorry, both of you I was making sure that the extra doors were all tightly closed and the special seals were watertight for our voyage to Bermantus, we go so deep". We were safe passing through rock tunnels at the deepest parts of the lochs, eventually passing into and through Loch Linnie, the sea loch and onwards into the North Atlantic Ocean. Botami took us through to a smaller room and told us to rest on the relaxing chairs and Eafi would bring us a refreshing drink. The whole incident will stay in my memory, it was very exciting, also nerve wracking, but even now hard to believe where I was going. I turned to Arthos after a while, perhaps an hour had passed when I asked him, "Have you heard how Yatop is? Is he safe?", "Yes, I've already received a message from Yaptap he's going to stay the night in Inverness, before he drives back to London, he will check our flats when he gets back and on a regular basis and our voyage continued. I leaned back in my chair and found it hard to believe that I had already been staying in Bermantus for well over a month. Time seemed to pass so quick when I was writing my stories from all my notes. From when I arrived, I was treated with such friendship, but also given so much time to write, also given such wonderful books to read, some so old that they must have been from antiquity. Some in languages or hierographic that were undecipherable by me, but I was told that certain Astrotars were coming to meet me and translate them, to increase my knowledge of past millenniums, where Astrotars had been involved in helping our planet. A knock on the panel and Millem entered, he was a very learned and wise Astrotar who said he had been on earth for a long, long time and had undergone more Relive Programmes then he cared to remember. Looking at him I immediately thought to myself, why is he not wrinkled and bent with age. He burst out laughing, a real hearty laugh and said, "Oh! Glen remember I can read your thoughts, you are funny. It's because of my Relive Programme that I have been able to live so long, granted by the power lords of the galaxy. When we were first coming here, just a few of us were selected to live on and assist with the educating and instructing the advancement of civilisation, we stayed at

Bermantus and other bases for stretches between our stays.

It was only after our planet Astrola was about to implode, and everyone that wanted to come to earth, came in many spacecrafts having many problems due to the speeds necessary and trying to avoid Galympite attacks and huge space debris storms. Some Astrotars refused to leave as they believed it really would not happen. Unfortunately, it did happen, and we lost many Astrotars which will be forever a great sorrow to the rest of us, many loved friends from our planet. During this exodus many Astrotars became sterile and many of the females died, therefore the great power lords of the galaxy, not wanting the Astrotar race to become extinct, gave them all the chance to have a Relive Programme enabling them to continue their work on earth to help you all survive. Obviously if any get killed then that Astrotar is finished and cannot use the Relive Programme. Anyway, my dear Glen I have met people you can only read about now, and with help they created things that people wonder how, not realising that our own civilisation was so far advanced that even today you on earth have not achieved this pinnacle of creativeness, but if only the people of earth worked together as we did on Astrola, instead of fighting and having wars, you also could achieve greatness. With our help the natives from thousands of years ago regarded us as gods, and some were given offspring from mating with Astrotars thus the natives were evolving into a different species. That is why in the human race of earth there is one DNA which has apparently not been traced as yet. We Astrotars bought knowledge to your planet sometimes I wonder whether perhaps we were too advanced, when our planet imploded or perhaps it was just a galactic happening, but luckily, we had already been chosen to help earth and had built bases, to move into and inhabit. Your scientists, geologists, historians, astrologists and people of religious to name some categories have always in the past tried to say that the natives of the time had the ability without help to build and erect fantastic creations, move huge stones from far distances, cut laser type straight edges, make huge statues, build fantastically accurate pyramids, all in alignment with solar star systems with strong magnetic forces from them I could go on and on, but I have much to say. I was once told by a friend of mine that the philosopher Socrates who was very wise, said that most wisdom the masses could show, or muster was to choose a wise rule or leader. That is what we always had in Astrola". He stopped for a minute then said, "Glen I have had quite a few talks with you, informative and interesting or do you find them just historical facts unnecessary to your writing?", "No", I said adamantly, "You are very interesting, and it only helps me to understand the length of time the Astrotars have been helping to mold our civilisation. It must be wonderful to live through so many advancements in history and to provide a way forward from the distant past, to build amazing structures that can't even be copied today.

History is only available to the average person by reading about it, but how wonderful it must be for you to say you have actually known, or have spoken to people who have invented such things to allow us as a civilisation to progress to this present stage. Obviously, you have been in the eras of many rulers of Great Britain when we were great in the eras of the Romans, maybe even Egyptians. Oh! Millem and you are so young and yet so old and wise". He smiled and said, "Alright Glen, I will leave you now and if you would like I will return in a couple of days and bring you some more facts for you to digest", "Yes please Millem, I could listen to you for hours, like a child that is being told a story by a parent and never wants the story to end", :"Well Glen", said Millem, "We will continue in the near future". Millem took his leave and quietly glided out of my room like a white shadow. After a while Eafi knocked and asked if I wanted refreshments as usual in the great hall or in my room, I said, "I'll stay here Eafi I've got some wonderful notes to write down, but have you heard how Arthos is on the Relive Programme?", "No one but the Great Astro knows", she said smiled and exited coming back about five minutes later with a goblet of juice and some food tablets. Obviously, tonight's meal I thought and smiled in return to her smile. As usual they tasted great, delicious flavours and a feeling of complete satisfaction, and a drink of liquid which made your thirst completely quenched. How strange Bermantus was, happy and complete but so different to that which I was used to in my normal life I continued writing till I felt tired and climbed into bed having already washed. A strong knocking on my door proved to be Ennovy, I recognised him from my first visit to Bermantus, "Quick Glen we have to rush to the great hall, the Great Astro has called an emergency gathering. As we passed along the passageway the lights were flickering and Ennovy was muttering, "Please hold", I wondered what he meant and what it referred to holding. On entering the great hall everyone seemed to be there, even the Great Astro. He held up his hands, and the room went totally silent, "All of you, my family and friends, listen, we are being attacked by a Galympite force, and unfortunately. It has breached some of our force fields. I have gathered as many of you as I can together here for your safety whilst we work against them and hopefully destroy them. As I said at the moment, we are in danger but have faith, I'm sure our aqua crafts from Base 1, with their doom ray blasters will give the Galympites crafts problems, as they are not expecting them. Those evil ones are not as advanced as our crafts, we just need them to arrive quickly". Suddenly without warning there was a terrible explosion, and the lights went out. There were general murmurs, and my heart was racing, as I was sure was the case for many other people. A flickering of lights, they came back on. The Great Astro standing firmly in the middle of us said, "Stand firm, have courage, all of you, we have moved onto our secondary system of lighting, which keeps our force fields in place, which in turn protects the other perimeter of Bermantus. The lights appeared to flicker again, and we all couldn't help but notice that the huge main doors were all closed, and the clear paneling with the oceanic view were no longer obvious. Time passed and a couple of the Astrotars came over to speak with me. I had been given a long white robe to wear with a plain sash, and I knew it made me feel I belonged in fact on reflection that was a couple of weeks ago, since then I had been given a further one to change into. The three of us stood together waiting for something to happen. All around the tension could be felt like electrical charges in the air. Every moment we kept on hoping for something good to happen, not ever losing hope, or having negative thoughts., "Yes" said one of them who had obviously read my thoughts. "I agree with you". Then the second one said, "Sorry we never introduced ourselves, I am Soldat, and my friend is Bandon, we are here having completed a successful mission in Casablanca where we caught up with some other Astrotars that you met with Arthos. "Oh! Yes, Youssef and Mohammed and Khalid, they were wonderful to me, I do hope I meet them again", I said. "We were trying to carry on as if all was well, but time was ticking by and deep down we were all worried", Then our attention was diverted to the far wall where it was noticeable that one of our aqua crafts could be seen, as the screens had started to move back, and the ocean outside Bermantus was to be seen again. The aqua craft appeared to be moving towards the end of Bermantus where the aqua craft station entrance that was well concealed, was situated. It was then that the Great Astro announced to all gathered, "Once again the evil ones have been repelled and you can all relax. Go back to your rooms for now we have an important and necessary job, all the force fields must be checked as they must stay strong. Hopefully it won't hurt anyone on the outside of the Bermuda Triangle, either in the sea, or the air.

We have already lost enough souls at Bermantus who we welcomed into the Astrotar family". With that the Great Astro left, and we all started to disperse. My two new friends had said goodbye and moved over to a group of their colleagues. Another Astrotar came over to me as I was leaving the room and said, "Glen can I introduce myself to you? I know you are very busy, and I haven't liked to bother you, but anytime you would like some company, send word with Eafi. Although I now look after the people that have been caught in our force fields, and are forced to stay here as they are damaged and cannot return to the outer world, I have to tell you I spent many years in the olden days amongst people that you have read about in history, and I would love to share it with you", "Marvellous", I said, "Please tell me your name so that I can call you", "My name is Wentas, and I would just like to say I'm so sorry that although we tried everything we couldn't save your lost love Leanne, but Glen, she died happy that she had shared a love with you", "Thank you Wentas", I said wiping away a tear, "Don't worry I have learnt to live with it now and will devote my time helping the Astrotars and my planet". He gave me an unexpected hug, smiled and said goodbye, then moved away. I went to my bed study room thinking how friendly these Astrotars were, and at the same time wondering how Arthos was. I had been told that the Relive Programme took about four weeks, but it seemed it had been far longer. I thought that, maybe he had been sent on another mission without me. I knew he had been on plenty before I arrived. I started to think about all we had spoken about and all the places and people I had met whilst with him and began to feel quite sad. He really was the very best friend I had ever had in my life, and more than anything I hoped he was all right. Well, I thought, before all that trouble and the meeting in the big hall, I was going to bed, in fact I had just got into it when Ennovy knocked for me, so I thought tomorrow is another day and I climbed back into my bed. I woke in the morning and realised that it had to be over six weeks since I had seen Arthos. I guessed that there must always be a slight danger to this Relive Programme, but what was wrong with me? Of course, he would be all right. Nobody had told me anything different. Then I started wondering if I would ever be able to undertake this experience or was that impossible after all I was only a human being, an earthling and smiled at myself for an attempt of humour at my expense. A sharp knock on the door and the panel slid back, I expected to see one of the Astrotars, but it was the Great Astro that entered my room, "Glen" he said in his powerful deep voice, "I have come to have a word with you. Are you enjoying your stay with us? Have you learned much about us? I know that the people of earth tend to think that any extra-terrestrial beings are dangerous, but we are aliens, and we are friendly, and our only wish is to help, we came at first to help civilisation learn and adjust to the future, now of course we live here and spend our time helping to eradicate the Galympites from earth. They are evil in every concept of the word and would take over your planet destroying everything you know. If only we can succeed with your books to let the world know that people from other planets are not necessarily bad and have in many cases over the ages benefited the earth with their knowledge and advanced tools. I'm sure that Arthos who is wise and friendly and many of the others have told you about the different periods of time on this planet, the different rises of races of people, the advancement then deterioration of a civilisation then a different race of people advancing and then again sinking again. Repeatedly over the centuries Millem will continue whilst you are here to enlighten you with the distant facts, as knowledge is a great strength to anyone, and in your case will help your writing. He is also an interesting character that has been on your planet for a very long time, thanks of course to our Relive Programme. Glen I would also like to get permission for you also to be allowed to participate in this programme and increase your lifetime. Every one of the Astrotars you have met all have a great love and respect for you, so there is hope, that one day Astrotars and earthlings can all live in harmony. We just need to destroy the Galympites. Glen is there anything you would like to ask me?". I looked at him and said, "How sir do I address you? Do I say Great Astro, or have I missed something I should know?" Astro answered, "Glen I know you respect my position so when we are alone, 'Astro' is fine. Everyone refers to me as Great Astro so when you wish to meet with me just say to one of the Astrotars could I please ask to speak to the Great Astro. If it is possible, I will meet up with you", "I am honoured to speak to you Astro", I said and smiled. He smiled in return and said, "Goodbye Glen we shall meet you again soon" and he was gone. I found the experience enthralling he was in fact the leader, ruler of the Astrotars and I was truly honoured. He had an aura of a great leader, power and love the two most important things to be in charge I picked up my pen and started writing again. The days and nights passed, and I had almost completed my third book, I thought just a few pages more and I could start the process of getting them published. That might awaken the world. Others in the past had written about 'Chariots of the gods' that had been seen by the natives and had been shown on the pyramids and on rock drawings. A great writer authored this book a Mr. Erich von Danikan and many people read them, making more and more people believe that we had been visited on earth in the past. Now I was writing my books and hoped that my reporting days were going to hold me in good stead as my stories hit the book stands. Millem regularly visited me even going on about the happenings of the past centuries and to the details of the Pyramids and their accurate alignment with the solar system. A knock on the door and it slid back, I couldn't believe my eyes, it was Arthos I rushed to him and hugged, I was overjoyed my Astrotar friend was back.

    The next day I was summoned to the Great Astro's room, he said to me, "We are going to get you to get ready to leave as they are getting the Zoom-Ray transporter ready for you, and Arthos will follow in a day or so. The reason for the need to depart was urgent business that you are being sent on, in about a week". He looked at me and then said in his deep voice, "Glen we love you and look forward to your return. Is it all right for us to come and get you in about an hour?". Although I was surprised, I said, "Great Astro I will be ready. Thank you for all your hospitality, I shall look forward to returning to this wonderful place". He smiled and lent forward and embraced me. I felt the power of his love, smiling I left and returned to my room. An hour later having collected my things together, Eafi came to my room and took me to Botami. When I entered the room Arthos and Botami were talking, Arthos said, "Glen I'll be with you probably tomorrow and we'll make our plans" We gave each other a hug and Botami helped me into the Zoom-Ray transporter, and put in my bags saying, "We all love you Glen, take care we'll see you soon". He touched my forehead and lowered the lid, and I felt my eyes close. Opening my eyes, I became aware that I was lying down on the ground in a place unexpected and unknown to me. It was cold wet and dark and as far as I could make out it appeared to be area of long wet grass stretching as far as I could see. My backpack and duffel bag were on the ground by my side, but where was I? I stood up and began to shake not only with cold but also an overwhelming fear of whatever had gone wrong as I certainly wasn't in my London flat. So what had happened when I was being transported from Bermantus? I began to try and take stock of my surroundings, no houses, no signs of life, just a windy road in front of me and what appeared to be boulders, shrubs of a prickly nature, probably gorse, long grass and across the road vague shadows stretching upwards obviously hills or mountains. Certainly, no sign of life to ask for help, maybe I thought it was just as well, as I didn't know where I was or if I was in England or somewhere else in the world. That was indeed a quite frightening thought. Without realising it I was nervously twisting my special green triangular ring that Astro had given me, when suddenly the silence was broken by a quiet voice I recognised as Botami. "Glen what is wrong?", "I'm lost", I answered, "Where am I Botami?", "Are you not in your flat?", "No", I said, "I'm in a vast grassy area with boulders scattered around nearby, with plenty of bushes. It's quite dark and cold and I'm wet from the ground where I was laying. As far as I can see in the dark there are no houses just a windy road that I'm quite near." Botami then said, "Don't worry Glen, we'll get you safe, just start walking along that road in the right direction whilst we check co-ordinates. Have you got your phone?", "Yes", I replied, "Well will you turn it on, and we'll use it in connection with our intricate satellite navigation co-ordinates to find your position and area, but don't worry we never desert our own and you are one of us." "But there won't be any charge in the phone", I said, Botami's reply was, "Hold the phone in your hand that you wear your special ring, and we will find you", "OK, I'm walking, I'm on the roadway off to the right", I replied. I continued onwards wondering how this had happened, and what would happen now. I was suddenly made aware of a car approaching from behind and a cheery voice shouting, "Hello stranger, can I help? Sorry only speak English". I stopped and starred at the car and driver, a man with a cheeky face, with rosy, red cheeks, wearing a white collar of a priest, with a black hat perched on his head and looking at me with intent, obviously surprised to find anyone on this lonely road. "Thank goodness you stopped sir", I said, "I'm lost". "Well," said the man, can I take you along the way?", "You certainly could, but it would help if I knew where I was, even what country I'm in", I replied. The priest gave me a strange look, obviously deciding I had mental issues, he started to move forward slowly. "Please stop", I said, "I can explain everything if you care to listen.

12

It's a rather unbelievable story, but it is true. I am certainly not mad, just confused as this wasn't supposed to happen". The priest then replied, "OK, I'll take a chance, can't leave you stranded. Oh! I'm Father Patrick O' Kearney by the way. Get in then", with that he pushed open the passenger door, I put my bags on the back seat and climbed in. "Thank-you so much, but before you say anything more, could you please tell me where I am, and I'll then tell my story". "Well, my friend, first what's your name?" he said, "I'm Glen Grant Wallace, I was for many years a world correspondent journalist for a large newspaper in London, but now the things I am writing about, will change the world I hope, and bring peace and understanding". "Well," said my listener, "You are at the moment in the region of the Galtee mountains in Southern Ireland, and I'm shortly going to turn off this road and follow the long and twisty road to Clonmel. I am renting a cottage for a long break as I have been very ill, and the powers that be, have made this possible as I am now retired and need to enjoy a restful holiday. The man who owns the two cottages is renting one to me, I know that you can stay the night and tell me your story, the cottage has two rooms". "Thank you so much", I replied and settled down to complete the journey. Eventually we arrived, it was a few miles to Clonmel, but he checked his letter and map and said, "Yes Glen, we are I think here", my eyes took in the two cottages standing beside each other with land stretching out on both sides, with a few trees around them. We got out of the car and the old priest went and knocked at the door with a large number '1' on it. The door opened and, in the doorway, stood a tall man with glasses and white hair tied back wearing dungarees. "Hello", he said, "You must be Father Patrick O' Kearney, and may I ask who this is with you? I understood the booking was for one person", "You are quite right my friend", said the priest, "But I thought you wouldn't mind as this gentleman is lost, so I thought I could help him for one night, as it is late", "Oh!" the man replied. As I went to thank him, I noticed he was wearing a ring just like mine, yes unbelievable but identical. My eyes went to his face and I pointed to my ring saying, "My name is Glen Grant Wallace, and I am a friend of Arthos and Botami. I guess we have some coincidental stories to tell?". I paused then saying to Father Patrick, "It is an amazing coincidence but meeting this gentleman will make my story even more believable to you". My new Astrotar contact then said, "I must introduce myself; my name is Ritchie, and I'll let you go and put your things into next door number '2' and then I'll come and have a word, but you can stay with me for a while". "Can I ask a favour", I said, "Could you contact Botami and let him know where I am, near Clonmel and staying with you please? "No trouble", he replied. I hesitated then said, "I think I owe Father Patrick an explanation of sorts, he saved me when I was desperate and quite scared, maybe I could see you later?"

 We entered the small cottage being occupied by Father Patrick and put my bags inside the door. I was hardly inside when there was a knock on the door and it was Ritchie who said, "Glen, just to let you know everyone is happy and relieved you are safe, when I contacted Bermantus, if you would both like it, I have come to invite you both into my house, so that we can all join in the story telling". "Marvellous idea" said Father Patrick, "We will accept with pleasure isn't that right Glen?". "Yes, thank you", I replied. Ritchie took my bags next door and we followed him after Father Patrick had quickly checked around and found everything extremely satisfactory saying, "I think already this break is going to be quite special, maybe the good Lord sent you". We went next door to Ritchie's house knocked a couple of times on the door and were ushered into a lovely little lounge with a blazing log fire, and cups and saucers set out for a drink. Coffee, tea and biscuits were put out, we were told to help ourselves. Ritchie and I had coffee whilst Father Patrick had tea. We all sat around in the fine comfortable lounge enjoying each other's company, as though we were old friends rather than new acquaintances. I began by saying to Father Patrick, "Father the story I tell you must not be told to the general public, as my books are to be issued when we are ready to bring everything to the attention of the world. You must keep our secrets like you would a confessional". "I certainly will", he replied, exclaimed with excitement in his voice. I looked at Ritchie and started my tale. "On a trip to Scotland for my newspaper I took time off to go walking by Loch Loyne, suddenly I fell through what appeared to be a deep void hidden in the tall grass. It was terrifying, and then the appearance in the dark when I felt I was suspended in a large web of a nearing large monster. It was all too much for me, I guess I fainted. On coming around that was my first introduction to the Astrotars, a wonderful race of people from the planet Astrola, also it was my first meeting with Botami, who has been a marvellous friend to me." I took a mouthful of coffee and caught the memorised look on Father Patrick's face, so I continued. "I had a fantastic trip in an aqua craft, a journey at the bottom of the Atlantic at depths impossible to normally imagine. I saw fish that I had never heard of before, the whole experience was mind blowing and surreal, I kept wondering if I was dreaming, which of course I wasn't. We eventually having passed through the Sargasso Sea the graveyard of so many different boats scattered about, and of course passing through an undersea mountain range, with severe currents and a Galympite attack. They are the most evil people that the Astrotars are trying to destroy to save the earth. When at last I arrived at Bermantus the wonderful undersea base of the Astrotars where I was being taken. I was privileged to meet the Great Astro the leader of the Astrotars who is trying with all others to get rid of the Galympites who are an evil race that are goat like in appearance, have the stance of a man but cannot breathe in our atmosphere, thus they wear breathing apparatus which gives off the smell of Sulphur." I looked at Father Patrick as my tale was unfolding, the face of the elderly priest had changed from disbelief to absolute amazement as he listened mesmerised by all the facts. Ritchie smiled at me and nodded obviously he had been told about me before. I then continued my tale, "The Astrotars have been coming to our planet for thousands of years, helping the advancement of civilisation only coming here permanently when their planet Astrola imploded. It was a marvellous experience and I found everyone I met so friendly and the undersea world they have created called Bermantus unbelievable. When it was time to leave this became a further adventure. I was returned to the Scottish Highlands by means of a transporter called a Doon-ray machine, at first, I thought it had been a dream, but before I travelled back to flat in London, I noticed this green triangular ring on my finger and remembered I was told never to take it off as it is your continuous with us. Shortly after my return to my flat I met Arthos an Astrotar and the best friend I have ever had. We travelled to Sicily and I met other Astrotars, and we had several adventures in our missions destroying Galympites or passing information to the bases. The Great Astro made me an Astrotar by adoption and my role as ambassador to them through my books, so I write down all the stories and will present them to the world. Arthos and I have been to Sicily, Tunas, Casablanca and then to the blue marble caves of Chile, and my life was saved on many occasions by the Astrotars. Father Patrick these people are not aliens they are true friends of earth. They gave me something to keep me safe." I once again then showed him my ring. "How can I believe all of this?" asked the elderly priest. I stood up stretched up my hand with my ring on it and said, "Botami please confirm to Father Patrick that I tell the truth about the Astrotars." The lights flickered went out, then came back on and Botami's voice softly spoken said, "Father Patrick you are a good man, we represent only good for the earth. The evil ones are trying to destroy the world with many catastrophises, but we will win. Please believe in us." It went all quiet and I sat down. Silence reigned for a few seconds then Father Patrick spoke, "Holy mother of God, I never thought I would ever meet an alien, even if he is good, but you aren't one, are you?", "No" I said, "But I'm sure that you will gain their trust and they will continue to get in touch with you." "Amazing", he said and continued, "Well the world certainly needs some help, it's in a terrible mess, that's for sure." Ritchie had listened to all of this and said, "Father Patrick you are a man of honour, and I sense you are completely trustworthy, so I will put my life in your hands with my secret. I am an Astrotar, we all have white hair and blue eyes and the way Glen, and I recognised each other was by the green stoned triangular rings we all wear, and never take them off, but never let anyone know that I am not an earthling, or they will destroy me." "Your secret is safe with me", the elderly priest said, "And I'm sure this holiday break will be the most amazing time of my life." "Well,", I said, "I will tell you both tomorrow some more of my adventures with Arthos but if it is possible after I have finished my coffee could I please go to bed? I am absolutely dead beat." "Of course," said Ritchie. "Before I leave", said Father Patrick getting up from his chair, "Please tell me how you ended up on that lonely road by the Galtee mountains, confused and needing help." "You are right", I exclaimed, "By God you are right", I turned to both of them and said, "The reason I was there, Botami told me that they thought I was home in London, but the transporter called a Zoon-Ray for the first time ever, was disturbed by some bad alien rays outside Bermantus and I was thrown off course to that road where you found me Father and saved me, even though you thought I was mental." This statement made us all laugh. This was when Ritchie stood up and said, "Well Father Patrick your fire is all backed up, so the cottage will be nice and warm. I've put some milk and bread in the fridge along with some other bits and pieces." "Oh, to be sure my dear Ritchie, you've really looked after me and I thank you so much." Richie opened the front door and saw Father Patrick to his cottage, and checked him saying, "Sleep well, we'll see you in the morning", then he came in saying to me, "What a lovely elderly gentleman he is. Come on Glen I'll show you to your room." I doubt I was in the bathroom more than five minutes then I was into bed and I was unconscious in sleep. Ritchie knocked at my door, I glanced at my watch to see it was already 09:00 and the sun was shining through the curtains. I was embarrassed and shouted, "I'm sorry I slept so late", "Does it really matter?", came the reply, "Come and have some coffee I've got something to tell you." Ten minutes later I was sitting in the lounge when Ritchie said, "Glen, I have been in contact with Bermantus, and they now know exactly what happened to you. At the moment the transporter was started a Galympite craft tried to break the through the force field and exploded, interfering with the transporter direction rays. They are so thankful that you are ok. Arthos is now in his flat in London and says if you charge your phone, he will contact you." "So, everything ends well", I said, "And I met you, another Astrotar thanks to Father Patrick. Thank goodness he turned up when he did because even the Astrotars didn't know where I was." Ritchie replied, "Anyway, I have got finish chopping the logs today and delivering them, do you fancy helping me after you had a bit to eat?" "Of course,", I said and grabbed another coffee. Outside we worked away sawing some trees into logs and filling the pick-up truck trailer with them. Then we got to work with the axes and made piles of kindling with which could use to help start their fires.

I learned from Ritchie the rent from the cottage along with the income from supplying logs and kindling around the area was how he supported himself. He told me that the Great Astro had supplied the money in the first instance for the purchase of the cottages, which were quite run down at the time, and Ritchie had renovated them.

He had been placed in the area because of suspected Galympite activity. So far though he had reported only the odd sightings, which he thought were coming from the direction of the Galtee mountains. He had been told by Bermantus just to report and not to take any chances at this stage. I found this information very interesting, of course it stirred my curiosity and imagination. We were just having a quick coffee break when my phone rang. It was of course my very good friend Arthos. He was back from Bermantus and in London, but was flying to Cork airport tomorrow, where he would arrange to meet us when he knew what time his flight was due to arrive. When asked, Ritchie said, "No trouble, I'll give him the route to Clonmel, and we'll meet him there." Ritchie started laughing saying, "Poor Father Patrick, when we tell him he's about to meet another Astrotar." That made us both laugh. Just ten minutes later Father Patrick himself popped in as the door was open saying, "Any chance of a cuppa for a lonely elderly priest? To be sure my dreams were unbelievable last night.", "No trouble", said Ritchie, "Oh! and by the way Father Patrick guess what? You are going to meet another of our friend's tomorrow, someone with whom Glen has travelled with extensively around the world." "Who's that?", said the elderly priest in amazement. "His name is Arthos and he's coming into Cork airport tomorrow." I said happily. "To be sure I'm excited I think I've died life is so good, I don't know whether it is a dream, or I've had too many whiskies, and the holy mother knows I'm trying to reform." "No, it's all real and we are trusting you with a secret of a lifetime, not to say anything to anybody, as it is not the right time yet." I said. "well, I'm amazed that Ritchie looks like us and not like they say aliens look like", "No", said Ritchie, "Different solar systems have different people, but we are like you on earth. We are not grey shadows of a tall thin statue with large heads and large oval eyes, but that doesn't mean that they are evil, they are just not an Astrotar from Astrola, but we always know what you are thinking as we can read your thoughts, so sometimes we answer your questions before you ask them." That made us all laugh and Father Patrick made us laugh again when he said, "Well in the name of god that's a miracle to start with, if anyone can read my brain". He was so uncomplicated and natural and obviously a very good person. Ritchie suddenly said, "Well, I think we've done enough work for today, so how about us going into Clonmel, the three of us? I'll drive and show you around." Father Patrick and I were made up with the idea, before we left the cottages, we backed up the fires, making sure the fire guards were in place. They were fixed with some hooks which fastened them to the fireplaces, with that done we were off. Father Patrick and Ritchie were in the front, I piled into the back of the car. It was an old Toyota with plenty of room for my long legs to stretch out. It wasn't a long journey, about half an hour then we were there.

We parked up at the shopping mall and walked round having a look at the different shops. I needed a few bits and pieces, and they were easily purchased. I then asked Ritchie if I bought some steaks, would he cook them for us, to which he replied, "That's fine we will have them tomorrow night when Arthos arrives. Tonight, I have organised a big pot of stew for the three of us." I was embarrassed I always seemed to be someone's guest, but I had to laugh at Father Patrick who exclaimed, "My god, I'm being fed and looked after and treated so well by people who I have only just met. I feel the angels must have sent you, 'cos I'm having the time of my life!" I went into the butchers which was sparkling clean and had everything laid out neatly, and was meet by the greeting, "Well, my good man, tis a pleasure someone, it's darn quiet this morning." He then added, "To be sure you're not from around here?" I answered, "No actually I'm from London, and just popped in here to buy some meat." He laughed and said, "Well, to be sure I know I have good quality meat, but people don't usually come that far to buy from me, I really must be special!" This made us all laugh, I then said, "Can you cut me four nice sirloin steaks?", "They will be my very best", he replied. Whilst he cut them, I studied him, he was a cheery character, quite rotund with rosy cheeks with a head of black hair and only the slightest of grey showing at the temples. His white coat was immaculate although his red and white striped apron was marked with his meat preparation. On his head he had a straw boater. After I had paid for the steaks, he shook my hand saying, "It's not every day I get someone who travels so far for meat, I hope I'll see you again?" I smiled and said, "If the steaks are good, I'll be back." Leaving the shop, we went and put the meat in the boot of the car, then decided to drive to 'St. Patricks' Well' a popular landmark Ritchie informed us. "With a name like that it's got to be good", said Father Patrick, to which we laughed. He was a really lovely old gentleman and was enjoying himself. Ritchie parked the car, and we started walking down the logging steps which were on each side of the pathway bordered by a wooden railing. It was so peaceful, with trees all around on the grass verges. As we went down the steps, we got closer to the water. A squirrel scuttled across the path in front of us and went up a tree at amazing speed. In the quietness of the area the only sounds were the choruses of birds. Everything was perfect even the weather was warm. Eventually we were able to get reasonably close, still walking along the path, we came to some tree stumps, so we sat down, as Ritchie and I were talking we noticed that Father Patrick who was a little further away from us seemed to be mumbling something, or talking to himself, or possibly saying prayers. Ritchie looked at me and nodded, he had read Father Patricks' mutterings from a far, I guess Ritchie had made an Astrotar connection, they were amazing people. I felt a wonderful inner peace sitting there. Ritchie broke the silence between us all, suggesting we move and maybe find time to go and see the old ruins of Corey's Castle.

It didn't take long to get back to the car, we tried walking slowly as Father Patrick was puffing and his cheeks were very red. Perhaps we were pushing him a little too much. I asked him, "Are you alright Father Patrick?", he quietly replied, "Don't fret about me, I'm just not as young as I used to be, and a little overweight!"

It would not take long to arrive at Carey's castle, we all commented on how peaceful it was at 'St. Patricks' Well', we all thought it was great to get out and see the sights. When we arrived at the destination of the castle, Ritchie parked up the car, we then walked across the grass to the ruined walls of the castle. I touched the stone of the building and felt my thoughts transported back to all the loss of life of long past battles, the deprivation and suffering. As we started walking around the walls Ritchie who had obviously been reading my thoughts said, "Glen, you have deep feelings for history and people, that is a major sentiment that was recognised by the Great Astro, when he had long talks with you. I had been told so much about you from the Astrotars I've come in contact with lately, never did I expect to meet you in this manner." "The lord works in mysterious ways", commented Father Patrick who had been avidly listening to the conversation. I was busy in my studying of the masonry which showed such precision in the way stonework had been placed; when suddenly the peace was shattered by a low flying plane that seemed almost to touch the treetops, obviously coming in to Cork Airport. This made think of flying saucers or alien spacecraft to be more exact. Turning to Ritchie I said, "Have any weird sightings been reported in the sky around this area?" To which he replied, "Well, actually that is why I was sent here a while ago, as some reports of strange things in the sky have been sighted over the Galtee mountains, especially around Lough Maskry.", "Well, if it is possible can we go tomorrow and have a look around? Maybe after I've helped you with the logs." I said. "No problem" said Ritchie, "How about you Father Patrick, are you game?" "To be sure I wouldn't miss it for the world, but I'll ask the Holy Mother to look after us." He then added, "I'm excited already", "Oh! I forgot to tell you, Arthos contacted me and said he was staying in Cork tonight and was meeting someone tomorrow morning but would be here by dinner tomorrow evening. There is a small bedroom in the attic of my cottage, he can also stay with me as well as yourself." Ritchie said to me. "And Father you can join us whenever you want", "Thank you so much" said Father Patrick, "You have given me a new lease of life, guess my guardian angel sent me here." "Well, if we are going to Galtee mountains tomorrow, let's hope your guardian angel looks after us all, you never know what we might see", I said.

We got back in the car and set homewards passing the main guard building which was very impressive with what looked like a tower in the middle of the building, but as we didn't stop, I didn't really get a good look. We continued on way chatting like old friends till we reached Ritchie's Cottage and parked up. The first thing we did when we arrived back was put on the coffee; Ritchie gave Father Patrick a small drop of the golden nectar as he was feeling cold and looked tired. We poked the fire and whilst I poured the coffee and a cup of tea for our elderly friend, Ritchie nipped next door to Father Patrick's cottage, and ensured his fire was backed up. When we had finished our coffee and some cheesy biscuits Father Patrick asked if we would excuse him, so he could go for a nap. It was only 16:00, and as he left Ritchie said, "Come back about 19:00, and eat with us." "Oh! The angels be praised, yes I'd love to if you can put up with me?" I was musing over the day and embarrassingly dozed off in the chair. A voice suddenly pulled me out of my mixed dreams, I realised I had been fast asleep. Ritchie said, "Don't worry it's nearly dinner time and it's all organised", "Oh Ritchie I'm sorry", I said, "I think I must be getting old falling asleep like that, mind you I'm not an Astrotar who never seems to tire" That made Ritchie laugh, "No", said Ritchie, "It's all the wood cutting, then walking and of course the change of air." The meal was a great success most enjoyable and extremely filling. We all recounted tales of previous experiences, with Father Patrick not to be out done telling us funny Irish stories and myths and tales of the little people, the famous Irish Leprechauns. The time passed so quickly, around 10pm Father Patrick went home next door, whilst I helped Ritchie clear up, then we both parted for bed, and in no time, I was in dreamland. After breakfast we backed up the fire and got ready to leave for a drive to the Galtee mountains. I popped next door to alert Father Patrick to the fact we were almost ready to have our outing. The door was opened, and he said, "Glen, I'm sorry can you both give me half an hour? I'm afraid I've slept in. To be sure it's my own fault I had a couple of whisky's before I went to bed, as I don't sleep well, I guess even the Arch Angel Gabriel couldn't have woken me this morning!" I said, "Don't worry we'll wait for you, we will have another coffee and pass the time." Just over half an hour later we were in the car on route for the mountains to investigate a little carefully of course. It was probably about an hour or so when turned off to the left and started driving along the road that I had started walking along the day before yesterday, when I was picked up by Father Patrick. He truly saved me, as I didn't even know where I was or what country I was in. We came to a small track off on the right side of the road which I think the main road was N74. We turned up the track but found it was becoming quite narrow and rough, the mountain side was so very black. We came to a place which was suitable to park with a great view, but Ritchie said, "I think I'll turn the car round in case we need to make a quick getaway. That done we all got out and Father Patrick said, "If you two don't mind I don't think I'm fit enough to clamber up those rocks, so I think I'll perch on one of these flat boulders and enjoy the view over the valley in front. I think it's called the valley Shehan and maybe if you are a long time I'll sit back in the car. I have a bottle of juice with me, honestly to be sure it is only juice!" We all laughed at him. He really was a pleasant man, never grumpy like some people, who can change after getting to know them. We agreed that this was the best idea and that we wouldn't be overly long. Ritchie had parked the car tight into a huge boulder so that it was not visible, also not in the way of anything else coming up the track. We set off walking and scrambling up parts that were accessible to us, as some slopes were too steep, and we had to find ways round them. It was a lovely mild May day, quite warm and thankfully not raining. I was hoping we would soon be near Lough Maskry, which on the computer looked quite desolate and eerie. We chattered walked and climbed forgetting time and slipping occasionally on rocky surfaces. We passed water filled crevasses which looked black and deep.

Eventually, after about an hour we reached Lough Maskry and as we came quite close to the edge, we noticed what appeared to be an under craft at one side. Curiosity took over so of course we had to investigate, not a very good idea! As we neared it, we stopped in our own tracks, an immediate impact on both of us, because a very strong smell of Sulphur was suddenly very prevalent around us. Was that possible? Was this a base of the Galympites. We both knew what that could mean, and we were in a delicate position. Nowhere to hide if necessary, so having taken note of the exact location we started to walk back around the Lough Maskry, stopping for a moment looking back, and to our absolute horror saw from the dark waters a silvery object shoot straight up sky wise. We hurriedly scrambled behind a large rocky projection and watched as the object shot across the sky disappearing behind clouds. We started back down the slopes, thank goodness it wasn't too steep and far easier going down than up. Next thing the silver object shot back across the sky much lower this time, as if checking all round. We pushed ourselves against the rocks to stop standing in view. Twice it passed across the area above us, we held our breath expecting discovery or to be killed by their death rays, which were capable if I remembered correctly when in Chile visiting Pedro at the blue marble caves, and we were lucky to miss that.

When I remembered the damage they did, "Stop it", said Ritchie, "I'm reading your mind and you are making me more nervous", "Right", I said, "Let's have another try at getting down before they re-appear, as we still have a quite a way to go." It seemed forever, getting down the slopes even though we were taken chances and sliding down parts to get back to the car as quickly as possible. Eventually we saw the car and got to it as fast as we could. As we approached Father Patrick, he jumped out faster than I thought he could, saying, "Oh! Thank the Holy Mother you are safe I thought you had been injured or something." Ritchie replied, "Something is right", then I said, "If those bad Galympites have a base up there, are you going to let Bermantus know?" "Don't worry", said Ritchie, "I'm ahead of you, I have already alerted them to the spot. I took the reading on my watch compass, which they immediately co-ordinate the position on their equipment and they will check them out and destroy if possible. They will immediately send out a spy craft from a base we have on the channel coast only known to the Astrotars and you I guess Glen, one day." As we were discussing the closeness of severe danger we had been in and how lucky we were when suddenly a round silver disc like shape shot back quite low in the sky, across the area we were parked, luckily have hidden by huge boulders. We silently prayed that we hadn't been spotted, but as yet felt it would not be safe to move. Certainly, a very wise move remaining hidden, as the object came back even lower, obviously it had been alerted to some people snooping around Lough Maskry. Then without warning it shot upwards in the direction of the higher hills and out of sight. Father Patrick said, "Holy Mother of God, I'll need a stiff whisky after all this excitement, but I'm so thrilled to be with you, but to be sure I prayed to all the saints." We thanked him, smiling at each other, he really was a dear old soul. Ritchie started the car and we moved down the track as fast as we dared, and back onto the main road which I think was the N74 towards the right turn off for the direction of Clonmel. We knew we still had a good drive to go, we all felt shaken by the experience. Father Patrick could be heard muttering something and bending over from the back seat. I realised he had his rosery beads in his hands and was praying. I said, "Father Patrick I'm sorry to interrupt your prayers, but don't think you are alone, we also were surprised and fearful, and certainly didn't expect that to happen. Ritchie has alerted the base and the Astrotars may with luck and ability and bravery eliminate another Galympite base. If that is the case, then our afternoon foray may have once again helped in our constant battle between good and evil." By this time, we had arrived at Ritchie's cottage and we were met as the door was opened by the phone ringing. Ritchie rushed to answer it, spoke for a while then came into the lounge where we were standing. "It was Arthos asking for directions from Clonmel as he has already managed to hire a car and got that far. Now I'll make some coffee, give Father Patrick a whisky and then he can rest it's only 17:00, then come back for dinner, we will eat around 19:30 if that's ok with you?", "Yes I'd love to come back." replied the old priest and drank his whisky and said his goodbye's and went next door. Ritchie and I had our coffees, I then said, "Come on I'll give you a hand to prepare dinner", we then set about getting the steaks, potatoes and salad ready, we worked as a team, when everything was done, apart from cooking the steaks, I asked Ritchie if he minded if I went and took a shower. He said, "No bother, Glen I'll have one after you." After we had both tidied ourselves up, Ritchie said, "It's 19:00, let's have a glass of wine and relax, any minute now Arthos will be here." A knock at the door came, "There you are I'm psychic" said Ritchie, we both laughed as he opened the door and in came Arthos who greeted us both with great affection. It was wonderful to see him again. He then turned to Ritchie saying, "So after at least ten years we meet again old friend and in the presence of my dear friend Glen, who is an Astrotar by adoption." The fire was glowing, and the room was warm and inviting, and the table was set. Ritchie took Arthos upstairs to show him his bedroom, whilst I answered the door to Father Patrick as he tapped very gently. As I let him in, he said, "Are you sure you don't mind being my here, in case you all want to talk?" "No, we want you to stay", said Ritchie entering the room again. "By the way Father Patrick this gentleman who has just arrived is our friend Arthos." Father Patrick held out his hand in friendship saying, "Well to be sure, no offence meant but the good lord has sent me into the company of very special people who aren't leprechauns, but just as secretive, and taller! Don't worry my friend, I've given my promise on the Holy Mother that I'll not tell anyone I have met you all, but unbelievably thrilled I now know that although you are aliens you are really Astrotars and are the good ones." Arthos held up his hand saying, "Father Patrick I know you are true; I can read minds and yours is good and honest. I'm pleased to welcome you to our gathering." He then added, "We all believe you'll keep our secrets and we'll be very grateful if your guardian angels look after us any protection is welcome, and it's lovely to meet you." Father Patrick was grinning like a Cheshire cat, he was so happy. We left Arthos having a chat with Father Patrick whilst Ritchie and I finished getting the meal ready. The smell of the steaks was making me hungry, as we buttered bread and put everything out on the table, salad, potatoes, onions, bread and butter as well as glasses of wine for three of us, and a whisky for Father Patrick. We then sat and enjoyed the meal together; it was rather perfect. We cleaned away the plates to the kitchen and the stories started. Father Patrick was enthralled with the tales Arthos told of bygone days when Astrotars visited the planet and helped civilisation move forward as well as all the different places in the world where they had visited, and how he had lived for more years than he could remember, by the help from the great power lords of the galaxy and universe who had made the Astrotars guardians of the earth.

    Ritchie and I then told Arthos about the experience we had earlier that day and how we had heard from others that bright lights had been seen over the Galtee mountains, and how we had watched the silver disc shape of the Galympite craft flying low, backwards and forwards, as though looking for something, obviously us. Arthos said, "I've got news for you, after Ritchie informed Bermantus with the co-ordinates, one of our crafts flew over that area, it will now be watched and destroyed sooner than later, I hope. Also, folks I'm here for a few days thanks to the hospitality of Ritchie. Maybe we'll take another ride up that way again, are you all game?". "Even I am", replied Father Patrick, "If you'll let me come along, I'll guard the car." This made us all smile, he was game for anything for an elderly gentleman, he then exclaimed to us, "You see I've been a priest for over forty years and I've never felt better or experienced more genuine friendship and the feeling of belonging or had as much excitement in all my years." I for one knew exactly what he meant; my life had never been happier. The evening was a great success, and it was nearly eleven before we all said goodnight. Arthos, Ritchie and I quickly tidied up, backed the fire up then went our separate ways to bed.

    Next morning, we were happy for the weather continued warm and sunny but Arthos said, "If we intend in going to the Galtee mountains today, all wear black, it will make us less conspicuous as we will blend in with the black rocks of the mountainside." Father Patrick said, "Am I allowed to come with you? I'll remove my white collar, even though I think I'm best at the car, I'll be all in black as well and as the car is black it will be invisible where we parked last time." We all laughed at him, Arthos patted him on the shoulder saying, "Of course you can come, you are the official car minder as I don't suppose you want to scramble up the rocks?" "Well, the saints be praised; you must surely have read my mind!" Father Patrick said. We all knew how true that was.

We all got ready, searching amongst our things for black clothing, with Arthos completing the look by providing black hoods. This started us all laughing as I said, "I hope no one comes and sees us getting into the car, they'll think we are off to rob a bank", "Oh, heavenly mother of god, I've never in my life had so much excitement", cried Father Patrick as he put his collar on the chair. We now peered out of the door, no one was around so we all clambered into the car, Arthos and Ritchie in the front with Father Patrick and I in the back seats. Arthos was speaking low at Ritchie as we set off, turning to me he said, "Glen, I've alerted Bermantus in case we run into trouble and need back up." "Well let's hope that is not necessary", I replied. It was warm to say the least as we were all dressed in black, we opened the windows and chattered away. Father Patrick regaled us with tales of Irish legends and leprechauns. He said they either help people if they like them, or cause mischief to people they don't like. Arthos asked Father Patrick whether he had ever seen one of these little people, to which he replied, "I think I saw some in my garden one summer night when I was a child, I was looking out of the bedroom window, of course no one would believe me, but it is said that they often appear to children." He hesitated for a minute then said, "But now I've met wonderful people from another planet, and sworn to secrecy, and the big surprise is that they don't look like aliens, life is full of surprises it seems!" We all burst out laughing he was such a funny genial character to have around. We had turned off left onto the road which passed in front of Galtee mountains, we were now on the lookout for the little side road which was on the left. It seemed as though we had missed it as we kept on driving when suddenly Ritchie spotted it. "Well," said Father Patrick, "Whether you believe in prayers or not, I'll bless you all and pray for your safety." We thanked him, all getting out of the car except for Ritchie who had decided to turn the car round and park it next to a large boulder, so that it was more or less invisible being black like the boulder. Father Patrick perched himself on a flat rock overlooking the valley and being able to lean back against a large boulder, "Well my friends I've got myself comfortable, I'll keep a look out for the car, but tis with fear I wish you all the blessings of the angels." As we moved away, I had the feeling he would be saying his rosary, hopefully he hadn't sensed trouble and was just praying for us. We started up the rocks barely talking as Arthos said, "Save your breathe as you climb it saves energy, also stops our voices carrying to the wrong ears, we don't want the Galympites alerted." It was lovely weather warm with just a slight breeze. I felt a sense of amusement as I realised how funny we all looked dressed in black with hoods to complete the look. Obviously Arthos and Ritchie needed to cover their white hair but needed to look the same. We certainly blended in with the rocks and we seemed to make quite good progress towards Lough Maskry. On route as before we passed the large crevasses we had seen yesterday filled with water, which looked deep due to the rocks being black. Some were quite wide, and others just wide cracks. Near one I slipped and was grabbed by Ritchie, "Take care", he said, "We don't want to lose you", "Thanks", I replied quietly watching more carefully where I was putting my feet. A little further along, we were there by the side of the large expanse of the black watery Lough. Yes, no doubt in my mind it looked menacing. Looking at Arthos he nodded obviously he thought so too. We looked across the watery depths to where the large overhang of rock was situated. Suddenly we became aware that there seemed to be bubbles coming from below the watery depths. "Get down low", whispered Arthos, "Lie flat on the rocks we will hopefully blend with the area and not be noticed. I feel something is about to happen." No sooner had he spoken when from the Lough burst a silvery torpedo shaped object which shot straight upwards heading Skywise.

It then circled the Lough a couple of times; we hardly dare breathe in case our breath showed. My heart was pounding, as I lay on my stomach quite near the edge of the water, I hoped we weren't too close for our reflections to be mirrored in the water. Arthos half turned and said, "It seems to have gone, let's move over quickly and get behind that big rock over there." This was about three metres from us. We scrambled and made a quick rush to the big rock and crouched beside it. Fate was on our side as there certainly wasn't many rocks that were big enough for the three of us to hide beside. Ten minutes passed with nothing happening, we started contemplating what should be our next move, when back into vision came the torpedo shape again, circling the Lough a few times. Was it aware we were there I wondered, "I hope not", said Arthos reading my thoughts? Then as its circular form was passing the overhang projection it changed course and dived straight below the watery depths. "Right", said Arthos, "Come on we are going back to the car, I've enough to report and hopefully destroy the Galympites." We started down the side of the mountain side I was slightly in front of the others as they were busy talking and entering co-ordinates on their phones, when without warning I suddenly felt as if I was surrounded by a thick mist, but it happened in a flash. Then a sensation of spinning and twirling and my body seemed to be out of control as if in an overpowering force. Then the mist seemed to evaporate, and I was dropped about two metres onto a grassy bank, I was overcome with a peculiar fear of what had actually happened to me. Then as I took a look round, I saw that I was by the ruins of a castle and I was on my own.

13

I felt for my phone remembering too late that it was left in the car. I wondered where I was and how I must contact Botami quickly as the others would be looking for me. What had happened? Something I just couldn't understand! I hadn't fallen down a crevasse all I could think of was I was being swallowed by a thick mist and then landing here, but where was here? I slowly moved my ring round my finger saying, "Sorry Botami, it's me Glen, I need help. I've been picked up by a swirling mist and dropped by an old, ruined castle. I don't know where I am or where Arthos and Ritchie are." True to form Botami was gently speaking to me, "Glen, don't worry, firstly I'll let the others know you are safe, as they are frantic. Please look around and see if there are any signs or notices to tell you where you are, whilst I talk to the others. I believe that you have been whisked through a time tunnel. Let's hope it's only a short one." I started to feel safer but still wondered where I was. Although it seemed such a short time ago since we were altogether. I knew the ruins looked familiar and if they were that which I thought we had visited with Ritchie yesterday, that was impossible. As I walked over to the actual ruins, I noticed a sign, impossible I thought Carey's Castle. Oh! My god that was at least three and half hours from where we had all been, and it was less than fifteen minutes since I was with them. "Botami", I said moving my ring, "I'm at the ruins of Carey's castle", his voice answered, "Ok, I'll let them know, thank goodness it's not that you've been dropped in another country, it can happen." "Oh no", I said, "Ritchie bought us here two days ago, it's the other side of Clonmel." "Get yourself comfortable, just wait I'll let you know what is happening", "Thank you Botami." I said. I found a warm patch by some trees at the back of the ruins, way out of sight of the road. I would hate to have to explain why I was all in black, but I had taken off my hood to look less like a bank robber. What a situation I was in I had no money or identification on me, and I certainly hadn't got an Irish accent. Then Botami spoke again, it was all quite surreal, sitting on my own when a voice starts speaking to you, and your scenery is an old, ruined castle. "Glen are you listening?", "Yes", I replied, "Well in about ten minutes Inkas who is a very capable aero craft pilot is going to take a chance and drop down for you. I know it is dangerous, but he knows the place and will pick you up and transport you by air to an arranged place. He was in that area checking on the Galympites and although as I've said he's offered to take the chance although it's dangerous he said he's heard of you and as you are now one of us, he'll risk getting you back to Arthos and Ritchie", he said. "Oh, thank you", I said, "And please thank Inkas". A slight humming noise made me look up and a silver approximately five metre circular craft came down quite fast behind the ruins where I was sitting. I jumped up as the hatch opened, and rushed over to it as a voice said, "Quick Glen, I'm Inkas this operation is very dangerous so before we get spotted get in." I jumped in and strapped myself into the second seat. Inkas fastened a special helmet on my head, the hatch closed and sealed, and whoosh we were soaring up. What an amazing experience, but Inkas immediately said, "Wonderful to meet you Glen, as I said this is very dangerous, let's hope the power lords are on our side." Up into the clouds we shot and above them at such a speed that made me glow, not sure whether it was adrenalin or fear. Suddenly Inkas said, "Right this is where I could meet them, oh! No, I've been spotted by a Galympite craft, say nothing just trust me." We zoomed in one direction then we went down, then across the sky like a bolt, then I saw it. It was a torpedo shaped craft coming straight for us, but so accurately and at tremendous speed, Inkas turned the craft pressing some large buttons, and shooting upwards at the same time. Immediately a loud bang could be heard echoing all around, and what looked like a huge fire ball lit up the sky and was gone. "I must deliver you quick" said Inkas, "That one has gone forever, but they could send out re-enforcements." "Oh Inkas", I said, "That was amazing you are indeed a fantastic pilot and I'm so proud to have met you." Inkas smiled saying, "Likewise Glen, I'm so pleased to have met you too, many times I've heard your name mentioned."

I realised we had come down to earth. "Quick", said Inkas, "I must be off straight away, I'm in terrible danger on the ground." I jumped out releasing the helmet, shook his hand and the hatch closed and whoosh he was up and away. A voice said, "My god, I bet that was some experience", it was Arthos, Ritchie and Father Patrick standing by the car which was by the field where we landed. This was after the turn off from Galtee mountains. We all climbed into the car and I said, "I'm glad to see you all again, but what an experience. Firstly, being transported by some sort of black hole or time tunnel, then being picked up by Inkas in the aero craft. Being in the craft whilst Inkas obliterated another Galympite craft. Let's get home, that's enough excitement for one day." Father Patrick said, "Glen, I am so thankful you are safe, but I'm overjoyed to see an Astrotar aero craft actually land and take off, oh the saints be praised." We all agreed. It was wasn't too long before we arrived back at Ritchie's cottage. I had dozed on the journey, but no one commented, just smiled when the car stopped and I said, "Gosh that was quick", but Father Patrick couldn't resist saying, "Well after all that excitement you deserved a snooze, and I bet you could kill for a cup of tea or coffee?" He then added, "If you gentlemen excuse me, I'm going home for a while for a quick nap and a couple of whiskies to calm me down" We all laughed and he added, "I love your company and to be sure I hate saying this but I'm going to have a small meal and go to bed early, even though I hate missing anything. Can I see you all tomorrow?" We all agreed, and Ritchie said, "Now are you sure Father Patrick, you know you are welcome?", "Yes my dear friends", he replied, "But I'm getting old and mustn't push myself." Ritchie saw him into his cottage, backing up his fire for him, and checking he had enough for his dinner. We were standing by the door waiting for him to come back and open it, whilst hoping no one drove past and wondered about the black outfits. We decided to make a huge omelette between us, complete with a salad, not a lot of mess and quickly prepared. We had really had a full day, too much excitement and it wasn't long before we decided to retire to our beds and save ourselves for tomorrow. The next couple of days passed without incidents. We chopped logs and kindlers, and whilst we worked Father Patrick regaled us with many stories about the different places he'd been as a priest and some of funny stories and people he had encountered along the way.

The time passed quickly, we only stopped for some juice and coffee. I delivered the logs with Ritchie, whilst Arthos and Father Patrick drove into Clonmel to get some shopping. I was trying to spend as much time with Ritchie and help him as I knew my time was limited and soon, we would be moving on, and I really enjoyed his company. Ritchie interrupted my thoughts with, "Glen, I know what you are thinking, and I will really miss you when you and Arthos leave. It gets quite lonely at times, maybe you will both be able to come back again for a break after your next travels?", "I hope so", I said, "Can I ask you something Ritchie?", I added, "Of course", came the reply, "Well I have been left quite a lot of money and I never get a chance to spend it, can I pay for a few extra months for Father Patrick if you haven't got any bookings already?", I asked, "Do you think he'd like that?", said Ritchie. I answered, "I think he's retired and not very rich he would love it, and I'll pay for his stay as well. Please don't say no, I really like the old man and he seems to have no one else, maybe I could adopt him?" Ritchie laughed, "Well, I haven't advertised again so that will be fine, but are you sure?", Ritchie said. I smiled and said, "As Father Patrick would put it, to be sure, I'm sure!" When Father Patrick was told what we hoped he would like, he burst into tears and hugged us saying, "I was dreading leaving, so I'm glad the Holy Mother heard my prayers", he then turned to me saying, "But it's not fair on you to spend your money on me, I'm a stranger", "Oh no you're not", I said, "As long as Ritchie doesn't mind I'll keep paying for you, and you can make sure that you know you are one of the family, and look after Ritchie when he needs some extra company, and if he doesn't you can enjoy this lovely countryside". When Arthos heard about the arrangements he laughed and said, "The money Glen inherited is burning a hole in his pocket, but I think it's a great idea, how about you Ritchie?" "Marvellous" he answered. Arthos turned to me and said, "Glen, I'm afraid that your days here are going to be short lived, we are off the day after tomorrow to Cork airport and on our travel once more. The Great Astro has spoken, and it's been great, but we have jobs to do, and you have your books to write." "Don't worry Arthos, the latest experiences are noted" I said. Father Patrick turned to me and said, "Glen, I'll miss you I feel so attached to you and yet I've only known you for a short time and now to be sure I can't believe that I'm to stay longer, I'll let them know back in Tipperary that I've met up with a second cousin and I'm staying longer, and It'll keep them from worrying that I might have had an accident." "Well,", I said, "I'll settle up with Ritchie for ten weeks including those first days as well." "Ten weeks", he said, "Oh my god I'm dreaming." "No, you're not" I said, then added, "Will you have enough money for food?" "No trouble", said Father Patrick I have my pension and my cottage in Tipperary is mine, so I don't owe rent, oh my god I'm so happy", he then hugged us all.

    The next day I washed and dried some clothes ready for further expeditions into the unknown, I also took a drive with Arthos into Clonmel as I needed some shopping, I also bought some more meat from the cheeky butcher who recognised me and made a big fuss. That was for Ritchie, I then bought some cheese, bacon, eggs and bread for Father Patrick, plus a small bottle of whisky. Ritchie said, "I bought some pork chops for dinner tonight which I will put in the oven to cook slowly", I said, "I'll bring back some nice red wine." "That's great", he replied. I went to a couple of other shops and asked Arthos if he needed anything to which he replied, "No, Glen I've organised our tickets from Cork airport tomorrow afternoon, landing at Heathrow, stay a night at the airport and then our travels really start. I'll keep you in suspense till tomorrow", he laughed, "I know how curious you are, and you can't read my mind", he laughed again, what a tease.

The four of us spent an enjoyable evening, but both Father Patrick and Ritchie said they felt sad, though we still managed to have a good chat and laugh, until it was time to part our ways for the night.

In the morning it was time to leave, we all gave big hugs, with even Father Patrick joining in. "You feel more to me than family", he said then added, "Mind you, I haven't any family, so I'll adopt you three, if that is ok?" We all laughed and told him we would be honoured and that he was to remember us in his prayers. I found out from Ritchie with great difficulty how much he charged for a week's rent of the cottage. Eventually with a little nudge from Arthos who knew I was serious he told me €250 a week, so I said, "Ok, here's a cheque for €3000, now you can bank that, I'll ring the bank and advise them so there is no hold up, and I have put some stuff in your freezer to thank you for the work you have done for me." "Thanks" said Ritchie, "Please come back sometime." "We will", said Arthos, "But come on it 09:00 and we have to be at the airport", we piled into the car, bags on the back seat and we were off. I felt sad but hoped that Father Patrick and Ritchie would be ok, and that I hadn't given Ritchie any further problems having a guest for ten weeks." "That was very kind of you to pay for Father Patrick", Arthos said, "Tell me, why did you do it?" I thought for a moment and replied, "He helped a stranger on a bleak road without thinking, I could have been an evil person, but he asked me my name and said I'll let you stay overnight at my cottage. I feel that he has a big heart, and I was left that money by Sam Juste the editor, and it's extra to my needs so it was a lovely feeling to be able to help someone who was worthwhile." Arthos looked at me and just smiled. Arthos was studying the map when we arrived at Clonmel, checking which was the best route to the airport, and how long it was likely to take. Having worked everything out in his usual manner he started the engine again and we were once more on the move. Arthos turned to me and said, "We have a fair amount of travelling over the next couple of days, so if you doze off whilst I'm driving, I'll forgive you." I laughed and replied, "Anything is possible", and settled down in the seat wondering where we were off to, after Cork airport to Heathrow International London. Arthos liked to keep me guessing our final destination, and with that thought in my mind I noticed him smiling, he had read my mind again.

Suddenly I became aware of Arthos's voice in the distance, and realised the car had stopped, and we had arrived at Cork airport. As I woke up with help from Arthos, I thought to myself what a terrible travel companion I was falling asleep for the journey, "Yes", said Arthos laughing and reading my thoughts once again. "You would be late to your own funeral, but come on, could you get the bags out of the boot, and check the back seats for our packs and coats, whilst I settle up the hire car" It seemed no time at all and Arthos returned, "Come on", he said, "We're off on our travels again." We passed through the main entrance and passed many people, making our way first to Air France desk to show our tickets, passports and boarding passes whilst also handing in our duffel bags, having declared we had packed them ourselves, and that they didn't contain any forbidden items. Now it was onto the interrogation and security entrance. This consisted of the usual questions and taking off of our jackets, belts, shoes and watches, placing them into a basket, plus of course our backpacks, which all had to go through metal detector and x-ray. Once we had got all items back, Arthos said, "Well that's us ready for the first part of the journey to Charles De Gaulle international airport and onwards. Don't you wish you could read my mind?" He smiled mischievously to which I replied, "I'm improving in that direction Arthos, I have already got mountains in mind how about that?" "But which mountains?", Arthos asked, teasing me. "Well,", I said, "As long as there aren't any active volcanoes, I'll cope", to which he turned quickly and studied me, whilst I tried to blank him. He laughed and said, "Well done Glen, we'll make you into an Astrotar yet." We continued chatting as we made our way into the executive lounge, showing our boarding passes to gain entry. Picking up coffee and sandwiches, we made our way to a quiet corner where AF178 would be able to be seen on the flight screen. We realised we still had an hour and a half before taking off at 1930hrs, due to arrive in Paris at 2230hrs, that includes the time difference. We barely had time to finish our coffee before our gate number was showing. We wasted no time and made our way to the priority boarding, through the exit, across the tarmac to our waiting plane. We climbed up the stairs and were shown to our front business class seat, much more leg room, even though this was not a very long flight. "So", I said to Arthos, "Where to next?", "Oh have a drink Glen, and relax, because you have a long journey after this one." I really wished I could read minds and closed my eyes, but only for a second, as a charming young lady asked what I would like to drink. So, with a smile at Arthos I replied, "Oh, thank you, may I have a whisky one ice?", "Certainly sir", she answered and passed me a glass with a cube of ice and a miniature bottle of whisky. Now I could relax and did so for about an hour. Suddenly the curtain that was across the aisle parted, and a tall man with long hair and a beard pushed in shouting at the air hostess, "Where's my drink, I asked you for more", he added some foul language in his rant, "Sorry sir", she said, "I'm afraid you've had enough, you a very inebriated and so we cannot serve you more." He grabbed hold of her saying, "Do as I say bitch, get me another drink, or I'll hurt you and you'll be sorry." Quick as a flash Arthos was up and only seemed to touch him and the man dropped to the floor. I knew it was Arthos's taser, it looked just like a pen, but it worked like a charm, and was powerful. "Quickly miss", said Arthos, "Get me something to tie him up with to keep him immobile till we land." She quickly bought some straps and I helped Arthos tie the man up before he could come round, "Thank you so much sir", she said, "It's ok", said Arthos, "Don't let on to anyone, but I'm on a case, so it was fate I was here", The pilot popped his head out and said, "Thank you gentlemen, we'll be landing in about fifteen minutes, we've alerted the police to come aboard and take him off. Are you sure he is secure?", "Oh yes", said Arthos, he's strapped up and tied to a seat, as well as being drunk, he'll be there till we land." We were soon landed, the plane taxied into position, the stairs were connected, and the door opened. Immediately three police officers came on board and asked us to move over whilst they disentangled the tied up the drunk into hand cuffs, roughly took him, still only half conscious off the plane. The air hostess told them that it was Arthos who had been able to subdue him, and that he is undercover with the F.B.I; this information seemed to please the French police, they thanked Arthos and shook both our hands. A short conversation between them in French ensued and then they departed. We were allowed off first with some others from business class and thanked again Arthos for helping them. I noticed that people in the other part of the plane were all trying to push forward to disembark but were told to wait. After leaving the plane we walked across the tarmac towards an open sliding door where a security officer was making sure we all went the correct way. I was surprised by the sight of some parts of the outside of the Charles De Gaulle terminals, which gave a weird impression of huge stripes of white plastic in a slotted effect. I found out later that the building and faichers were totally cement and only designed to give that peculiar effect. All along the base was window and at higher level I noticed were viewing windows for people probably in the departure lounges. In actual fact other parts of the different terminals were completely different. The French police were very impressive and out in force. Everywhere you looked there were groups of them and unlike the British police they were armed. I jokingly whispered to Arthos, "Do you think they are expecting us?", "Shush", he whispered back, "They may be able to lip read or even read our minds." The queues were long, and I was wondering if we had enough time between flights, when Arthos suddenly said, "Yes", reading my thoughts, "Too much time actually."

At last, we were at passport control, showing them our passports and waiting whilst they scanned them, and double checked them. We then made our way through to the notice board to check which terminal we needed. Arthos then said, "We don't have to collect our bags, as we are booked right through, hopefully we will collect them at the destination." He hesitated for a moment, then said, "Mexico City international airport, so now you know", "Great", I said, "I was there many years ago, though I'm sure it has all changed since then. It was definitely some twenty years ago, now I'm showing my age!", I laughed. Surprisingly Arthos said, "Glen, what a coincidence I was there around the same time, and had some amazing adventures, as I'm sure I will tell you whilst on our travels." I felt excited, because deep down I knew it was dangerous in this part of the world, though the fact was danger found us wherever we went. Charles De Gaulle airport was massive and extremely complicated with its many terminals, and the need to travel from one to another, sometimes by a small bus, or internal train, it needed to be well studied. As I looked up, I noticed that the arched ceiling was also concrete and covered in rows of square lights. There were many shops, bars and cafes, with places to buy everything needed for travelling. All this time I was looking around watching the hundreds of travellers using the escalators which appeared to crisscross everywhere. Arthos was hell bent on getting us to the correct terminal before we could settle down. Eventually we reached our long-haul terminal and using the priority section entered the security to be put through the usual procedures which luckily this time went smoothly, passing through with ease. We checked the flight notice boards to see where we would be departing. It was now 2350hrs and our flight with Air France was not until 0625hrs. "No problem", said Arthos, "We will go to the international executive lounge and find a quiet corner, obviously making sure we get someone to wake us if we fall asleep, especially you Glen", he laughed because nowadays he knew me so well. The entrance door to the lounge was quite ordinary, but on opening found it was spacious on the inside and tastefully decorated. An official in uniform sat at the entrance desk, checked both our boarding passes and passports, speaking in very fast French to Arthos, who replied fluently, and we were ushered into the room. Arthos said, "I've advised that official at the desk our flight details, and said we are on an important mission and if asleep need to wake up at 0545hrs, and that I would make it worth his while to do so." We found a quiet corner where there were two sofa chairs, we decided to take it in turns to go for food and drink. Arthos went first, quickly returning with a chicken salad, coffee and fruit juice. I decided I would have the same as it was late for a heavy meal. When we had finished Arthos said, "Glen use your backpack as a pillow, putting your arm through the strap just in case someone decides to lighten our loads! Think what a nightmare that would be without passports and our Mexican visas etc.", "I agree", I said angling myself as Arthos had suggested, before long I was asleep. I awoke hearing voices to see Arthos talking to a tall important looking gentleman, immaculately dressed, and wearing dark glasses, holding a briefcase. Obviously, he was someone quite high up in Air Canada, as I noticed the badge on his jacket, I was wondering who he was. As I sat up Arthos said, "Glen, I would like you to meet a friend of mine. I haven't seen him for a long time, he spotted me when we came through security, but couldn't speak as he was busy, but was determined to find me." Whilst Arthos was talking I was listening but trying to see whether he was wearing a green triangular stoned gold ring but found this impossible as he was wearing black leather gloves. He looked straight at me and smiled saying, "Glen, my name is Mikel, and don't strain yourself, yes I have a ring like you." With that he took off a glove and held out the hand to me, then put his glove back on. Mikel then sat with us and started telling us how he had been with Air France for many years, transferring from London to Germany, then to Paris, and had unfortunately lost contact with Arthos. He said, "I always knew that one day our paths would cross, and we would meet again." They were very pleased to see each other, it never ceased to amaze me how magic the bonds were that these Astrotars had for each other. He told us how he had taken a couple of weeks holiday last year and stayed with Conrad in Berlin, another Astrotar who had lived near when he was working in Germany for a few years. "Actually", he said in his deep voice, "We were often talking about Arthos, as he has always been a leader and is quite wise, but don't let him hear me praising him!" We all laughed. I turned to Mikel and said, "The circle keeps getting bigger", "Not really", he said, "There are only about five hundred or so left of us, because of accidents but we all care deeply for each other. We are a loving kind people, not like our enemies the Galympites, which I'm sure you have already come across them Glen? Anyway, Arthos let me know when you are coming back and we can meet up for a couple of days, I can show you round Paris. I'll give you my special number actually", said Mikel stopping for minute, "I'll be called for my relive programme, how about you?" Immediately Arthos replied, "Mikel can't you tell how young I look? I'm just back from Bermantus". They laughed but Arthos did not leave me out saying, "Mikel, the Great Astro is trying to get permission to put glen through it, if they think his body and mind as an earthling could be able to cope. He has been accepted by the Great Astro and is our ambassador on earth writing our stories and history into books. He is an ex-journalist of renowned capabilities; we don't want to do anything to lose him." I felt tears in my eyes as I looked at them, such praise and friendship were unbelievable and they both gave me a hug. Mikel asked if we had already had our boarding passes to which Arthos replied, "Of course Mikel, we have to have business class, it's a twelve-hour journey we have to face, and the Great Astro is very generous with us all." "You are right Arthos", said Mikel, "He is wonderful to each and every Astrotar, a true leader amongst people how lucky we Astrotars really are!" At this point Mikel looked around saying, "Dear friends I must leave you, I have some high security jobs to authorise, and I sense that they are looking for me." He smiled, "Please keep in touch, and I'll look forward to seeing you both in the future. By the way there are many staff around, so be offended when I shake your hands, I have to treat my position with a lack of soft heartiness". Winking at us he left with a wave. Arthos laughed and said, "It's several years since I met up with Mikel, but he has never changed. He has two sides, a business side and a social one, you've just seen both." Arthos checked the board for flight times, and we said that it was only 0530hrs, so Arthos said, "Glen we still got nearly an hour till we fly, so I'll have a walk round and listen to others who are our travelling companions, do you fancy coming?" "Why not", I said, "We'll be sitting a long time when we are on the plane to Mexico." As we went to go out the door, I saw Arthos slip something to the official, and say something to him in French. They both nodded and smiled. Arthos hadn't forgotten his promise I thought. We walked towards the area of the terminal where the long-haul screens would show our gate number. "Arthos", I said, "What are we looking for, or rather are you listening or mind reading for, have you got a bad feeling, or had a tip off?" Arthos looked thoughtful and said, "I always go on gut instincts and Mikel told me we have reason to check security very carefully at present, for people that cause harm. Hopefully not on our flight, but he did say, "Anything overheard, or you get the vibes, to report immediately as we have that ability being Astrotars and able to mind read, and hear whispers from afar, if I hear anything, I will ring him." We wandered around and noticed group of three men sitting away from everyone, looking at laptop, definitely looking furtive. Arthos said, "let's go and sit down near them and pretend to doze, whilst we wait for our flight. Talking we walked to the window appearing to be looking at the planes. Arthos started to yawn, so I followed suit, "Come on", said Arthos, "Let's us go and set down." We went and sat nearby, but not too close to the group that would make them suspicious. We wrapped our arms through our backpacks and pretended to sleep. I could tell Arthos was concentrating. Ten minutes passed, I began to think Arthos was asleep, when he opened one eye, winked at me, so I kept my silence saying nothing.

Arthos suddenly said to me, "Glen, just going to the gent's bathroom, I'll be back in a minute", off he went. Five minutes later, I saw him walking at the far side of the departure lounge, gradually making his way back along the windows edge of the room, and facing outwards as if watching the planes, though I knew he was up to something. He then started walking nearer, but still at the windows edge and slightly passing the aisle where I was sitting, he then stopped again, still looking out. I was so curious but knew of old, that I must not move, but keep looking relaxed. A tannoy announcement asked several people by name to return to security. The three men in the next aisle of seats behind me got up and left departures to security, and I immediately saw Arthos coming towards me, "Ok?", I said, "What's going on?", Arthos replied, "Well I got to know a lot when I was sitting by you and concentrating on those three men behind us. Mikel had warned me earlier that there could be some trouble and he'd be grateful if I kept listening and reporting. He even said that there were three men travelling onto Mexico that were worth watching, so that is why I chose to sit where I did and tune into them. When I left you, I found Mikel and told him what I'd heard and what one the men were constantly running over in his mind, something about the hidden compartment in the case hoping that the plane would not be delayed, and everything would stay concealed. His manner was extremely anxious and was noticeably watching the flight board for the gate number to be called, I was watching him all the time, I was wandering around to deflect suspicion from us. Anyway, Mikel says that security now have returned all their luggage to security and they will not be on a flight but are being interrogated at the moment. I'll find out more later but must admit I am greatly relieved that they were stopped before they were trouble, and maybe more then we yet realise. As we were chatting about its Mikel came into the departure lounge and came straight over to us, saying, "Hello, thought I'd just come and say a big thank you and goodbye for the time being", then in a lower voice continued, "Thanks Arthos we found the panel, very well hidden. It had managed to pass through security, and it wasn't just drugs we were looking for, it had some weird devices that are being investigated that might have been controlled by them from the plane. Anyway, they won't bother you, for they won't be travelling for a long time, thanks to Astrotar intervention. So once again goodbye dear friend, I can't wait till I see you again, socially", and with a wave he was gone. Priority was called, so we made our way to the gate, showing our passports and boarding passes, then crossed the tarmac to the waiting plane. At the top of the stairs, we were shown to the business class seats. We settled in whilst the usual niceties were given. A warm flannel was passed to each person, to use to refresh our face and hands. I realised I was getting used to this type of travelling and pampering as Arthos' travelling companion in the fight against the Galympites.

Next, we were offered a drink; I had my usual whisky with ice. Arthos had a white wine, and we both settled back listening to the flight regulations being conveyed by the air hostess from Air Canada. I later learned her name was Natasha and that she was from Scotland. The male steward returned enquiring if I wished for another drink, which I declined much to the surprise of Arthos, especially as I ordered a coffee instead, in an attempt to stay awake for a while. I made Arthos laugh when I said my ability was to sleep and it was greater than my ability to stay awake. Arthos looked at me saying with a laugh, "How true." The take-off was extremely smooth. I watched the small screen in front of me showing us how far we had to travel, and as yet had hardly made an impression on the distance. For a while Arthos and I discussed the airport incident and commented on the fact that it must have always helped Mikel to get on in life with his Astrotar abilities. At this point Arthos said, "Glen, it has its good points, and its bad ones too. You always have to be careful not to bring suspicion on yourself or make enemies by being too clever, or even worse say things you shouldn't have known. People often wonder why we don't take girls out or is there a reason for this? If so, what is the reason? Well, we are not going to tell them, we have to adopt to situations by working hard, being members of men's clubs meeting up with other Astrotars, or in my case meeting with my friend Glen." I looked at him and said, "Thanks Arthos." We settled down putting our feet up, as we adjusted the chair into the bed chair, which was very comfortable. We were both given a blanket for extra warmth by the attractive air hostess Natasha. The lights were dimmed and relaxed into a welcome sleep after twenty-four hours awake. I was dreaming that I was at a fairground, I felt as though I was on a rollercoaster, extreme shaking about and that horrific feeling of dropping, then the sensation of climbing quickly again. I opened my eyes and realised we were passing through a storm, then the realisation oh my god I'm in a plane. I looked at Arthos who said, "Well I thought even you wouldn't sleep through this, I hope the galactic power lords are looking after us, this truly must be a nightmare to fly this plane through this." I pulled up the blind and was looking out at the blackest of clouds that we seemed to be attempting to rise above, but the turbulence was still very unnerving. An announcement from the pilot followed, "This is your pilot Captain Edwards, sorry about the bumpy flight, hopefully the atmosphere pressure and turbulence seem to be calming down a little. We are now flying much higher to avoid the severest part of the storm, hopefully we will be able to descend to a lower altitude shortly. If anyone feels sick of faint, and feel you may need some oxygen, you will find the oxygen masks above your seats, the cabin crew will assist you if you need assistance."

  I was looking out at the clouds and the horrific blackness below us, when suddenly a flash of silver seemed to shoot past my window, "I saw something silvery shoot past my window", I said to Arthos, "Well if you did", he said, "I sincerely hope it's one of ours", he hesitated and continued, "Or let's hope it's your imagination playing tricks on your eyes." We both kept looking, then a man on the seat in front on the opposite side of the aisle, who was also watching the storm shouted, "Good god, did you see that? I'm sure I've just seen a flying saucer, it was going too fast to be a plane, anyway it was too close for that. I'm in the British Airforce, so I'm not idiot with an overzealous imagination. Did anyone else see it or anything strange?" Arthos turned and leaned forward saying, "I actually thought I saw something, but maybe it was the rays from the sun playing tricks it was just a quick flash." The male steward who we learned was called Scott came and asked if there was a problem, the man turned to him and related what he had seen, then directly pointing at Arthos said, "Even that man thought he'd seen something." The steward went and used the phone that was connected to the cockpit and spoke to the pilot saying what had been said. Scott then came back and told us what the pilot had said that he had not seen anything, but both navigators and he would be more alert. He finished with, "The pilot is sure that it was only lightening reacting with the clouds." Arthos looked at me and whispered, "If it is one of ours, I mean an Astrotar spacecraft, perhaps Mikel has alerted base for someone to keep an eye on our plane in case we have any problems with the Galympites and with the raging storm, or maybe it's purely a coincidence that one of our crafts is on a seek and destroy mission against the Galympites and was flying higher to avoid the storm. Their extraordinary speed which is not only anti-gravity propulsion but even more advanced, would be so fast we would only see a quick flash of silver as it passed, and maybe even circled us." It was at this point the pilots voice came over the tannoy, "This is the captain David Edwards your pilot speaking. Just to let you know that we have now descended to a lower altitude as the storm appears to have abated, I hope you can now feel a bit more relaxed. The cabin staff will bring around some food and drink shortly, so please try and relax and enjoy the remainder of the flight." I turned to Arthos and said, "God I'm starving and thirsty, I could eat a horse!". Arthos laughed at me saying, "I think you are out of luck; they aren't serving up any horses!" The air hostess asked us if we were ready to eat, I think she thought us both mad when we both burst out laughing. "Sorry", we apologised we were just talking about something and didn't mean to be rude. Within minutes our meals on trays were served up, with a couple of small bottles of champagne. "Glen", Arthos said, "You took over very well with your quick explanation when we both burst out laughing, we certainly didn't want her to think we were rude. We are definitely equaling out", "Thanks", I said for it was indeed unexpected praise. The rest of the journey was uneventful, I read some of the magazines that were provided, had a couple of coffees, and a walk to stretch my legs. During the flight Arthos had spent about an hour and a half telling me tales of Mexico and the history of the people. How there were many places where we would be alright, but other places which could prove dangerous. It was 18:00hrs I noticed on the screen in front of me and as I did, we were advised over the tannoy by the pilot that we were now about twenty minutes from landing at Mexico City International Airport, and that we would find the weather was very warm, about 37°C and dry. So, this was it the point I didn't enjoy, we were descending, engines were roaring as they went into backward thrust, to slow the plane down. We made several bumps as we landed, then we were heading to our allocated position at the terminal. As we disembarked, we felt the heat it was hot and only late afternoon. As we passed through the terminal, and security where there was a large presence of police and army, we got to control where the official spoke to Arthos in Spanish, who told him I was his secretary but couldn't speak Spanish. After long hard looks at both us and our documents he stamped our visas and waved us through. After collecting our bags, we started towards the exit door, there were two officials in front of us, both very tall, and barring our way. With a Mexican accent and looking at Arthos one said, "We were awaiting you; we were told you were on this flight."

14

Arthos looked at them and said sharply, "What's your problem?", then he suddenly leaned forward and burst out laughing, I thought we had got ourselves in trouble. Then one of the men said, "So we caught you out, I thought you would be too astute, you must be tired." Arthos turned to me and said, "Glen, guess what? Mikel put them up to this I bet. I'll introduce you. This is my special friend Glen, and these two 'hit' men or so they pretend to be are Luis and Ramos, and yes are Astrotars, but I think they dye their hair", we all laughed, Ramos saying, "Mikel rang us and told us all about you, and said that Glen was a good sport, so please forgive the joke", "Of course", I said. They told us how they had been helping out Mikel as temporary security, and he had employed them on occasions. They told us they were semi-retired but had been involved working for the F.B.I in the past, which then got them the jobs. I told them that I had been warned there could trouble in Mexico, and I thought not already, as I pointed out my disadvantage of not being able to mind read. "We will teach you", said Luis. We went outside as Arthos had intended to hire a car, but the men said, "No need we have our car waiting outside, and if you aren't in a hurry like Mikel said, we have decided you are staying with us for a couple of days, for a catch up." We all climbed into their car, I was still in a state of shock and thought to myself, wait till I next see Mikel! Arthos and I were in the back, Ramos half turned in his seat to talk to us saying, "Arthos did you really not recognise us? The dyed hair was our blending disguise. Out here you really have difficulty blending in with blonde hair and blue eyes. We've been here over four years now taking over from Gustaf and Lantos, who have moved on to Peru. There have been many sightings over the Pacific, I guess that is where you and Glen are heading too? Do you realise how dangerous it is by car taking a journey from Mexico City to the Pacific, and how long it will take, what is the name of your destination?" Arthos replied, "Well, I'll have to check but area maybe around Volcan Orizaba has been studied and onwards that mountainous area of Balsas and Oaxaca, following the route through Sierra Madre Del Sur.", "Are you mad?" said Luis that area has many groups of bandits and other dangers, I'm sure there is a safer route to the Pacific. We'll discuss it later, but you are coming back to our part of Mexico City and staying with us for a couple of days, is that ok with you?", "Fine", said Arthos, "Have we any choice?", "No", said Ramos laughing, "It's wonderful to see you again." As we were driving to where Ramos and Luis lived, they were pointing out different things and places to us, showing us how the ancient historical remnants of Mexico City and the modern and popular parts are all cross sectioned, by the massive Mexico City metro, which is daily used by hordes of people, not only working there, but enjoying restaurants and infectious Spanish and Mexican music and culture. Records show population at approximately twenty-one million people and is considered one of the most desirable cities in the world to visit. There have been many rebellions and outbursts but still continues to be a great and diverse place, and financially rich. I was fascinated with Ramos's information as this was always good for my books. I had been totally absorbed in his excellent relating ability of Mexican information. Time flies when you are talking and listening in the company of extremely knowledgeable and interesting people. The car pulled up. "We're here", said Luis, "We have two flats next to one another, both have two bedrooms so enough room for the four of us." They were both on the ground floor, front doors next to one another, they were smart in appearance, the stonework of the buildings was a pleasant mixture of old and new, blended together. We went into Luis's flat first, he said, "Glen you can stay with me, is that ok with you? Arthos and Ramos have not seen each other for years and they have been friends for a long time." Immediately Arthos gave him a fake smack and said, "Well respect your elders then!", then turned to me and said, "Don't believe all you hear Glen, I told you that we have to stand much teasing from each other, but the banter is all fun, no doubt you will come in for plenty?" Arthos went net door with Ramos, whilst Luis showed me my room, which was extremely comfortable and spacious. "Thank you, Luis", I said, "This is really lovely and most kind of you." "Well,", said Luis, "I'm going to put on some coffee, and change as the dark suit was only to meet you both and pretend you were in trouble!" "It worked", I laughed. Ramos and Arthos were soon back, and we all enjoyed the coffee. It was decided as it was late, we should hurry and get ready and go for a meal. The restaurant was busy, but as Ramos and Luis appeared to be regulars, we managed to get a table for four in a quiet corner of a large dining room. Wine was ordered, and steaks with all the trimmings was ordered by us all. We chatted for a short while, then the meals we served, "If they taste as good as they look, then I'll enjoy every mouthful", I said. We arrived back at the flats just before midnight, I said, "Will you three please forgive me, as I who's only semi-Astrotar needs some sleep! I'll see you all in the morning, if someone could be so kind as to wake me", it was agreed, so I went to my room and straight to bed and asleep.

After being woken up for a late breakfast, everyone else had already eaten, I apologised for sleeping in, then poured another coffee. Arthos started talking, saying, "Let's get out the map and check exactly how and where we are going to be making for when Glen and I set off on our mission." "Well,", said Ramos, "I personally think your best option because of the distance from here to the coast, is to fly to Oaxaca airport. Then if you must take the main road through Sierra Madre Del Sur mountains to the Pacific coast." He then added, "Sorry Arthos, but you are mad because there are bandits, different groups and you are only two against many, especially as it is possible to fly from Mexico City to Oaxaca airport, then onto a Pacific coast airport, there are plenty of them." Luis then spoke, saying, "Arthos, you know from old that life can be hostile around the mountainous regions, we don't want anything to happen to you both. Please is there a real reason or are just being stubborn?" Whilst they were talking, I was becoming more and more worried about the journey, "Stop worrying, Glen", said Luis, "You'll be safe with Arthos, he has more tricks up his sleeve, more than you can ever imagine, all to do with survival, he has gained over the years." The map was spread out and the conversation was like a geography lesson about this area, then that area, my mind was buzzing. In the end Luis, said, "Right my friends, it's coffee time" and went off to make it, whilst Ramos was busy coping the route into a notebook, whilst quietly studying the map, "Right", he said, "I think I have worked out a suitable plan, we can change it if you don't like it." We gathered round and he started, "Mexico airport to Oaxaca De Juarez airport by plane obviously, it's about an hour's flight and cost around £60 per person for a return flight.

Then Oaxaca airport by hire car to Puerta Escondido which is around 160 miles, should take about six hours if you're lucky. It is a very lonely route and passes through part of Sierra Madre Del Sur mountains which could involve coming across some Mexican bandits, who are not to be messed with. According from what I have heard they can give travellers a hard time.", "Well", said Arthos, "No problem, in the past I had a very good relationship with a senior bandit and his family, I shall check and see if he is still their leader. His name was Senor Rodrico" "What connection did you have with him?", asked Ramos, "I'll tell you all the story tonight, I've even got a number for him if it still works.", said Arthos and that was the end of the matter, it was temporally closed. Who doesn't he know I thought and even though it was only a thought, Arthos looked at me and smiled, I guess he'd read my thoughts again? Arthos leaned over Ramos's shoulder looking at the map, and tracing down from Oaxaca De Juarez airport and started reeling of the names, "We pass Monte Albany on the right on this main road to Ejutia de Crespo following the same red road for about half way to San Pedro Pochutla airport, turning off to the left down the smaller blue road through the Sierra Madre Del Sun mountains to Santiago Jamiltepec turning onto the red main road again to Puerto Escondido where we will stay for a couple of days. I think the main red road is the federal highway 200." "Why chose that route?" said Luis joining in the scrutiny of the map, "Knowing Arthos", said Ramos, "He's obviously got something up his sleeve, hope it's a good thing not a scorpion, and you don't get stung." "I hope not as well", I said, but added, "I have never known Arthos to put a foot wrong yet." Ramos laughed saying, "Glen always a first time." We all had another coffee washed up and went out to the car, as Arthos and I were being taken for a short Mexican City sightseeing tour, then out for a meal. As we got into the car, I thought how wonderful and how different all these Astrotars were, yes, I thought they are all different but all kind friendly and wonderful to know, "Thanks" came an Astrotar chorus, Oh! I thought, caught out again with them reading my thoughts, I smiled at my mentors and said, "Well my friends I'm going to have to learn how to block my thought and torment you." This actually caused a chorus of laughter. When we set off, the car was warm, I had my notepad ready to write down specific things to add to my book notes. It isn't always easy to remember names afterwards, and points of interests always made books more factual and believable. They pointed out to me the National Palace Government building which holds national archives and is home to the Federal Treasury. The walls inside are decorated so I was told with murals by Diego Rivera, telling Mexican history thousands of years. Then there was the Cathedral Metropolitan which was enormous and had taken over two hundred and fifty years to build taking many mixed architectural styles in the process of its completion. Then Ramos started talking, taking over from Luis by saying, "Mexico City's main square is apparently the longest in the world, and is a huge expanse of paved area with a large Mexican flag depicted in the centre. As this is the very heart of Mexico City, it is where many festivals and events take place, not forgetting protests. There are many clubs of different types of restaurants and bars, some quite chic, and others more crowded extremely noisy, and is not for the faint hearted. I'm still trying to work that out", Luis interrupted suddenly added more information for me. "Glen, this is Zocalo one of the largest plazas in the world. It was used by the Aztecs for religious and spiritual ceremonies. Shortly we will show you the Imperial Residence in Mexico City, called Chapultepec Castle. This huge park, castle and museum is one of Mexico City's most scenic and beautiful places and was treated as sacred by the Aztecs who used to live there." As Luis stopped talking, Arthos said, "Well you two, I'm well impressed and I'm sure Glen must be as well. Have you two ever thought of becoming city guides, or does the security employment keep you too busy?" "Anyway, let's park up somewhere, and see if we can get an early evening meal. I don't know about you three but I'm starving." We all agreed and, on the way, back to the flats we came to a lovely hotel set back from the road called, 'El Magnifico'. So, without delay we parked up, climbed out and went in. Arthos asked the doorman in Spanish, whether we were too early, he waved us through into the hotel with a smile. I asked Arthos what had been said, the doorman quickly looked at me saying, "Oh you wanta me aspoke Ingleesh?" Ramos immediately said, "We all speak both Spanish and English, so it's fine with us." Pointing he said, "Oh! And that gentleman is deaf that is why we asked" and winked at me. We entered the dining room, which was extremely comfortable with a Spanish décor, though I did notice the mixture of Mexican history about the room. We were surprised to see that several people were already eating as we were shown to a corner table for four by a large window which looked out into a beautiful garden. When we were all seated, we were handed the menus, in a short time we all decided to order the lamb specialty with Mexican salad, new potatoes and garlic bread and two large bottles of the local red wine. The meal was excellent, and the conversation turned to Arthos's meeting years before with a bandit chief, though he kept us all in suspense saying, "I'll tell you the story when we get back to the house, you never know who is listening." We were soon finished and ready to head back home. The being paid and thanks given in Spanish we left; I was once again amazed at how many languages Arthos could speak fluently.

    We arrived back at the flats ready to enjoy the rest of the evening together and hopefully finishing our arrangements for getting to the Pacific coast. We all gathered in Luis's lounge as it was the bigger of the two for all of us to seat comfortably, Luis bought out two large bottles of wine with four large goblets, which when filled he passed round. "Well,", said Ramos, "I presume Arthos you won't keep us waiting with bated breath to learn about your meeting with the bandit chief, who you told me was called Chico Ramirez, so how long ago was this?" "Yes, his name was Chico Ramirez, and it must have been around twenty years ago now", said Arthos and continued, "I was travelling from Mexico City airport to the coast, using connecting flights, changing at Oaxaca De Juarez then catching another plane to either Salina Cruz or Puerto Escondido. I was travelling with Gintas an Astrotar friend who actually lives in Rome these days. I'm sure Ramos you've met him, or maybe you Luis?" "Yes", said Luis, "I met him about two years ago in Bermantus when I was there." "Anyway, as I was saying", continued Arthos, "We decided to hire a car and finish the journey from Oaxaca airport by road rather than wait a day, as when we arrived on the plane from Mexico City the planes had been cancelled, till the next day at Oaxaca. The hired car was the only option available; it was a rather beaten-up VW Beetle." Arthos shook his head, "What a fool I was, all I needed to do was wait till the next day and get a flight, but I thought I knew best and Gintas being a good friend trusted me. We set off taking the less important red road on the maps which we thought would be more interesting, although it was hilly and twisty going through the forest of pine and oak trees and hoped that this would be quicker although quite lonely to follow our route towards Ejutlade De Crespo which appeared to be one hundred miles. In some parts it was thick forest on each side of this extremely twisty road. The weather was similar to now, sunny and warm, but as we were driving along, we noticed we seemed to be the only ones travelling along the route, and wondered whether I had chosen wisely, but because we were Astrotars so I thought no problem, we will be fine." He grimaced and continued, "We passed a few shacks and small holdings which no one seemed to be inhabiting. It was a mountainous terrain, then the area would open up, but it was still craggy. I seemed to be driving for ever when it suddenly started getting dark, and the rain came down, heavy wasn't the word for it, there was thunder and lightning, so we pulled into the side in an area with large boulders that gave us some shelter. Eventually the storm seemed to abate, so we set off again. I remember Gintas saying, Arthos do you think we should have taken the main road? I told him that it was much longer, and we would soon be at Ejutia de Crespo where we could grab a coffee and something to eat." "About an hour later we arrived, the town was not that big just a few houses, a general store, a garage and a shanty type hotel. We pulled up outside and felt a little wheezy, as it had a very strange name, translated it was, 'The dead stop'. We pushed open the door and walked in, there were several people sitting just inside, the place then went silent as we approached the bar, luckily quite near the door. The bar man had a typical Mexican look as depicted in the movies, with a thick bushy moustache and very dark eyes, with a rather unfriendly face. He looked at me and said, 'Hey Amigo ye wanna drink? Where yer going?' I said, "Yes drinks would be good." He replied, "You wanna tequila amigo?" Before I could answer he passed three, and drank one himself and said, 'You pay me?' He charged me enough for about four, I didn't argue I realised it was a rather hostile atmosphere, and ten minutes was long enough especially as others around that bar seemed edgy and I was getting rather aggressive thoughts coming from some of them. Having already paid I put down a few notes on the bar and said give these amigos a drink from us travellers, and we left quickly. We jumped into the car and we were off, Gintas said to me, 'Arthos I felt we were in for trouble, how about you?' I told him I agreed that was why I left some extra money for them to have a drink, and whilst they argued over it, we could get away, to which Gintas thoroughly agreed was the best thing." Arthos stopped and said, "Any chance of a drink, I'm parched", "Yes", said Ramos, "I'll nip next door, I've got plenty and can always replenish it tomorrow". Within five minutes he was back. Drinks were poured and like three children listening to a bedtime story, we asked Arthos to continue. "Well, my friends", he began, "We drove as fast as we dared through the twisty road which was passing through parts of Sierra Madre Del Sur mountains and the forests that surrounded as we made our way through to San Pedro Dochutla. We drove, mile after mile, having to stop about five miles outside of Etutlook De Crespo, as we were almost out of petrol. Fortunately, I had packed a five gallon can of petrol in case we needed to refill on route away from civilisation. We filled up as quick as possible as we were worried, that we were being followed, then off we went through heavy showers and difficult terrain, but we never saw any traffic coming from the other direction. Suddenly after about an hour the car started making some weird noises and finally cut out. I maybe many things, but a mechanic is not of them, so Gintas said to me, 'I'll have a look', opening the bonnet we saw steam coming out from the engine, and he said that radiator was empty and needed water, but we would have to wait for it to cool down first. We closed the bonnet and waited. It must have been around twenty minutes or so before we thought of where we could get some water, and that we had better check the car to see if it had stopped steaming. Then from around a bend in the road came several men all on horseback looking very fierce and dressed in mostly black wearing Mexican style hats, most had moustaches and beards. All of them had guns slung around their shoulders. I noticed that one of the horses had two men on it, one of which looked injured or ill. The men were shouting in a mixture of Spanish and Mexican, who were we. I jumped out of the car and said we were travelling to the coast, but our car had broken down. The man doing most of the speaking was youngish and said that his father was ill and pointed to the second man on the other horse being held on by another man. Having over the years learnt much about medicine, I asked if I could help as I was a doctor. The man said, "Why yer wanna helpa me? We are bandits, people are scared of us" I told him that we weren't scared and only wanted to help and my name was Doctor Arthos, then asked him his name. He told me that he was Chico Ramirez son of the ill man, who my brother Enrico is holding on the horse, he then asked me to help them. They put the sick man in the car, I could see instantly that he was very ill, quickly I told them my car needs water, immediately one of the men dismounted and opened the bonnet, then from a bag he poured water into the radiator. I tried the engine, which after a couple of splutters started again. Chico said to me, "Yer not able to turna yer car rounda, yer justa follow me" All the men on horseback started turning around, one of them stayed behind us. Suddenly we came to a turn off almost hidden, if we hadn't been with the men, we would have missed it. We followed up a mountain path, potholes and stones, not great for driving on, but somehow, we managed it. The path was windy and steep, but suddenly on a bend we came to a clearing hidden from view by trees, here there were three houses, Chico jumped off his horse, he and his brother Enrico carried their father out of the car, telling us to follow them. Gintas and I went into the house behind them and found it very pleasant inside, not luxurious but homely and clean. There was a downstairs bedroom, I asked them to put their father on the bed and leave Gintas who was my assistant and to help his father. They looked very wary, I knew time was of the essence, I took out of my wallet a fake ID like my F.B.I one I had used earlier, this ID showed I was Doctor Arthos Grant. They were happy with this and left us, I asked the great power lords to help us. I took out some small tablets I carry for emergencies like this, which was given to me by

Xedato the doctor Astrotar at Bermantus. I put one on his tongue, as by now he was only semi-conscious, I started putting my hands on his head saying to Gintas to concentrate on his heart improving, I'll pull him back, we worked nonstop. I had loosened his shirt and was rhythmically pressing on his chest and then putting pressure on his head, mind controlling him back. Slowly he opened his eyes and said in a whisper, "I have been to strange place, and seen people I know, that are gone. I think I died, and you saved my life. Who are you?" I told him not to talk for a while, and just to breathe deeply. It had been a success I was relieved, because he was a human and my Astrotar methods might not have worked on him, but thankfully they had. I think the power lords of the galaxy were with us. We called Chico in and told him that his father was back with us, we have been lucky as we nearly lost him, he was unconscious when we started, and he really must have lots of rest. I told them he had suffered a heart attack, and if we hadn't of met, he would have died. We told Chico that we were happy to help, and that now we would leave them in peace. He answered immediately telling us that we must stay with them and eat with the family, leaving in the morning. We are bandits and were taking my father to that village you passed through, but because we are not welcome there, we would have to threaten them to save him, but I fear it would have been too late. I agreed with him and said it was fate that we chose to take the minor red road. It must have been written in the stars said Chico, he gave us both a hug which amazed us, as he was fierce in appearance and said that if we were ever stopped by bandits tell them you are part of the family of Chico and Enrico sons of Rodrico Ramirez, and you will always be safe. Chico continued that it was fate that his father was taken ill, and we had broken down, or we might never had met on the road, and we could have been robbed or taken prisoners and asked the government for ransom money. He then started laughing heartily saying that he was only joking, and they weren't that bad, only perhaps firstly a few cows, and surviving by any means we can. He said that the bad people were the drug lords, but we don't mix with them, we just live in the mountains. Chico took us upstairs, I was amazed to be shown several small bedrooms, with a wave of his hand, issued us each one. Someone bought in our bags from the car and told us Juanito was Chico's cousin, and a good mechanic who was looking at our car so we wouldn't have any more trouble. We were told as soon as we were ready, we could go down for something to eat, to which we glad as we hadn't eaten for a long while. We hurriedly went down the wooden staircase and noticed that there were two places obviously left for us, we were told to join them. I noticed that there were two Mexican ladies one young, and an older lady obviously the mother, both were serving out huge plates of a stew type meal consisting of meat, vegetables, and potatoes in gravy. It tasted as good as it smelt. We were all given big mugs of homemade wine, which was strong but thank goodness it was drinkable as we wouldn't want to have left it. Someone started playing a guitar and started singing, even the women joined in playing the castanets. It really was most entertaining, and I felt I was dreaming as it was after one in the morning when we went to bed, but what a night it had been.

    Next morning, we rose early, but our hosts were all up and on the go. I counted the people, there were about ten men, and three women, with others floating about. They told us that there were many bandits in parts of the Sierra Madre Del Sur mountains, but they all followed one code of honour, if you were accepted by one group, then the other groups would allow safe passage without any harm coming to you. We were given breakfast and as we were saying our farewells Chico said, "Mea padre yer musta see my father before yer go." I was surprised to see him sitting in bed drinking coffee, looking remarkably well considering he had been at deaths door the night before. He addressed me saying in pretty good English that having saved his life he was in my debt, and if I ever needed help or his families help, no matter the danger, to find a way to contact us, he then gave me a secret telephone number and a small picture of a steer with a weird brand on it and told me this was his mark, and may we always keep safe and maybe one day you will come back to see us. We shook hands, and we returned down the mountain path back to the road. With renewed energy and a feeling of sheer disbelief and excitement we drove for the next two hours passing through a small town called San Pedro Dochutla and with no need to stop after all the hospitality we had received, we kept on driving. As we came to the end of the town and down more twisty roads, we came upon a group of men mounted on horseback tucked into the trees, on the side of the road wearing exactly the same outfits you would expect bandits to be wearing. I stopped the car and called out to one of them who happened to be the nearest, as to if there was a problem ahead. He replied that there was and that his cousin Chico had called him and asked him to look after us, as were family friends. Apparently, there had been a rock fall and the road was blocked. After the man checked to see I was doctor Arthos, and I had shown him the steer picture that Rodrico Lopez had given me, we were told to follow the men, and they would show us a way round. Just a short way down the road they took us off the road onto a track type road through the mountains. It was quite a road, some parts were steep, the car shuddered but managed to keep going, it was also full of potholes making it difficult to drive along, but the men kept waiting for us. One part was very intimidating as there was a sheer drop on the side, I was glad when we had passed it without trouble. We drove for about an hour following the men, until we came to the main road again, they gathered round the car and one got off his horse, so I opened my door and held out my hand. I told him I was very grateful to which he replied that he was the younger brother of Rodrico's Ramirez's wife and he was Pedro Lopez. I then slipped some money in his hands, and again said how grateful I was, he smiled and wished us all the best for the travel. With a wave of his hand, he mounted his horse, then many gravelly voices shouted, 'Adios amigos' fired their guns into the air, then they were gone.

    It wasn't long before we realised that the diversion had taken a huge part off our journey and we were now on the main Federal road F200 to Puerto Escondido. The miles were so much easier now and the car was running like a dream after Chico's cousin had worked on it. When we arrived in Puerto Escondido we made for a large hotel. We parked up and entered the hotel and managed to book two rooms, that my friends, was my story of meeting the bandits," "Now I am exhausted, and as it's nearly midnight I think we should call it a night", said Arthos to us. Arthos then turned round and said, "We'll stay tomorrow if we may? Then we can make all the arrangements for travelling the following day." We said goodnight to Ramos and Arthos who went next door, then Luis and I cleared up and retired to our rooms. I couldn't help wondering if we would come across Chico on our travels, I then settled down to sleep. We spent the next day out and about seeing local Mexican architecture, having a walk round a large shopping mall, and buying a few odds and ends that I had long run out of, as I hadn't been able to get to London for a long while. We chattered and listening to stories of Mexican history. I certainly enjoyed seeing and mixing with so many different nationalities and colourful characters that we encountered each time we got out of the car to look around. We eventually made for Mexican City airport where we parked the car, and all went inside. Ramos, Luis, and I whilst waiting for Arthos went and found us a coffee bar and ordered. It was just up my street, people watching, or in other words watching the world pass by hearing different languages and seeing many colourful attires. I have always studied people and find that while you can almost always work out what their nationality is by their different outfits and voices. Ramos bought my attention back saying, "Are you still with us Glen?", I apologised and told them, "I'm sorry I was born nosey, that's why I became a reporter then a world correspondent." Ramos and Luis were both worried about how we would both cope with this journey that Arthos and I were about to undertake. Mexico City to Oaxaca De Juarez then to follow in the footsteps of Arthos and Gintas twenty years before. Thinking about it I became a little apprehensive of the unexpected encounters I might have to face. I turned to Ramos and Luis and asked them if they were actually working in Mexico City, to which they told me they had two jobs, one being taxi drivers, which was their main occupation but occasionally helping as part time airport security. They explained that coincidently prior to hearing we were coming they had decided to take a couple of weeks at least off from work, as they had been busy with some Mexican festivals so actually it had worked out great all round. I thoroughly enjoyed my coffee and noticed that Arthos was on his way back to us. He sat down saying, "I've had an idea", both Ramos and Luis answered, "We know" at the same time. Ramos followed up with, "Have you checked Arthos, with the Great Astro", "Yes", said Arthos, I listened and interrupted with, "Excuse me my friends, but I am in the dark, remember I can't mind read, what's going on?", "Well", said Arthos, "I thought that all four of us could travel to Puerto Escondido and spend some time together, whilst checking out the Galympites sightings. Then we could return to Mexico City and you and I, Glen return to London for a short time at least. It would be extra sensible to have a decent exploration of the areas, as many flying objects have been sighted from the coast, flying about, and in many cases diving into the Pacific Ocean, by many people and notably recorded as such. Maybe we are lucky and spot one of their bases, and once again be lucky in helping to destroy it." "We are one hundred per cent in agreement", Ramos said, "So that's agreed?", said Arthos finishing his coffee. "I better get back to organising another two tickets." I looked at the others and said, "See I'm always at a disadvantage, you two knew immediately what he was thinking, anyway I'm absolutely thrilled, because I've now got three watching my back and hearing my cries for help", they started laughing. Arthos was soon back saying, "Well we had better get back to our flats, as we've got to be back here by 08:00 in the morning, and I'm sure you've both got arrangements to do before we leave? Plus, a little packing. We've just got a duffel bag and a backpack each, that's all you'll need, basics. On the way home I'll buy us a Chinese banquet meal, so we won't have to wash up afterwards." "Marvellous idea", said Luis, "It's ages since I had Chinese food." We wasted no time, picked up our meal which we ordered over the phone, and soon we were back at the flats devouring the meal in a very short time. It was then time for them to do the packing, which was done quickly, then advising friendly neighbours and asking them to keep an eye on the flats whilst away. Arthos and I just sat with a coffee whilst Ramos and Luis completed their chaotic fast sort out of jobs for a safe leaving. Suddenly Ramos appeared saying, "Everything is complete, we are both done so now for some sleep, as tomorrow we must be fit and able to follow Arthos's directions and may the great power lords of the galaxy universe be with us. It was just 05:30 when I heard a knock, time to get up. It was in my usual dazed way that I got myself up and dressed, shaved, and packed and downstairs for toast and coffee. Everything was checked before leaving in both flats, and as they locked up, both Ramos and Luis said, "Well here's to our future adventures", I had a feeling of apprehension once again. We left for our travels, this time there were four of us, and arriving at Mexico City airport, we parked the car in a long stay park. As we entered the airport, I noticed it was exactly 08:30, so we prepared for the usual checks involved in booking in, as usual it was rather unnerving with all the armed security and police personnel walking around.

Ramos whispered, "Who told them we were coming?", Arthos immediately said, "Be careful your voice could easily be overheard, then we would be trouble.", "Okay boss!", replied Ramos and we all had a smile at him as he wasn't wrong. Arthos was definitely in charge as usual and had over the years earned that respect from everyone. He looked at me and smiled, he'd been reading my mind yet again. Our flight was due to depart at 09:50, it was just an hour's flight to Oaxaca De Juarez then to face that long road trip. Our gate was called, '13' I immediately thought I hope that's not a bad omen, as I looked around the others were laughing saying, "Are you superstitious Glen?", now I have got three people to tease me. It wasn't a large plane being an internal flight, we were all sitting together, two on each side of the aisle. A party of eight men boarded the plane, one was obviously the boss and was treated as such, being well dressed with dark glasses, quite heavy built, but all of them his dutiful employees when there is so many in a party, all of them dressed in black gave you a few worries in case they were up to no good, I just hoped that they were not trouble. The engines were roaring as we raced down the runway and rose into the sky, I looked at Arthos and he said, "Glen, not every time we fly it is going to be trouble, but of course you never know." The cabin crew bought around drinks, we had white wine, whilst Arthos had a juice, as he was driving. Luis went to the bathroom, coming back I saw him lean over where the men were sitting talking to the obvious boss, who seemed to be speaking loudly, wondering what was wrong. Arthos left his seat and went down the aisle and started talking to him as well. Then Arthos immediately learned over to someone sitting next to him and appeared to be doing something, I said to Ramos, "What is going on?", to which he replied, "One of the men I think it's the boss's son who seems to have pains in his chest, and Luis let Arthos know by telepathy, so he's acting as a doctor and checking that he's not too bad." Ramos said, "We'll soon see what happens." I saw that the man sitting next to the person who had taken ill, being asked to move from his seat so that Arthos could sit there, as he needed to check him over. After fifteen minutes or so, with Arthos bent over the sick man, Arthos stood up and said to the boss man, "He'll be alright for now, but he's had a close shave, I luckily had some tablets that calms the heart down, only one can be given but it has temporarily stopped him from going into a full heart attack. Please take him to the hospital when we land, I think they will assure you that with plenty of rest he will be fine, but seriously, just in time my assistant signalled me that I was needed, I was glad to be of assistance." Arthos turned to Luis saying, "Well done recognising the symptoms and calling me, now come and sit down, we will be landing soon. The boss man shook Arthos's hand saying, "Take my card, if you need help let me know, I'm in your debt.

It is my only son who you have helped, my name is Paulo Del Figaro, I have many businesses, keep safe and ring me if you need me, I'll sign it so that you have proof", which he did. Arthos and Luis came back to their seats, one of the cabin crew came to him saying that the pilot had asked her to come and thank him, as they are very important, and it will give the airline some credit. She then said, "This incident could have been disastrous for the airline." The engines started their backward thrust, roaring as we descended then we landed with a slight bump, and we taxied to our allocated dock, and we were ready to disembark. As we prepared to walk across the tarmac, I could not resist saying to Arthos, "Can we go anywhere without you becoming involved? I'm sure that there is nothing in this world that you can't do, I feel so safe with you." "I wish that were all true, but sometimes however hard you try you cannot succeed." I wondered what he meant but he just looked away obviously something he did not wish to talk about. The four of us were soon through security, we were surprised when the eight men gathered around us shaking our hands and wishing us well. The boss man called Paulo asked us where we were staying, so we told him we were hiring a car and driving to Puerto Escondido, taking the route through the Sierra Madre Del Sul mountains. He said, "Oh my god, do you realise the dangers? Why don't you fly, look I'll buy the tickets?" Arthos thanked him saying, "This is a nostalgic journey, I'm sure we will be alright", then added, "Sir we can always call you if we are in danger", Paulo quickly answered, "That my friend is if we can get there in time." Oh my god I thought, I hope it won't be that bad. As we moved away having said goodbye, we all noticed the strange looks we were getting from security personnel, we thought that perhaps these men to whom we had been talking were not as good as they seemed. Ramos said to Arthos, "Perhaps, they are involved in drugs. I've heard there are very rich drug barons in South America", Arthos answered, "Not our problem, we were only passengers on the same plane, not customers", we all smiled.

  Arthos as usual took charge and hired a VW saloon, black and in pretty good condition. He booked it for approximately a week, and said if it needed to be extended, he would contact them. Ramos and Arthos were sitting in front sharing the driving, whilst Luis and I were in the back. We had plenty of water, soft drinks and sandwiches had been bought for the journey, following the journey that Arthos and Gintas had driven twenty years previous. Remembering back to Arthos's story I was quite sure that the first port of call would be a hotel bar in a small town called Ejutia De Crespo, but we had many miles travel first along a road that was mountainous, Ramos, Arthos and Luis were all chatting about past experiences and people they knew, which was very interesting, though after a while the heat started to get me, and I slid into complicated dreams of drug barons taking me to prison.

  I woke with a start when Luis sitting next to me said, "Glen you are all confused and erratic, don't worry we'll save our energy to protect you and fight the Galympites", "Anyway", said Ramos, "We've just arrived at our first town, we'll stop here for the night." The building was called 'El Greco's', I said to Arthos, "Is this the same bar?", he replied, "Can you see any other one?", "No" was the only possible answer. We pushed open the swing door, and entered the building, which was like turning back time to Athos's story, men sitting round, about six of them all talking and drinking, then silence. The four of us walked to the bar behind which was a man in his forties, with a black bushy moustache and dressed in a colourful shirt with black trousers and a rather unfriendly manner. He spoke to Arthos who as usual took charge saying, "Where you amigos off to?", Arthos replied, "Amigo we go all the way to the Pacific through the Sierra Madre Del Sur mountains, we have many friends in the mountains who expect us." The man looked surprised and said, "What you want to drink?", quickly Arthos said, "Four of your wonderful coffees, we have a long journey still and we need to keep alert and awake, always ready." As the man prepared our coffees Arthos caught his attention, "Have you had the bar long? I remember many years ago speaking and having a drink with an older man, not unlike yourself", the man who had to know had looked unfriendly, broke into a smile saying, "Oh, so you remember my Papa, he was a good man. I am so happy that even strangers remember him." With this I suddenly noticed everyone was now talking, so far so good, I thought. He started talking to Arthos, he was leaning on the bar counter and I couldn't quite catch what he was saying, but it sounded like, did we need protection? Did he know there were bandits? I expressed to Arthos my concern about whether we were ready if we got attacked, Arthos suddenly said quite loudly, "Grec, you said your name amigo was Grec didn't you? Well don't worry as I told you we have more protection than you could imagine, as for the bandits, no worry, yes, we are prepared, well dear friend that would be telling, my secret, but thank you for your concern." The three of us were highly amused as the barman in the next breath said, "You like me to make you bread and ham and more coffee?", "Good idea" said Arthos, smiling at the man. He came out quickly I guess someone else was in the kitchen, he bought out large spicy ham sandwiches, more coffees which we took to our table. As we finished Arthos said, "We need to pay and move quickly, I'll tell you what I know to which Ramos said, "Arthos, Luis and I know and Glen will have guessed", Arthos went to the bar and paid Grec, adding a tip for him and telling him we would be back on our return.

Then half turning to the others, he said, "Oh Grec, here's some money to buy the men a drink and let them all know that it's good of them to consider helping us, but we've many friends to do that." We all shook Grec's hand and bundled into the car as fast as we could, then we were off again. I said to the others, "Bit tense in there wasn't it?", "Not a bit", said Luis, "A hell of a lot", Ramos quickly added, "Did you notice how taken back they all were when Arthos said we had many friends in the mountains, and it was nice of them to think of helping." I said to Arthos, "Gosh Arthos you are so quick the way you think us out of difficult situations, you certainly are a survivor" The miles went on, Ramos and Arthos taking turns with the driving, the road was definitely not a main road, but just as Arthos had told us in his previous journey. It was considered an 'A' road with its continuous twisty and hilly state, though it wasn't actually bad. Either side of the road the forests became thicker, and, in some places, the treetops stretched across the road blocking out the light. Ramos was driving and jokingly said, "If we climb anymore, we'll be at the top of the mountain", "Well", I said, "I hope it's not a volcano", "Trust you", said Arthos. I heard Arthos speaking in Spanish but obviously not to Ramos, I wondered who, but then it was his business, I closed my eyes, ten minutes passed when suddenly I heard gun shots and heard Arthos say, "By the powers of the universe, we are being attacked. Don't say anything, leave it to me". He got out of the car, it was surrounded by men on horseback all dressed in black clothes, with big sombrero hats. One man who appeared to be their leader jumped off his horse and approached Arthos with a gun in his hand, Ramos said "Oh Arthos why this way, what now?" Suddenly the man shouted, "All of you out of the car."

15

We quickly got out, they then all started laughing, the man who had held the gun was embracing Arthos, and said, "It was joke, this man Arthos saved my Papa's life many years ago, although we spoke a couple of times over the years, I had always hoped we'd meet again. Guess what? Even better. My Papa is very old now but still alive, this will be a wonderful surprise for him. Arthos rang me asking if I still remember him and that he had some Amigo's with him, could you play a joke on them. It was good, now you will all follow us and stay for the night, we will have a party, my Papa always said, Doctor Arthos will come back, he promised" Chico then said, "So few people even help the bandits, but he did it without force, so he saved my Papa's life and that was a forever favour." Ramos said, "I thought it was real at first and wondered why you were blocking me, then I guessed what about you Luis?", "Well I guess both Glen and I fell asleep and waking up I got quite a shock and looking at Glen I think he's still in shock." Ramos said, "Well Arthos you maybe one up, but wait the week is still young"

They told us to follow them, having formed up in front of us once we were back in the car, and we did so for about a mile, then they had us leave the road following them up to the left, through the trees up a mountain track, full of potholes, making driving an art form trying to avoid them. Eventually we entered the clearing that Arthos had described, which now had about six houses scattered around. On what appeared to be the main house, steps leading to a porch sat an elderly man in a wheelchair, who waved to us, and Arthos leaped out of the car and rushed over to him hugging him saying, "I told you I would come back one day", Senor Ramirez smiled and said, "And I waited for you" We were all introduced to Senor Ramirez then to Chico's brother Enrico. Chico said! Listen amigos you will meet everyone tonight at dinner. We will have a party to welcome our guests, come with me I will show you your rooms. We went into the house from the porch and up the wooden staircase and we given a room; I couldn't believe it even if I tried, I could not write fiction like this. It was all amazing. After about an hour we were called downstairs, which was great because it was long enough to change and have a shave. Chico then showed us around, first taken to the stables, with his beautiful horses, then he showed us with delight his goats, some sheep and a couple of cows with calves. I really thought how incredible it was, hidden away high in the mountains. I thought to myself how different this could have been if we hadn't excepted as friends, once again it was thanks to the friendliness and capabilities of the Astrotars. I remembered how Arthos had explained that approximately twenty years before he had saved the life of Chico's father when he had a heart attack, coming back to now, Chico was leading us back to the main house, saying my Mama insists we are on time, as we entered, we saw a huge table now laid for dinner. We were all slotted in between others so that we could enjoy everyone's company. I was sitting between Chico's brother Enrico and a man called Sandy. I noticed Arthos had been placed by the old man who was at the table in his wheelchair. Ramos and Luis were already chatting away with some of the other men, it was indeed an excellent atmosphere. After we had a splendid meal the table was cleared by the wives and daughters who I guessed had eaten earlier. Out of the blue a couple of the men started playing guitars and they played very well. Within minutes everyone was singing and dancing. The women folk came back in and started squeezing in around the table sitting on some of the men's knees, a young woman came and squeezed in between Enrico and I and told me she was Chico's eldest daughter, and she was called Raquella. She was very pretty with long shiny black hair, wearing a colourful dress long with gathered frills, Enrico said, "Glen watch it, I think she fancies you!", I quickly laughed and said, "Now then Enrico don't make me blush." She started playing the castanets as did all the girls. I was fascinated, under different circumstances I could have quite easily fallen under the spell, but I was part of a different lifestyle these days. The night passed quick; it was late when everyone started making their way to bed, before I had a chance to stand up, Raquella threw her arms round my neck and gave me a long passionate kiss. I disentangled myself and said, "Raquella you are beautiful but please don't do that, your father will shoot me." Everyone laughed and I knew I was blushing, as we thanked the hosts and went upstairs. Ramos started teasing me saying, "Well, well Glen you really a quite a dark horse, with the ladies, we saw the passionate kiss", I answered him saying, "No one was more surprised than me" that made them laugh, then Ramos said, "I noticed Arthos left with the gentlemen a couple of hours ago, I wonder what he is up to, I guess we will find out when he decides to tell us" It was late so that was the end of the conversation as we went to our rooms, the night had passed so quickly, but now as I got into bed I would have no trouble getting to sleep.

Next morning Ramos woke Luis and I telling us it was 08:00 already, and senora Ramirez hade made breakfast. Quickly we got up and went downstairs. Ramos asked Chico, "Have you seen Arthos? He's not in his room, has he gone without us?", Chico replied with a grin, "Oh, no senor Ramos, he is with my father, he has been since very early this morning, I might add he was with him for ages last night, even I was not allowed into the room, not even Mama, I do not know what they are to, do you?", "No", said Ramos, "I'm afraid it must be a secret to them and not to us, but we can enjoy your mothers coffee and wait, are we in the way?". "No never my dear Amigo may I just call you Ramos now as we are all friends and you will always be welcome here?", "Thankyou" we all chorused, and Chico smiled. We moved from the table and all perched on the wooden steps and watched as everyone worked cutting wood, mending fences, and hanging laundry out. Eventually Arthos came and joined us pushing senor Ramirez in his wheelchair and said, "Well sad as I am to say goodbye, but as you understand we have unfinished business to attend to in the Pacific, but will return to you on our way back. I have given you my word it will be in a week, certainly not much more and probably less." Enrico had come to say goodbye and turned to me and said, "Glen, you have made a big impression on my niece Raquella, are you sure you are not looking for a wife?" To this I immediately said, "Enrico, most definitely not, but dear friend please don't take offence, I am a free spirit, and a job keeps us always on the move, but she is very beautiful." I could feel myself blushing as the others started winking at me, "Okay", I said, "Let's go and say goodbye to everyone", with that I bent and shook senor Ramirez's hand and thanked him and his family for the hospitality. It was time to leave, so we all piled into the car, at the last minute Raquella came dashing up saying, "Goodbye Senor Glen, I love you please to come back, you good man, I'll tell my Papa", I shouted, "Bye Raquella see you next time", and quietly to Arthos, "Will you hurry up and leave I am so embarrassed", that then set them all off laughing. As we left, I thought 'What next', Ramos broke the silence, "Okay Arthos what was so special about senor Ramirez, that you had so much time with him last night, and several hours this morning, are we allowed to know or is it a private matter? I have to tell you I never tuned into you, as it was obviously private, and of course at first didn't know that you were with him." "Yes of course I will tell you about what our hours were spent talking about", said Arthos, "But in a million years you won't believe all that I intend to tell you." Ramos was driving and Arthos leaned back in his seat and began talking, "Senor Ramirez said to me, can you come to my room, I need to talk you. He told his wife that she was not to allow anyone disturb us, not even herself. I must admit I began to wonder myself if he was going to admit to some terrible crime, what do they call it? Death bed confessions. We excused ourselves discretely so as not to spoil the party and left. In his room he said to me, Arthos many years ago when I was a young boy, I lived at the foot of the Andes mountains in a small village, in Peru were very poor, I always used to say Mama I ask god to help me find a fortune for you as you work so hard, and I know Papa works hard as well. I used to go out having had some bread and maybe some jam, Mama had made from berries, that was all. I would wander around on the mountainside always checking for birds' eggs or berries, or maybe I thought I might find some gold like they had in times before. As I was scrambling up the rocks where there lots of small stones and crevices on the mountain side, I thought perhaps today would be the day I would find some gold, when suddenly my foot slipped and went down a crevice and a bigger rock slid over and held my foot tight. I tried and tried to free it, but the more I did the worse it became. I started crying I was so frightened thinking a wild animal might come and kill me, or I would die of thirst. I was only about ten years old, and really didn't know what to do, I began to tremble with fear and thought I don't want to die, I wish I had help, but this horrible sick feeling started to take me over. Then in the distance I spotted two horrible looking things emerging from what must be a cave, and they slowly started approaching me. They were each about a metre in height, with what looked like a big helmet on their heads. I was terrified I tried to pull out my leg, but again nothing happened, when suddenly there was a huge flash and explosion, and they were gone. Then down from the air came a huge round disc shaped thing, a door opened, and someone jumped out. He had a helmet on, which he took off and then said in Spanish, "Thank goodness I noticed from the sky that you were in trouble and also destroyed those horrible people that would have killed you. Do not be frightened I will get your foot out." With marvellous strength he moved the rock away from my foot and freeing it. He then said, "I am from another planet, I am called Oracet and I'm an Astrotar. Those other things I destroyed were called Galympites and are evil. We Astrotars only want to help people on earth, now tell me is your foot sore?" I told him 'Yes', so he held it and it got better. He said, "Now do as I tell you and go home, these people are very dangerous so tell me why you come up here on your own?" I told him how poor we were, I hoped to find some gold to help my Mama and Papa. He gave my three pieces of gold, saying "I must go quickly because I am safe in the air, goodbye and good luck, adding remember do not come up here on your own again, promise me?" I said 'yes' then he climbed into the craft and it shot up into the sky and was gone. I was so frightened I ran all the way home and told my parents that I had found some gold and gave them two of the pieces this was how we were able to afford to move to Mexico, and we lived in the hills and we came with two other families and have lived here ever since. Then senor Ramirez opened a little locked drawer and showed me his third piece of gold, it was the size of a walnut and we continued talking. I often wished I could thank that wonderful man as he definitely saved my life when I was a child, then you did when I had the heart attack twenty years ago. I have always wanted to tell my tale to someone, but no one seemed right till I met you, why are you so different? This is where I said, "Senor Ramirez I am about to trust you with a huge secret, so I told him that I like Oceret am also an Astrotar." I told him our story through the ages, how we live and relive, because how during our travels when our world imploded, our crafts had to be fast, faster than they should and how it affected us being able to continue our lives. So, the Great Power Lords of the galaxy and universe gave us a relive programme, so that as long as we weren't killed, we could be put through a coma type programme and life extended on and on in order to continue to be guardians of earth and try and totally get rid of the evil forces of the Galympites. I told him how Oracet was a very special craft pilot, but in dropping down to save a young child in trouble on the mountains it was very brave as a Galympite craft could have been signalled and blown his craft and him up, and that

I would let our leader the Great Astro know, as Oceret indeed needed recognition. I told him about our under-ocean city of Bermantus and some of our adventures and how people thought it was the Loch Ness monster when the aqua craft picks us up sometimes in Loch Ness at night, as it comes slightly out of the water and is the same colours. That made Senor Ramirez laugh, I also told him that Ramos and Luis both of you are Astrotars and that Glen is an adopted Astrotar writing our stories ready for when it is safe to go public, but the world is not quite ready for us yet and would destroy us. I said you are definitely someone who as a leader can be trusted. Unfortunately, many leaders cannot as they are only self-important and untrusting of anything that they personally don't understand or might endanger their personal space or importance. I then said I am going to give you a couple of examples that this is all true, sit quietly and watch. I held up my hand bearing my green stoned ring and said Botami hear me. I am Arthos and I am with Rodrico Ramirez and he has been very special to us, and although we trust him, would you speak to him. The lights flashed off and on, then a quiet voice said, "Rodrico you are honoured to be trusted by Arthos as he is very wise, and as you have been good to the Astrotars they will be good to you, listen to all he says, and he will help you. You have been ill for a long time, you will start feeling stronger every day, because I will ask our leader the Great Astro to look kindly on you" The lights flickered again, and I sat down. Senor Ramirez sat with an amazed expression on his face, he looked at me and said, "Arthos, you and your friends have indeed honoured the Ramirez families and we are so happy to have met you. At last, I have an answer to what happened to me when I was young, I have been truly blessed to meet you. I love your stories and I wish it were possible to let all the family know, but don't worry I will tell nobody." I then gave him one of my tiny tablets that our Astrotar doctor Xedato had given me for emergencies and told him that if he felt really ill before I get back to put this tablet in his mouth and let it melt. Lying down and breathing deeply and to keep resting till I returned Then he said, "Arthos I noticed you all wear a most unusual green stoned gold ring, may I see it?" He held out his hand to which I said, "I am sorry senor Ramirez it is impossible for any of us to take off our rings, or our lives are virtually forfeited. They are our strength and wellbeing; each is given by our leader the Great Astro and only that person can wear it and must never take it off."

"At this point I knew that Senor Ramirez will never let us down, but I am wary I think of telling his family", "I agree" said Ramos, "Time will tell, I will have to get in touch with Oceret" said Arthos, "He would love to hear that story", Arthos sat up in the seat saying, "So what do you think about all that? Isn't it amazing the tricks life plays, and the way life catches up with you? Anyway, when we go back, maybe we'll tell him more stories of our past." We were amazed and quiet for a few minutes then the questions started. "How did you know you could trust him?", "What made you disappear with him last night?", "Wait please", said Arthos, "I'll answer all in good time. Firstly, why did we trust Franchesco in Sicily? The answer is everyone these days are talking about visitors from other galaxies, but the fact is, if they don't know where we live, they cannot harm us, but I felt an infinity with him and remember he has never ever told his sons about his past experiences as a boy and he was so thrilled to be believed. I was taken back when he remembered the name Oracet, and that he was an Astrotar he struggled remembering Galympites saying the bad aliens were Gala something, but as he said he was a poor hardly educated little boy, but those things stuck in his head. Your question about last night, Senor Ramirez at dinner asked if I would mind coming to his room at the back of the house downstairs, as he wanted to ask my advice about something that happened to him when he was a boy. Guess what we got out a map, and he showed me exactly where he had that experience and where that cave was in the Peru Andes mountains marking it with a cross. So, guess what I've used my minicomputer and sent it to Gustaf and Lantos who stay in Peru, and believe it or not they are less than forty miles from that area they intend to advice Base 2 and have the cave destroyed and just think that could destroy another Galympite base, because they won't expect it after so long. The stories and conversations between Arthos and Senor Ramirez were unbelievable but after all we wanted the eventual story of the Astrotars to be told, so maybe these gradual events were the right way forward till my books were out for general reading. We talked about the evening the people we had met and how Arthos's past experiences twenty years before had all been reborn for us to enjoy. Then they started teasing me about Raquella, Chico's eldest daughter and whether I fancied her, and become a bandit. My answer was, "If circumstances were different and I wasn't an adopted Astrotar who knows what I would have felt", "Well stated Glen", said Arthos, "We've got too much to do for you to get involved", "Thanks", I said, "I'm glad you aren't trying to get rid of me." On this particular journey we had stayed on the red road, having not been met by Chico's cousins like

Arthos has the first time, and before we knew it, we were passing through San Pedro Pochutla, and onto the main F200 route taking the left route to Puerto Escondido. Now we found ourselves travelling along the coastline of the Pacific Ocean, which was on our left-hand side. We still had approximately one hundred miles, but as we had the windows open, we were getting the warm breeze from the sea. Arthos had taken over the driving from Ramos and we were not long on the road when we noticed a small roadside café and pulled in for some cool drinks and a few sandwiches. The man who served us spoke quite good English with a strong Mexican accent, being jovial and quite efficient, we were served quickly. His problem was his nosiness, he started by saying, "You are strangers eh?" then we just smiled so he continued, "Have you come far? Perhaps from San Pedro Pochutla?" to which Arthos said, "Yes, we passed through the town", "Ah, I understand you came from the airport?", "No", said Ramos, "Not that one", "Senor your funny, now I guess right I know it is Salina Cruz", "No" said Luis. Then Arthos said, "Senor we have finished our coffee and sandwiches you will give me my bill? We still have far to travel." The man looked puzzled and just could not work out where we had come from and is probably still guessing." As we left Arthos said, "Is it true that many people have seen strange objects flying out of the sea, and maybe even diving into the ocean, do you think that they are aliens?", "Yes" said the man, "Sometimes we see flashes and see long and round things in the sky", "Perhaps", said Arthos "We could hire a boat and go out and see if we could see anything", "Senor you must be mad, a fishing boat was attacked recently a bright flash hit the boat and one man was injured, the other two were hiding below decks, now everyone is scared", "Oh perhaps it was lightening", said Arthos, "Anyway thank you for the story, it was great." Arthos paid the man as we climbed into the car, and I guess he gave him a tip as he was busy shaking Arthos's hand and telling us to all to take care. As we sped off Arthos said, "So the Galympites are here, it was only by chance I mentioned it, and we found out more than we expected, but we will have to be careful." Arthos said, "Number one priority is to let Base 2 know about these latest developments", Our conversation was on what we should do, and how we should prepare and as we talked the excitement and fear ran through us all. We decided that the first pleasant looking hotel we come to, whether it be large or small, is where we would stay. As we hit the town we came to stop, it wasn't a large hotel, but it was quaint and colourful, and appeared well kept and clean. Arthos said, "You three wait in the car, I'll go in and check it out." Five minutes later he came out talking to an elderly lady, very smartly dressed, and indicated for us to bring all our bags, plus his and follow him in, but first lock up the car. As we entered, we were all introduced to the lady who was the owner, her name was Terercina and she was Peruvian originally, and spoke excellent English, which was good for me, it was a lovely accent that she had. There were eight ensuite rooms, we booked four for about five days to a week. We then had some food, then we were given our room keys. After I had showered, shaved changed and relaxed for a bit, we went downstairs for few glasses of red wine. We chattered away and after the glasses were cleared the owner Terercina came over and said, "Senors may I ask why you are visiting our town?" Ramos quickly said, "To meet the charming lady Terercina", she gave a loud laugh and said, Thanks, it's been a long time since I had a compliment, but joking aside, are you here on business?", Arthos said, "I'm from London and have met up with my colleagues as we are scientifically interested in the phenomena apparently seen in the skies around here, but more over the Pacific, we are all wondering how true it all is, and whether it could be alien forces, what do you think?" Gosh I thought Arthos thinks of some quick stories and looking at Ramos and Luis, they both nodded at me. She looked at him saying, "Senor I think that there are definitely strange things happening around here, but what they are heavens only know" Then Arthos said, "My dear lady, do you know of anyone who would hire us a boat, we would love to take a short trip around the coast, if so can you let them know I hold certificates for sailing and a pilot's license to captain a boat?", "Okay, I will ring around tomorrow and get someone to come and see you, is that alright?", she said, "Marvellous", said Arthos, standing up, "Now do you want me to settle now or pay it altogether on leaving?", she answered quickly, "Oh, I'll trust you till you are going just put it all on the bill", "Thanks", said Arthos, then, "Well come on my friends it's bedtime we've had a long drive and last night was a late night, can we have breakfast at 09:00?", "Certainly senor", she said we all said goodnight and went to our beds. After a good sleep, I felt ready for anything whatever that maybe. I went downstairs for breakfast, which we all eat very quickly, then the conversation turned to hiring a boat, and whether the hotel owner would be able to get somebody to come and see us, about hiring a boat. I suddenly said, "Listen, would you all mind if I take a short walk down to the sea? It's not far from here and I could do with a little sightseeing.", "Okay", said Arthos, "See you back here in around two hours, keep your eyes peeled for any sea divers, and remember to duck!", the others started to laugh, but it had made me feel nervous yet again, even though I knew it was Arthos subtly telling me to be careful.

On arriving at the sea front, I took off my trainers, tied the laces together and slung them around my neck, and walked on the sand feeling the sand between my toes, and the refreshing breeze coming off the sea. The beach was very clean, I noticed although it was long it appeared to be semi-circular the end on the right side was covered in trees and bushes with houses on the cliff top. I noticed in the distance on the left side, which was the direction I was taking a long projection of land forming a peninsular going out into the sea. I appreciated that the tide may be coming in, so would need to be careful in case I got cut off, but for now kept walking as it fascinated me the density of the trees, bushes and rocks. I wanted to climb and see what else was up there, again I checked the sea to check the tide, and decided I had sufficient time to climb up and have a look around and walk along the edge. I put my trainers back on and started to climb the rocks. On making it to the top I found it was at least four metres wide, and as I climbed down to the section, which was partly underwater, I was amazed how blue the water was. On the other side I was fascinated with a tiny inlet, it was almost closed off from the sea with another form of island protection forming another peninsular on the far side a few metres into the sea but appearing to almost meet the end of the one I was on. The inlet was nearly underwater now, and I realised I had better go back before I got cut off by the incoming tide. I took a final look at this almost man-made creation, the way the rocks met out at sea, when I noticed an almost concealed cave entrance, fairly large but not immediately noticeable, due to the large overhang of the bushes and rocks. If I hadn't climbed up, I would never have seen it, and as I thought about it, I realised it was almost impossible to reach by the sea. My god I thought, maybe this is a Galympite base, it could easily be, as it was so well hidden. I decided I needed to go and let the others know of what I had seen and quickly in case it was a base and I got caught. I started down the rocks, quicker than what was save, I slipped trying to save myself from falling, when I banged my head on a rock and all went black. Back at the hotel the others were concerned as I had been gone so long, and they had seen someone about the boat hire and the arrangements were made for the next day. As two and a half hours had passed, and knowing I liked to be on time, they became increasing concerned. They left it for another half an hour, then with no sighting of me, they headed down to the sea front. I was nowhere to be seen, and the tide was coming in rapidly. When deciding in what direction to search, they were drawn to the rocky side. Arthos said "I'm being drawn to towards that rocky peninsular in the distance over there, we know Glen comes from Scotland, so I'm sure those rocks would attract him, but tell me are any of you getting any message from him?" As they said no, they agreed I must be in trouble. They told me afterwards that for strange reason they all felt they were being pulled in the direction they had chosen. As they got to the rocks and started to climb, they called out my name without any luck. They in hastily started to rush towards the area where the sea was lapping around below, having suddenly noticing my body lying on a rock that was projecting out over the sea, another foot and I would have landed in the sea. I was unconscious so with great difficulty they managed to manoeuvre me gradually on to a higher safer ledge which was flatter. There was still no response from me, and panic started to creep in amongst them, Arthos checked my pulse which was very faint. They agreed that it would take all their energies to save me with their Astrotar deep mind abilities. Arthos first put some liquid on my head where I was bleeding, Ramos held the gash closed, whilst Arthos and Luis worked on pressure points, and Ramos working on my head. They combined all their healing skills with Astrotar medicine, Arthos told me he thought they had really lost me, but they had kept going and didn't give up. After about thirty minutes my eyes opened, I turned my head slowly asking Arthos in a weak voice, "Where did you come from?", he answered, "Looking for you and saving your life, it has been touch and go", then Ramos said, "Do you remember having an accident?", I replied, "All I remember is my feet slipping, trying to stop my fall, then everything went black." As I tried to sit up, with the others kneeling over me, there was a nearby roaring sound, something shot out of the rocky peninsular straight upwards into the sky. Arthos immediately said, "Quickly lay flat" we were all aware to what the object that had shot into the sky was. Arthos then said, "Well, Glen, on your own and you seemed to have discovered a Galympite base, but for now we have to leave quickly, do you think you can walk Glen?", "With help, of course I'll manage" I said. How we managed it I'll never know, but with their help we climbed down, I'm sure Ramos almost carried me. The ocean tide had receded somewhat, we slowly worked our way back along the edge of the sea, luckily by now the tide was on its way out. "How did you find me?", I asked. Arthos answered, "I can only think we were guided by the power of our rings connecting with yours", then he added, "If you had been a foot nearer the edge you would have been swept away in the sea, it was already lapping around you on that lower ledge, how are you feeling Glen?" I answered rather faintly, "Shaky, feeling sick with a horrendous headache, but grateful to be alive, and of course thrilled to maybe have found a Galympite base, because surely it must be with that thing shooting into the sky." We had reached at last the part of the beach where the entrance to the roadway was, Ramos said, "You three wait, I'll run back to the hotel and get the car", he was off like greased lightening, what speed I thought, and Arthos smiled. Suddenly Arthos said, "Quick, we must all get down, I see it circling keep down in the bush." Just then the black object shot in the direction of the peninsular, Arthos stood up and said, "It has suddenly dropped down below that rocky projection and out of sight" at the same time we heard the horn from the car, its Ramos, already back with the car, I was glad to get in as my legs were like jelly. We returned back at the hotel in one piece thanks to my friends.

    As we arrived back, Arthos said, "First, things first, Glen you go to your room, I must check your head and everything else, as when you fell you don't know what else you may have done, Oh Ramos could you go and have a word with Terercina and order all of us coffees and cakes, as I'm sure we all need some sugar for shock, especially Glen" The hotelier Terercina came out of the kitchen as we were climbing the stairs, she asked if everything was ok. Arthos told her that we would tell her about me afterwards. When we got to the room, Arthos used a small clean towel and gently dabbed my head which incidentally had miraculously stopped bleeding since they had treated it. Arthos still checking the wound, sprayed something on it and said, "This tiny bottle is a miracle cure and healing agent used by the Astrotars, hopefully it will work on you, an adopted one" "Don't worry, I'll be careful", I think he thought I might collapse, "Yes you're right", he said reading my mind. When we got downstairs the other two were waiting patiently, we were bought coffee, and cakes immediately. They had told her enough, just I had climbed on some rocks, slipped and banged my head and had been knocked out, she said, "Oh, you didn't go and climb on that peninsular, that goes way into the sea on the far-left side, did you?", I replied, "Yes why?", she said in a quiet shocked voice, "Well you are lucky, some terrible things have happened at that end of the bay. Apparently, a couple of fishermen had climbed onto them to fish from the side, one had been talking to wife on his phone, when suddenly it went dead, they were both found dead, with awful burns on them, when they washed up to shore. I'm sorry I forgot to warn you about that area. It's only a small area, but I've been told there are two peninsulas that almost meet, the local people say it's an evil area. Did you feel it was bad?" Immediately Arthos said, "I agree, when we found Glen we got away as quick as possible, obviously we were lucky." With that we started pouring out coffee and talking about the boat, and whether I would be ok the next day, as if I would miss anything! Arthos said that that the three of them were going for a walk, he was insisting on me going to lie down, for at least an hour. It was only mid-afternoon, but I agreed as I felt shaky still, and had lost a lot of blood, and with my headache I knew it was the sensible thing to do. I told them I would see them later and told them to wake me up if I slept too long.

When Arthos woke me it was evening, although I went to get up, he said, "No, Glen you are very white, your pulse is still very erratic. I'm going to have your dinner brought up here for you, something light and a drink of juice. We will come and chat with you when you have eaten, which we are about to do, don't think we are going to desert you. We will then have a reasonable early night and see what tomorrow brings. After all Glen we are already ahead with our programme, we have whereabouts of an evil base, which must be destroyed. Importantly we have advised our Base 2 in Peru about it, so maybe this base of the evil ones is about to be destroyed. Therefore, the first part of our mission is almost complete, so Glen rest and recover." I had eaten washed and changed and lain back in my bed, whilst turning over the events of the day, and appreciating how lucky I was to still be alive, when I remembered words of my father from years before, 'Glen your nosiness and inquisitiveness will be your undoing' it nearly was, I always took chances just in case I missed something. Well, I thought in my defense I did sense a form of danger when I was up on top of the peninsular, it was just bad luck I slipped. I smiled to myself and thought I wonder what my parents would have said to know that my very best friends, came from another galaxy. There was a knock at the door, I called "Come in", as I had left the door unlocked. They came in the three of them, the first thing Arthos said was, "Glen you should have left the door locked, and not be so trusting, have you forgotten what happened at Puerto Tranquillo with the Galympites?", I said, "Don't Arthos, some things I like to forget." Well, that started the stories, the four of us enjoyed the next two hours until Ramos said, "Ok, I don't know about you, but I'm for an early night?" We all agreed and decided on a 08:30 breakfast would be excellent. Arthos checked my head and said that it was already healing nicely, and hoped my headache would be gone by morning, as were all supposed to be going boating." Arthos had booked a large motorboat and the sea air would do me good. Luis added, "As long as we don't have any bad experiences", trust him, I don't want any bad dreams. The next morning at breakfast, Arthos told us all that Base 2 was now on the case of the possible destruction of the Galympite base which we had alerted them to, probably being on the other side of the peninsular to where I had my accident. They were told that we weren't sure whether the craft had erupted at speed from the cave, or straight out of the sea, the main thing was the Astrotars knew the details. Just as we were leaving Arthos who had gone upstairs for his backpack came rushing down saying to us all, "Laximo is dead, I know Glen knows him, do you two?" My heart broke at the news, such a kind but troubled man. "What happened?", said Luis, I was almost in tears as I had really got on well with him and spent a lot of time with him in Chili, I also noticed Arthos was visibly upset as well, he replied, "It is still being investigated, he had gone back to Balmaceda, when he left Bermantus he lived near Ricardo and Paulo, he apparently decided to go and visit Limrod, Flipsi and Ottol in Puerto Tranquillo as he had fully recovered, he actually bought a little car with his savings they said he was so proud of it. One day whilst he down visiting, he had gone for a drive, when he didn't return by the evening, they went out looking for him, eventually finding his car near the waterside in a desolate place, burnt out, his body was unrecognisable. Had he come across a Galympite base by accident? Perhaps had spotted one of their craft with his high velocity binoculars and they saw the sun flash on the glass, so terminated him. He was interrupted partly through a message to Base 2 but they only received part of it. It was the number plate which was recognised and that is how we know who it is." Ramos said, "The people in Puerto Tranquillo must be devastated?", "They are", said Arthos, "And have paid for him to be buried, as the authorities have decided there must have been an explosion in the cars motor, though many people are suggesting that it is those damn aliens again. I wish they would realise that it's those damn Galympites, some people from other galaxies are good like us Astrotars, not everyone is evil. Apparently, the case is closed and is listed as a terrible accident. I certainly don't think so, I will get in touch with Paulo and Ricardo, in the meantime Ramos can you ring the boat man, say we've had some bad news, and can we book for tomorrow instead." Ramos said," Luis you go and ask Terercina if we can all have some coffee, as we had to cancel the boat hire today, duc to some bad news we have just received, and we need to sort some stuff out." I said, "What can I do?", to which I was told go and sit at the table in the lounge, and we'll join you soon.

Arthos joined me in the lounge fifteen minutes later, we were all sad and tearful, Laximo was a kind special friend. Suddenly Arthos said, "The Great Astro has been told and expects us all to think positive, think of him with kindness, and not to dwell on it, or we will lose our spirit. He then said, Arthos tell all the others it is written by the Great Power Lords of the galaxy and universe, that his spirit will live forever, and the name Laximo will be in the golden book." I looked around they were all smiling through tears and said to me, "Glen, you are adopted now, try and think like us it helps." We drank our coffee and Arthos said, "I am going to contact Ricardo and Paulo, would you like to speak to them Glen? Remember the Great Astro's words." I told him, "Yes, I would love to speak to them with a smile if possible, in my voice, however hard that maybe." Ricardo and Paulo were happy to speak with me saying how much they missed us and was there any chance of us coming back for a visit to Balmaceda. I told them I would really love that, but it all depended on what plans were ahead. I told them that I was happy I had met Laximo and would always think of him with love and true friendship. I then asked how Ottol was, and how I'd enjoyed his stories and company, and if they saw him to send him my best wishes. We then said our goodbyes, and I passed the phone back to Arthos who said, "We'll be in touch soon", as Arthos finished his call he turned and said, "Well done Glen, you did good." Arthos had many calls to make, due to his senior rank, he told us he would see us all shortly, as he left for his room. Ramos said to him "Arthos, why not come down to the back garden and the other two can go out for a while, you could go for a drive whilst I stay and help", Ramos then said to Luis, "Be careful both of you, no heroism, we will be too busy to rescue you", Luis replied, "Thanks friend, I'm sure you don't mean that", I had to smile, friendship was always there. We drove for about ten miles and found a nice spot to park, near a small café, where we went in and got some cold drinks. We went past the car where there was a small wall, with sand on the other side of it, we climbed it and sat down on the ground leaning against the wall. It was peaceful, ahead of us the ocean, so blue with frothy white waves rolling in, though still a fair way out. Behind us were many trees, so the silence was only broken by bird song. Luis broke my thoughts, "Glen, your thoughts are exactly as mine, isn't it truly wonderful to find true peace?" It was warm where we sat, and we talked about our life's experiences. Luis wanted to know all about my family, and my life growing up and how I first came to meet Arthos, then the details of the adventures we had up to now, and the different Astrotars I had met. He told me about his many times reprogramming he had been through, the places he had visited, the near-death experiences he had encountered, friends he had lost and even things I had never been told about the planet Astrola, where he had come from when he was young, he even said many things that had happened when he was young had been obliterated from his memory due to the relive programme, as it moves you forward and helps to forget the distant past. Sharing our stories bonded us, I found myself drawn close to him, he asked if I had any brothers or sisters, I told him I was an only child and that when I was in my twenties, just out of university my parents were killed in a car accident, and left me reasonably financially sound, but I felt lonely as we were a very close family. I then told him when I was travelling with Arthos, my editor had died and left an amazing amount of money to me, so I was free to travel with Arthos and still keep my flat in London. Luis then said, "Maybe the Great Astro will allow me to come and visit you in London, could I stay with you?", "Of course, we shall always be bonded by our friendship", I said. We had talked for ages, I loved hearing about Astrola, it sounded a beautiful place with oceans and forests like earth, but how sad it all ended. He agreed reading my mind saying, "And even better Glen, the people were not war like, they were peaceful and kind, and what I can remember which is limited, there was so little warning, and life changed forever. Apparently, the Great Power Lords of the galaxy and universe had already made the leaders of Astrola the guardians of the earth, the Astrotars had been visiting for thousands of years help civilisation move forward. They had many problems as they taught the people as they were quite war like and believed in human sacrifice, but they learnt quickly. Many acquired advanced with ideas which we tried to help put into practice. All this time we had built bases here on earth so that we could keep helping, like we had been chosen to do, so when the implosion was about to happen, many as possible escaped to earth. We have been here ever since, doing our best to rid the planet of the Galympites, who would like to take over the earth." I found myself feeling a special link with Luis as both Ramos and Arthos were leaders, and we were followers. We never realised how long we had been gone, as we swapped our in-depth stories, the hours had passed like minutes. We had left the hotel around 10:30, I couldn't believe it when Luis's phone rang, it was Ramos asking if we were both ok. Luis replied, "Of course we are, why what time is it?", Ramos said, "It's 16:00 as you had both been gone for five hours, we naturally started to worry", Luis replied, "We've had a lovely afternoon telling each other stories of past years, sorry we stayed away so long", I then said, "Arthos and you I suppose have been so busy sorry we stayed away for so long, we'll come straight back, I guess we'll be about twenty minutes or so, I've just realised how thirsty I am." Once in the car, we were soon back at the hotel, we both started laughing it was like being late home and your parents were getting angry, but we just entered smiling, in case we were indeed in trouble. Arthos said, "I'm really glad you enjoyed yourselves, you can tell us about it all soon, but we have some news. Glen, Luis, you will both be pleased like we were hearing from Base 2 in Peru they have reported that Oracet on one of his missions spotted the area that Senor Ramirez told me about, and on circling he spotted a couple of Galympites doing something to a craft of theirs, obviously feeling safe away from civilisation on the plateau in the Andes, So Oracet dived down from the clouds and blew them up along with the craft and sent fire into their cave, I wonder how many more he killed? They must have had peace for years as it's over fifty years since many people moved from the foothills. That was number one, then Incas was told about what we found at Puerto Escondido at the peninsular, and the way the other peninsular seemed to connect in the sea, we explained how it formed a small inlet with an almost concealed cave, and the water seemed to stay deep. Well, he checked this out called for backup, and another pilot staying at the base from India called Surgier joined forces with Incas went back to Puerto Escondido, as there was nothing around the area to endanger people, they landed in the trees and rocks, they blasted the ground from the entrance of the cave, which bought out the craft from the water which was destroyed.

Then something started to emerge from the cave entrance, which was half collapsed, that to was destroyed. They circled for a while but nothing else happened, but are coming back tonight, just to make sure. What a commotion in town about aliens attacking, although they haven't damaged any properties or people, but still the army and air force have been sent for to come and investigate, so I've been told. I have let Surgier, and Incas know and told them to be careful. So, my friends I think our work is done in this part of the world, we will stay another day to make sure, isn't that marvellous?" we all agreed that we got first the sad news, but now the news had turned good, the way of the world, I guess. Ramos then took over speaking, saying, "Arthos, sorry to interrupt but I think a drink would be in order, let's go and ask if we could go and sit in the back garden, as it is nice and peaceful there." Ramos went through to the kitchen and asked Terercina if we could order some drinks and sit in her garden, her reply was immediate, "Of course, just all come through this door, it's very private isn't it?" She asked what we would all like as we sat down in the garden. Ramos said, "Well, can we start with some coffee and cakes, then another good bottle of red wine", she laughed, "Are you celebrating or spoiling yourselves?", "Yes", said Ramos without further explanation and smiled. The garden was very prettily laid out, with shrubs, trees with fruit and blossom on them. All around there were tubs full of flowers, after the last few days, this was a small piece of heaven. We talked about our days since we came and what had happened, then talk turned to today's events. Arthos and Ramos told us what they had done and what was ahead for our future plans. Luis and I described our leisurely day, feeling slightly embarrassed as we had only enjoyed each other's company and thoughts Arthos said, "There is nothing wrong with that, both of you gave extra knowledge to one another, and you may never know when that might be useful." We both smiled. As we were sitting drinking and eating, our eyes were drawn by Arthos to an object which darted across the sky a couple of times, even maybe two objects we couldn't be sure, they seemed to fly out to sea, we immediately went out of the side gate, and dashed round to the front of the hotel so we could watch the sky over the ocean. There plenty of clouds in the sky, but flashes of silver kept flitting in and out of them, something then came from nowhere and shot upwards black in colour, and a more oval shape. It had come from the left, we all gasped and hoped that Incas and Surgier were ready for it. Obviously, the silver flashes had been the Astrotars, who were not convinced that all the evil things had been destroyed earlier and were checking the area again. A clap of what sounded like thunder as our eyes were glued skywards, we saw a flash like lightening, then all sorts of objects falling into the sea.

16

Our hearts stopped for a couple of minutes, waiting, praying and hoping, then it happened, two flashes above us, we waved frantically, and one came low, dipped then shot skywards again, then they were gone, obviously job done, and back off too Base 2. We started laughing how cheeky was Incas, he had obviously seen us, and decided to acknowledge it by dipping then shooting up,

Arthos said, "Yes he would know it was us, as he knows where we are staying, he was only bowing to his audience, isn't he something else?" We went back to the garden letting Terercina know we were back, telling her what we had seen, Ramos commented, "This is great Terercina, a boy's dream is always to see spaceships and whether it was or not, it was quite exciting", she said, "weren't you scared?", Ramos said, "No I was with my friends", this made us laugh. Arthos then said, "Obviously they were content with what those two pilots had accomplished, job done, and back to base. We thought they had already finished here but they must have been sent out once again to check that this area is hopefully complete. When you think about it otherwise those Galympites could have reconstructed their base. That craft came out of the sea and must have been held in the cave. The great Astro will be pleased and Alimo will be complimented at Base 2." "Isn't he the chosen leader there?", I asked, "Yes" said Arthos, "He earned that leadership with some remarkable deeds he has done. I will tell you all about him one day. I don't think everyone knows a lot about him", Ramos and Luis said together, "Arthos tell us about him as well", "Yes", said Arthos, "I'm sure we will have time on our hands shortly, and I will tell you all then." They all decided to go and have sometime in their rooms and meet up again at 20:00 for dinner. As agreed, after having a rest I met the others downstairs and asked them if they had ordered, "Yes" said Ramos, "Hope you like fish, we've ordered the Mexican fish specialty?" Before the food arrived, Terercina came out of the kitchen saying, "Did you all miss the excitement this afternoon? There were some flying objects and a great clap of thunder, followed by a flash of fire from the sky, we had the air force and army here investigating, they think it could have been aliens, I bet it's not, it's just America testing something new, and it went wrong, what do you think?" Ramos with a straight face turned to Arthos and said, "I told you it wasn't thunder and lightning, I never thought aliens though, gosh I hope we are safe?" Immediately Terercina said, "I hope it doesn't make you leave any earlier? Don't worry the air force and army are keeping an eye on us, so you will be fine." Arthos said, "Oh that makes us feel so much better!", Luis then said, "Terercina dear lady, is it possible for us to eat now, as we are all starving?", "Oh so sorry", she said, "I'll bring the food straight out." After dinner the arrangement were made for the next day, to still hire the boat just for a few hours, getting to the boat yard at Playa Principal for 10:00, and afterwards to go to town and have a look round. Arthos said, "Glen, if you don't mind, I'm going to come up to your room and check your head", as soon as we got up there, he said, "Ok sit down", he checked my wound on my head, joking, "Marvellous doctor you saw Glen, in such a short time, you an earthling and it's almost healed up, I guess you must be changing into an Astrotar?" He laughingly gave me a hug and said, "Goodnight my friend, take care in the future", and was gone.

As arranged, we were all organised and ready for the trip by 09:45, and arrived at Playa Principal by 10:00, there were all types of boats moored up, with others on the sand in the shelter of the trees and bushes. The port of Puerto Escondido of supports commercial fishing, and deep-sea fishing to a certain degree, I found it all very interesting. We gave the man who owned the boat the car keys, then got into the boat. Apparently, the car keys acted as a deposit for the return of the boat. The sun was high, with a warm breeze on the ocean, it was very pleasant as we set off. Ramos and Arthos were in the front whilst Luis and I were in the back. Ramos then spoilt the relaxed atmosphere by saying, "Did you see that black shape shoot across the sky?", we all started to look, he started to laugh and said, "I just thought I might have missed something", "Behave yourself", said Arthos smiling, "We have already been through enough and today hopefully is just for relaxing."

As I said before Arthos and Ramos were in the front, Arthos the captain and Ramos obviously the lookout. Luis and I were quite content with our back-seat position as usual, Luis smiled reading my mind, we intended to keep a sensible distance from shore, but we didn't want an oceanic cruise, just a small boating experience. A couple of hours was our intention, we were going in the direction of Salina Cruz but obviously not intending to go that far. As we motored through the waves, we suddenly spotted dolphins leaping out of the sea, then submerging again. Arthos said, "I hope they keep their distance, because if we are tipped out there are plenty of sharks around." One of the dolphins came close and seemed to stand on its tail, with his head out of the water. They were great to watch and came quite nearing appearing to be following us, then just as quickly disappeared. We were looking back at the far end of the beach, we saw that the land went quite high, there were many houses on it, I guess that was the start of a town being constructed. The we noticed at the edge of the point was a light house. It is situated above Playa Marinero beach which with some waves reaching over fifteen feet was popular with surfers. Luis said, "Very interesting, I've been reading your mind, where did you find that out?" I answered him saying, "From a book in my bedroom when I went to bed with my cut head.", "Well" said Arthos, Terercina said, "Don't go swimming in the ocean as there are strong undercurrents which can pull swimmers under, that and the high waves which can be lethal, so make sure no one falls overboard." Ramos laughed, "I don't think she wanted us to drown as we haven't paid yet!", Arthos said, "Ramos don't be cruel she was just being kind", I interrupted, "Anyway I don't fancy being a sharks supper."

In the distance we could make some large ships, Arthos thought they were probably making for some nearby port. We saw a fishing boat which was nearer than we thought, we realised we had drifted further then we had intended, then we were aware of a sailor shouting to us over a loudspeaker. Arthos turned the motor off so we could hear, the sailor shouted again, "You lot, be careful there is some funny things shooting around, in and out of the clouds. Some of our colleagues have been hurt from rays from one of them. Apparently, it was like a black oblong, so we've decided to call it a day. I'd go back to land if I were you as you wouldn't stand a chance", Arthos shouted, "Thanks my friends, I hope you've had a good catch." We immediately turned the boat round and started back to Puerto Escondido or rather the boat yard where had hired the boat. We had been out for longer than we thought, it was now 14:30, as we neared the little harbour and made for the jetty, we spotted a flash silver, then another. Ramos said, "I wonder what our friends are up to?" When we walked to the boat shed, we saw a flash of black, then it disappeared, we went up to the man still watching the sky, Arthos spoke to him, paid him and got back the car keys. Before we got into the car, we went down to the harbour wall, looked up and saw a black flash shoot of the cloud, then behind some more. Nothing happened for about five minutes, then there was a horrific bang, we froze, watched and waited, suddenly in the distance out to sea we saw things fall out of the sky into the ocean. Everything went quiet, no flashes of silver, nothing, we didn't know what had happened. Ramos said, "Let's get back to the hotel and check, I can't make contact out here, I've got to use the device that shields where we are calling from, so that we can't be found by a satellite director finder. I can't stand the worry and suspense, we can only hope the Power Lords of the galaxy and universe are protecting them, as Incas and Surgier are good not evil so they will be more protected, but even so, their job is dangerous." As we left the man knocked on the window of the car, Arthos wound the window down and the man said, "If yer wanta go tomorrow please ye coma mea senors ma noma est Carlo", "Ok", we said, "Thank you

Carlo", and we drove off.

As soon as we arrived at the hotel, Arthos ran upstairs to his room to ring Alima and find out about the two Astrotar pilots. When he came back, he said, "The Power Lords were with them, Incas returned intact, but Sergei's craft was damaged, he made it back but was very shaken. The good news another Galympite pilot has been destroyed." We were morbidly happy at this news. We ordered sandwiches and coffee and sat in the back garden of the hotel to try and relax. As it was our last night Ramos said, "I've got an idea, why don't we just pop down to town and have a look round, and back for a meal for this evening?" We told Terercina we would return in time for supper, she advised us of the best place to park in town, and we left. The middle of town is not a plaza, but is called Perez Gozga Avenue the locals call it, 'El Adoquin', it's street is made of paving stones with a statue at the start of the town Benito Juorez. There were bars, small hotels, cafes, restaurants, corner stores and night clubs, with plenty of outlets selling scuba equipment. We went into a craft shop and had a good look around, I ended up buying a shirt and three dolphins made out of stone. I then handed one each to my fellow travellers saying, "Dolphins are reputedly clever and save many lives, so I have bought you each one to say thank you for saving me, and they will bring you luck." We then went and found a café and ordered four glasses of wine. As I went to pay Arthos said, "Sit down Glen, I'm paying I want to hear what those individuals over there are talking about." He spoke to the man behind the counter and said, "Can I have a private word with you?", the man said, "Yes", and took Arthos behind a curtain. We wondered what was going on, then Arthos came out carrying a tray with four glasses of wine, he sat, and we started to drink them. Suddenly two police officers came from the back, with a further four coming in from the front, and headed straight to the table where the men were sitting.

Arthos said, "Be in deep conversation and do not look up", we all had our heads down and were speaking rubbish to look intent. The men got up and went outside with the police. We then noticed that the police had drawn their guns, whilst two of the officers were hand cuffing the men together. A police van pulled up, and the men were put inside the prisoner's cage at the back of the van, then they and the police left. "Ok", said Ramos, "What was all that about?", "Well I thought they looked suspicious, so I went to the bar and ordered wine, but listening to what they were whispering and thinking about, I learnt they had just robbed a bank today at Salina Cruz, and were considering robbing this place. I warned the man, saying I was F.B.I and showing him my I.D. fake of course! told him to ring the police and tell them they were sitting in your bar, and for him to take the credit and reward, saying that he had overheard them talking about their plans." Next minute the man came over to Arthos and said, "Thank you senor, how did you do it? You are clever, the police are happy with me, and will come back and see me again later", "Well I've told you what to say", said Arthos, I only heard because I have a special earpiece, which is essential for my job. Anyway, good luck, and I'll pay for the wine", "No, no", said the man, "My gift to you my friend", we all said thank you and left. Ramos started the conversation as we walked back to the sea, "Arthos, can we not even go for a glass of wine, without you playing detective?", Luis was laughing, "Listen" said Arthos, "Those rats were going to rob that poor man and he told me, he has had a good week, and he needed to do so, as he was robbed not so long ago and stole all his takings, the police have said he will get the reward for the arrest of the men, so that's great for him.", "Ok", said Ramos, "You win again", we all had a good laugh about it. It was just 19:00 when we got back, in time for a quick shower and ready for the meal. After dinner it was decided an early night was in order, for an early start in the morning. At 09:00 we were saying farewell to Terercina, who said, "I am sad to see you go, you are lovely Senors", she thanked Arthos again for generosity, Ramos said to me, "Arthos paid for six nights even though we were only there four nights". "Luis", I said, "You are very quiet, what's wrong?", he answered, "I'm just wondering what will happen to us next, I'm hoping it's just my thoughts, but I have a feeling of dread, and it's giving me a bad headache", Ramos quickly told him to calm down and added, "Look I just think we've all had quite a lot to take in, and we need to think positive thoughts."

    The car started and again we were off, along the F200 main road. As we were driving, Arthos said, "Are you all willing to call at Chico's again? I personally would love to see senor Ramirez", we all agreed it was a good idea, but Ramos said, "Arthos you had better ring and check that it is ok with them", "Of course", said Arthos, "I'll do that shortly." The miles continued to pass, with us discussing the events of the past few days, when we noticed we were already about to pass the café that we had stopped at on our incoming journey five days before. Immediately Arthos stopped and decided we should get some coffee, to break the journey as it was a hot day, and outside the car was the breeze from the Pacific Ocean. As we walked into the café the man recognised us saying, "Oh thank you senors, you come back, you happy mea, happy too, four coffees you want more things?", Ramos told him, "No thanks, but when we leave will buy some juices to take with us", Ok, I go ye giva mea five minutes for your coffee." We went outside to the patio where we could feel the breeze. We had hardly started to talk, when he returned with four coffees and four pieces of cake, "I give you the cake, cos you come back, thank you", he said, "Can I ask you senors you hear we see things in the skies, you see too?", "Yes", said Arthos, "We heard all about them, it will probably bring lots of tourist and investigators to the area with this sort of news", "You think so?", said the man, "I thought people no come because scared", "Well", said Ramos, "We came to Paulo Escondido stayed and enjoyed it, like we are going to enjoy our coffees before they go cold", "Oh sorry senor", and the man went inside. Arthos started laughing saying, "Oh! Ramos that was so sarcastic but funny", we all laughed. We were soon on our way again taking the turn left which was the eventual direction to Oaxaca Juarez airport, but first we were heading towards Ejutia de Crespo, but didn't intend in stopping there. I heard Arthos talking to Ramos, he appeared to be talking on the phone in a weird language, even Luis seemed to be having a doze, as the car was very warm, due to this I obviously dozed off myself. I awoke hearing a loud voice, I sat up startled and realised it was Ramos saying, "I came round the corner after driving for miles through continuous forest along the twisty road, I came round a hair pin bend and it was stop immediately, road blocked. A lorry strewn across the road after jack knifing and spilt the load" On the left-hand side Arthos commented that there was a huge quarry carved out of the hillside. I said, "Maybe the lorry was leaving the quarry and it's skidded, or its wheels hit the ditch of the side of the road." "Does it really matter?", said Luis, "They will sort it out soon." As we sat watching, Luis and I spoke about the quarry, obviously it was lunchtime as there were many machines standing idle, around the gravelly ground there appeared to be a pool of water or oil spilt from the machines. On the high ground at the back of the quarry a man was standing on top of the quarry that they had been digging into, he was waving his arms and generally gesticulating to those behind him and busy half turning to the back of work being done, you could see he was shouting.

Suddenly the ground at the top gave way, as he was standing on the edge, he went falling down head first scattering rocks and gravel over the lower gravel creating sparks and in turn set fire to the pools of liquid, which was obviously flammable started erupting all over the area, before anyone could stop Luis, he bounded out of the car vaulted over the small boundary enclosure and raced across the burning area attempting to avoid the flames as best as he could, in order to reach the unconscious man. In the meantime, Ramos had his hand placed on the horn to try and get attention. People came running down the side of the hill, others came from the roadway in front us. Luis was dragging and half carrying the man, who was rather large from the fiery gravel which would have consumed him if not for others arriving and helping them both from danger.

The police, fire and ambulance services arrived for the truck, but as the man was only bruised and shocked, they immediately turned their attention to putting the fire out and getting to the unconscious man and Luis. We were all outside of the car frantic for Luis and his safety, and if he had been badly burned. The paramedics and police bought them back to the road, while many of the workers all came to help sort out the lorry. The paramedics had the unconscious man in the ambulance taking details from one of the workers who was interviewed by the police. They were also putting burn dressings on Luis's hands, his face also had patches on it. His trousers had been singed. They wanted to take Luis to hospital, but he said if he needed to go, Arthos would take him. Then the two police officers said, "Can someone give us details of this brave man", Immediately offered as the others were taking care of Luis, I said, "Senors, I am sorry I do not speak Spanish, but I'm sure you gentlemen could speak a little English", "That is correct", said one of them, "As long as you speak slowly" I told him what we had seen how Luis before we could stop him ran through the fire whilst we kept the horn hooting for attention. That Luis had dragged, and half carried the unconscious man to safety, and where the man's colleagues had arrived down the hill and taken over, and now he is with you. Then he said, "What is your friends name?", I said, "Luis MacDonald we all come from London and are all scientists studying the phenomena of the possibility of space craft in your area, which has been made into a government mission and you must realise it is still secret", he said, "I understand thank you for the information." Then I said, "Will you please excuse me now I need to see what is happening to my friend" The road had been cleared ahead and Arthos asked Luis, "Would you like to go back to Salina Cruz to the hospital", to which he said, "No, Arthos that cream you have I'm sure will work for me. I am alright for the moment they have put some spray on it which is helping, and they have put burn dressings on my hands. Remember I told you I had a feeling of dread, I knew something was going to happen and it did" The work men and fire, ambulance even the police were crowding around as Luis got into the back of the car all shouting, "Thank you", then to Ramos, "Please let's go I feel a bit sick." Arthos gave him a juice and said, "Get some liquid down you, and swallow this tablet", he gave him a little tablet. I noticed he was so white with two big red blotches on his face, I said "Oh, Luis I was so frightened for you, we all love so much", he just half smiled and closed his eyes. Arthos turned to me and said, "Thank you Glen we were all so shaken you were amazing the way you handled those police officers; you are indeed one of us, I will let the Great Astro know and also about Luis and his bravery", I was thrilled with such praise from Arthos that I handled the police statements correctly. We drove for miles and I noticed that Luis had gone to sleep which I mentioned to Arthos who said, "Glen, just keep an eye on him, I'm a little worried that he is more affected than perhaps we realised. After a short time of driving Ramos having looked round said, "Arthos, I think we should stop immediately whilst you check Luis, he's ashen and may have gone into severe shock", "Right", said Arthos and pulled into a grassy verge in between the thick trees, he jumped out and opened the back door, and checked Luis's pulse then he said something to Ramos which was in a language I didn't understand. He jumped out of the car in the front and told me to change places quickly, I saw them as I half turned in the front pushing on his chest, then putting pressure on his head. Then Arthos put something in Luis's mouth, whilst they both continued working on pressure points, as I was told afterwards and blending their minds with his, as only Astrotars can. It is their healing process and unbelievable in its strength. We had been stopped for at least half an hour before Luis opened his eyes and spoke, "What's wrong", he uttered, "You dear friend", said Ramos, "You didn't only scare yourself, you nearly scared us to death, how do you feel now?" Luis answered very quietly, "Rather sick, exhausted and terribly thirsty", "Right", said Arthos drink this water we have in the car, even if it's a little warm, it's fluid and we'll stop as soon as we can, "Thanks", said Luis, "Sorry to be such a nuisance", "Just rest", said Arthos, "But if possible, please stay conscious." "Glen is Luis alright?" Ramos asked me, "Yes", said Luis before I had chance to reply, "I'm just not feeling too good, but thanks for everything I have to admit my hands and legs are painful, and my face feels numb in places", "Don't worry", said Arthos, "I'll try and sort things out as soon as I can stop", then after a short hesitation said quickly, "The road is getting quite steep, and twister here, that last hair pin bend was tight, I'd hate to be driving a bus or a lorry, I think we are climbing the Sierra Medora Del Sur mountains again, we'll soon be there", "Where", I said, "Oh I know, Ejutia de Crespo", "No", said Arthos, "I think when we turn the next corner or so, you'll see an amazing sight." That was an understatement as there they were about ten men on horseback waving their hats at us, I realised it was chico and Enrico and some of the other bandits, I should really say our friends, I looked at Luis he was still very quiet and white, but was trying to smile and said, "Maybe Arthos you will help me in a short while, as I'm in awful pain." I saw Arthos turn looking worried, and he said, "Luis hang on, try and concentrate on something if possible, for just a short time, and I'll fix things I promise." We turned off the roadway following the men on horseback up a hidden trail, through dense trees, out of sight from the unaware on the left of the road. Up the path of the mountain side, it was bumpy, windy with a huge drop on one side, quite treacherous if you were to skid, "Don't" said Ramos, "Glen stop those bad thoughts." At last, we turned another corner, we had arrived at the Ramirez's secret settlement. Amazingly senor Ramirez walked towards Arthos slowly, as he had jumped out of the car, "Welcome back my friends", senor Ramirez said, giving Arthos a hug, then explained quickly about Luis, before any of us spoke he was, helping Luis out of the car, and with the help from Chico and Enrico, took him straight into the house. Senor Ramirez came towards Ramos and I and said, "See it is a miracle senor Arthos has helped me walk again, but only slowly, but it is marvellous", Enrico collected all our bags and with one of the men carried them and we followed senor Ramirez, Chico and Enrico's mother welcomed us saying, "Wanna coffee you?", "Yes please we all agreed and sat down, waiting for Arthos to come and tell us how Luis was feeling. Ramos said, "I wish I knew what was happening, with Luis and Arthos. I really think that Luis is not only in pain but severe shock, he rushes in to help anyone without even considering the consequences, but that is Luis, he has a lovely kind and warm personality, and Glen, he confided in me that he thinks of you as his special friend. I guess you two confided a lot in each other. That makes an unbreakable bond. Here comes Arthos, let's find out what he has to say." Before we could ask, Arthos said, "I have asked senor Ramirez if we can stay for a couple of days, obviously we will pay our way, and help out if they can give us jobs. I must keep healing Luis's hands as they are badly blistered, we never realised how badly he was hurt. He is lying down and has been given some top Astrotar healing tablets, I've dressed them plus his leg and face with some special cream. I am so grateful to doctor Xedato from Bermantus for supplying me with emergency medical supplies, Astrotar style, not of course for a minute expecting to have to use them. However, thank the Power Lord of the Universe that Luis is no worse, Although I admit to being very anxious. I still may have to get him airlifted to Base 2 if his condition doesn't improve, it's not only his burns it is his whole nervous system has been put out of order.

 Now, I have to speak to senor Ramirez and ask him some things which I need to ask both you, Ramos, and you Glen, it has to be a collective decision. 1, Can I trust his family with our secrets if I have to call Incas to collect Luis, or maybe even Ocelot. 2, Are we a nuisance staying here longer even though I intend to pay for our keep? 3, Is there anything we can do for the family to help out whilst we are here, as we obviously would like to be useful. Now how about your thoughts, what do you both think?" Ramos looked at Arthos and said, "Well dear friend we respect and value you as a leader, so whatever you decide is alright with me, and I know Glen is thinking the same", "Quite right", I replied, "Now can I go and see Luis, or Arthos can he not be disturbed?", "Well Glen give him an hour or so, then go up, is that ok with you?", "Of course", I said. Just then Chico and Enrico came in with senor Ramirez, Arthos said, "Senor Ramirez I need to ask you some very important things." He then started firstly saying, I need to know whether I Arthos could talk to senor Ramirez's sons and the other people on the settlement about the secret matters he had previously discussed with him, as nothing could be leaked out till the world was ready, Chico and Enrico looked puzzled, first at Arthos then to their father asking him, "What is the big secret?" Senor Ramirez said looking directly at Arthos, "We are all men of honour and if we say we will not report it, anything we are told in secret, we will keep to our death, taking it to the grave. A curse would fall on anyone breaking the bandit oath of silence" so we told them that what we wanted to tell them would be tonight after dinner so it was a good the suspense would be broken. Senor Ramirez told Chico and Enrico to tell everyone they must meet in the main house, some were eating with us, some in their own houses, but all to be ready to swear the bandit oath of silence, men and women. Arthos asked about his worry about being a nuisance staying longer, but we would pay our way. Ramos said, "So if you are allowing us to stay for a few days whilst Luis recovers, please, let us help with the work, we would love to be part of your life." "Senor Ramos",

270

said Chico, "I would love the help, we have many jobs so please you can all help tomorrow and as friends I no longer call you Senor, I call you Ramos and Glen, and perhaps doctor Arthos", Chico then said, "How can we help you with your sick friend?", "Actually Chico, I am grateful but I must be the one checking on him regularly as I have decisions to make in the morning." Then both Enrico and Chico apologised for not taking us up to our rooms and show us where they were. "I hope everything will be alright for you all, we all look forward to hearing your very secret stories after dinner, which we will pledge never to repeat. Obviously, my Papa already knows as he and you doctor Arthos are very close friends." We had the same rooms as last time. I wondered how Luis was and started concentrating to let Arthos know I wanted to know. Ten minutes passed and there was a knock on the door, it was Arthos, "Sorry Glen" he said, "I know how worried you have both become so close, but we are still in the same boat, worried sick. At the moment Luis is sleeping with the medicine I have given him. He is having plenty of fluids and senor Ramirez is making some soup for later. I can assure you if there is no improvement tomorrow, or even later tonight, I am going to send for Ocelot to take him to doctor Famusa at Base 2. I have been in touch with the Great Astro and Alimo head of Base 2. I am speaking with everyone tonight in case we have to clear the area, then Ocelot will quite safely land in this secret environment. Hopefully all will go well, and Luis will be back with us in a few days. Now have a quick rest and I'll make you are ready for 19:30 dinner." "Please Arthos", I said, "When Luis wakes up tell him I miss him, and for him to hurry up and get better." Arthos smiled, he knew how close we had become, as were we all. We went downstairs for 19:30, and this time we were seated together rather than mingled as before, I guess this was for the story telling. Senor Ramirez seated himself next to Arthos as he wanted to show everyone that he was in charge. After the ladies came and cleared away after the meal, they too also squeezed in with mugs of wine for everyone. Arthos had popped upstairs to check Luis and let him know what was going on. As he came back and sat down, Senor Ramirez stood up and clapped his hands, immediately it was silent, and a feeling of excitement ran through the room, as he said, "I Senor Ramirez head of the family, demand that every last one of you stand and swear on the honour of our family that on pain of death what you are about to hear will be secrets you will honour for ever. All hold up your right hand and say the following, 'We pledge on our honour not to reveal anytime what we are about to be told' As they as one chorused the statement, then were allowed to sit down again. Then Arthos stood up saying, "What I have already confided in full to Senor Ramirez, I am about to reveal to all of you, we have become sworn brothers by the statement of your leader, my very special friend and we as your new friends swear to honour your friendship into eternity." They all clapped and then the room fell silent. Arthos took a sip of his wine and started with his story. "At first as I tell our story, I must insist you do not interrupt as I will give you proof, I am from a far-off Galaxy and came to this planet to stay when our planet imploded. It was Astrola and in many ways like earth, but not as violent." He told the whole story of bygone days and how they had travelled back and forth across the galaxy, helping civilisations over the thousands of years and trying to increase the knowledge of people and stop the war like tendencies of earthlings. They have a constant battle with the Galympites who are evil and would destroy the earth as it is at present, adjusting it to suit their needs. The Galympites are ruled by the most evil of beings called Galumpus Diavelo, and they come from the planet Galactic Doom Star. They have the stance of a man, but a head of a goat with a Sulphur breathing mask, they cannot breathe earths air, that's why they cause so many volcanoes and other disasters hoping to destroy earth as you know it. We Astrotars are constantly destroying them at extreme danger to all of us." His story telling was magic, he bought into it how I as an earthling had been bought in, and become totally involved, how I was now adopted by the Astrotars and how even their father had experienced a connection with us when he was only ten years old, and how he had always been scared to talk about it, even though his life had been saved by Ocelot, a very skillful aero craft pilot when he was about to be caught by some Galympites in the Andes mountains. Then he said, "Before I say anymore I want you to listen very carefully", he then continued, "Glen, Ramos stand up, point your Astrotar rings upwards," We did this, then as we stood there with our arms outstretched upwards, Arthos called out, "Botami, with permission from our leader the Great Astro please tell our special friends gathered here that all I have told them is true.", The lights dimmed, flickered and a voice of deep serenity said, "You have been chosen to be our Mexican friends, we trust you, the world is not ready to accept us yet, but we Astrotars only fight for good on earth, trust us, these four, Arthos, Ramos, Luis and Glen will always remember your kindness and we will make sure you will be looked after." The lights flashed went out, then came back on. Senor Ramirez called out, "We are extremely blessed to have you as friends and amazed to hear the words from Botami." Athos then said, "I must pass you to Ramos to continue the story as I must go and check on Luis." He left the room as Ramos stood up and started telling them about Bermantus, the under-ocean Base 1 situated beneath the Bermuda triangle, and about Base 2 in Peru and that there were other small bases situated in different parts of the world. He then told the gathering of people that Senor Ramirez now had a tale to tell them. Senor Ramirez stood up and told them his experience when he was only ten and very poor and up in the mountains hoping he might find some gold to help his parents and how he was stuck and couldn't move with his foot in a crevice and the Galympites were drawing close to him, when there was a huge flash, and they were destroyed, and an aero craft had come down from the skies and the pilot said his name was Ocelot and he told me never to come back to that dangerous area, then he took three pieces of gold and said that they will change your luck, and it did. Then he held up a piece of gold and said, "This I keep safe the others helped us all to move from Peru and form our settlement." Then I stood up and said, "I know you must think this is all a dream, I did, but it is real, mine is a long story that can be told another night, but for now let me tell you, they are the kindest, most generous, friendly people you could ever wish to meet, and maybe if Luis isn't any better, he may have to be taken by Ocelot, the aero craft pilot to Base 2 in Peru to see Doctor Famusa. If the aero craft comes here, we will need to clear an area in front of the houses for him to land. Astrotar medicine is far more advanced than ours." Everyone had started talking, amazement lit everyone's faces up, they were asking questions from Ramos and myself, when suddenly Arthos came in the room and said, "Sorry to break up the happy mood, but Luis is worse and it leaves me no option, I've called Ocelot to come and take him, to get medical help. Now can everyone go outside and make the area clear of obstacles, in order that the craft can land, I hope this is ok, Senor Ramirez?", "Of course", he said, "But may I ask, is this the same pilot that saved my life as a boy?", "Yes", said Arthos, "He is on his way now", Arthos left to go and get ready, whilst everyone went outside to make sure the area for landing was clear. Arthos arrived with Luis who I noticed was so white and was visibly shaking, I went to him saying, "Please get better soon, I miss you", I then gave his body a small hug, frightened of hurting him. I noticed everyone looking up, as we had pointed car lights to area, slowly and quietly the craft descended into the middle of the patch, immediately the hood went up, and Ocelot jumped out. He walked to Arthos and said,

"Let's get Luis in the craft, and get his helmet on", he turned to Senor Ramirez saying, "Senor, so glad you took my advice over fifty years ago, when you were just a child. Thank you for looking after my friends, I will bring Luis back as soon as he is better, maybe a few days treatment, and maybe in a few days if it is safe, I can spend an hour with you. Of course, it will be late at night as that is the safest not to be spotted by the Galympites, I will let Arthos know the night-time of my arrival", He turned to the gathering and said, "I will be back and maybe have a chance to speak with you all, goodbye my Mexican friends", then as he left saying to Senor Ramirez, "Tell your family to watch out for those Galympites in the mountains, if you see any, steer clear of them and call Arthos, even after he leaves, he will give a number to call, and we Astrotars will keep you safe, and destroy them." He shook hands, then rushed over to the craft, put on his helmet, jumped into his seat, checked on Luis, closed the hood of the craft, and a slowly and silently it ascended up, once past the treetops, it was off like a streak in the sky. Ramos went and turned off the car lights and engine, and we all trooped back into the house. Arthos said to Senor Ramirez, "Would it be possible for us to have a coffee?", he replied, "No problem, or would you prefer wine?", "No thank you, coffee would be wonderful" said Arthos. Arthos turned to Senor Ramirez who had a big smile on his face and said, "I guess you never expected to meet and talk with Ocelot again, did you?", "No", he said, "Not in a million years" then Enrico said, "I still believe that this is all a dream, but it is a wonderful experience." Then Chico said addressing the three of us, "Thank you so much, your secret is our secret forever", then everyone chanted, "Yes, yes."

17

As everyone was talking Raquella came by me saying, "Ah Senor Glen, you come back see mea again?", "Raquella", I said, "Yes we will come back to see you all one day", she snuggled up to me, I pretended not to notice, it just wasn't going to happen. Everyone was asking questions and hypnotised by all that happened, perhaps an hour had passed, and it was close to midnight when Arthos got up from his chair and dashed out of the room. Everyone stopped talking, and we were all wondering what was wrong. Five minutes passed, and Ramos and I were starting to panic, had something gone wrong on their return journey? Arthos reappeared saying, "Good news, they have arrived at Base 2 and Luis is now with Doctor Famusa, I have a feeling all will go well now, and he'll be back with us as soon as he is cured" Everyone cheered, and it was really wonderful to know for the time being they were both safe. It seemed strange the next morning without Luis, although obviously he was in the best place possible to be cured. I kept wondering what was happening to him and whether he was going to alright. As I drank my coffee and ate my breakfast. Suddenly from nowhere Ramos said, "Glen, that's enough", I looked at him and said, "What's wrong?", "He said we are all worried about Luis, but we must realise he is going to be back soon, as he will recover with, Astrola medicine as our planet was far ahead of that on earth, so don't worry. Let's go and offer our services to Chico and Enrico." We thanked Senora Ramirez and went outside, as we did so Senor Ramirez called Arthos, we teased him saying, "Well played, you sit and talk, whilst we work!", he answered, "Well I said I was the boss, so my good friends I'll see you later" Ramos and I were laughing as we went over to the stables where both Chico and Enrico were standing. They laughed when we said, "Any overalls or old jeans we can borrow, as we haven't much with us", "No bother", said Chico, "Come with me", he gave us some old dungarees that were hanging in the shed by the stables. We went to their well-stocked kitchen garden to collect salad and vegetables. I was amazed how they had cultivated their land up in this mountain. We brushed the horses, helped to clean out the stables. We worked hard all day, enjoying banter with the men, sometimes I didn't understand as these lapsed into Spanish. Arthos came out for ten minutes and said, "Sorry about this, but I'm intrigued with the history that Senor Ramirez has been telling me about. I of course have been telling him about the Mexican and other South American history that the Astrotars have been involved with, to help people move forward, he is an avid reader, which is amazing because he taught himself to read, as they were poor and he couldn't go to school, but of course the others have helped him. He has read about Egypt and the pyramids and pharaohs, even about the Greeks and the lost island of Atlantis. So, I have told him things he couldn't read about, he was thrilled.", we said, "Have you heard how Luis is?" "I thought you would never ask", replied Arthos, "Actually, he is responding well to treatment, that's all I have been told." With that he went back into the main house, just as we went back to stables a young woman carried out a huge tray of mugs of juice and sandwiches. The evening was another meal and more storytelling, my tale this time, plus some of our adventures, then it was bed ready for another day's work. The next day was much as the first, filled with jobs like mending fences. Four of the men disappeared into a big shed which we wondered what it was for and found out as they carried out a huge box of meat, it was their abattoir and they had been butchering their meat ready for the kitchen. The evening followed the same pattern apart whilst eating our supper we heard from Arthos that he had received news that Luis was making good progress, and needed a couple more days, everyone cheered as we were all happy.

  The next day we went outside and were told that Arthos and Chico had gone out in the car very early and would be back later. I wondered where they had gone, Ramos said in a whisper, "I'll tell you later." We went outside ready and expecting to work as we had done, but Enrico came out of the shed with a couple of horses, we carried on into the shed and got changed. As we came out we saw a man holding two horses, Enrico was already on a beautiful black stallion and said, "Senors, today I take you out on a ride, have you ridden before?", I said, "Well not really, but I'm willing to have a go", "Yes", said Ramos, "But I admit I am a little worried, I can't afford to break my neck, and it's been years since I had the opportunity", Enrico started laughing, "Don't worry", he said, "We've given you both very gentle horses, whilst they are held, put your left foot into the stirrup and swing your right leg over the back to the other stirrup. We have given you western type saddles as they have a slight raised section on the front which you can always hold on to, if you feel nervous. Now hold the reins over your hands so that you have control, and we will walk around this open part of the settlement till you feel comfortable" I was very nervous but at the same time elated and excited to try something new. Ramos called to me saying, "I feel exactly the same", which made me feel much better. After circling for a while, Enrico said, "Good we are ready to go for a mountain trail ride now, I will go first and you will both follow me, my two cousins Janus and Datino will follow behind." Then he had to scare us saying, "They will watch your backs to make sure nothing attacks you from behind.", and then laughed, was it possible I thought or was this, his sense of humour? We rode in a line through quite a dense tree area which had been made into a rough pathway, just wide enough for horses to pass through. I had to admit it was exhilarating being high up as we passed between the trees. Suddenly the trees opened up into what appeared to be the location of a lake, hidden from the world in this dense forest. We were able to ride right around the lake, as a pathway had been cleared. At the far side Enrico suddenly noticed a large patch of mushrooms, "Let's dismount, my Mama would be pleased to get a basket of these." Everyone got down, the two of us managed it very slowly, he had a few bags rolled up in his saddle bag and passed them around. It was fun as everyone was talking about Ocelot and the stories, and we were able to tell them more things, and before we knew it, we had filled three bags which Enrico said was more than enough. We now had the job of mounting the horses again, I remembered the foot in the stirrup and throw the right leg over, which wasn't that easy, the horse refused to stand still, everyone including Ramos was in their saddle, this infuriated me, so foot in stirrup and with determination, I threw my right side to what I thought to be seated, but foot came out of the stirrup and I went right over the other side into the lake, as my horse was standing right on the edge. It was a shock as I plunged headfirst into the icy cold mountain lake. Before I had time to panic one of the men hysterically laughing, jumped down and pulled me out. He apologised for laughing, but by this time even I realised how funny it was, and we all enjoyed my pitiful wet being, "Well", said Enrico, "I guess we are going back now, but if you stay for a few extra days we will go further next time." They helped me back up, soaked to the skin, and we were off continuing around the lake, and back through the forest path to the settlement. As we came into the clearing, others around were highly amused at my disaster but as quick as I could I dismounted and went into the shed to discard my soaked clothes. I put on my shoes and in my wet tee shirt and shorts I went straight to the main house to shower and change. As I entered Senor Ramirez said, "Please giva mea the wet clothes I wash, you ok senor?", "Yes thank you", I said and went upstairs to get a quick shower and change. When I came downstairs Ramos was inside having a coffee and talking to Enrico, whilst his mother was making some sandwiches. When she came in with the tray Ramos jumped up and took it from her and in fluent Spanish, he thanked her for her kindness. She was taken aback, obviously not used to compliments. We were all outside again and Enrico said, "I suppose you wouldn't mind helping me to chop and store some logs? We have cut down trees and we need to chop them into logs for the stove fires.", "Great", I said, "Maybe it will improve my muscles", "What muscles", said Ramos, we had to laugh but I actually meant it, swinging an axe was a new experience. We worked at the forest edge Enrico was using a power saw, I said in all innocence, "How do you get the electric supplied all the way up here?", Ramos replied, "Glen, for a clever man you are so funny at times, haven't you heard of generators. That's how they have electricity up here', he burst out laughing. I think it was Janus who joined us with another power saw and they cut up the trees they had already cut down, and stripped of foliage into large chunks, which we in turn had to chop into smaller logs with our axes. I had to stop every so often as I'm afraid that I am not the most physical person. Ramos seemed as strong as the other two but on several occasions previously he had amazed me with different feats of strength and athleticism. Suddenly a car horn was heard, it was Chico and Arthos, at last I thought now I'll find out where they have been. We had been so busy I had forgotten to ask Ramos where they had been. Senor Ramirez came out of the house to welcome them back, and asked Arthos before we could, "How is senor Luis, do you know?", Arthos answered, "Yes", then sat down on the wall next to Senor Ramirez saying, "He has greatly improved, and Doctor Famusa said all being well Ocelot will bring him back tomorrow night." "Isn't that marvellous", I said, and Ramos agreed saying, "We will be four again", then Chico said, "Papa come and see Doctor Arthos's car, the inside is full of goods he has bought us. Senor Ramirez slowly walked to the car and seemed amazed, I was dying to see why he looked so surprised, and then I began to understand, it was box after box, bag after bag of things, firstly for the food stores, coffee, sugar, butter etc., then things like a few boxes of beer and things for the kitchen garden, nails for the fences a drum of fuel for the generator, cleaning materials, bags of grain for the horses. Then there was chocolate for the ladies, plus wine and a bottle of special whisky for Senor Ramirez. Then I noticed there was bacon, eggs, sausages, bread flour and tea bags. Oh my god Arthos had done them proud, "Please Arthos", I said, "can I pay for half?", "No" said Arthos, "This all comes from the Great Astro, in thanks for their loyal non demanding services." Whilst they unpacked the car, Senora Ramirez was smiling, she was obviously thrilled with all the goods, whilst the unpacking was going on, Arthos went inside with Senor Ramirez. Later I found out that he had been instructed to also give an amount of money to the old man for emergencies. The evening meal was served at 20:00, Senora Ramirez had cooked an amazing roast dinner with all the trimmings. After the meal the guitars came out again, they sang very joyously it was very enjoyable. It made a change from the previous nights of stories and questions. I realised they had asked how the Astrotars knew so much from the past, or why Ocelot still looked so young, yet it was over fifty years ago since he had made contact with Senor Ramirez. Were we going to have to tell them about the re-live programme? That started me thinking about it, wondering if I would ever be considered to participate in it, or as an earthling maybe I wasn't able to be considered, but even if it was a risk, I'd like a chance, to think how wonderful to have longer with my special friends.

All my life I'd wanted real friends, but had been let down often, and being an only child, I tended to be lonely, but now I had real friends I wanted them for always. Ramos suddenly said, "Arthos could you come with Glen and I?", "Yes" said Arthos, "What is wrong?", "Nothing I just need a word." The three of us excused ourselves for five minutes and went up to my room. "What's wrong", I said, Ramos replied, "Glen I need your thoughts, you were miles away and Arthos was busy, and I wanted to tell him", Arthos said, "Ok, Ramos what's wrong?", "Well", he said, "Glen was deep in thought about the re-live programme, firstly wondering if we were going to tell them why we are involved in it, then he was sad knowing his time is limited with us, and us being the friends he always wanted. Then wondering if he will ever get a chance to go through the programme, willing to take that life and death chance to remain a friend and brother Astrotar to us", "Oh", I said, "I am embarrassed that you have read my thoughts, but I admit it is all true, but I would not have told you. It was only in my deepest thoughts.", "Well", said Arthos, "It is time I should ask for a private word with the Great Astro, and tell him that all I say can be reiterated by so many Astrotars but only he can decide whether to ask the Power Lords Of the Galaxy and Universe whether it could be attempted.", I looked at Arthos and said, "Oh, Arthos I'm sorry to not be sufficiently grateful for what friendship you have already given me, I must stop being greedy." They both gave me a hug as we were all rather tearful. "Right", Said Arthos, "Let's go downstairs, I'll follow in a minute, I'll just check on Luis, and tell you the news when I come down." When we got downstairs Senor, Ramirez asked if everything was ok, I said, "Yes", then added, "I just needed to ask if there was anything, I could buy for you, as I would also like to say thank you", "No, no we have received too much, in all my life nobody has been this kind to myself and my family." Everyone then started to sing, and a warm friendly atmosphere prevailed, I thought how strange, what a combination you wouldn't be able to write a fiction story where company was so diverse, made up of a mixture of friendly aliens, Mexican bandits and a Scotsman, all enjoying a wonderful evening together.

    The next morning Chico and Enrico said that seeing today could be our last day together, he wanted to take us somewhere special, they bought some horses out of the stable, two men who I had already been introduced to as his cousins, Janus and Datino were also bringing out some horses, Chico said Arthos, "Doctor Arthos have you ridden a horse before?" The answer amazed us, "Yes many times, but years ago why?", "Because Senor we are all going to my cousins ranch on horseback." Arthos was given a horse and without any trouble he jumped into the saddle, Ramos and I were given our horses, they were really good and held the horses whilst we mounted. Then out came Enrico and Chico, and like a double act they both bounded to their horses and with a couple of spring like steps they were in their saddles, I said, "Good god, I thought I was either in a cowboy film or the circus: everyone laughed, I guess they were showing off, but I have to admit they were good. Janus and Datino were the last to mount up, then Chico told everyone the order of riding, he went first with Arthos, then Janus, then Ramos, Enrico and myself, and last was Datino. "Is that ok with everybody, now folks we are the magnificent seven, does anyone else remember that film? I know it is an old film, but it was really good" We started forward and took a slightly different route than the day before. It was still narrow and deep into the forest depths although they appear to have made a pathway over the years. Eventually after about an hour, we came to a clearing in the mountains, the air was very fresh, I realised we were quite high up. There were stables near the house, obviously this was his cousin as a man came dashing out of the house shouting "Welcome, come on in, Senors I am happy they are bringing you to my house." I recognised him as a person when the story telling was happening, he had sworn his oath of silence, so we were safe. He said, "Come on my Maria she macca cakes and coffee, or wine you want better", we decided on coffee, "I might fall off my horse again", I said, and they all laughed. We had a great afternoon we talked and laughed, his wife maria sang for us with a fabulous voice that amazed us. We all clapped, and Angelo looked so proud of her, she started blushing and ran out of the room, back to kitchen. Then Angelo showed us his horses, he took great delight in showing us a tiny foal which had been born to one of his mares the night before, it was already standing looking at us beside its mother. Angelo said with great pride that it was a baby stallion which will be worth something as it comes from good stock. Chico laughed and said, "Oh Angelo, what's the betting you keep it?" Time passed, as it got to late afternoon Enrico said, "Doctor Arthos, how is Senor Luis? Everyone wants to know", "Well" said Arthos, "I've just heard that he is coming back tonight, around midnight, if there isn't any trouble in the sky. Chico we will have to make sure the landing area is clear again.", "Yes of course", he replied. Then Angelo said, "Enrico, can Maria and I stay at your house to night, so that we can see the aero craft land?", "Yes", said Enrico, "But just you two", "Okay" said Angelo. We went outside and all mounted our horses, I was thrilled I managed it on my own. Chico started, "Can everyone from the same pattern of riders, I do it for a purpose", I wondered why, but as no one said why, I thought I would ask later. Everything went to plan, and when Angelo and Maria said they would follow later, Enrico said, "I think you should come now; we will wait the forest is no good at night on your own", "Okay", said Angelo. A man came out of the stables leading two horses, tackled up and said, "Don't worry Maria, I'll lock everything up and keep watch over your house." So now we were the magnificent nine I noticed they tucked Maria in line not at the end, I wondered why, Enrico insisted that the forest was bad at night, ah well I guess it's ok in the daytime, I did notice they all had their guns handy. About an hour later we all arrived back at the Ramirez main house, I was relieved to dismount, amazing myself that I managed this on my own as well. I went to my room to wash and change before the evening meal and take time to relax as I had a couple of hours to play with. It was 20:00 and I heard a banging at my door, it was Arthos attempting to wake me up. "I'm sorry, I was shattered after the horse riding, and all the manual work I have done recently" Laughing we dashed downstairs and enjoyed yet another exceptional meal. The evening passed quickly with everyone excited at the prospect of actually seeing the aero craft again. Arthos had heard that Luis was coming back, but under orders to take it slowly for about a week, though it should still be ok for us to travel the next day. Arthos asked if the landing area was clear, Senor Ramirez said, "Yes, it has been done, but I am so sad to see you go, we will perhaps never see you again" Ramos tried to lighten the mood saying, "Don't worry we will be back for your wife's cooking, it is wonderful." That bought about some laughter, the old gentleman kept saying, "Doctor Arthos, I will miss you, maybe if I want, I can call you?", "That is fine, I will leave some contact numbers", said Arthos. It was close to midnight we all went outside; everyone had found a place to stand, Arthos put on the car lights pointing to the centre of the clearing, with some of the exterior lights on as well. Arthos shouted, "Okay, they are nearly here", slowly and quietly a large circular shape descended into the middle of the clearing. The hatch then opened, and Ocelot jumped out, putting his helmet on the seat, then he helped Luis out. They rushed over to us, we all hugged them both. We were thrilled to see Luis's hands had healed perfectly, no scars what so ever Senor Ramirez pushed forward and shook Ocelot's hand saying, "An old man's dream has come true, it has been wonderful having your friends to stay, they will be sorely missed when they leave tomorrow", he then added, "If you ever get a holiday, come and stay with us, maybe you could get dropped off, I would love to have chats with you" Ocelot thanked him saying, "Senor Ramirez you are very kind, I will remember your invitation" Luis showed us his hands and legs completely healed, slightly pink, but no scars, his face just looked the same as it always did. The Astrotars cured him, I asked him how he felt in himself, he replied, "Glen I was a wreck after the fire, it affected my whole nervous system, it started to shut down, but now I feel great, everyone was so kind, the only thing I missed were you three so much. Ocelot true to his word went round the gathering, shaking hands with as many as he could, explaining how time was limited as it was too dangerous for him to stay on the ground too long, as going from land to sky was time, he had to be so careful, in case he was attacked by the Galympites. He turned and wished everyone well, shaking hands once more with Senor Ramirez and warning him to beware of the Galympites, as they may be in the mountains, and if he or his family saw any to run and call Arthos who in turn will let Base 2 know, and they would come and destroy them. He then gave the four of us a hug, and ran to his craft, put his helmet on closed the hatch, and silently ascended into the sky. Arthos said, "Okay everyone he will let us know when he reaches Base 2 now perhaps we can go inside and scrounge a coffee and have a quick chat with Luis", "Well its magic to be back again with you, Arthos thanks for the care at first, I was told by Doctor Famusa that my intricate Astrotar nervous system was at the point of closing down and if you hadn't done what you did, I would be dead before I got to Base 2." We were all shocked but relieved, you never know what's around the corner. We went inside everyone was asking Luis what it was like to fly in the space craft and said, "Faster than fast" and rolled his eyes. We laughed at him; he hadn't lost his sense of humour. After we drank our coffee and decided we should go to bed, as we found out we needed to leave by midday. Our flight was at 17:30, so we didn't want to miss it, we knew we had about a two to three-hour drive and hand the rental car back. Just then Arthos received a call from Ocelot he was back at base 2 but had seen he thought a flash of black when he was passing over the Andes in Peru, he said he would sort that out tomorrow when they weren't expecting it.

    It was sad saying goodbye to Ramirez family, as it was true, we may never meet again. I really hoped so. We packed the boot of the car, checking we had left nothing behind. I was embarrassed by Raquella coming over to me and saying, "Senor Glen, you wanna stay? Mea Papa say you good man", "Sorry Raquella, my life is travelling and writing, you are lovely and one day you will meet someone special, but it's not me, sorry.", I told her awkwardly, she leant forward, grabbed me and gave me a kiss, I untangled myself and said, "Bye, Raquella", I knew the others would torment me, but no one was more surprised than me, so I just smiled at them saying, "Sorry friends, but the ladies love a Scots man", they all laughed. The men mounted their horses, as we got in the car, Ramos was driving with Arthos next to him. Luis and I were in the back of the car, he smiled, "Glen, back to normal", I agreed with a smile. Arthos although in the car was still having to shake hands with Senor Ramirez, who was saying, "Doctor Arthos, don't lose touch, call me when you are free, I have your number for emergencies but will not bother you otherwise." He had tears in his eyes and running down his face which seemed out of character for a bandit chief. As Ramos started the engine Arthos gave the old man a final hug, then closed the door and we moved forward slowly following the men on horseback leading the way with two following at the rear. It was a scary journey with the narrow path, the trees in places hiding a sheer drop, not a road for winter. Eventually we reached the main road, I noticed the men lined up at the side so that we could draw out onto the left. This done we shouted, "Goodbye", waved and as we did, we heard a series of gunshots, and they were all waving their hats. We drove for miles along twisty roads and round some scary hairpin corners. We finally passed through the small town Ejutia de Crespo, after another half hour or so we pulled into a shaded part of the verge. Arthos then got out and got some bottle of juice and some sandwiches. We headed off again with Arthos driving, we were talking, telling Luis what had happened whilst he was away, the swearing of the oath of silence, our horse-riding expeditions and of course my falling in the lake! Luis laughed so much saying, "Poor Glen, you must have felt so daft?", "I did", I said, "And wet, but the others were better riders than me, after all I'm just a writer!" Luis then went on to tell us how they had a narrow scare on their way to Base 2, but luckily Incas was circling in case of trouble, and got us away. Guess what he even managed to blow the evil being plus the ship out of existence. He then went on to say that Doctor Famusa was lovely but seemed old, but with a young face, guessing he had been through the re-live programmed at least once.

    Eventually we were there, Arthos drove the car back to the hire car firm, we climbed out and checked the car, whilst Arthos paid for the hire. We went into Oaxaca International airport where it was only 16:00, which was good as we had plenty of time to spare. We purchased the tickets, and bags handed in with seats organised for our 17:30 flight to Mexico City. We went to the security gate where we passed with no trouble. Once we got to the VIP lounge for departures, we all got ourselves a drink and something to eat and sat down and waited for our flight. At 17:15 our gate was shown as open on the notice board, we were allowed out by the security guard, to walk across the tarmac and board the plane. Once we had taken off, Arthos quietly said to me, "Glen have you always enjoyed your time with us? Wouldn't you sooner be settled down, perhaps with someone instead of constantly travelling around the world, on constant flights or continual battles with the Galympites, with all its pitfalls and dangers?" I answered without hesitation, "My time with you and all the Astrotar friends I have made, who have risked their lives at times for me, have been the happiest time of my life. Nothing ever seemed to have a great deal of meaning when I tragically lost my parents so suddenly in a car accident, my life now has meaning, and I wish for it to never end, though sadly I am not an Astrotar, and I will become old and be unable to be any use to you, apart from writing my books, if only I was an Astrotar I might be chosen to undergo the re-live programme, and life with you all would be extended." Arthos said to me with a serious face, "Glen who knows what the future holds", Ramos then asked Arthos, "What are your plans when we land in Mexico City?" The reply made me laugh, "Well Ramos for a start we are coming back to stay at your flats, then we will decide, maybe if you are lucky, we'll invite ourselves to stay for a few days.", "Marvellous", said Ramos, "You can buy the supper tonight because I'm not cooking" Luis who had been quiet then piped up with, "Well, I'm so pleased, I thought you were going to leaves us at the airport, and continue on your next flight, remember I missed out on your company for a few days." With all the chatting we were soon landing, and with a bump and the brakes roaring, we raced across the tarmac. When then went through security and collected our bags, Luis said, "Come on, let's go the car park and collect my car." "Should I hire one?", asked Arthos, we'll need to get back here in a few days, "No need, Luis and I are taking an extra week off as he has been unwell, and don't know when we will see you again.", "True", said Arthos, "We truly live a nomad's life, always on the move." We got in the car and set off, Ramos said, "Shall we buy a takeaway, or go to a restaurant?" Arthos replied, "A restaurant that is my boss type decision", we all laughed, then he added, "Ramos your job is to find a decent restaurant, I really fancy a big meal, how about you three?" We all agreed on that. On finishing our meals and an evening of music and chat, we headed back to the flats. We hurried inside with all our bags as it was raining hard. Luis and I shared one flat and Ramos and Arthos shared the other as we had previously done. We sat talking for a while over coffee then headed to bed for an early night.

Next morning, we made breakfast and sat in the garden, and chatted again about our adventure. Luis shared his experience at Base 2, how it was situated with a large hidden entrance in the Andes on the Peru-Colombia border. The entrance was controlled opening to allow aero craft to enter without problems, their large base was completely hidden from the sky and sea and goes deep into the Andes mountains and continues under the Pacific Ocean, something like Bermantus with many rooms and even an under-ocean base entrance for aqua craft. Arthos said, "Actually, Luis have you never been there before?", "No", replied Luis, "I have been to Bermantus Base 1 and the one in Australia many years ago, Base 3, I believe there are others but of a smaller size.", Ramos then chimed in, "Well I've been there and the one in Australia", "Stop showing off", I said, "I've only been to Bermantus, perhaps they don't trust me?", "Oh it's because you are only a new Astrotar", said Arthos laughing, "Time will tell", "Only if I live long enough", I said, "Well", said Arthos, "We are hoping for that for all of us." Arthos also started telling some interesting stories about Senor Ramirez and how when his father was given two gold pieces from him his son, they all decided with some other poor people to make their way to Mexico by boat, knowing the Pacific Ocean, it was a long journey from the Andes landing near Puerto Escondido. They quickly moved to Sierra Madre del Sur mountains and formed their settlement. Gradually they spread out keeping to the mountains, as they found this better as they were different from the local inhabitants. They used their survival skills, a bit of hunting, poaching and were targeted by other bandits.

The journey across the Pacific was long and arduous, they had acquired a fishing boat and had to use their skills as fishermen to stay alive. Some of the weaker members of the group sadly died, as did one of his younger sisters, it was fortunate it was summer, if it had been winter, they would have never survived the journey. Once they landed, they made their way up the mountains where they felt safe. The boat they sold was sunk during a storm a few days later, Senor Ramirez believes god was on his side. "Actually, I think the piece of gold that Senor Ramirez still had, which was Astrotar gold, maybe the Power Lords had something to do with their safety, after all Ocelot had given it to Senor Ramirez when he was young and that is how they were able to leave Peru", "Who knows?", said Ramos. It started to rain so we all moved indoors, Arthos excused himself saying he had important phone calls to make but would be back in an hour. We all sat chatting about Galympites and the battles around the world with them. Arthos returned and said, "I've got something very important for us to discuss, I've been waiting for conformation on the matter that has been in the hands of the Great Astro for a while. Also, some matters I've had to sort out, so sorry I took so long. Right where shall I start?" We were sitting waiting for him to tell us what this great thing was, and before Arthos could speak, Ramos said, "Arthos, am I right what I'm thinking?", "Yes", said Arthos. He turned to me and said, "Right Glen I am about to say something, the answer you give must be really well thought through it is not easy", I looked puzzled, I wondered what this was all about. "Glen, The Great Astro has received permission for you and you alone to go through the re-live programme. The only earthling that the Power Lords of the Galaxy and Universe are willing to permit. It is dangerous you have to decide, you will not be promised absolutely that it will work, you are not an Astrotar, but they reckon you have because of your make up so like us in bodily functions and organs and your attitude a strong chance of success, but it has to be your decision. You would enter the re-live programme saying goodbye to us, and for a period of time we will not know whether you have had your name put in the golden star book, or whether you will come back to us. It is a hard decision and only you can make it. If you are successful the re-live programme will be safe in the future for you, but Glen, are you brave enough to take that chance? You will have to make sure you sort out everything you own before you do it, if you say yes, but if you say no you will still be part of us, for as long as you live." I couldn't believe it, I was desperate to be able to participate, but now I had been offered it, I was scared to accept, what should I do? Arthos said, "Glen don't make us ill, talk to us, see if we can help you make a decision but don't do it if you are not sure. Give me your answer for the Great Astro later tonight, as it will have to be arranged, plus of course your journey to Bermantus." I looked at him, tears running down my face, "What an honour?", I said, "How can I say no? But please forgive me for being scared. I am sure I already know the answer, I'm going to give, yes, is the only way forward." They discussed with me all that they knew about it, but their knowledge was all they were allowed to know. They said once you enter the special life compartment chamber with the Great Astro you remember no more, it is obviously a coma induced sleep, so that whatever happens you cannot tell anyone about it, and you are missing for a while. Arthos said, "Well Glen, I always secretly hoped that one day it would be decision time and deep down always knew that you were destined to be one of us." Arthos continued, "So Glen, have you found the courage to take your chance, am I right?", "Yes", I said, then Arthos said, "I will get in touch with The Great Astro who awaits your answer." Ten minutes later Arthos came back into the room and handed me his special Astrotar phone, I immediately heard the strong deep voice, "Glen it is Astro your future leader speaking, Arthos says you are ready?", "Yes Great Astro, I am", I said, my hands and body quivering as I heard his voice starting to talk to me again. "We are all thrilled that you want to join us in body and soul, we realise that to make this decision you are brave, and my judgement when I first chose you was correct. I also realise that you have the necessary courage needed for the re-live programme for we realised that you have certain qualities. Arthos will make all the arrangements for you, and I look forward to meeting with you again, and may the Power Lords of the Galaxy and Universe be with you", and he was gone.

"So now you have spoken with the Great Astro and told him yes, I am now instructed to start making any necessary arrangements for you, for your personal ones, and your travel ones.",

"Well", I said still in a state of shock, especially having spoken to the Great Astro, "I own a flat in London, as you know I have monies of a considerable amount in the bank, If I draw up a will, and give you power of attorney saying that if anything happens to me, everything becomes yours. Then you can do what you like with it and the P.O.A will allow you to make all the arrangements. Also, you will have to finish writing my books as we have to get these books out into the world. They are almost complete, just the last one to finish. Anyway, I am going to think positive and hope that this trip to Bermantus will be one of many." "Anyway", said Arthos lets order supper tonight and make it a night of celebration, we all notice you are being sad and tearful, stop it immediately, lets enjoy every minute together, then tomorrow I will start making arrangements for calls to London and plans for a trip to Bermantus. So, Luis gets out the wine and let's toast to the future. Our friendship, Ramos, Luis, Glen and I Arthos, and our reunion when Glens re-live programme is over and everything in our lives is a success.

Word count 132075

Printed in Great Britain
by Amazon